COLD NOSE, Warm Heart

MARA WELLS

sourcebooks
casablanca

Published by Sourcebooks Casablanca, an imprint of Sourcebooks
P.O. Box 4410, Naperville, Illinois 60567-4410
(630) 961-3900
sourcebooks.com

Printed and bound in the United States of America.
OPM 10 9 8 7 6 5 4 3 2 1

*For Nicole Resciniti, career-wrangler,
deal-maker, curse-breaker.
Thank you for changing everything.*

CHAPTER 1

RILEY CARSON'S BUTT BUZZED. SHE PRETENDED NOT TO feel her phone's vibration through the denim of her cutoff jean shorts and lifted her face to the morning sun, sucking in a lungful of humid air.

"Ah, nothing like late summer in South Florida." She kept an eye on her toy poodle, LouLou, who galloped around the patchy grass of the neighborhood dog park alongside her best dog park pal, a black Labrador ten times her size. Well, it wasn't really a dog park, more an empty lot that the good dog folk of the surrounding area had commandeered as their own. And Lady wasn't really a Lab, more a mix of large breeds with a Lab head and soulful eyes.

"If only there were more mosquitoes." Eliza, Lady's owner, batted half-heartedly at a few early-afternoon pests. "And more humidity so one hundred percent of my clothing can stick to my skin instead of the usual eighty percent."

Recently retired from her legal practice, Eliza was a dog park fixture, bringing Lady from their home across the street multiple times a day. She'd been the one to find LouLou, abandoned in a cardboard box with holes punched in the top, just outside the lot's entrance.

Riley crinkled the ever-present plastic bag in her pocket, remembering meeting Eliza on her door-to-door search to find the poodle's owner. "I can't believe it's been over a year since you brought LouLou into my life."

"Love at first sight, wasn't it?" Eliza dabbed at her

steel-gray hairline with a tissue. White streaks at her temples defied gravity and frizzed around her face. "She was a pathetic thing, wasn't she? So dirty and with the worms."

"Nothing a body shave and a trip to the vet couldn't fix." Riley didn't like remembering those days. LouLou had been skeletally thin, her apricot coat sparse and matted. She'd been weak, her survival touch and go, especially given her advanced age. Now, she was the picture of health, clearly finding joy in herding her giant friend around the perimeter of the chain-link-enclosed lot.

"They're quite an unlikely pair, aren't they?" Eliza tracked the dogs' progress while they ran the fence. Clods of dirt flew from under Lady's paws, and LouLou chased after them as if they were toys. The fact that the clods crumbled in her mouth didn't stop her from chasing the next one, but it did remind Riley that she needed to bust out the dog toothbrush. Poodles had notoriously bad teeth, and Riley figured there was nothing wrong with a bit of prevention. Luckily, LouLou liked both the vanilla-mint flavored toothpaste and the extra attention.

"Opposites attract, I guess. I'm glad they're such good friends." That Riley was also grateful for Eliza's friendship went unspoken. Morning, afternoon, and evening, the two met up to let the dogs run, and somehow that had turned into long hours of conversation, day after day, that left Riley hoping when she reached Eliza's age, she'd have half as many funny stories to tell about her life as Eliza did. Right now, though, her life was the opposite of exciting—work, work, and more work.

Riley's butt buzzed again. She winced and pulled out her phone. She texted a quick reply and added another item to her to-do list. Although she wasn't technically always on call, in practice, it certainly seemed that way. "I'm sorry. I know the dogs both love a good run, but we have to cut it short today."

"Butt problems?" A smile was never far from Eliza's lips, and they stretched into a grin at Riley's sigh. Eliza patted the tissue behind her ears and down her neck before stashing it under her bra strap, hidden by the neckline of her floral blouse. Riley had seen her pull a key and a driver's license out of her blouse. She wondered what else Eliza stashed in there.

"Mr. Cardoza problems." Riley thumbed through a few more messages, turning the screen so Eliza could see her to-do list of the day. "Duty calls."

"You're good to them, those pesky residents of yours at the Dorothy. Sure keep you on your toes, don't they?" Eliza patted Riley's arm and called Lady. The big dog slid to a stop a mere inch from crashing into Eliza, head lolling to the side with a doggy grin. Such a large dog for such a small woman seemed incongruous at first, but Riley had quickly learned that they shared an irreverent sense of humor and a great love of pâté.

"You know it. But after the disaster at my last job, I'm grateful for the work. See you this evening?"

LouLou came running, too, now that Lady was leaving, and Riley bent down to clip on her leash.

"Wouldn't miss it." Eliza threaded Lady's leash through her fingers. "Kiki and Paula got back from Italy yesterday. They'll bring Princess Pugsley, which will be a nice treat for Lady, and I for one can't wait to hear about every moment of their trip."

"And see every picture, right?" Riley smiled at Eliza's enthusiastic nod.

"You know, they met right here at the park. Kiki had that old Maltese, God rest her cranky soul, and Paula started bringing Princess Pugsley when she was a puppy. Gosh, that must be five years ago now."

"A real doggy love match." Riley pulled her hair back into a sloppy ponytail and secured it with a band from her wrist, following Eliza through the gap in the fence they used as the dog park entrance. Two poles, meant to hold the chain-link upright, tilted away from each other, creating a slot large enough for humans and dogs to slide through.

"But it sure wasn't love at first sight. Those dogs hated each other. Kiki and Paula on the other hand..." Eliza winked. "Just you wait, Riley. Maybe the dog park will bring someone special your way, too."

"Thanks to you, I have my someone special." Riley squatted to give her poodle a good scratch behind the ears. "I don't need anyone else. Come on, LouLou. Maybe Mr. Cardoza has some treats for you."

"You're skeptical," Eliza called to Riley's retreating back, "but I'm usually right. You'll see. I have an excellent sense for these things."

"No romance for me, thank you very much. Work your matchmaking wiles on some other sucker." Riley waved but didn't turn around. Getting into it with Eliza about her failed engagement was a topic for another day. And the name of that day was Neverday.

Riley'd shared a lot with Eliza about growing up in the area, how her mom's job working for a cruise line had her out of the country for weeks, sometimes months, at a time, leaving Riley's grandmother to mostly raise her. She hadn't shared much about her love life, though—neither her disaster of an engagement nor how she sometimes fantasized about the cute UPS driver with the sexy accent who delivered Eileen Forsythe's medications on the first Tuesday of every month. No, for now, her job, her poodle, and her Grams were enough commitments in her life. Who had time for anything more?

LouLou followed Riley along the sidewalk that led back to the Dorothy, the Art Deco apartment building where Riley spent her days—and quite a few nights—troubleshooting maintenance problems for the residents. Another failure. Her gig at the Dorothy was a long way down from her position as an assistant manager at the luxurious Donovan Resort in downtown Miami, but when the whole chain was sold off due to a series of political and financial scandals that ended up with the CEO in prison, she got laid off, and she didn't have a choice. It was the job at the Dorothy or no job at all.

Really, she was grateful for the strings her Grams had pulled to get her hired. It meant she was an elevator ride away from her favorite relative, the woman who'd provided the only stability in her young life, and she was certainly learning a lot of new skills. Skills she'd never thought she'd needed, but who wouldn't want to add handywoman to their résumé?

Sure, she missed her Donovan Resort team, the inside jokes, and the after-shift drinks at the bar. She missed greeting returning guests and welcoming new ones for their first stays. She missed her not-too-shabby paycheck and how putting on the Donovan Resort's requisite black blazer and pulling back her hair instantly made her feel like a kick-ass professional.

She did not miss being unemployed, though, and after wrestling with plumbing and electrical problems, single-handedly regrouting the lobby bathroom, and negotiating lower rates from the cable company, she didn't need a blazer to make her feel kick-ass. Her Dorothy uniform of cutoff jeans and thrift-store T-shirts was more comfortable anyway. Oh, who was she kidding? She did miss that blazer. Who would've noticed if she'd never returned it? The Donovan Resort, and every one of its sister properties, would likely never open for business again.

Riley and her poodle circled around to the front of the building, and as always, Riley admired its graceful lines. Although a bit faded in places, the cheerful pink façade never failed to lift her mood. She'd loved coming to Grams' as a child, imagining the building had been painted her favorite color just for her. When her mom popped into town, they'd lived in a series of one-bedroom apartments in neighborhoods near the port—not always the most kid-friendly places in Miami. It was a relief to be dropped off at Grams' when Mom's job took her away for long stretches, and Riley cried every time Mom picked her up when the cruise finished. "You'll be back soon enough," Grams said each time they said goodbye, and she'd been right.

Mom moved up at the cruise line, assigned to lengthier charters and adventure cruises until it wasn't uncommon for her to be gone for six or eight weeks at a time. Grams and the other residents at the Dorothy welcomed Riley and made her feel like part of a large, loving family. Now the Dorothy was Riley's home, too, and her job was to make sure that all those who'd helped her through her childhood and rocky teens were safe and happy. Really, she was simply returning the favor.

Inside, LouLou panted with excitement as they neared the elevator. Riley wished there was something in her life she loved as much as her poodle loved a ride on the elevator. The car shook on its slow ascent; a lesser dog might be afraid of the movement, the noise. Not LouLou. Her tail never stopped wagging. As soon as the doors rumbled open, LouLou dashed inside, tugging Riley along. The building was only a two-story, but the elevator took its job seriously, stretching out the ride so that it felt as if more than a mere one floor of distance had been covered.

At the ding, LouLou was as excited to exit the elevator as she'd been to enter it. Dogs. Riley knew she should be taking life lessons from her pooch about the importance of living in the moment, but it was hard to shake off the feeling that she should be doing something different. Something more. She just didn't know what. Or how on Earth she'd ever make time for more, whatever that might be.

"Ah, my favorite girls are here!" Mr. Cardoza opened his door before Riley had a chance to knock. A proud "eighty-five and still alive," as he liked to say, Mr. Cardoza cut a dapper figure in his tailored chinos and navy suspenders. His thick head of gray hair and status as a longtime widower made him the most sought-after of the silver foxes in the building. His refrigerator was always stuffed with offerings from the female residents of the Dorothy—casseroles and lasagnas, homemade pies and mango preserves. He should be thirty pounds overweight, but his strict regimen of daily walks and trips to his senior-friendly gym kept him fit.

"What can we do for you today?" Riley kissed both his cheeks with genuine affection. When she was fourteen and going to her first high school dance, he'd driven her in his old Saab and explained in excruciating and embarrassing—at least back then—detail how a young man should act around her. And exactly what she should not allow, on or off the dance floor. Thanks to his thoroughness, she'd been perfectly happy to dance with a group of her girlfriends and sit out the slow dances.

Riley cocked her head at the familiar grinding sound coming from his kitchen. "Is it that new garbage disposal? I told you to stop jamming chicken bones down there."

"The ad said it could grind anything." He tucked her hand into his elbow and escorted her to the kitchen, LouLou trotting behind them, her fluffy ears brushing Riley's calves. "Anything."

"Anything but chicken bones. As we've discussed. Many times." Riley unclipped the leash, and LouLou promptly nosed around the kitchen, finding bits of who-knew-what in the hard-to-clean space between the floor and cabinet lip. "Alright, Mr. Cardoza, let's take a look, and if it's chicken bones again, I'm leaving you to fend for yourself. Also as we've discussed. Many times."

Mr. Cardoza nodded solemnly and slipped LouLou a sliver of chicken from a plate of already precut-to-poodle-size bites. "You won't leave before you let me make you my famous café solo?"

So it was chicken bones. Again. But pass up his hand-ground dark-roast coffee? Riley placed a hand to her chest. "Never!"

She opened the cabinet under the sink and pulled out the

flashlight and pliers she'd bought especially for Mr. Cardoza's apartment. It was both her nature and her Donovan hotel training to anticipate guests' needs, and she'd known from the first call from Mr. Cardoza about his unauthorized garbage disposal that she'd be back again and again. Easier to keep supplies here than to haul them back and forth on the daily. She looked over to where Mr. Cardoza sat, LouLou in his lap taking bites of chicken from his fingers. *The things I do for caffeine. And chicken. And Mr. Cardoza.*

Riley's butt buzzed again, and she grabbed the phone. Grams' Google wouldn't Google. Riley shoved the phone back in her pocket and flipped off the power to the garbage disposal. It was going to be a long day, but what else was new?

At least the long hours of her job kept her from thinking too much about her life, but sometimes in the wee hours of the morning, with antiseptic and Band-Aids freshly applied to whatever scrapes and cuts she'd acquired during the day's maintenance challenges, she did worry. Was her blazerless status at the Dorothy her whole future? Would she be patching stucco and unclogging drains for decades to come?

When she thought of her careful plans so carelessly destroyed, she could cry. Did cry. But crying never changed anything. She firmed her chin, got hold of a semicrushed chicken bone, and yanked it out of the drain. The bone popped out with a slurp and a cheer from Mr. Cardoza. Riley turned to give him a thumbs-up before diving in for the next one. For now, it was enough to be needed.

CHAPTER 2

"YOU'VE GOT TO BE KIDDING ME." CALEB DONOVAN checked his phone for the address, hoping it was a mistake. This couldn't be the property Grandpa William thought was the answer to their problems. But no, 1651 was definitely it. The Art Deco façade, once painted in a Miami Beach palette of pastel pinks and oranges, had long since faded. Latex strips hung like old palm fronds in need of trimming. Sagging gutters promised roof problems, and the overgrown crown-of-thorns shrubs flanking the entrance threatened to jab someone in the eye with their spiky branches.

Grandpa William had said "quaint." He'd said "charming." He'd said "original period details." Caleb should've known real estate code for *money pit* when Grandpa William first said "fresh start," something Caleb could really use after the chaotic, life-altering disappointments of the last two years but seriously doubted this old apartment complex could provide.

But he was here. Might as well take a look, even if Grandpa William's plan was half-baked and, well, surprisingly sentimental. The surprise wasn't that Grandpa William wanted to rebuild the family business but that his plan apparently also included rebuilding the family. Or at least the part of the family currently not serving time for fraud, embezzlement, and a slew of other state and federal crimes.

Caleb slammed the door of his carmine Porsche Boxster, then immediately patted the door handle apologetically. In the left-behind neighborhood not far enough south to be part of the upscale South Beach scene but not north enough to technically be part of North Beach, either, the Boxster was distinctly out of place on a block full of aged Volvos and family-oriented SUVs.

A coconut fell from a curbside palm tree, bouncing off the Porsche's front bumper with a loud *thump*.

"Son of a—" Caleb kicked the coconut into the street and inspected the bumper and front grill. No visual damage. No chipped paint. He ran a hand over the area to be double sure then glared up at the offending palms when he felt the slightest indentation above the bumper. A half-dozen lawsuits-waiting-to-happen hung high above the sidewalk, ready to attack a vehicle or a litigious neighbor out for a power walk.

Wasn't there supposed to be some kind of manager on-site? Someone making sure the coco palms were trimmed regularly so that innocent bystanders weren't thunked on the head by coconut bombs? Of course, it'd be terrible if someone were hurt—he'd read somewhere that falling coconuts killed more people than sharks—but at the very least, the manager should make sure the building wasn't liable for injuries and damages.

Caleb thumbed through the notes on his phone until he found the name. Riley Carson. Hired a year and a half ago. His trained-from-the-cradle real estate developer's eye took in the three boarded-over windows on the front of the old apartment complex, two stories high, and the peeling paint on the portico's stepped columns. So far, not so good.

This Carson guy might think he could get away with collecting a paycheck from Grandpa William for doing nothing, but Caleb wouldn't let anyone take advantage of his grandfather, not on his watch, and especially not now that he feared Grandpa William was growing soft—definitely in the emotions, but maybe it was impacting his business sense, too. With Caleb's parents on frequent, prolonged business trips and his two older brothers striking out on their own, cutting ties with their father before Caleb was even in high school, Grandpa William was the one person he could count on.

Although the past two years had made Caleb question a lot of things about what it meant to be a Donovan, his love for his grandfather never wavered. The very least Caleb could do while scoping out Grandpa William's claim that the crumbling apartment complex had "unlimited potential" as a condo conversion was to put the fear of God—or at least a fear of the Donovans—into this do-nothing building manager.

Caleb strode toward the double front doors, cutting across the front lawn that was more sand than grass. Okay, he admitted to seeing some potential. Install a bit of lush landscaping—a bougainvillea or two and a handful of traveler's palms—and the curb appeal would improve one thousand percent. Above the arched front door, the name Dorothy stood out in relief, a pale reminder of how many buildings from the era were named after women. Original details, indeed.

"Well, Dorothy, I can't say it's a pleasure to meet you." Caleb stopped at the call box that was easily as old as he was and punched in the code Grandpa William'd given him. The box wheezed and the door locks clicked, but when he pulled on the handle, it didn't open.

Fantastic. Not only did the place need a serious make-over, but the technology was both outdated and inoperable. He knew from viewing dozens of foreclosed properties that the possibilities for disaster were endless. But this wasn't a foreclosure. It was Grandpa William's secret weapon, a property his grandfather had separated from the company holdings before the authorities confiscated all of Donovan Real Estate Group's assets.

"One property at a time," Grandpa William had said last night over drinks on his deck overlooking the Intracoastal Waterway. *"That's how you build a solid business."* Caleb had bought into the fantasy that he'd somehow restore the family name and bank accounts.

Now, Caleb wondered if he was being naive. He'd only done one thing in his life—follow in his father's business footsteps. For good or for bad, real estate development, especially in the hospitality industry, was his specialty. Hotels, casinos, time-shares—that was the world he knew, and the one his father so carelessly lost with his less-than-legal approach to dealing with city officials and the IRS. Residential real estate wasn't Caleb's thing.

But things could change, even his things. They had to. Since the trial and his father's subsequent conviction, he couldn't rely on his father's example anymore. Robert Donovan wasn't the respected and powerful businessman he'd portrayed himself to be. He was a criminal. Caleb hadn't believed it at first, not at the indictment, not at the beginning of the trial. Seeing was believing, though, and as the prosecution slowly and methodically convinced the jury of Robert's guilt, Caleb became convinced, too, and he'd lain awake many nights after, cursing himself for his gullibility. His blind faith.

He should've seen the fall coming, should've listened to his brothers' numerous warnings over the years. But he hadn't, and he'd lost the business right along with his father. Caleb fingered the metal key chain in the pocket of his pressed trousers, the keys his grandfather had tenderly handed over.

"Lots of good memories in that building." Grandpa William wasn't usually nostalgic, but he had a distinct gleam of tears in his sharp blue eyes. *"Never could part with it. Figured I'd go back someday and make something of it. Now it's your turn, Caleb. Rebuild. Make the family whole again."*

Grandpa William's plan included Caleb's half brothers and Caleb convincing them to work on this project with him for the good of the family. The family they'd wanted so little to do with that Knox joined the Marine Corps as soon as he was legally old enough to sign the paperwork himself, and Lance started his own construction company, refusing any jobs their father tried to send his way.

Somehow, though, Grandpa William had faith in Caleb, that he could do this. Rehab a building, reel his brothers back in, take the nightmare of the past few years, and turn it into some kind of American Dream fairy tale. It was unrealistic; Caleb had thought so when Grandpa William spelled out his terms, but now, looking at the run-down Dorothy, he wondered if it was downright delusional.

When Caleb's father had argued that Caleb didn't need college, that he could learn everything he needed on the job, it was Grandpa William who'd paid Caleb's college expenses. Grandpa William who showed up at parents' weekend, helped him deck out his dorm room, and was the only family member at his graduation. At the very least, Caleb owed him a walk-through.

He used the key to open the front door and stepped into the lobby. Original terrazzo floors, pockmarked and stained, would need to be restored. Rattan furniture circa 1970-something would have to be replaced and, judging by the mold growing on the cushions, possibly torched. He checked his phone again. The manager's apartment number was 101. Mr. Carson was about to get an earful, for sure. Or maybe Caleb would simply fire him with no explanation. Florida was an at-will employment state, after all, and Mr. Carson shouldn't need to be told that he was seriously derelict in his duties.

Caleb was about to take the right hallway, following the placard's directions that apartments 101 to 108 were to the east, when straight ahead, a single elevator dinged. An older woman, white-haired and thin, pushed herself forward on a cheery yellow walker. She angled her path toward the five-foot-high bank of mailboxes against the lobby's south wall. She wobbled as she walked, and when she held out the mail-box key, her hand wobbled, too. Wobbled so much the key shook right out of her hand and hit the floor. He rushed to her side, bending to pick up the key.

"Here you go, ma'am." Caleb pressed it into her palm, glad that Grandpa William, though well into his seventies, was in good health. There'd been a scare a few years ago, right at the start of the legal troubles, but he'd pulled through. He walked with a cane—an intimidating hand-carved contraption with a silver handle specially molded to his hand and engraved with his initials—but he was still as headstrong and opinionated as ever. "Slippery things, those keys."

The woman exhaled a labored breath, and for the first

time, he saw the clear tubes snaking from her nose to a small oxygen tank mounted on her walker. "Aren't you the gallant one? Thank you, young man."

"No problem. You take care now." It didn't surprise him that a woman of her age lived in such a run-down building. It was a sad truth that those on limited retirement incomes often couldn't afford any better. A rush of gratitude flooded him. Thank goodness Grandpa William separated his personal holdings from the Donovan business when he did so he could keep the home he'd custom-built over twenty years ago.

A high-pitched yip brought Caleb's attention back to the elevator—not a cute Deco-style box with brass trim that would make a great selling point but a clunky 1970s-era contraption that, no surprise, clearly needed updating. A tiny dog, some color between orange and pink, dashed out of the ancient elevator before the doors stuttered to a close. The fuzz ball, no taller than eleven or twelve inches, turned dark eyes up to him and let out a soft woof.

"Ma'am?" Caleb called, and when the woman didn't turn around, he tried again, louder. "Ma'am? Your dog?"

"That's not my dog." She angled her walker back toward the elevator, a few envelopes in her left hand. Her shoulders sloped dramatically in her faded housedress, and she leaned more heavily on the right side than the left. "Never had a dog. I'm a cat person myself. How about you, young man?" Even her smile was a bit crooked.

"I don't have any pets." Caleb slid his hands into his dark trouser pockets and rocked on his heels. "Never have. At least, not of my own."

"Isn't that a shame." She shuffled a few steps forward

before resting again. "Everyone needs a little unconditional love in their lives, don't you think?"

Caleb straightened, her words hitting him almost as hard as Grandpa William's *"You owe it to your family to try."* He cleared his throat before saying, "I thought cats were too independent for that kind of sentiment."

She blinked rheumy eyes at him. "No one loves more fiercely than an independent creature. It's too bad you don't know that yet."

Caleb didn't know what to say so he stuck with a safe "Yes, ma'am," and she made a humming sound of agreement before continuing her slow progress toward the elevator.

Something soft and damp nuzzled against the tips of his fingers. He looked down and found the fluff ball gazing up at him with a clear—though to him, unreadable—plea. Guessing, he scratched behind her soft ears. She stood on her hind legs, placed her front paws on his thighs, and bounced. Mr. Pom-Pom—hey, he didn't name his mother's Pomeranian—used a similar move when he wanted to be picked up, so Caleb crouched down and scooped up the poodle. Her little heart beat fast against his hand, and her soft, springy fur curled around his fingers.

"LouLou!"

Caleb heard the frantic voice seconds before the stairwell door slammed open, and a young woman emerged, blond ponytail collapsing, sending wild curls springing every which way. She was tall, leggy, and long, with brown eyes that dominated her round face.

"Patty, have you seen my LouLou?" Barefoot, the blond rushed toward the woman with the walker. "I was just leaving Grams' when the elevator dinged. You know how she is about the elevator."

Patty smiled her crooked smile, scrunching up the wrinkles around her eyes. "She rode down with me. Such a sweet girl. You know I always enjoy her company, but right now, she's enjoying someone else's."

"What do you—" The blond's eyes caught on Caleb's dark-brown Gucci loafers and traveled up his legs until they landed on her dog. Her brows pulled together, and she angled her face up, one hand to the base of her throat. "What're you doing?"

Caleb wasn't sure if the question was for him or the dog. Patty shuffled back to the elevator, leaving him alone with the poodle and her short-shorts-wearing owner. Suntanned legs and delicate bare feet with hot-pink nail polish. He'd never considered himself the type to have a foot fetish, but the flip-flop tan across the top of her foot was definitely turning him on—making him wonder what other tan lines she might have. But he was here for business, and he never let anything get in the way of business. Time to hand over the dog and be on his way to find and fire Mr. Carson.

He hesitated, though, strangely reluctant to let go of the dog or the view of that flip-flop tan line. LouLou's warm body grew heavy, so he shifted the poodle into a more comfortable position and scratched under her chin. "LouLou's a cute name. How old is she?"

"She's a rescue so we're not completely sure. The vet guessed around eight or nine years old." Riley's back pocket buzzed. She pulled out her phone, frowned at it, swiped, and tucked it away again. "Should've named her FloJo, though."

"Is that a rapper name or something?" Caleb continued

to pet LouLou, but apparently he wasn't doing it exactly right. The poodle maneuvered her head so he could get behind her jaw.

"FloJo? Florence Griffith Joyner, the fastest woman of all time?" The woman laughed, a light and airy sound that hit him like a shot of his favorite sipping rum—straight to the gut. "My girl here loves to run. A bit too much, I'm afraid."

"She's a getaway artist, huh?" He didn't usually chat up residents of buildings he was scoping out, but he was curious about her and her dog. When was the last time he'd been curious about anything? Anyone? When the judge's gavel came down and his father's sentence was announced, Caleb's whole world had turned upside down. He'd been scrambling for so long to put things to rights that he'd forgotten what it was like to simply be, to have a conversation with a stranger for no other reason than she and her little dog interested him. The gentle smile he'd given the woman with the walker spread to a full-out grin. "An escapee? A dog dodger?"

She laughed again. "Indeed she is. Luckily, everyone in the building knows her. She rarely gets far."

"This building?" Caleb didn't care for the sound of that. Pets could do a lot of damage in a small space, especially in a situation where all the units were rentals. Owners fixed up their places before selling, but renters moved on. "I thought no pets were allowed."

The blond flushed, turning almost as pink as the polish on her nails. "That's what the lease says, for sure, but you can, you know, get special permission from the manager. In special circumstances. That are, you know, special."

So pet damages were another thing Carson would have

to answer for. The list of grievances grew by the second, and Caleb felt even more justified in his decision to fire the guy as soon as possible. But none of it was this woman's fault.

"She seems like a special dog." A special dog who didn't live here. The woman was visiting; she'd said as much. Maybe her Grams had a cat or something. That was why she'd been flustered. Didn't want to rat out her own Grams. He roughed the poodle's fur and widened his smile.

She smiled back, and it did weird things to him, narrowing his focus until all he could see was her. The wide lips, the way her eyes tilted at the corners, the color still staining her cheeks. Would she say yes if he suggested a coffee date? Drinks? Dinner? Her left hand darted up to tuck one of those wild curls behind her ear. No ring. What was her name? That was what he should ask first. *Say something, say something.* But nothing came out, and the silence grew longer and more difficult to break.

She licked her lips, drew in a deep breath. Maybe she'd ask his name. Ask him out. The dog squirmed in his arms as if even she knew someone needed to break the awkwardness.

"Come on, LouLou. Let's go." The woman reached for her dog.

Caleb knew he should hand her over, but then LouLou turned her head so he could dig in behind her ears, which he did. She grunted a doggy sigh of satisfaction and angled her head, encouraging him to scratch the other side.

"I'm sorry." The woman sighed, too, so forcefully that a curl bounced on her cheek. "It's a bit embarrassing how shameless she is. Her first owner must've been very affectionate. She's sweet and well socialized. I can't imagine anyone giving her up. But they did. In the cruelest way. People are terrible sometimes, you know?"

"They certainly are." Caleb flashed to his last visit with his dad, separated by a pane of glass, surrounded by other inmates and vigilant guards. "Even people you think you know."

Her surprised eyes locked with his. "Isn't that the truth? Luckily, dogs are good through and through. All the way to the bone, you could say."

Her optimistic words washed over him, soothing the tightness in his neck that never quite went away. The lilt of her accent sounded local but more musical than that of a typical South Floridian. She settled a hand on the dog's back, just below the hot-pink collar. Their hands were an inch apart, then half an inch when she slipped her fingers under the band to give a good scratch. The poodle's fluffy tail thumped double time against his arm.

What would it be like if he moved his hand that small distance to touch her? Although he kept up the steady pressure under LouLou's ear, his mind wandered to how the woman's skin would feel. As warm and soft as it looked? He was holding his hand very, very still, careful of her space, careful not to spook her, when Riley's finger slipped from under the pink collar and brushed against his.

Contact. Pinkie finger to pinkie finger. Accidental? Or had she wondered, too, what it would feel like? It was like he'd imagined, only better. Warmer. Softer. Both of them stopped petting the dog. He stared at their fingers. She stared at their fingers.

He wanted to slide his hand until it covered hers, but

that wasn't like him. He didn't touch women he just met, no matter how soft the skin or how good they smelled. Was it strawberries? Something fruity filled his nostrils, and he inhaled deeply, reminding himself that he didn't do random hookups like his father. He was sensible in his romantic life, dating women with similar interests and incomes so they were always on a level playing field. But he also couldn't move his hand.

She didn't move either, not toward him or away. Then her fingers curled in LouLou's hair, and when they uncurled, she'd put a few breaths of space between them. He itched to close the gap and feel her skin again. *Inappropriate,* he scolded himself. *You're not some kind of caveman who can't control his urges.* But he felt like one.

Then he felt something else. The frantic wiggle of a dog with a mission. He'd been around Mr. Pom-Pom enough to recognize the signs, so he crouched down to let LouLou go off to do her doggy business. She didn't go far, though, before copping a squat.

"Oh no! Oh my gosh." The woman pulled at his arm, and he let her drag him away from the scene of the dog crime. "Oh, I'm sorry. Really, really sorry. No wonder she beelined for the elevator before I could get her leash on. Hang on, I'll be right back."

She dashed next to the elevator where, like many Miami Beach buildings that boasted a common-area lobby, a door displayed the stick figures universally signaling a public restroom.

Soon, she was back, miles of paper towels heaped in her hands and trailing behind her. "The lobby restroom's mostly used during the holiday party in December and sometimes by the mail carrier. Oh, and that time Rhonda in 202 forced some questionable sausage on the cutie-pie UPS guy when he delivered her new shower seat. It's usually not a high traffic area, but I will definitely need to restock the paper products after today."

She tore off a few feet of paper towels and handed them to him, then stooped to drop some on the floor, still chattering in what was apparently a nervous habit. He found himself leaning toward her, the sound of her voice, waiting for the next syllable to fall from those berry lips. About a public restroom. Good Lord, what was wrong with him, waiting to hear more about delivery folks with intestinal distress and paper-restocking protocols?

"She's really a very good dog." The woman gave him another wad of towels, although he wasn't sure what she expected him to do with them. She swiped more around on the floor with her bare feet. "We were at Grams' longer than usual, and we were on our way back to the dog park when she ran for that stupid elevator." Swipe, swipe. She pressed more towels, and more words, on him. "And she is getting older. It's hard to find homes for older dogs, you know? I couldn't take her to a shelter, not knowing what might happen. That's how I ended up with her."

"I'm sorry I waylaid her." He finally found his voice, although it didn't sound much like him. Rusty, croaky. He cleared his throat and tried again. "It's okay. These things happen."

She nodded so vigorously that more hair flipped out of her ponytail to wave wildly around her face. "Sadly, they happen pretty often with her. At home, she has her pads and the patio, but there are still accidents." She stopped wiping the floor for a moment to inspect him from head to toe. "Sorry about the shoes."

Shoes? He looked down. Sure enough, they'd taken a bit of spray.

Her bottom lip shifted back and forth as though she were chewing on the inside of it. "I can have them cleaned for you? Do dry cleaners even take shoes? I'm not sure. Maybe it's easier to give you money for a new pair? What do you prefer?"

Prefer? He'd prefer that she stop throwing paper towels at him and look him in the eye. Her raggedy cutoffs, her Grams living in this old building. She didn't need the extra expense of designer shoes.

He didn't have to force his smile. "I said it's okay. It was an accident."

She fluttered her hands at him, up and down. "There must be something I can do."

"Have dinner with me."

He got his wish. Her eyes flew to his and locked there. Shocked.

She squashed the last clean paper towel in a tight ball and let it fall. From the waist up, she was motionless, but her toes tap-tapped a nervous beat. "You don't even know my name. I don't know yours."

"That's easy to fix. What's your name?"

She shot out a hand to shake his. "I'm Riley, Riley Carson. And you are?"

He didn't take her hand. He couldn't. "I'm here to fire you."

CHAPTER 3

"FIRE ME?" RILEY'S OUTSTRETCHED HAND DROPPED TO her side, and she took a step back, heel sliding in her rush to put distance between them. "Don't be ridiculous. How could you possibly get me fired? Besides, I said I'd replace your shoes. Geez, it's not even LouLou's fault. Her age makes her somewhat incontinent is all." Her eyes darted guiltily to the expensive loafers that she for sure couldn't afford.

Why couldn't he have been wearing some dollar-store sandals? The precise crease down the front of his trousers, the rolled-up sleeves of his button-down revealing a watch that probably cost as much as her eight-year-old Mazda, if not more, all indicated this guy didn't buy anything at the dollar store. Chalk up another credit-card expense to the joys of dog ownership.

"I can. I should. This place is a disaster." The man raked a palm down his face. His familiar face. She swore she recognized him but couldn't quite place from where. He didn't know who she was, though; maybe he had one of those faces. But no, the combination of eyes so blue she expected to see a dolphin swim by and the strong line of his jaw was not a common sight. At least not for her. Local TV anchor maybe? Someone she might've seen but who'd never seen her?

Riley sniffed, and her lips tightened. "This place is historic. Maintaining it is complicated." To think she'd liked the guy, liked him enough that when their fingers touched, she'd fought off the crazy urge to cover his hand with hers and gaze at him as adoringly as LouLou gazed at Mr. Cardoza when he slid her a few bites of chicken. That was when she'd remembered what a mess she was from spending two hours becoming intimately acquainted with Mr. Cardoza's garbage disposal—the one he should never have installed with pipes as old as the ones in this building—pulling chicken bones out of places chicken bones should never be. Again. "I'm not coming back," she'd told him, shaking a slim bone covered in slime at him. "I mean it this time."

"You are too good to me." As usual, Mr. Cardoza ignored her scolding and continued making his delicious café, knowing that once she'd cleared his drains, she'd sit and chat with him for a while. He always had news to share about his sister in Spain and his grandson, a philosophy major in Tallahassee, who'd taught him how to use Facebook so he could see the family's pictures and posts.

Riley'd gritted her teeth and gotten back to work, suspecting—not for the first time—that Mr. Cardoza clogged his drains on purpose for the company. Then Grams texted with another of her nonemergency emergencies, and she and LouLou had to scram before she got even one drop of her café solo.

Maybe that was why she was feeling off. Nothing was better than Mr. Cardoza's hand-ground coffee, and between Grams needing her to reboot her computer so she could check her lotto numbers and LouLou's escape, Riley'd missed out on some much-needed caffeine that would've helped her more quickly put together precisely why this guy thought he could fire her. But on second thought, you know what?

"No, just no. The only person who can fire me is the owner of the building, and since that person happens to be my grandmother, I don't even want to hear it from you right now."

"Your grandmother doesn't—"

Riley shut him down with a hand chop through the air between them. "I know she doesn't handle the day-to-day or get involved in running the place. Are you from the management company?" Technically, Grams' management company, Rainy Day, hired her and could fire her.

He took a long time to answer. "You could say that."

Her stomach did a little twirl, but LouLou's comforting presence helped her stay calm. "You work for Grams, not the other way around. You can try to fire me, but I'm not worried. I've done good work since I took on this job."

"A good job? A coconut bombed my Porsche!"

"Oh, your Porsche. How tragic. Next time the tree trimmers cancel on me three times in a row, and the new service I ask to come give me a quote never shows up, I'll be sure to put out a *Beware of Coconuts* sign for the local Porsche owners." Riley backed away, feet slapping the terrazzo with every step. "And you can be sure I'll let Grams know how you threatened to fire me. I'd be worried about my own job if I were you."

The guy's jaw worked up and down, like LouLou when she got peanut butter on the back of her tongue. If he were like LouLou, it'd take him awhile to work through whatever he was chewing on, so she left him there in the lobby.

Left his icy gaze that should feel cold when it hit her but instead made her skin heat and brain scramble. Left his tall, trim body that should look stuffy in his chambray button-up and high-end loafers but only made her imagine what he'd look like when all the layers were stripped away. Left him saying, "But I don't, I mean, your grandmother can't possibly—" because her grandmother did a lot of impossible things for someone her age. Left his familiar face behind because she was getting a sinking feeling that she knew exactly who he was. *Damn it.*

"Wait!" His voice stopped her, the voice she was pretty sure she could find in online video clips saying how his family was innocent of wrongdoing and his father's trial would prove it. *Ha!* He didn't work for Rainy Day at all, the liar. If he was who she suspected, his family was guilty of destroying her career. Now he was sniffing around her grandmother's building? Oh no, she was not going to wait.

A hand on her arm stopped her retreat. "Please, I shouldn't have said I was here to fire you. I'm here to look around."

Riley pressed LouLou to her side. He wanted to look around? She'd gladly show him the exit. But even as the thought surfaced, two things occurred to her. One, no way would she let him off the hook that easily—the man had ruined her life once, and here he was, threatening to do it again. Two—and this one pained her to admit—she doubted he'd be that easy to get rid of. Nope, not this guy. If he was indeed the Donovan heir apparent, he'd move heaven and earth to get his way. That didn't mean she'd make it easy on him. *Nuh-uh. No way.*

"Hoping for a tour?" She owed Mr. You-Could-Say-That a bit of a hard time, didn't she? Perhaps they'd start in the laundry room, and he could enjoy the symphony of twenty-five-year-old washers on spin cycle. Or the water-heater closet where, no matter how many notices she posted or emails she sent, residents insisted on piling boxes and beach chairs in a giant fire hazard she had to clear out at least once a month.

"That's right." He reached out to pet LouLou.

"You're not old enough to rent here." Riley snapped her fingers to get LouLou's attention and was ignored. The traitor dog covered his hand in doggy kisses.

Why didn't that hard jaw crack when he grinned up at her? "I can assure you, I'm well over the age of consent." He threw in a wink, clearly intent on charming her.

He was flirting with her? Flirting? After she'd been given zero days' notice of being laid off and spent weeks sleeping on Grams' sofa? She stopped outside her apartment door, kicking a pair of flip-flops off her *Home Is Where the Dog Is* welcome mat to clear the way. "It's a fifty-five-plus building."

His eyebrows shot straight up, but then he quickly got them back in line. "Of course it is. But don't you have an empty unit I could see?"

"Is your wife over fifty-five? Because that's the only way you could rent here." She wasn't fishing for marital status. She wasn't. Everyone in Miami knew his wife left him the day after his father was found guilty. And no, she wasn't trying to be spiteful or mean-spirited—although the man *did* threaten to fire her—but she couldn't resist prodding a bit to see if his façade would slip.

"It's for—" His jaw worked the peanut butter again. "—someone else."

"Your father?" she suggested with narrowed eyes, opening the door. LouLou ran for the patio. Maybe he'd come clean and tell her his father was in prison, maybe admit why he was really here.

He didn't. Riley turned to block the entry to her apartment, hands propped on the doorframe on either side of her.

His smile slipped. "My grandfather. Do you have something available or not?"

Truth was, half the building was empty. Residents passed on, moved to assisted living or in with relatives, or simply moved away, and no one was knocking down the door to rent here. Riley loved her neighborhood, had essentially grown up here, but the Dorothy was no longer in her prime. Riley acknowledged that, but fifty-five-plus renters were on limited incomes, and the building had long ago spent its reserve budget on hurricane windows and doors. In her old job as an assistant manager at the Donovan Resort, she'd had an entire staff on call to make repairs. Now she had a long list of to-do items right next to the budget spreadsheet that said she couldn't afford them.

Thank God for YouTube videos. She'd learned to snake drains and regrout tile with the help of DIY channels. She didn't need some Donovan coming around and telling her the place was a disaster. Like any aging woman who'd spent too much time in the sun, the Dorothy might need some cosmetic repairs, but Riley was proud of how she'd kept the essentials running on such a tight budget.

"Give me a minute." She closed the door in his face. LouLou followed her to the bathroom where Riley washed up before changing into longer shorts, a pale-pink T-shirt, and a well-loved if slightly ratty pair of Skechers. She grabbed a dental chew from the box on the kitchen counter and bribed LouLou outside to enjoy a bit of sun on the screened-in patio.

One more thing and she'd be totally ready: a quick Google. Caleb Donovan. Smiling, frowning. With his father, his mother, his ex-wife. In newspapers, on the covers of tabloids. How had she not recognized him immediately? He was everything the Donovans stood for—wealth, privilege, and now corruption. A quick scan of a few articles said he'd lost millions, so what was he doing here? Scoping out run-down properties to buy at a deep discount? Grams would never sell the place; he was welcome to waste his time making offers she wouldn't accept.

When Riley reopened her apartment door, he was no longer the Friday-casual businessman.

He was hottie-on-the-way-to-the-gym, his sneakers so high tech with their crisscrossed cords and rubberized tongue adorned with the Ferragamo logo that she figured they did the workout for him.

"Had my gym bag in the trunk." He tugged on his wrinkled gray shirt, releasing the scent of fabric softener that said this was a going-to-the-gym outfit that hadn't actually made it there yet. "Thought I'd change my shoes, but it's pretty hot today, isn't it?"

"It is August." She had to reach down deep to remember how the general manager praised her mere days before she'd been laid off, saying she was the quickest rising star on the management track, and if she stuck with it, she'd have her own hotel to manage before she was thirty-five—a full five years ahead of the schedule she'd painstakingly laid out for herself when she'd started working the front desk of a smaller Donovan property out in Doral. Managing this place was paying her bills, but it wasn't making her dreams come true, and no amount of muscled bicep should make her forget that.

She dragged the mop bucket along behind her, ignoring the fresh laundry smell even though it reminded her of how much she loved to snuggle down in her bed when the sheets were still warm from the dryer. Great, now she was thinking about Caleb Donovan on her sheets and in her bed. And she didn't hate the picture it made.

She shoved the mop at him. "You don't mind helping, do you? Now that you're perfectly dressed for the next event of my day?" She flashed him some teeth, afraid the expression came off more as a snarl than a smile, but he bought it. Chuckled when he dunked the mop in the soapy water and gamely mopped away, though he'd clearly not had much practice.

Riley crushed the flare of disappointment she felt when they were done. Was it evil of her to enjoy a Donovan doing janitorial work at her building? She resisted the urge to snap a photo.

"Have I earned the right to see inside an apartment yet?" His blue eyes lightened with humor, and her heart hammered a too-loud *thump-thump* that she attributed to pushing around the weight of the industrial-size and filled-to-the-brim mop bucket. It wasn't because Caleb Donovan was flirting with her, that was for sure. She was on to him, but he didn't know it. If she kept her mouth shut, how long would he stick with his I'm-looking-for-a-home-for-my-grandfather story? Did he really think she'd just up and forget his threat to fire her?

They'd fallen far, the Donovan clan, but surely not to the

Dorothy level. No, he'd given himself away with that I'm-here-to-fire-you nonsense he'd lobbed at her after asking her out. Donovans didn't rent. They bought; they developed. She felt a hostile takeover brewing. Wary and not really sure what to make of Caleb, Riley tilted her head and considered how to play this. Call him out and let the chips fall? Bide her time and see if she could figure out exactly what his plan was so she could warn Grams? In the end, she decided to go along with his ploy to see how far he'd push it before showing his true Donovan colors.

"Let me show you the empty unit," she said like there was only one.

"I'd appreciate that." He knelt to double-knot his laces, and she found herself staring at the breadth of his shoulders, the nimbleness of his fingers. But now was not the time to get distracted. He still hadn't introduced himself. Caleb Donovan was definitely hiding something.

She stuffed the mop in the bucket and busied herself arranging it so it wouldn't tip over. They'd never met in person, of course. As far as she knew, he'd never been to the Donovan Resort while she worked there. She had no reason to be mad that he didn't know who she was. Who she really was—one of the many employees who'd relied on his family for their livelihoods, their futures, and been cast aside like so much collateral damage.

"Which one is vacant?" Caleb helped her wheel the supplies back to her apartment, where they left them outside her door. It was hard to stay angry at someone amenable to cleaning dog pee off the floor, but it was easy to be mad at herself for so easily forgetting who he was. Who she was. And why they could never be friends.

"Unit 207 is across from my Grams' with the street view, but it's got a nice view of the dog park on the other side of the building." She led the way to the elevator, hands stuffed in her back pockets.

"Your grandmother live here long?"

"My whole life." Unexpectedly, Riley found herself telling him about life at the Dorothy—the weekly potluck dinners at Grams' and the monthly excursions to the Hard Rock Casino. "It's a great place to live," she was saying when the doors opened onto the second-floor hallway.

She'd imagined shabby chic as she'd arranged a few of her college textbooks on the table across from the elevator doors for decorative effect, but looking at it through the lens of the Donovan Resort, it was just plain shabby. At least the walls looked nice. She'd painted them a pale yellow with fresh white trim a few months ago, and the light color never failed to cheer her up. But the carpet was threadbare, and the table leaned a bit to the right, kind of like Patty on her walker.

Who were they kidding with this charade? No Donovan was going to live here. Why was she bothering with her "welcome to the community" speech? Caleb probably didn't even have a grandfather.

"My grandfather would love it here. He's been isolated ever since—" Caleb cleared his throat and started up again. "—ever since some family trouble. It'd be nice for him to make some new friends."

Suddenly, it occurred to Riley that perhaps the Donovans' fall from grace had been a true plummet. This man had lost his company, his father, his wife. Perhaps all his financials had been seized as well, and now he was

focusing on his grandfather's care. She understood that—
the need to care for a loved one, especially an elderly loved
one, whose days might be numbered. Lord knew her own
Grams could be a handful, but Riley'd do absolutely anything to keep her happy.

She walked him all the way to Unit 207, finishing what
had suddenly become an orientation tour. "Everyone looks
out for one another in the building. Your grandfather will
be safe, and if he's got your looks, the ladies will drown
him in casseroles and invitations to fix their plumbing."
She winked, copying his earlier move and feeling her old
assistant-manager persona come out to play. He laughed
with her. God, it'd been so long since she laughed with a
man for the simple pleasure of it. Could he hear how out of
practice she was?

"Thanks for the info." He rocked forward and back on
his heels. "Do you mind if I check out the place by myself?"

"Do you promise not to fire me?" Riley teased, finding it
easy, too easy, to give him the benefit of the doubt. Where
was the rage she'd nurtured for months?

"I'm sorry about that. Old habits, you know?" He ducked
his head, and when he looked up again, his blue eyes caught
hers, and she was trapped in the whirlpool of emotions she
saw in their depths.

"You're in the habit of firing people?" She forced her
gaze away, flipped through her keys for the master.

"I'm in the habit of being in charge."

"And you're not anymore?" *Introduce yourself.* Somehow,
if he'd say his name, admit who he was, they could start over.
She'd tell him how his fall from grace had been hers, too,
and they'd have that in common and maybe even laugh.

But he stayed silent, so she reached past him to open the door, giving him a sarcastic bellman's sweep of the arm to guide him inside. "I'll be across the hall if you have any questions."

"Thanks." He slipped into the apartment with a final nod and shut the door.

Click. Riley was left alone in the hallway, wondering why she felt locked out of the building that was her whole life. She clutched the key in her hand. Maybe Caleb Donovan really was the down-on-his-luck man the media portrayed. Or maybe his machinations were carefully calculated to lull her into trusting him. After all, the Donovans weren't known for their compassion and community service. They were business sharks, and the Dorothy was simply their latest prey. Whatever Caleb was up to, she wouldn't give him the chance to ruin her life a second time.

CHAPTER 4

CALEB WATCHED THROUGH THE PEEPHOLE IN THE DOOR until Riley disappeared into her grandmother's apartment, the gold-plated 6 in 206 rocking when the door swung open. Riley Carson was a woman, a beautiful woman, and because he'd opened his stupid mouth and said that thing about firing her, she didn't like him. Not much anyway and rightly so. Sometimes he could hear his father's words coming out of his mouth, and he couldn't stop himself.

Business was business, but he had the feeling Riley Carson was a lot more than business. He couldn't decide if it was cute or delusional that she thought her grandmother owned the building. *Definitely leaning toward cute.* Too bad she was going to straight up hate him when the condo conversion notices went out. He pushed down the sense of loss, pushed the image of dark eyes—both hers and her dog's—out of his mind, and turned to check out his new future.

It wasn't easy. He kept thinking of Riley's downright pleased smirk when she'd put him to work mopping floors, the flex of capable muscles under that ragged T-shirt while she worked alongside him. And all those shoes outside her door. If he were a neighbor, public shoe storage would be an outrage. Worse, he found it adorably quirky, like her sweet poodle, and that was more troubling than her willfully ignoring the line between private and public space. Equally troubling was how hard he found it to focus on the business at hand. Inspect the apartment. Take notes. Plan for the future. He strode toward the small kitchen, the heart of the home and the perfect place to start his analysis.

Twenty minutes. That's how long it takes for a dream to die. Caleb ended his tour of the one-bedroom in the living room. If all thirty-two studios and one-bedroom units were as run-down as this one, it was going to take more money than Grandpa William was willing to loan him to upgrade the place. Galley kitchens, tiny bathrooms, broken tiles. He was no architect or engineer to evaluate the sturdiness of the building itself, but the basic construction seemed sound enough. Cosmetic repairs alone, however, were already totaling tens of thousands in his head for this one unit.

Maybe it wasn't so bad. Riley Carson wasn't the complete screwup he'd imagined at first, and maybe with an influx of cash from the renters buying into the condo conversion and some skilled management... Oh, who was he kidding? The renters would most likely not be able to afford to buy into the conversion, at least based on his study of the median income in the neighborhood, so he'd be kicking out Riley's grandmother and all her friends.

On paper, it'd made sense to go for a higher-end market, and he hadn't thought much about the renters who'd be displaced. If they'd found this rental, they'd find another, he'd reasoned. Now he wondered how long Patty had lived here and where she and her walker would go once the renovations started.

Robert Donovan would never feel the guilt gnawing at Caleb's gut—he'd do what had to be done to make the place profitable. And that was what Caleb needed to do, too, for his grandfather and his brothers. If he could get his brothers to play ball. Grandpa William's stipulation circled in his head, a puzzle he couldn't quite solve. He took some pictures with his iPad, hoping something would pop out as the missing piece that he could present to his brothers.

Maybe he'd figure out something else for Patty and the other renters. He could already hear his father's laughter. "Why bother?" he'd say. "It's only a bunch of old people." But his father hadn't met Patty, hadn't seen her wobbly walk and wobblier hands. Caleb couldn't simply kick her out, but maybe she'd be better off in an assisted-living facility. Yeah, that was what he'd do. He'd find more accommodating accommodations for the fifty-five-plus residents. They'd be happier in their new homes where their needs were better met.

How he'd do that, he had no idea, and he knew for sure his father's legal team would advise against it. But they were gone now, as soon as the last check was cashed, and Caleb would make his own decisions. He was building his own company, not his father's. Well, not quite his. That damn stipulation of Grandpa William's needed to be addressed, and he needed his uncooperative half brothers to do it.

"Call Lance." Caleb bit the words out tersely, and soon the phone was ringing. Once, twice, voicemail. Just like the last five times. "Dammit, I know you're screening me. Call me back." The same message he'd left yesterday. "It's about Grandpa William. Seriously, you need to call."

It wasn't a lie. Grandpa William was the reason he was trying to reach his brother—both his brothers, actually— but Lance was closest, still in the Miami area, and if Caleb could get him at least to offer some advice or do a minor job on the project, maybe Grandpa William would bend on the stricter stipulations of his business proposal. Give him props for good-faith effort. Maybe cough up some more cash.

Caleb hoped so because Knox, the oldest of Robert Donovan's three sons, was not an easy man to track down. Getting him to agree to Grandpa William's conditions would be tricky. Knox was career military and had never shown an ounce of interest in the family hotel business. The business their father, Robert Donovan, bankrupted and destroyed but that Grandpa William was sure a helping of family togetherness could put right.

Family togetherness? The last time he'd seen Knox was when he left for basic training sixteen years ago. And Lance? Caleb had sat in the back row at Lance's wedding and had a few too many manhattans at the reception. Lance was divorced now, must be over three years ago. Sure, the three of them had different mothers, but they were still brothers. How could so much time have passed without any contact?

Honestly, he didn't blame Lance for not calling him back. If the tables were turned, he'd want nothing to do with the brother who'd stuck by Dad's side, even stupidly defended his actions in court, either. Knox and Lance had seen their father for who he really was early on, but Caleb had held out hope that their father had a larger plan, that somehow it would work out, and he'd let his father's fight with his brothers become his own.

Stupidly, he was as guilty of pushing them away as his father had been. He could only hope that his brothers would eventually hear him out and maybe even forgive him. Grandpa William wouldn't sign the deed over to Caleb alone. All three brothers needed to be in business together. Caleb didn't like having his hands tied, but a deal is a deal, as Grandpa William liked to say, and Grandpa William had been adamant that without all three brothers, there was no deal.

Even more pressing, though, was his need to find out how their lives away from Robert Donovan had turned out. Without their father pulling their strings, what kind of men had they become? And could they help him figure out how to keep the best of being a Donovan while leaving the worst behind?

Pacing the boxed-in living room—really, had no one thought to knock out the kitchen wall and open the place up?—he made one more call to the most recent number he had for Knox, even though it rang and rang and never went to voicemail. He stopped at the entrance to the kitchen, fingers gliding over the pencil marks on the door-frame. Someone grew up here, someone long gone now, but their progress from three feet, two inches to five foot ten remained behind, like a crab leaving its shell when it grows too small. He knew it wasn't Riley's life marked out on the wall, but he pictured her anyway, growing from year to year, her Grams marking time and keeping her close all these years.

Caleb tried to imagine his father—always on the phone brokering some deal or another—taking the time to measure him at the beginning and end of every school year. The picture was even more ridiculous than trying to envision his mother with a pencil and measuring tape in hand instead of the tiny Pomeranian whose paws rarely touched the ground. Perhaps one of his nannies would've done it if he'd asked, but none of them ever lasted an entire school year.

Midday sun blazed through the back-facing window, and Caleb slumped to the floor, heedless of the dirt and dust, and sat cross-legged on the chipped pine. Elbows propped on his knees, he rolled his neck and took a few deep breaths.

This project wasn't about his parents or his brothers or the past. He was supposed to build the Donovan future, and although he'd worked for his father's company since graduating from Duke with his business degree eight years ago, he'd never singled-handedly headed a project of this type before. Conversion? He gazed up at the lopsided ceiling fan with the cracked blade. It'd be easier to raze the building to the ground and start from scratch, just like he was having to do with the business.

He pushed aside the memories of the day the feds came to the office and took his father away in cuffs, of the endless days spent in the courthouse while the trial dragged on, the slam of the gavel after the guilty verdict was delivered. His mother's useless tears; the lawyer's even-more-useless assurances that the business was protected. All that was in the past, and if he wanted to move forward, then he had to make this condo conversion work. Maybe his father's less-than-legal business practices cost the family everything, but that didn't mean Caleb hadn't learned a useful thing or two from his old man. People liked new; they liked shiny, sleek, modern. And Caleb would deliver.

"LouLou!"

The familiar shout shook Caleb out of his reverie. He walked to the window that looked out over the back lot, an overgrown plot of land that, according to the blueprints Grandpa William had shown him, was technically part of the property but had never been developed. An aging chain-link fence enclosed the land, and a handful of people congregated in one corner while half a dozen dogs of many shapes and sizes roamed the grass. A German shepherd and a black Lab raced the perimeter, and a Chihuahua barked from the top of a tree stump every time they ran by. What had Riley called it? A dog park?

"LouLou!" she shouted again.

He leaned into the window, craning to see her. There she was, T-shirt showing a tantalizing flash of belly when she raised her arm. LouLou danced on her hind legs, catching Riley's shorts. Caleb held his breath, wondering if he was about to get an eyeful, but all he could make out was a flash of hot pink, just like her toenails. Riley laughed, brushed the dog away, and hitched the denim back over her hips.

"LouLou, fetch!" she yelled and used some sort of catapult contraption to fling the ball. The poodle ran toward the far fence before the ball even left the catapult. Soon, she was flying back toward Riley, bright-pink ball in her mouth. Though Riley threw the ball again and again, LouLou never seemed to lose interest or energy, always back in a flash and ready to go again. Age and incontinence weren't slowing that dog down one bit.

Caleb couldn't help himself. He locked up Unit 207 with the master key Grandpa William'd given him, took the elevator down, and ambled toward the back lot. LouLou saw him coming before Riley did and, with an excited yip, ran toward him. He crouched down on one side of the chain-link fence while the poodle tried to lick him through the diamond-shaped holes.

"I see you, girl." He scratched behind her ears, and she leaned against the fence, curls pushing through to his side.

"You found the dog park." Riley leaned against the fence, too, arms raised above her head to hang onto the chain-link. He didn't look at how her breasts strained against her T-shirt. He didn't.

The lot was filled with patchy grass and a few tree stumps. "Not much of a dog park, is it?"

She laughed and scooped up LouLou. "It's not the dirt that makes a dog park. It's the dogs. Come on in, and I'll introduce you."

Caleb had done his research. He knew the zoning regulations and where the nearest schools were, but her offer would give him something he couldn't find in county records or on the internet—a real feel for how the community would react to the proposal he'd submitted to the city.

"Hang on." Caleb located a gap in the fence that looked well used as an entry point, chain-link bent back so the pointy bits didn't point at him. He saw another opening across the lot, two poles leaning away from each other to create an odd door—an upside-down triangle through which a middle-aged man in a business suit was trying to coax a reluctant Yorkie. Caleb pushed the broken chain-link a few inches more to the side, careful of the sharp ends where someone had clearly cut the chain. Vandalism. Was there no end to the problems with this property?

"Watch your step." She offered her hand as if he'd need help squeezing through. He wasn't an old lady to need assistance crossing the street, but considering what a butthead he'd been—*You're fired*, indeed—he felt lucky to be offered this olive branch. He placed his fingers against her soft palm. And discovered a different problem. He didn't want to let go.

Her cheeks were bright with color, and a dimple flashed in each one. Every muscle in his body tensed. Not in the oh-crap-what-has-Dad-done-now way of the past year, but more like an oh-crap-she-is-so-damn-beautiful fashion.

Their eyes locked, and with a gentle tug, she guided him through and let go of his hand. He tightened his muscles to keep from clenching her fingers in his and pulling her back against him. Her long body would fit snugly against his, he could tell, her head high enough that all that curly hair would tickle his nose.

Riley bent her knees, placed her dog carefully in the grass and, if he wasn't mistaken, took a steadying breath. Lord knows he needed one, too. He dragged air into his lungs. Pushed it out. Reminded himself they'd just met, and he'd bungled asking her to dinner to such a degree that trying again would be an idiotic choice.

Riley's dark eyes studied him from under darker lashes. Her berry lips softened the severity of her angular cheekbones and aquiline nose. At this angle, strawberry highlights streaked her hair to almost the same shade as her apricot poodle. A matched set.

Really, he needed to stop thinking ridiculous things about her hair and contribute to this conversation. Something real. And businessy. So she'd know he didn't usually stand around in dilapidated lobbies fondling other people's pets. All he could think of, though, were her wide lips and the memory of her bare toes. Luckily, she didn't need him to keep a conversation going.

"Lady." She tilted her head, for all the world reminding him of her poodle again, and he had to fight the urge to reach out and push a few of her escaped curls behind her ear.

"What?"

Her lips twitched like she was about to smile, but she reined it in and pointed beside him. "Meet Lady."

When he dropped his gaze, a black dog that must weigh in at seventy pounds or more sat on its haunches, one paw gracefully extended like royalty expecting an air kiss above the knuckles.

He obliged, bowing his head over Lady's paw. "It's an honor, my Lady."

"Oh, she'll like that. Thinks she's the Ambassador of Dog Park, greeting everyone who enters," a voice said behind him. He turned, and an older woman only a foot or so taller than Lady placed a loving hand on the big dog's head. "She's never met a stranger, but that's how Labs are, of course. Mostly anyway."

"Mostly? She's not friendly?" Caleb didn't see anything about the dog that seemed aggressive, but he took a cautious step back just in case.

"Goodness no. Kindness and people-pleasing are breed traits. I meant Lady's a little bit of this, little bit of that, and a whole lot of Lab. A mostly Lab, if you will. That's the fun of a rescue, isn't it? Never knowing exactly what you've got on your hands?" The woman cackled and tugged on Lady's ear, a move that sent the dog into ecstatic leg thumping. "New around here, are you? Which dog is yours?"

"Oh, I don't—"

"He was checking out the empty apartment." Riley jerked her chin toward the Dorothy, and the older woman's eyes narrowed.

"Thought about moving in a time or two myself." Her eyes traveled from his recently cut hair to the shine on his shoes. "But I'd have to give up my house"—she pointed her chin east—"because it's really too much for one person, you know?"

"You're not missing much." He tried his charm-'em smile on her, but it only made her squint more. "Until you look out the back windows." His gesture encompassed the dogs frolicking in the middle of the lot as well as the ones lounging near where their owners chatted with one another under the shade of a mature mango tree. If he wasn't mistaken, a few were looking their way.

"Neighborhood loves its dogs." The woman's hand slid from Lady's ears down her thick neck. "Riley'll tell you. This dog park is the beating heart of our neighborhood, no doubt about it. Right, Riley?"

"Right." Riley pushed humidity-frizzed curls behind her ear. "Mostly apartments and small lots around here, so it's good to have a spot where the dogs can get in a nice run. We're lucky to have this place."

Caleb chewed the inside of his cheek, thinking how he and Grandpa William had discussed that this lot was ideal for a parking structure. "Can't build anything on the Beach these days without including a parking plan," Grandpa William had groused. Without parking, the conversion would never succeed. High-end clients do not park on the street. Still, it was fun to watch LouLou engage Lady in a game of chase with an enticing play bow and a yip. Lady wagged her thick tail, and they were off. Even more enjoyable was the smile on Riley's face as she watched her pet dash through patches of grass.

"What about the No Trespassing signs? This isn't part of the Dorothy, is it?" Caleb was fishing, and he felt a twinge of guilt for playing dumb. But fishing was all part of the research. One of the biggest hurdles for any developer was community acceptance. How big of an obstacle was this unofficial dog park going to be? Was Riley going to claim her grandmother owned this lot, too?

"Oh, no one minds," Riley said breezily, waving away his question like a mosquito. She tightened her ponytail, and he caught another glimpse of her smooth belly, skin a few shades lighter than her arms and legs. His gut clenched, knowing his next words were going to make it so she never reached out that soft hand to help him again. But they had to be said. Rip off the Band-Aid, if you will, and let go of the stupid fantasy he was building in his mind about how Riley would taste when he kissed her. Sweet like the sound of her voice? Strawberries like the highlights in her hair? Whatever it was, he was never going to find out, because he was the big, bad landlord about to evict her grandmother. Even if he found every resident the poshest retirement home in Miami, there'd be no coming back from that.

"I think someone does, or at least will, mind." Caleb crossed his arms over his chest. "When he builds a parking structure on this lot, you'll have to find another dog park."

"There's nowhere else in the neighborhood." Riley took a step backward, tripping over a Chihuahua running by. She landed on her butt but pretended not to see his hand when he extended it to help her up.

Caleb tucked his rejected helping hand into his pocket. "I'm sure you'll find somewhere else." He knew he sounded like an ass. Like his dad. She was going to hate him—hate him more, he corrected—and he didn't blame her. He kind of hated himself right now. "Your days of taking advantage of an absentee owner are over."

"Why would you say that?" She cocked her chin at him,

the picture of defiance. "I told you my grandmother owns the place."

"That can't possibly be true." He'd seen the paperwork himself. How did he gently break it to her that her grandmother was indulging in a senile fantasy?

"Well, it *is* true." Riley crossed her arms and leveled a glare at him hot enough to make sweat pop on his forehead. The neighborhood, or at least this neighbor in particular, seemed to believe this lot was theirs. Her quick defensiveness proved they weren't just going to pack up their dog toys and go home when the bulldozers rolled in.

Matching hot-pink accents or not, Riley was trouble. He had to get his head back in the game and remember why he was here. "Honey, *I* am the owner, signed deeds and all, and I have big plans for this property."

Hand to heart, Riley stared at him with those wide eyes.

"Oh, this one's *special* indeed." Lady's owner cackled and placed a wrinkled hand on his shoulder. "That's nice, dear. You go on and make your plans. You know what they say about the best-laid ones, don't you?" She shuffled off to the group of people at the mango tree, leaving him with Riley. Planning a coup, no doubt. Lady was a lady, but he could tell by the way the dog owners checked him out after a few words that Lady's owner was the designated dog park gossip. Caleb suddenly had a bad feeling, the kind usually saved for reports that the foundation was compromised or a Cat 4 hurricane was barreling its way toward one of their hotels during the height of tourist season.

"Wait a minute, Caleb Donovan." Riley's fingers fluttered on her chest. "Are you telling me you swindled my Grams out of her property?"

"You know who I am?" He couldn't help the flick of pride that she'd heard of him. Maybe she'd read about the timeshares down in the Keys or the resort in the Bahamas.

"Of course." More heat flashed in her eyes, and the flick of pride died an even quicker death. She knew the headlines. Knew about his dad. The worst of his family obliterated any good he'd ever accomplished.

He should know her. He saw it on her face, the careful way she watched him. How could he have forgotten a woman like this? He couldn't place her, and it killed him to have to ask, "We've met before?"

Her curls shook with her denial. "Why would you recognize any of the thousands of employees whose careers you ended?"

He sucked in a breath. It was true he'd ordered the terminations days before the assets were seized. "I didn't have a choice."

"You made a lot of choices."

LouLou jumped at Riley's hip, the bounce-bounce of pick-me-up, but Riley ignored the dog to glare at him some more.

LouLou turned her attention to him. Bounce-bounce. Caleb scooped up the dog, a move that sent the poodle into a licking spasm. Soon, the underside of his chin was thoroughly dog-slobbered. She was a godsend, this tiny tornado of tongue, lick by lick elevating his mood from the bleak thoughts Riley's accusations triggered.

He didn't like to remember the dark days right after the trial, when everything was up in the air and no matter how he crunched the numbers, there was no way to save his family's business. No way to save the hotels or the jobs. He'd liquidated assets and cashed in stock options, and none of it had mattered in the end. His father had thoroughly screwed the company, and Caleb was glad for the hefty prison sentence the judge proclaimed with a smack of her gavel.

What he hadn't anticipated was that as the one left behind, he'd be facing the consequences of his father's actions in the real world. It didn't seem fair that Robert Donovan got to hide out in a prison cell while Caleb dealt with the fallout. That was what he deserved, he supposed, for believing that while his father occasionally lied to get his way, he would never lie to his own son.

By now, LouLou was sniffing his ear, and if he didn't put a stop to it, he suspected a thorough ear-cleaning was coming his way. He tilted his head away from the dog, which only inspired her to cover his neck in doggy kisses.

"What a little love," he cooed, stroking the dog's back while supporting her hind legs on his forearm. She agreed with more vigorous licking.

"Traitor," Riley mumbled at her dog. She took custody of LouLou, holding her in a loose grip under her arm. "First pee, then slobber. I'm sorry to inflict so much doggily fluid on you in one day, but this one is a nonstop supervisory nightmare. Aren't you?" She punctuated the lighthearted scold with a kiss on the top of LouLou's poofy head.

No doubt about it, he was jealous. Of a dog.

LouLou squirmed in Riley's arms, wiggling around until she could butt Riley's chin with the top of her head. He'd never thought much of Mr. Pom-Pom, but now he realized he missed having a dog around.

"It's okay," he found himself saying, wishing he was still holding the dog so he could at least get Riley to look at him.

"Dogs will be dogs." Riley hugged LouLou to her side. "It's not like I had a *choice*."

Caleb winced. "I'm sorry, too. If it helps any, that was the worst time of my life."

Riley considered him, head tilted, cataloging him from head to toe. "It kind of does. Were you miserable?"

No one had ever asked him how he felt about the whole thing. No one had noticed if he was miserable or not. The words crowded into his throat, but all that came out was, "Yeah."

"Good." Riley's fingers covered those soft-looking lips, the pink tips pressing into her cupid's bow. "You really think you're the owner? I don't understand how that could be."

He nodded because he was *practically* the owner. Once Lance finally called him back and they somehow got Knox involved or Grandpa William to change his mind, he'd own every square inch of this run-down money pit.

"That doesn't even make sense. Why would you want this place? The neighborhood is residential. You can't build a hotel here." Riley tugged at the fabric of her scooped neck, righting the havoc LouLou's wiggling was doing to her neckline, and revealed another flash of hot-pink underneath. Sighing, she bent down to let LouLou run wild again, and the swells of her breasts pushed against the material in a drool-inducing way. *Down boy*, he told his inner hound. Hot pink wasn't even his favorite color, and he for sure should be keeping his eyes above her neck.

"Zoning ordinances can be changed." He was definitely looking at her eyes. Her big, brown eyes that were none too happy with him. "But I'm thinking more of a condo conversion."

"You've been here all of two seconds, and you want to completely change the neighborhood?" She planted her hands on her hips and notched her chin up. LouLou scooted closer to his leg and nosed the back of his knee. "Are you kidding right now?"

He squatted and soothed a hand down the dog's back. "It's just business, honey."

"Well, *honey*," Riley sniffed and tugged LouLou toward her. She eyed him up and down like he was something she wouldn't touch with a doggy bag. "I hope you have a backup plan. No one's touching Grams' place."

Riley stomped off, LouLou watching him over her shoulder like she'd never see him again. Thunder rumbled and a few large splats of rain quickly turned into a torrent. In seconds, Riley and her dog were out of sight, and he was soaked to the skin.

CHAPTER 5

HONEY? HONEY? RILEY KICKED OFF HER MUDDY sneakers outside her front door and leaned against the wall, grateful once again for the enclosed hallway that kept the elements out and the AC in. With LouLou tucked under one arm, she reached down with the other to peel off her wet socks. Luckily, she was an expert at balancing a freaked-out poodle while accomplishing tasks like brushing her teeth or putting dishes in the washer.

When it rained, LouLou got nervous. When it thundered? She was an anxiety ball, and no homeopathic pills or overpriced thunder shirts would calm her. Dr. Morrow, LouLou's veterinarian, offered to write a prescription, but Riley hated the idea of drugging her pooch, especially since thunder was a daily occurrence during the summer. Besides, LouLou was fine as long as she had ninety-nine percent body contact with a human. Riley stepped inside, grabbed a towel she kept on the entry bench for rainstorm emergencies, and gave the shivering poodle a brisk rubdown.

But seriously, *honey*? Riley wrapped LouLou in the towel and walked with her to the kitchen where she poured some water into her Keurig, prepping for a late night of research. Grams always told an entertaining story but not always a true one. Public records were the way she'd get to the bottom of this mystery. Who did Caleb Donovan think he was, calling her honey while threatening her dog park and her grandmother's gorgeous building? When she found proof her Grams did own the building, he'd be eating those words. With honey.

In the bathroom, Riley tossed the wet towel in the hamper and ran a dry one over her own out-of-control curls.

"Zoning ordinances can be changed." Her singsong, high-pitched voice was meant to calm LouLou, but the words themselves still infuriated her. LouLou perked her ears and tilted her head, more relaxed now that they were inside where the booms of thunder were muted.

The sound of the Keurig finishing its cycle brought Riley back to the kitchen, LouLou's favorite room. The storm outside still troubled LouLou, so rather than spin in circles in front of the refrigerator door until Riley gave in and gave her a treat, she cowered under the breakfast table until Riley sat down. Then, she levered herself up Riley's legs until Riley had no choice but to reach down and pull her the rest of the way onto her lap.

One hand wrapped around her mug, Riley propped open her laptop with the other. The second bedroom was set up as a home office-slash-guest room, but fifty years' worth of the building's records took over most of the room. Riley found it easier to work in the kitchen. Closer to the coffee, and she could watch LouLou when she used her doggy door to go outside on the patio.

Honey. She couldn't get his voice out of her head, the deep rasp of it and how she'd found herself leaning toward him to better catch the sound. She'd liked him—the light-brown hair cropped close to his scalp, the way his hand felt in hers, his gentleness with LouLou—a lot. Right up until he'd gone all smug and possessive about the building, the dog park, her job. No way he was the owner. No way.

Sure, she had a long day tomorrow of some pretty grueling work on the stucco, but she couldn't sleep until she proved Caleb Donovan wrong. Riley angry-typed the address into the search bar and followed a convoluted trail through public records until she found it. Rainy Day Holdings. Grams' management company, or so she'd told Riley when the on-site manager position became available and Rainy Day hired her. *"Don't want the neighbors to know I'm the one collecting rent,"* Grams had said in a low, dramatic whisper. *"I like to play at being one of them."* Play? Grams was the queen of the Dorothy, and everyone knew it.

If Riley's friend, Marina, a real estate paralegal, weren't about to give birth any day now, she'd leave the background check to her. Why had she never dug deeper into Rainy Day? Probably because she'd wanted to believe Grams. Searches for Donovan and Rainy Day brought up nothing but a bunch of articles about Caleb's father and the crumbling of his empire. Could Caleb be the money behind Rainy Day? No, the transfer of ownership happened long before either she or Caleb were born. Didn't that prove he couldn't be the owner? What would Marina do next? Riley kept typing until she found the answer she wished she'd had years ago.

William Donovan.

Oh, her Grams was such a liar. Riley let the information sink in for a moment, and then she picked up her phone.

"More tea?" Grams held the flowered teapot aloft, but Riley waved her off. Two cups of tea, four finger sandwiches, and one pear tart later, Riley still didn't have the answers she'd come for. She'd need to unbutton her jeans if she drank another cup.

Riley crossed her ankles so that the toe of her sandal dug into the plush burgundy carpet. "Grams, you have to tell me. How did William Donovan buy the Dorothy back from you?"

Grams' face, still beautiful underneath her carefully styled and sprayed-within-an-inch-of-its-life white hair, tightened in disapproval. Years of Botox injections made it so very few emotions were obvious on her face unless she wanted them seen. Grams wanted Riley to know she was annoyed. Too bad. Riley was annoyed, too, and needed answers.

"You always told me that the Dorothy was the only good thing you got out of your first marriage." Perhaps a bit of prompting would get Grams talking about her past with William Donovan, a past she'd mentioned a few times over the years but, in very un-Grams-like fashion, never elaborated on, no matter how much a younger Riley'd begged. She didn't think being one degree of separation from the Donovans influenced her hospitality-centered career choice, but she also couldn't rule out her fascination with the one ex-husband Grams never wanted to talk about.

"That man." Grams could've been discussing any of her three husbands or one of the many boyfriends she'd had since divorcing Number Three and swearing off marriage. Grams loved to fall in love, but she never stayed there long.

Grams waved an airy hand and then settled it on Henry the Prince, the Persian cat sitting daintily beside her on the mauve sofa. The Prince blinked his blue eyes at her, and Riley became even more annoyed because they reminded her of Caleb Donovan and how his baby blues had admired her. At first, anyway.

"Did you know he owned Rainy Day?" Riley was good at keeping residents, who often mistook her maintenance visits for social calls, focused on the business at hand, but her tricks didn't work on Grams.

"No."

At Riley's skeptical look, Grams leaned back, straining the buttons on her paisley silk button-down. "I may have suspected, but I didn't know."

"What did you know?"

"That man. The third one. I told you about his gambling problem, didn't I?"

Riley shifted in her seat, remembering what a rapt audience she'd been as a child, soaking up Grams' glamorous love stories. As a proud descendent of Husband Number Two—the only one who'd died rather than getting tossed aside in favor of a newer, more glamorous love—Riley gloried in the drama of Grams' descriptions of European travels and men who let her down. Who needed telenovelas when Grams was your grandmother? "He gambled away your love. That's what you told me."

Grams snorted. "More like he gambled away our home. Lost the Dorothy in a poker game."

"How terrible!" Riley was sucked into the drama like she always was. She found herself leaning forward, teetering on the edge of her seat. "William stole your building in a poker game?"

"I didn't know it was William." Grams covered Riley's hand with her own. "That good-for-nothing Number Three said he didn't know the guy's name, but he described him.

Sounded like William. Back then, I didn't want to know. Not really."

"But you guessed?" Riley eyed the tarts. They were so good, and she could work the calories off pulling weeds or maybe finally installing the new drainpipe.

"When I got a letter from some lawyer saying I could live rent-free for the rest of my life, well, who else could it be but that skirt-chaser William trying to make up for all the times he cheated on me? I accepted the terms, and you know the rest."

"Terms?" Riley lost interest in the tart. She'd heard about Grams' rocky first marriage but never about any lease conditions. "What terms?"

"The usual." Grams elegantly flipped her hand, a left-over move from her beauty pageant days. "No subletting, no pets. Funny thing, too, you know it didn't become a fifty-five-plus building until I turned fifty-five? I'd complained to the manager about the couple downstairs fighting at all hours of the night. Next thing I knew, they were gone, and no one under fifty-five was allowed to rent. I always knew someone was looking out for me. Even in the bad ol' days."

The "bad ol' days" were the years right after the divorce from Number Three. It was the end of Grams' luxurious lifestyle. She'd done the best she could, raising her only child, Riley's mom, on the salary she made as an office manager for a local accountant, but it was no secret she missed her high-roller lifestyle.

"You should've told me." Riley filled her in on Caleb Donovan's appearance yesterday, and Grams paled.

"So he's dead. William's dead." Grams swallowed and

gathered the Prince to her ample chest. "Oh, the greatest love of my life is gone! What will I do now? I can't possibly go to my hair appointment while I'm in mourning." A single tear dripped into the Prince's coat.

"I'm sure you'll rally by this afternoon. You never miss your weekly 'do date with Kelly." Used to and certainly amused by Grams' dramatics, Riley did a quick search on her phone. "Besides, he's alive. I guess Caleb must be part of Rainy Day now."

"That bastard!" Grams straightened so quickly, the Prince was offended and jumped to the carpet where he put his full attention to cleaning his back paw. "How dare he still be alive after all this time!"

Riley laughed. "Grams, I'm sure you'll outlive him. You'll outlive everyone."

Grams smiled and poured herself another cup of tea. "That's what I'm counting on, Riley. That and you keeping the Dorothy away from the bastard and whatever he has planned."

Riley rose to go, looping the long strap of her cross-body bag over her shoulder. "I'm not sure what you expect me to do. He owns the place."

Grams took a long sip, eyeing her over the rim of the dainty, flowered cup. "We women have our ways. You know what I'm talking about."

"Grams, don't be disgusting." She leaned down and kissed Grams' powdered cheek. "I'll find out what Caleb Donovan is up to, and I'll stop him."

"Kiss that cutie-pie dog of yours for me." Grams held Riley close for a moment and then let her go. "And if you see that bastard William, tell him I'm dead."

———————

The main reason Riley liked her current job was that it kept her close to Grams. Mom had done her best by Riley, but working her cruise-line job to pay for private schools hadn't left them a lot of mother-daughter bonding time. It was Grams who watched Riley while Helen was away for weeks at a time, who signed field trip permission slips, who came to watch Riley kick ass in her high school debates.

"Where's that puppy dog?" Riley added her sandals to the pile of shoes collecting outside her front door. At some point, she'd have to bring them inside, but her shoe-buying addiction meant she could put off that chore indefinitely. Inside, she shook out her hair and clicked her tongue for LouLou.

LouLou usually met her at the door, a furry tornado of excitement. It was raining, though, so she might be in one of her thunder caves.

"LouLou?" First, Riley checked her closet. LouLou loved to snuggle up with Riley's dirty laundry and chew on a shoe or two while waiting out a storm. Nope, no LouLou. Next, she checked the bathroom. LouLou sometimes scrambled into the old 1950s iron tub between the curtain and the side. Still no poodle.

"Come on out, LouLou." Riley checked under her bed, a less usual but not unheard of hiding space. Under the breakfast table. In the office? Living room? Riley wouldn't let herself panic. LouLou was around here somewhere.

The rain outside picked up weight, hitting the covered patio at an angle and soaking the two Adirondack chairs. LouLou wouldn't be out on the patio in this kind of weather, but Riley was running out of options. She slid open the door.

"LouLou?"

Spray filtered by the three floor-to-ceiling screens misted her hair and made her clingy white T-shirt even clingier. Riley checked under the Adirondacks, inside the igloo-shaped dog house LouLou never used, behind the giant potted aloe.

That was when she found it. Not her dog. The hole in the corner of the screen, low to the ground and just big enough for one terrified poodle to make a run for it.

Riley ran for the screen door and flung it open. "LouLou!" Her shout was drowned out by a crack of thunder so loud the patio roof shook. "LouLou!"

Still barefoot, Riley ran into the storm and out to the street. The rain blinded her, or maybe it was her tears. Lightning flashed. "LouLou!"

CHAPTER 6

"Lance, call me." Caleb didn't say any more, didn't really even need to say that much, but somehow he couldn't give up on contacting his brother. He slid his phone into the back pocket of his khakis and rested his hands against the tile countertops of Unit 207. He couldn't start work on the building until the permits were approved, but he'd returned to the Dorothy today for another walk-through. Should units be combined to make more spacious accommodations, or should he jump on the small space-big style trend with minimalist Japanese décor and the ability to shoehorn more condos onto each floor?

There were a lot of decisions to be made before he met with architects and designers. He wanted the ideas to be his and his alone. He'd always been the numbers guy on his father's projects, the second-in-command. Now, he wanted to be involved in all aspects, which meant he had a lot to learn, and he relished the challenge of launching a project on his own. The Dorothy wasn't just another Donovan property; it would be a Caleb Donovan creation.

Or, if his brothers ever bothered to return his calls, perhaps a Donovan brothers creation. Not likely, though, and not what he wanted, either. Working with family again? Family he hadn't talked to in years? It seemed a recipe for drama and disaster, his two least favorite things. His brain traveled through options, trying to find a loophole in Grandpa William's conditions. What would satisfy his grandfather but leave Caleb with the Dorothy, free and clear? If it were his father on the other end of this deal, a large profit margin would be enough to sway him, but the way Grandpa William reminisced about the past lately made Caleb worry the only way out of this mess was to see it through.

Unable to solve that particular dilemma at the moment, Caleb looked out over the dog park, or rather, empty lot. He better not start thinking like the locals, but it was hard to think of it as anything else with the constant stream of dogs and owners passing through the area all day. He even recognized Lady, regally resting her head on one of the hacked-up tree stumps.

Like every day this summer, the storm blew in around five o'clock. Lady and the other dogs were called in by their owners, and one by one, they left through the gap in the corner of the lot where one chain-link pole listed far from the other. Some people had umbrellas, but most simply made a run for it, their dogs trotting beside them.

Today, he was nice and cozy inside, enjoying his solo trip through all the Dorothy's possibilities. Measuring tape in one hand, he sketched out configurations on his tablet while rain beat against the windows. Maybe Grandpa William was right and residential property could be his thing. It was different to think of designing a home rather than a vacation getaway fantasy.

Thunder rolled and lightning lit the room while he debated the pros and cons of solar panels. The rain seemed to be letting up, but with another crash of thunder, it poured even harder.

A yip pulled his attention from the puddle and out the window. A soggy mess of a small dog sat outside, paw raised like it was hurt. The dog shivered. Caleb looked up at the sky that wasn't about to clear anytime soon, shrugged, and headed out to get the dog.

The dog stayed where it was, shaking and obviously too terrified to move. When Caleb got close, he squatted and held out his hand to be sniffed.

"Hey there, little one. What's going on?" He opened his hand and turned it palm up. The dog gave a tentative lick.

"Let me see that," Caleb said, gently turning the dog's paw. A small sliver of glass bisected the pad. "Ouch, I bet that hurts."

The dog whined and nosed Caleb's hand.

"Okay, buddy, let's get you inside so we can get you patched up." Caleb kept his voice soft, and the dog didn't object when he placed one hand under its belly and lifted. The dog shivered and shook, pressing itself into Caleb's side and burying its nose in his armpit.

It was a relief to be out of the downpour, but when Caleb tried to put the dog on the countertop for a closer examination, it clung to his arm.

"Poor little guy," Caleb said, raising its chin with his finger to see its hot-pink collar. He flipped the tag. "LouLou? How can that be you? I thought you were a poodle, not a drowned rat."

LouLou blinked trusting eyes at him, and he couldn't believe he hadn't recognized her immediately. Sure, she was about half the size she'd looked yesterday with her poofy curls plastered to her skin, and her fur was so pale that when wet it simply blended into the pinky-gray of her skin. Still, he should've recognized that sweet face and smooth tongue. Riley must be going out of her mind with worry.

"I bet someone's looking for you right now." He kept a steady stream of small talk while he extracted the glass from her paw and wrapped a fast-food napkin he found in his pocket around the injury. "Don't worry, we'll find your Riley and get you home safe and sound."

LouLou nosed at the makeshift bandage, perhaps catching a whiff of burrito, then huffed and lay down on the counter, wrapped paw gingerly held an inch above the tile like she was afraid to put it down. Caleb checked her collar again and found a phone number under her name, but when he called it, no one picked up and the voicemail was full. He didn't question the impulse, just saved the number in his phone under Riley-LouLou.

"What next?"

She tilted her head like she was listening to him but didn't offer a plan of action.

"Shall we take you home?"

When he placed her on the floor, she lifted her injured paw and leaned against his leg. So that was out. He'd definitely be carrying this poodle around, at least until he found something more secure for the wound than a Taco Bell napkin.

Riley's grandmother! She lived across the hall. With LouLou held tight under his arm, he knocked on the door hard enough that the number six danced against the cream-painted wood. He waited a few moments and pounded again. No answer. Now what? Riley's place, of course. He held the dog on the elevator ride down, but like her grandmother, Riley wasn't home, either. Maybe they were out somewhere in the storm together?

Caleb thought of the people leaving the dog park, the

ones who must come every day, must see Riley and LouLou every day. Someone knew this poodle. All he had to do was find a dog park regular, and LouLou would be all set with a sitter until Riley got home.

"We're going to be very wet, LouLou, but don't you worry because we'll be together."

LouLou seemed content enough in his hold, even when he walked through the front lobby, out the entrance, and into the rain. She shivered and snuggled closer to him, twitching whenever thunder rumbled, but she didn't try to escape or run. Surprised at her trust, he held her tight against his side and knocked on the door of the single-family house to the east of the apartment building. No one answered, so he dashed across the street to the next house down.

A deep bark warned him not to knock again on the hunter-green door, but a dog in the house was a hopeful sign. He knocked again, and the dog barked louder. The door opened a crack, then widened to reveal Lady's owner holding Lady back by her jewel-encrusted collar.

"LouLou!" she said, waving them in from the rain. "However did you end up with Riley's dog?"

"I was at the apartments, and she was outside in the rain. She's hurt." He held up LouLou's paw, and Lady gave it a thorough sniff, tail wagging hard enough to create a breeze.

"Damn kids and their beer bottles." The woman gave a sniff every bit as loud as Lady's. "I've got some creams and gauze in the kitchen. Follow me."

"I met Lady yesterday, but I didn't catch your name. I'm Caleb." He followed her through a living room cluttered with handmade political signs declaring *Keep Our Parks, Give Bees a Chance,* and *I Can't Believe I Still Have to Protest This Shit.*

"Oh, I know who you are, Mr. Donovan." She pulled a plastic bin out from under the marble-topped breakfast bar and lined up small scissors, a roll of gauze, surgical tape, and an antiseptic cream. "Name's Eliza. Bring poor LouLou over here."

Eliza made short work of doctoring the cut, telling him about how she'd lived in this neighborhood her whole life. "Before all that development down on South Beach, you know? Good place to raise a family."

"Did you?" Caleb kept his hand on LouLou the whole time, and she switched back and forth between licking his hand and Eliza's.

Eliza let out a surprised cackle. "No, I did not, but this neighborhood's like a family to me. Know everybody on this block and the next one over."

Caleb smiled. "Does that mean you know where Riley might be?"

"Probably out looking for this mutt." Eliza put the supplies away with short, economical movements. "She'll be overjoyed to see her little troublemaker, won't she?" Eliza touched her nose to LouLou's and got a tongue up her nostril as a thank you. "For you." Eliza slipped the poodle a treat out of her pocket and fed another one to Lady.

"What should I do?" Caleb rubbed the back of his wet head. "She doesn't pick up, and her voicemail is full."

"Got her number, did you?" Eliza cackled and gave Lady a strong pat on her broad head. "She sometimes forgets her phone. She'll be out scouring the neighborhood is my guess. Probably best to wait it out at her place. She'll eventually come home."

Caleb thought about the calls he needed to make, the

plans he needed to get in order. "I don't suppose I could leave LouLou with you?"

Eliza inspected him, from dripping hair to soaked footwear. "I don't suppose you could. Go on, take that dog home yourself."

The Lab followed them to the front door. From the protection of her covered front porch, Eliza pointed to the Dorothy. "Get on with you. She might be there already."

"Wish us luck!" Caleb dashed across the street without waiting for an answer, but he heard Eliza's cackle over the pounding of the rain on the pavement. He opened the double doors that led to a small lobby and once again found himself in front of Riley's door.

Heels, sneakers, flip-flops, ankle boots, knee-high boots, loafers. The line of shoes outside the front door made him wonder if Riley had enough closet space. It also showed what a safe neighborhood it was, to leave personal belongings in a public space like that. He used the poodle-shaped doorknocker to rap twice. No answer. He used his fist. Still no answer. He tried calling again. Nothing.

"Try to do a nice thing for someone, and they're not even home to appreciate it."

LouLou did not share his frustration, seemingly content to let him carry her around forever. Her weight was surprisingly comforting, and since they were both soaked through, he didn't mind her wet dog smell.

Where could Riley be? If Eliza was right, probably out searching for her dog. So where would a frightened pooch go during a thunderstorm?

"Where's your favorite place?" Caleb made eye contact with the dog as if that would facilitate mental telepathy or something. LouLou stopped shivering long enough to wag her tail. And then he got it. The dog park! That was why she'd been outside the window. She'd run to the dog park, then spotted him in the building. In her rush to get to him, she'd walked across some glass. It all made sense.

"Back to the park?" He tried eye contact again since it seemed to work last time. She wagged her tail harder, and they headed back into the rain. It only took a few steps before LouLou's ears perked forward, and her tail beat his bicep like a broom.

"LouLou!" a hoarse voice called. "LouLou!"

"Over here!" Caleb yelled, not sure where the voice was coming from but hearing the pain in it and wanting to do anything in his power to make that pain stop. What could he say? Rescuing furry damsels in distress brought out his mushy side.

Through the sheets of rain, he spotted Riley limping along the sidewalk across the street from the dog park. She didn't look much better than LouLou had, hair flattened and plastered to her head, clothes sticking to her as though she'd taken a dunk in the ocean. And was she barefoot? All those shoes outside her front door, and she'd run out in the storm without so much as a flip-flop to protect her?

"You're a pair, aren't you?" He whispered to LouLou, waving frantically to get Riley's attention. "Over here! Riley, I've got LouLou!"

Riley looked across the road, and he knew the moment she saw them. She collapsed to her knees, hands over her face, and a giant sob racked her body. So they'd be staying out in the rain a little longer. He crossed over and knelt beside her, the soaked poodle between them.

"It's okay. She's okay. You're okay." He sounded like an idiot. He knew it, but he kept saying stupid things anyway. "I've got her. She's right here."

Riley sucked in a big breath and looked up at him with her tilted eyes. "Thank you." She held out her arms for LouLou.

He shifted the dog's weight to Riley's hold, but LouLou curled her paw around his wrist, tight.

Riley's chin sank. "I deserve that."

"No, it happens." Caleb didn't know what he was talking about. What happened? Rain? Dogs running loose in the streets? "You didn't do anything wrong." He knew that part at least was right.

"I couldn't find her." She scrubbed at her face with the heels of her hands, eyes red and lids swollen from crying. "And now she's hurt. What happened to her paw?"

"She's fine, just a small piece of glass." He pried LouLou's paw off his wrist and handed the dog over, surprised at how giving her back felt like a loss. If he felt this attached after such a brief time with the dog, how bad must Riley have felt when she realized LouLou was missing? The impulse to make Riley feel better kept his assurances flowing. "Eliza patched her up, and she'll be good as new in no time."

"Thank you." She buried her face in LouLou's fur and stood, but as soon as she did, she lost her balance and keeled over with a squeak.

Caleb reached out to steady her. "What's wrong?"

Riley closed her eyes and leaned heavily on him. "Think I stepped on something."

"Let me see."

Feeling a sense of déjà vu, he crouched to inspect the bottom of her foot, dark with dirt and specks of gravel stuck to it. "Looks like a bad bruise. Maybe from a rock."

Riley bit her lower lip. "Sounds right."

"Can you walk?" He levered her back to standing on her own.

"Of course." One careful step forward. Then another. "Thanks for taking care of LouLou, but you don't have to hang around." She winced and took another step, face as white as the knuckles clutching her dog. "I've got it from here. No problem."

It was painful to watch. Still, she'd said to back off, so he did. Until she stumbled, almost dropping the poodle, and a car horn blared at her for hogging up the road.

"This is ridiculous." He scooped her up, exactly like he'd done with her dog. Unlike LouLou, she wasn't grateful.

"Hey! What're you doing?" Riley couldn't bat at his chest because she was holding onto her dog, but she glared. "You can't swoop in and take over everything."

"Hang on tight. I'm taking you home." Caleb clutched Riley and LouLou against his chest, her legs over his arm like in some damn rom-com movie, and strode back toward her condo. If he wasn't mistaken, he could hear Eliza's cackle following them, but didn't care. It felt good to save LouLou, and it felt even better to have Riley in his arms.

CHAPTER 7

RILEY'D NEVER BEEN CARRIED OVER A THRESHOLD LIKE a bride in an old movie before, and it wasn't going to happen today, either. Not because Caleb wasn't willing, bless his well-meaning heart and strong biceps, but because she couldn't get the keys out of her soaked jeans without dropping LouLou. Caleb gingerly lowered her to the ground, making sure she leaned on him to keep weight off her bruised foot. She set the poodle down, only to have her immediately jump back up with her bouncy-bouncy-pick-me-up signal. Caleb apparently liked holding creatures with injured feet because he held LouLou while Riley fished out her keys.

"Thanks." Riley opened the door and grabbed the dog towel. She wrapped it around LouLou and extracted her from Caleb's hold. "Really, really thank you. Thank you so much. I don't even know how to thank you enough."

"I don't suppose you have one of those for me?" Caleb pointed his chin at the towel.

Caleb was as soaked through as she and LouLou were. "Oh! Of course. Please come in. I should've offered. What was I thinking?"

He swiped at the water running down his face with the back of his hand. "That you met me yesterday? That I threatened to fire you? That I own the building and am technically your boss?"

"You know, suddenly I'm not feeling that much like

inviting you in." Riley pushed the door open a bit wider with her elbow. "Just kidding. You saved my dog. Everything else can be on hold until we get you sorted out."

"Thanks." He stepped inside and dripped onto the tile floor. "Sorry."

"No worries. Why don't you make a dash for the bathroom?" Riley used the arm not holding her dog to point down the hallway. "Toss your clothes out, and I'll pop them in the dryer."

"And then?" He was already on the move. "A towel toga? Not that I mind." He flashed a wink at her over his shoulder.

Riley buried her suddenly overly warm face in LouLou's damp fur. "Why don't you take a warm shower? You'll feel better, and it'll give me a chance to hunt something up for you."

Riley took a step away from the doorframe and immediately regretted it. She hissed in pain and leaned back against the wall. Stupid foot. She raised it, crossing her ankle over her knee to have a look.

"Let me see." Caleb was back, still dripping, but then so was she. He dropped to one knee and took her ankle in his hand. "Does this hurt?" He pressed gently on several points until he found the one that made her wince. "Should we go to the ER? Maybe you should have this looked at."

"No, it'll be fine. It's only a bruise." She slid down the wall to her butt, LouLou squirming against her. "I'll sit here until it heals. LouLou has enough dog food in her bowl to make it a few days. I'll be fine."

"I think you're the one who needs a warm shower and a change of clothes. And some ice?"

"Ice would be nice." Riley's head thumped against the

wall. Of all the stupid ways to get injured. Running out into the storm without shoes. He'd never believe she was competent at her job now, and if he really was the owner and really did have big plans for the Dorothy, she wanted him to respect her. Maybe he'd listen to her about what was best for the building, for the residents, for the neighborhood. *Yeah, right. A Donovan who changed his plans because of community input.* It'd been a stupid thought to begin with, made even stupider by her stupid injury. *Stupid, stupid, stupid.* Her second-grade teacher, Ms. Garcia, used to say that *stupid* was a bad word, but Riley couldn't think of a better one to describe her current situation.

"Here." Caleb pressed one of her cold packs—wrapped in her dancing lemons kitchen towel—against the sole of her foot. "Better?"

Riley closed her eyes and nodded. He slid down next to her, and the warmth of his body cut through the chill of her wet clothes. She fought the urge to snuggle against him, to soak up all that delicious body heat for herself. She settled for a long inhale, enjoying his earthy smell. Some kind of cologne, she guessed, smoky and peppery with a hint of leather. Or maybe that was just his soaked footwear.

"Dammit, we've ruined another pair of your shoes." She opened her eyes to check out the second pair of loafers her dog drama had damaged. "I should go ahead and hand over my credit card to you now. What's this gonna set me back?"

Caleb curled an arm around her shoulders, pulling both her and LouLou against his side. He tilted his head so that his cheek rested on the top of her head. "Don't worry about it. They're only shoes."

She took a moment, then another, to soak in the

situation. Sitting on her tile floor, soaked to the bone, with her former—er, current—boss snuggling beside her. Surreal didn't even begin to cover it. But his scent up this close was even better, clean and crisp, and the man did put off heat like the Dorothy's old-style radiators. It might be surreal, but it was still really nice.

"The important thing is that you and LouLou are safe." Caleb gave her shoulders a squeeze. "Do you think if I help, you can make it to the couch?"

Since her couch was pleather—a decorating decision she'd made after LouLou threw up on her chenille sofa a few too many times for Riley to feel like it was ever truly clean—she nodded. "LouLou should probably go outside to the patio for a few minutes, but there's a rip in the screen. Behind the aloe plant in the corner. That's how she got out."

"I'll take care of it." Caleb removed his arm, and Riley felt the loss of heat but refused to reach out the hand that wanted to clutch at him and pull him back to her.

In a few moments, Caleb was back from the screened-in patio, crouched in front of her, even more wet than before. He held out his arms for LouLou. "I blocked off the corner with some furniture. She should be safe until we get someone out to patch the screen. Maybe you should think about something more substantial for the bottom few feet, like aluminum or something. You know, to be safe."

If the Dorothy's finances were a wreck, Riley's weren't much better. There was nothing in her budget for any kind of remodeling, especially not something on the outside of the building that would require permits, and goodness knows, she didn't need city inspectors taking too close a look at the Dorothy. Not until she'd finished a few more repairs herself. The last thing they needed was to be fined by the city for violation of some obscure building code.

"Sure thing, boss. I'll add it to the list." The never-ending to-do list. A to-do list that would soon be his responsibility. Her mood lightened at the thought of Caleb Donovan painting hallway trim. Not that he'd do it himself. No, a Donovan would surely have minions for that sort of thing, but in her imagination, it was Caleb in rough work clothes, sleeves rolled up to the elbow, sweating it out while he wrestled with power washing the front walkway.

"Here, let me take her out." Caleb held out his hands, breaking Riley out of what had quickly become a handyman fantasy. She was so soaked it had apparently turned even her brain to mush.

LouLou leapt into Caleb's hold, licking at his wrist, and Riley dealt with the double loss of heat. LouLou's furnace-like body had been warming her belly, but now the cool breeze of the AC made Riley shiver. Caleb kept up a steady stream of nonsense to LouLou while he carried her to the patio, then stood guard to make sure she didn't go near the aloe plant. She liked how he was protective of her dog. She liked it a lot. God, she was a mess, and in front of Caleb Donovan, no less. Well, she'd fix that. She could get herself to the couch, no problem.

Riley rolled to her side and gingerly crawled toward the couch. She learned along the way that her floor wasn't nearly as clean as she'd thought it was. When she reached her destination, she levered herself up and flopped onto the cool pleather with a grunt of satisfaction and, truth be told, a little pain.

"You really couldn't wait for me, huh?" Caleb stood over

her, shaking his head and tsking like one of Grams' second-floor friends.

"I can handle it." Riley heaved herself into a more comfortable upright position and strained to reach one of the dog-bone-shaped pillows. "Thank you for the help." She swept her arm to encompass LouLou out on the patio, happily sniffing at the new furniture arrangement, and her own couch-bound self. "You're still welcome to that shower, and I think there are some sweats from an old friend in the coat closet."

"An old friend. Do you mean an ex?" He waggled an eyebrow at her, and she laughed.

"Yes. He never showed up for the traditional exchanging of box-of-stuff-left-behind. I've been meaning to donate it." For over a year. Since before she'd moved into the Dorothy. Why had she even brought that stupid box with her? Losing her job and Aiden—it was a big blur of shattered dreams. Like keeping her CPR training current, she guessed that box was a safety net, a what-if of hope she hadn't been ready to let go of yet.

Caleb plucked at the neck of his shirt, pulling the cloth away from the defined muscles of his chest. "Sad-sack-ex clothes or not, I'll take 'em. But let me get you set up first."

He maneuvered the dog-bone pillows so that one propped her foot and the other protected her back from the hard edge of the couch arm. It had looked comfortable enough online, but there wasn't a lot of padding between the frame and the pleather. Someday she'd have the budget for a couch that was both comfortable and dog friendly, but for now, she made do. Caleb pulled her favorite fuzzy blanket, the one she used for cuddling up for a good binge-watch, off the back of the sofa and tucked it around her legs. "I'll be right back."

Riley wasn't sure what to make of this Caleb. He was nothing like the guy in the park yesterday, so sure he was in the right. He'd rescued her dog, in the rain no less, and her poodle clearly adored him for it. He'd reunited her with her runaway pooch not once but twice and was now rooting around in her kitchen, talking to himself under his breath too softly for her to understand the words but clearly trying to figure something out.

"Let me just…" He was back with the lemon dish towel packed with ice. He held it against the sole of her foot and cocked his head. He took the edges and created a rough knot on the top of her foot. It was bulky and already slipping off. "I don't have a lot of experience with first aid."

"That's, um, clear." Riley had to fight to keep from laughing at his concentrating-hard face. "I'll scoot down." She wiggled until she was lying flat and could balance the ice pack between her foot and the couch arm. "I got it."

"It's okay?" He crouched to inspect the setup more closely.

"It's lovely. Thank you." She found her eyes drifting closed. Adrenaline crash, no doubt. "Would you please go take that shower and stop dripping all over my floors?"

"Okay, okay."

She watched him back away through squinted eyes, and she fell asleep to the sound of the shower running.

———————————

Riley woke up to kisses. Doggy kisses. And if she'd been dreaming about another kind during her unplanned nap, well, no one needed to know but her.

"Feeling better?" Caleb appeared over her, behind the couch, Aiden's old UM sweatshirt stretched tight against his shoulders, so tight it looked like a sudden movement might tear the seams. She scooted up to sitting, bundling LouLou onto her lap for some snuggles, and saw the matching sweatpants ended well above his ankles. He looked like a little boy who'd had a mighty growth spurt. She found herself wondering who'd bought his clothes when he was young. Who made sure his shoes were never too tight and that he wore the right kind of footwear for whatever sports he played?

Riley picked up LouLou's injured paw. Eliza had done a good job with the bandage, so she didn't want to unwrap it yet. The poodle wriggled in her grip but didn't act bothered by her foot at all. Riley prodded it gently, and it didn't seem to cause LouLou any pain. Riley blew out a breath of relief. "LouLou's apparently recovered from her ordeal."

"She's been racing around on that foot like it barely bothers her. I think she'll be fine."

"Is that your medical opinion?"

"Absolutely. But if you want to take her to a vet, I wouldn't blame you. My medical degree is based solely on years of watching *Grey's Anatomy* with my mom at an impressionable age."

Riley laughed, really laughed. "Me too! My mom adored that show."

Caleb didn't join in, just watched her, lips quirked in a crooked smile. Finally, catching her breath, she said, "I'll keep an eye on her paw, and I'll take her in if it seems to bother her. In the meantime, I'll go with your prognosis, Dr. Donovan."

"Doctor. I like the sound of that. Should I have some business cards made?"

She threw a dog-bone-shaped pillow at him.

He caught it and raised an eyebrow at her. "You escalate to violence rather quickly, don't you?"

"I don't usually escalate to violence at all." One hand curled in LouLou's fur, she looked up, up, up at him. He hugged the pillow to his chest, and their eyes locked.

"Guess I bring out the best in you." He leaned forward.

"You certainly bring out something." Riley resisted the urge to prop herself on her elbows and lift her face toward him, but it frightened her how easily she could picture it. The distance between them closing. Their lips touching.

And then it did happen. Hands on the back of the sofa, Caleb bent down and brushed her lips with his. His eyes stayed open, watching her.

Her eyes were wide, too, and when his muscles flexed to pull away, she wrapped her free hand around the back of his neck.

"It's okay?" His breath feathered against her cheek.

"It didn't suck." She stretched her neck the smallest fraction of an inch, and their lips met again.

One hand braced beside her head, he grazed his lips against hers, a back-and-forth motion that awakened a thousand nerve endings she'd forgotten she had. And they weren't all in her lips. With only the slightest pressure, he had her yearning for more. She clutched his neck and pulled him closer.

A tongue licked her neck. But it wasn't his tongue.

"LouLou, down." Riley had to turn her face to the side to talk to the poodle, but LouLou wasn't listening. She sprawled across Riley's chest, tail wagging, watching Riley and Caleb with avid interest.

"That's a little unnerving." Caleb stayed in position, half bent over the sofa, one hand planted in the cushion, the other cupping Riley's face. He traced her eyebrow with his thumb, and she shivered.

"LouLou, down."

LouLou ignored her command. The poodle's tail thumped double time, and then she sprang to all fours and barked excitedly at the telltale click and swoosh as the front door swung open.

Caleb froze in a kind of half push-up above Riley.

Riley recognized the fragrance—Chanel No. 5, of course—and the crisp *clip, clip* of heels on the tile. "It's my grandmother," Riley whispered.

Caleb executed a less-than-graceful roll onto the floor.

Riley sat up. There was her beloved dog, yipping happily at Grams, who promptly scooped her up.

"Not much of a guard dog, you useless thing," Grams muttered. "How could you let a Donovan inside your home? If I've told Riley once, I've told her a hundred times you need to be sent to obedience school." Grams made her pronouncement with all the dire threat of a parent threatening an unruly teen with military boarding school. LouLou licked her cheek.

"You have never said anything about obedience school. Not once." Riley tucked the blanket around her hips, avoiding eye contact with both Grams and Caleb.

"Well, I've thought it." Grams huffed.

Caleb was on his feet and on the move toward Grams. Riley couldn't see that going anywhere good. "Uh, Grams, he was just leaving."

"Not before meeting your charming grandmother." He held out his hand to shake.

Grams offered her hand limply and scanned him head to toe. "Your grandfather was better looking. But you certainly have the look of a Donovan."

"You knew my grandfather?" Caleb smiled, taking her hand gently in his own.

"Know him?" Grams studied him over her knuckles and wrinkled her nose. "He took my virginity, that scoundrel."

"Grams!" Riley shoved a pillow against her face to keep from both laughing and combusting from embarrassment. "They were married," she said for Caleb's benefit.

"Briefly." Grams clicked her tongue in that way usually reserved for morning show hosts who annoyed her into changing the channel. "Very. Briefly. I hardly remember it."

"That's, uh, wow. Okay." Caleb clamped his jaw shut, and Riley smothered a smile. He was so clearly uncomfortable, but he rallied. "Hi, I'm Caleb." He shook her hand and then seemed to have trouble knowing when to let go.

Grams extracted her fingers to scratch behind LouLou's ears. "You think I don't know who you are?" She set the poodle down and strode toward the couch. "Here to take over my building. Oh, Riley told me what you're up to. And now I see it's worse, much worse, than I thought."

Riley straightened, flushing with guilt. How could she have let a soft pair of lips distract her from the imminent loss of her home, her job, her dog park? She was worse than Grams with her telenovela drama. At least Grams had thought she was in love every time she did something stupid. Riley had no such illusions. She was being stupid, and she should be grateful to Grams for interrupting before she did something even stupider.

But she wasn't. Her heart beat a tad too fast in her chest.

If she closed her eyes, she could still feel the heat of his skin against hers, smell her own shampoo in his hair.

"And what is he wearing?" Grams' voice rose in pitch. "Are those Aiden's old things?"

Riley gave a mortified nod.

Grams tsked. "Riley, my tales of romantic woe were supposed to be dire warnings about the faithlessness of men, not an inspiration for how to pick a mate. Good Lord, it's like you've never listened to a word I've said. How many times have I said it? Never give one of those skirt-chasing Donovans the time of day. And certainly don't let them anywhere near your..." Grams rubbed the air in front of her, shoulder popping as she covered all the territory from shoulders to knees.

"You've never said that. Not once. You only talk about your first husband when you've had a few too many glasses of chardonnay."

"I never have too much chardonnay."

Riley sucked in her lower lip to keep from laughing. It was laughable, wasn't it? Even Caleb looked like he was biting back a smile.

"Grandpa William mentioned his first wife a few times over the years. He never told me her name, but I do remember him talking about how beautiful she was. And smart as a whip, he'd say, which puzzled me when I was younger. How smart is a whip anyway?"

Grams wagged a finger at him. "Don't try that Donovan charm on me. I am immune."

But Riley wasn't. She pictured a small Caleb sitting on his grandpa's knee, wondering about whips. Frogs in the throat. A bird in the hand. She'd been jealous of her friends who carpooled. She'd imagined them sitting in a back-seat

Jacuzzi while she had to walk to school. She'd been so dis-appointed when Emma's mom took pity on her desire to ride in the car pool and picked her up one day. No Jacuzzi. No pool or pool toys. Just a bunch of kids strapped into the back seat playing drums on their plastic lunch boxes.

"Right, Riley?" Grams pulled Riley out of the past with a sharp question.

"Sorry?" Riley shook off the image of a small Caleb asking cute questions and rested her chin on the pillow.

"I said I'd like to have a word with you." Grams fixed a glare on Caleb. "Alone."

"That's my cue then, isn't it?" Caleb pulled on the too-short sleeves of the sweatshirt and eyed the door behind Grams. "I was just leaving."

"I bet you were." Grams snorted and stepped aside.

Caleb grabbed a plastic Publix bag full of his wet clothes off the counter and walked barefoot to the couch. He dropped a quick kiss to Riley's forehead.

"You're all right?"

"Of course."

His eyes narrowed. "Of course."

"Of course."

He straightened. "I'll call you?"

"You're a funny one." Grams cleared her sinuses. Loudly. "Riley won't be taking your calls, not after she hears what you've done."

Riley gripped the back of the couch. "What has he done?"

Caleb took a step backward, crinkling the plastic handle in a tight grip.

"What have you done?" Riley swung her legs to the ground and hopped to one foot.

"Margo says they're holding a special City Commission hearing this week. He knew before he ever showed up here that he was going to throw us out of our homes." Grams propped her hands on her improbably tiny waist. She still loved a good foundation garment.

"Caleb?"

He cleared his throat. "I did file some paperwork with the city. My grandfather may have called in a few favors to get it expedited."

Riley glared at the couch cushions as if they'd betrayed her, but the real traitor was LouLou, who'd circled over and was sitting at Caleb's heel for all the world like she'd been obedience-trained to do so. She gazed up at him with the same fondness she had for tiny bites of chicken.

"How expedited?" Riley's voice was low, but he heard her. He just didn't answer.

"Margo says tomorrow." Grams quoted her longtime friend and former mayor of Miami Beach. "She may be retired, but people still tell her things."

"*Tomorrow*?" Riley leaned heavily on the couch arm. Her whole body felt achy, like the day before the flu strikes hard. She wobbled in her one-footed stance.

"Tomorrow." Caleb squatted to give LouLou a few scratches behind her ears before standing again. "Guess I'll see you there?"

"Oh, we'll be there," Grams muttered.

Riley touched a finger to her lips, rubbing away the memory of their kiss. "Lose my number."

CHAPTER 8

THE LARGE CONFERENCE ROOM AT CITY HALL WAS comfortably decorated in the city's signature pastels—pinks and pale blues—but Caleb couldn't relax. He shifted on the padded chair, checked the time on his phone for the fifth time in as many minutes, and watched the door. So far, no Riley. He should be worried about his presentation. The fact that he was pivoting from a complete condo conversion to a slightly different, less radical approach after less than twenty-four hours to get his facts and figures in order should've had him sweating. And he was sweating, but not from any lack of confidence in his business plan. No, he simply couldn't forget the image of Riley's face when her Grams dropped the bomb yesterday.

He would've told Riley himself. Of course he would've. Not at that exact moment. But a later moment, for sure. She didn't have to look so betrayed by the information. He'd been up front with her at the dog park about his intentions. He hadn't hidden anything from her. Not really.

Then it happened. The door swung open, and Riley's grandmother swanned in, a tiny woman with a big poof of powder-white hair and a formfitting coral business suit. Behind her, dressed in black slacks and a drapey hot-pink top, Riley limped in. She was walking on her own, a good sign, but definitely favoring her injured foot.

Caleb stood. "How're you feeling? How's LouLou's foot?"

Grams breezed past him like he didn't exist.

"We're fine." Riley addressed the American flag pin holding his navy-and-red-plaid tie in place.

She limped away, taking a seat on the other side of Grams and about as far from him as it was possible to get in the room. An older man sat on Grams' other side, a paper cup of coffee in his hand.

One by one, the commissioners ambled in, taking a few minutes to make the rounds and greet the handful of people already gathered.

"Good to see you, good to see you!" Commissioner Santos greeted Caleb with a wide smile and firm handshake. "Thought your grandfather might make an appearance today. How is he?"

"He sends his greetings." Caleb pumped Santos' hand. "He's sorry he couldn't make it, but now that he's retired, he's got a standing golf game on Tuesdays that he never misses."

"Now, that's the kind of life I'm looking forward to one day." Santos wasn't anywhere near retirement age and, by all accounts, was looking to leverage his City Commission position into state politics. He was on the young side of middle-aged and looked good on television with his dark skin and gleaming white teeth.

"I believe we only have one thing on the docket today, so let's get it over with."

Commissioner Jackson, a former school principal turned politician, frowned at Santos. It was no secret the two were often at odds. She opposed commercial development on the Beach, while Santos was all for anything that brought more tax dollars to the city and more tourists to the local businesses.

Commissioner Jackson crossed over to where Grams and Riley sat, greeting both with a hug and an "It's been far too long, Gloria. Whatever have you been up to?"

Ignoring Santos' pointed throat-clearing, the two older women launched into a long discussion of bunco strategies while Riley looked on with a fond smile. One by one, the other four commissioners filtered in, followed by a harried Caroline Weir, recently elected mayor and the person Grandpa William had advised Caleb he'd most need on his side. Before he had time to greet her, though, Commissioner Jackson took her seat.

"Let's call this special session to order so we can all get back to work."

Ouch. Caleb arranged his face into a neutral expression. It was clear which commissioner he'd have to win over. The other commissioners took their seats at the long table at the front of the room, but Caleb kept his focus on Jackson. She was known to be tough on developers, but she was only one person. Surely, the board would follow Santos' lead.

"One agenda item; let's get to it." Santos rubbed his hands together. "And not much to discuss, either. You've seen the proposal from Caleb Donovan?"

Four commissioners nodded. Jackson thinned her lips and shuffled papers in front of her.

"All in all, a solid proposal. Beautifies an overlooked neighborhood, enhances our potential tax base, will bring in more residents for local business." Santos looked left down the table and then right. "Any discussion or should we approve it now?"

"Excuse me?" Jackson's voice growled. "I don't believe we've had time to properly vet the many ramifications of

Mr. Donovan's hastily filed plan. For example, I believe the building in question has a number of fixed-income residents living there. What will happen to them?"

Santos covered the mic in front of him and whispered something to Commissioner Graves on his left. He uncovered the microphone. "We hear your concerns, Claudia, but residents can be relocated to more suitable housing. I'm sure Donovan will make them a fair offer."

Grams gasped, hand to her throat. "Leave my home of over thirty years? How heartless can the commission be?"

Santos shifted in his chair, clearly uncomfortable.

"Obviously, we need to consider the impact on the community." Commissioner Jackson jotted down notes on the papers in front of her. "No decisions have been made, Gloria. This is far from a done deal. I, for one, need more information to make an informed decision."

"Stronger tax base, beautification. We've got all the information we need." Santos pointed at the papers in front of him.

Jackson sniffed. "I don't find these projections very convincing. Nor do I like the rushed nature of these proceedings. I move that we delay until we have time to fully consider the proposal and also have time to solicit feedback from the community."

"We speak for our communities," Santos snarled. "That's why they elected us."

"Which is why we should listen to them." Jackson straightened the papers by tapping them on the desk, aligning the edges. "Shall we reconvene in a week? Gloria, Riley? I expect you'll want to gather some testimonies, perhaps present something to the board yourselves?"

Santos' mouth opened as though he would protest, but three other commissioners quickly stated their support for a delay to gather more information. Santos' jaw clapped shut like a snapper catching a tiny fish as it swims by.

"We're agreed then." Jackson stood. "Always nice to see everyone." She exited the room, fairly floating on her sensible half boots.

Caleb rocked back in his chair, a bit stunned by how quickly everything had gone. Grandpa William told him it was practically a done deal, that Santos was on their side and had the ear of the whole Commission. Caleb's only job was to show up, be personable and presentable, and then appreciative when the Commission voted their approval. Now he wasn't sure what to do. Approach Santos? That was what his father would do, slap him on the back and offer to take him out for a drink. A cigar. Maybe some steaks at Smith & Wollensky's or some stone crabs at Joe's.

What Caleb really wanted to do was walk over to Riley and ask how she was feeling. How was her foot? Was LouLou fully recovered from her dramatic escape in the rain? Would Riley be interested in a drink? A cigar? Steaks or stone crabs?

Grams pointed two fingers at her own eyes and then at him. Riley turned to see who her grandmother was threatening with the famous I'm-watching-you gesture, and when her gaze crashed into his, she froze, hand midway between her shoulder and neck as if she were about to brush her hair back but suddenly forgot to move.

He crossed the distance between them. "That sure didn't go as expected."

Grams sniffed. "I'm sure you expected everything to

turn up peaches for you. Well, surprise, surprise, Donovan Junior. There are people in this town who look out for people like me and Riley."

"How's your foot?"

Riley blinked at him, then looked down at her foot. She lifted her knee, dangling the sandal-clad foot in the air. "Mostly fine. Still a bit tender."

"Is there anything I can do?"

"You can withdraw your proposal and leave me and my granddaughter alone. I'm surprised your grandfather wasn't here to see me thrown out of my own home." Grams dabbed at the corner of her eye as if she were crying, but there weren't any tears to wipe away.

Caleb's jaw hardened. He hated feeling manipulated. "My grandfather's building, you mean?"

"My home for decades." Grams continued to dab at her dry eyes. "Riley's home. She grew up there, you know."

Riley dug through her cross-body bag. "Not completely. Mom had an apartment near the port. I split my time."

"Riley grew up there," Grams continued as if Riley hadn't spoken, waving her wrinkled but still dry tissue at Caleb, "and now you want to rip her away from everything she's ever known."

"I did go away to college. Not too far, just FSU in Tallahassee, but I have been out of Miami-Dade County." She offered Grams a fresh tissue.

"All she's ever known," Grams repeated, wadding the two tissues together to make a mega tear catcher. "Not only her home but her livelihood. Are you going to fire her like you threatened? Because I'd like to see you try. After what I saw yesterday, she has a strong case for sexual assault. You know how that goes these days." She crossed her fingers like a hashtag and mouthed the words *Me too*.

"Grams!" Riley smacked at her Grams' hashtag fingers. "That is not what Me too is about, and you know it."

"You millennials." Grams straightened and examined her nails with a snort. "Always so touchy with your PC this and don't-be-offensive that."

Caleb was torn between amusement and horror. Before he could decide, Riley was pulling her grandmother out of the room by her elbow without even a goodbye glance. He shouldn't feel so let down. But he was. He shouldn't be wishing he were the one Riley was so eager to take home with her. He shouldn't feel a lot of things he was feeling. But he was.

Caleb's phone vibrated in his pocket, still on silent from the meeting. He figured it was Grandpa William calling to get the news. News he wasn't exactly excited to share. He thought about ignoring the call, but by the third buzz, he figured it was time to rip off yet another Band-Aid. When had his life become about telling people things they didn't want to hear? But instead of Grandpa William's name, the word *Lance* flashed across his screen. Video chat? Surprised and cursing the timing, he accepted.

"Baby brother!" Lance's voice carried loud and clear through the device, the sound of traffic in the background. The visual was mostly his chin, square with a hint of blond stubble.

"Lancelot!" Caleb's revenge for being reminded of his younger brother status: break out the dreaded full name.

Lance retaliated by making cooing baby noises. Caleb repeated, "Lancelot, Lancelot," for every *goo-goo*, *gah-gah* his brother threw at him.

"Alright, alright, you've upped your game since you were twelve." Lance finally broke their standoff with a low laugh. "I see you called a time or two."

"Maybe three or four." Caleb took his brother on a walk down the hallway to a smaller, empty conference room. He settled into a chair and propped his phone on the oval table. "You know you have video on, right?"

Caleb's face was framed in the tiny box, but Lance's phone jiggled between views of his neck and ear.

"Yeah, yeah. Damn things." Lance righted his phone and his face came into view, the strong cheekbones he'd gotten from his mother more gaunt than Caleb remembered ever seeing them and dark circles under the Donovan blue eyes the brothers inherited. "Thought we should catch up in person."

"Sure, when?" Caleb searched Lance's face for clues about how the past few years had treated him. A few crow's-feet around his eyes, no doubt from squinting in the sun all day while out at construction sites. His pale hair slicked back with gel that made it a shade darker but didn't quite keep his long bangs off his forehead.

The Lance Caleb remembered took pride in his appearance, and it wasn't that Lance didn't look good. Women no doubt still followed him around like the girls in high school had. He looked different. Older. It was unsettling to think that Lance, always bigger than life, might have changed. Caleb found himself curious. Did he actually want to get together with his brother? He did. "My schedule's pretty flexible these days."

"Now. We're catching up now. That's what the video is for." Lance glanced down at something out of view. "You've got approximately twelve minutes until I reach my job site to tell me what the panic is about."

"It's not a panic." Caleb scrubbed a hand across his scalp and squelched the disappointment. That was what their relationship was based on, wasn't it? Caleb disappointed when Lance decided to live with his mom, leaving Caleb behind with their father. Lance disappointed when Caleb followed their father into business. A two-way street of disappointment with years and years of wrong turns and dead ends. "Not exactly."

Lance narrowed his eyes, gaze bouncing between the screen and his windshield. "Exactly what is it, then?"

So Caleb broke it down into the ten-minute version, minus Riley. Minus Grams and Grandpa William's former marital status. Minus the special commission meeting.

"That wily old goat must be getting soft in his old age." Lance chuckled. "But his tricks won't work on me. When I said I'm out of the Donovan business, I meant it."

Caleb nodded. "Things are different now. Dad's out of the picture."

Lance snorted. "You think he's not still pulling strings? You know he and Grandpa William are still tight, right? They're playing you, little brother, and once again, you're falling for it."

"I'm not falling for anything. Believe me, I learned my lesson." Caleb leaned in, eyes and nose getting bigger in the frame. "We have a chance to make something better. It's a unique property." Inwardly, he winced at using one of the terms Grandpa William used to lure him in. Outwardly, he kept his gaze steady, his voice calm. "We can make it whatever we want."

"Two minutes." Lance stayed focused on the driving, but a muscle twitched in his cheek. "Give me one real reason to help you with Grandpa William."

Caleb thought of Riley. He thought of Grams. Of Patty and her walker. LouLou in the rain. What happened to all of them if the Dorothy went on as it was, genteelly disintegrating until another developer swooped in and demolished it? He was their best shot. They didn't know it yet; Riley didn't know it yet. But they needed him. So he swallowed a big old chunk of pride and looked his brother in the eye.

"Because I need you."

Lance's face showed his shock, one eyebrow launching above the other. "I thought if I could see your face, I'd know if you were lying, but I can't tell if you mean it or not."

"I mean it."

"It's something Dad would say to get his way." Lance's eyebrow descended, and he kept his eyes on the road. "You look so much like him, you know?"

Their father was a handsome man; it shouldn't be an insult, but both brothers knew it was. Caleb's back teeth locked, and he consciously relaxed his jaw before saying in the most even voice he could muster, "I'm not Dad."

"Me either." Lance glared into the distance, cheek muscle twitching.

Caleb leaned forward until his entire face filled the screen. "Then you'll help."

"I'll think about it." Lance looked down and off camera again. He looked up. "I'll be in touch." The screen went black.

CHAPTER 9

It was dog park o'clock, that time right after work and right before sunset when the field was full of hounds of every size and shape. From a sprightly Jack Russell terrier trying to hustle other dogs into a game of chase to Lady lying with her head propped on her favorite stump, dogs enjoyed the freedom of being off leash and surrounded by exciting smells. LouLou was part of Team Jack Russell, running circles and figure eights.

Riley let out a long breath she hadn't realized she was holding. "Basically, we've got one week to figure something out."

Eliza planted her hands on her hips and stared up at the sky. "Did I ever tell you what kind of law I practiced?"

"I always thought it was something to do with civil rights. Are the Donovans infringing on our civil rights? Our right to a community dog park, official or not?"

Eliza barked out a laugh. "Oh, that's funny."

"You do go to a lot of rallies."

"That I do. But my bread and butter was real estate law. Specifically Florida law. Specifically in Miami-Dade County."

"Oh." Riley's eyes widened. "Gotta admit. My hopes are rising. Like, a lot. Are you going to ride in and save the day with some obscure law the commissioners overlooked?"

"Wish I could, sugar." She adjusted the handkerchief she'd tied around her hair and spritzed on a bit more mosquito repellent. "Tell you what, though. Why don't you come over tomorrow, and we'll strategize. I'm sure plenty of these folks will show up if we ask. No one wants to lose what we've got here."

Riley looked out over the dogs. How could anyone want to put an end to this? Neighbors of all ages clustered together, chatting about their days. Riley took for granted seeing the same people day in and day out. She loved her residents at the Dorothy, but the dog park people were her real people.

"You know what we need?" Riley cracked her knuckles, ready to get to work.

"Me to offer my services pro bono?"

"Obviously." Riley rolled her eyes. "But we also need a dog park party. A social. For everyone to relax and have a good time."

"Before we ask them to take off work to show up en masse at city hall and cause a big stink?"

"Yeah, that too."

Eliza chortled. "I like how you think. What're you thinking?"

"Dog Days of Summer."

"Perfect."

A dog park party obviously had to include dogs, and of course the most obvious place to accommodate all the dogs and owners was the dog park. Riley designed flyers and printed them out on her old laser printer and spent a couple of days hitting the dog park at different times, chatting up the regulars, and getting them to agree to the Saturday evening party. Riley's clipboard listed the things they'd need—tables, chairs, coolers for drinks, food for a buffet, dog treats, and space for things she hadn't even thought of yet.

"What a wonderful idea!" the Chihuahua's owner gushed. The dog's name was Chewy, but Riley didn't think she'd ever learned the woman's name. She'd scrawled Sydney in the chairs category and the number four. "Will beach chairs be okay?"

"More than okay."

"We should've done this before." Sydney cuddled Chewy in her arms, not seeming to mind how he smeared dirt down the front of her trendy white tunic with split sleeves. "It's too bad we're only getting around to it now that the park's being closed down."

"What do you mean?" Riley dropped her pen in her surprise. She'd thought only she and Eliza knew about the impending Donovan takeover.

"Everyone's been talking." Sydney lowered her voice. "Guess the Dorothy's being sold or something, and this lot is part of the parcel. It's a shame, thinking they'll put up condos or some such, and then where will poor Chewy get his exercise?"

"Parking structure," Riley corrected her.

"You've heard?" Sydney leaned in closer. "Do you know more details?"

Riley tapped the pen against her clipboard. "I'm the on-site manager at the Dorothy, so yeah, changes seem to be on the horizon."

"This dog park—I mean, I know it's not a real park, but

still, when I was looking at apartments, I saw everyone out here and what else would you call it?—is a big reason why I rented in the area. It won't be the same once it's gone."

"There might still be something we can do." Riley hadn't meant to mention anything until the party, but she ended up telling Sydney everything.

A few minutes in, Sydney set Chewy down to let him go exploring. She planted her hands on her slim hips. "You need anything, I'm in."

"Thank you. That means a lot." Riley clutched the clipboard to her chest, moved by Sydney's offer. Caleb's plans definitely impacted the Dorothy's residents, and although she'd hoped the neighbors would feel as strongly as Eliza, she'd also been afraid they'd collectively shrug off the development plans and find somewhere else to take their dogs. That Sydney's immediate response was to jump in and help promised that the party's secret agenda—getting dog owners riled up enough to sign her petition—would succeed. Hope Riley hadn't felt since the disastrous commissioner meeting bloomed in her chest, like the tentative purple flowers of matchweed poking their heads up in the dog park grass after a good rain.

"I've got an idea." Sydney cleared her throat and lowered her voice. "And don't take this the wrong way, but I've never seen you in anything but dog park clothes. You need an outfit for the next city hall meeting?"

"No, I'm good." Riley didn't want to admit that her dog park clothes were pretty much her everyday clothes. She still had a few suits in her closet from her hotel days, but her Dorothy uniform was casual. Super casual. Maybe too casual? She pictured herself standing before the commissioners in one of her outdated Zara suits. Definitely not confidence building.

"Oh, I've embarrassed you." Sydney's forehead crinkled with concern. "Please don't take it personally. I'm a stylist. I can't help myself." She laughed and tucked her long bangs behind one ear. "I've got racks of clothes left from my last big job. Why don't you come over, and I'll hook you up?"

Riley'd felt underdressed at the meeting. She imagined walking into the meeting in a power suit with her PowerPoint ready to go. She smiled. "How can I say no?"

Sydney clasped her hands in front of her chest and squealed. "Wonderful! Now, hand over that clipboard. I have some ideas for other things we'll need for the party."

Riley held out the list with the pen stuck in the clip, and Sydney immediately propped it against her hip and started writing. "We'll need extra dog treats to give out as prizes for the contests, and of course, we'll need people to volunteer to judge the contests."

"Contests?" Riley swallowed. With such short notice and no budget, she'd been happy people were willing to sign up potluck-style for snacks and drinks and that Eliza already had two folding tables she said she could bring over. "What kind of contests?"

"We can do some version of a cake walk. A dog-walk cake walk?" Sydney jotted down a need for five cakes. "We'll come up with a better title. Cutest dog trick? Dog who most looks like its owner?" She scribbled her ideas as they came out of her mouth. "Who comes the farthest to our dog park? Who's been coming the longest?"

Our dog park. The blooming hope in Riley's chest

flowered. "Maybe some obedience commands? Who can sit-stay the longest?"

"Excellent!" Sydney pointed the pen at Riley. "Keep talking. We've got a lot to work out and not much time. Lucky for you, last minute is my specialty."

Kiki and Paula entered through the gap in the fence, Princess Pugsley already off her leash and running to catch up with LouLou and Chewy.

"A few too many gelatos in Rome!" Paula patted her rounded stomach with a laugh.

"Please." Kiki sucked in her own gut to get through. "It's always been a tight squeeze for you."

"Are you saying I'm fat?" Paula fake-punched Kiki's arm.

Kiki played like the punch had hurt, rubbing her bicep with an exaggerated grimace. "You, my love, are perfectly plump in all the right places. It's the fence that's the problem. We should widen that gap, stop pretending like it's not an entryway."

"Good point." Sydney jotted it on the clipboard. "I'm Sydney. That's my Chewy over there." She pointed to her Chihuahua, currently in the process of sniffing Princess Pugsley's butt. "The one with the questionable manners."

Kiki and Paula laughed and introduced themselves. Within minutes, Sydney recruited them as judges for the contests, and they even signed up to bring a cake. When they heard about the petition, Kiki immediately volunteered to help collect signatures, and Paula raised a fist in the air. "Viva la Rover Revolution!"

CHAPTER 10

GRANDPA WILLIAM'S HOME DIDN'T NEED A WOMAN'S touch. It was expertly decorated in a Mediterranean-meets-tropical style carefully cultivated by his longtime interior decorator, Maisy Cantor, with every bell and whistle a retired real estate tycoon could want. Wine cellar, automated blinds, high-end kitchen appliances he never used but that his personal chef insisted were necessary for her job.

Chantel, the full-time housekeeper, poured Grandpa William his usual two fingers of Scotch.

"Just one for me." Caleb raised a polite hand. He still had to drive home to his sad rental. It wasn't so much that he missed his downtown high-rise or his sunset views over the water—okay, he did miss those things—but more that he missed the comfort of knowing nothing was out of his price range. His accountant handled his finances, and his main financial worry had been making sure he had enough cash on hand to tip the valet. Now, he had to think about things like which gas station had the best prices, and he'd actually learned to grocery shop for himself.

He didn't mind that part really. There was something comforting about all the food in a store, the ritual of winding up and down the aisles, choosing meals for a week, deciding which indulgences were in the budget. Learning, thanks to a wine-tasting set up at the end of an aisle one Saturday, that he could in fact tolerate wines that cost less than forty dollars. That he maybe even preferred an Australian Shiraz to the merlot he'd kept stocked in his undercounter wine fridge.

Caleb lifted the Scotch to his lips and inhaled deeply. Nothing like a good whiff of Scotch to clear the sinuses.

"To what to do I owe the great honor of your presence?" Grandpa William sipped his Scotch slowly, reverently.

Caleb took a small sip and held it on his tongue for a few seconds before answering. "You didn't tell me your ex-wife lived in the building."

"Met Gloria, have you? She's a fine woman, isn't she? A fine woman indeed." Grandpa William closed his eyes for a brief moment, then opened them to stare down at Caleb. "How was she? In good health?"

"In fighting spirits. She's none too happy about our plan for the building."

"No, Gloria's not one for change. She doesn't let things roll off her back." Grandpa William's unfocused gaze wandered the room. "She doesn't forgive, and she doesn't forget."

"She called me a skirt chaser. Or rather, she called all the Donovans skirt chasers. What happened between you two?"

Grandpa William tilted his head back and stared at the stars overhead. "You have to understand, it's how things were back then. Everyone I did business with had a woman on the side. There were nights we went out together, to the Fontainebleau to see Roberto Durán box or down near the Omni for the showgirls at Les Violins.

"I couldn't take Gloria to those. She'd tell the other wives. Then who would I do business with? And I couldn't go alone. What would the other guys think, that I couldn't get some? That I was in love with my wife?" Grandpa William shook his head. "The other wives turned a blind eye, but not Gloria. She was up in my business, always asking questions. And when she found out for sure there was another woman? Faster than you can say 'alimony,' she sued my ass for divorce."

"Were you really that surprised?" Caleb knocked back more Scotch. It was bad enough that his dad was a felon; now he had to find out that his grandpa, the man he'd always looked up to for his business savvy, was a cheater? That he'd cheated on Riley's grandma?

"I knew she wouldn't like it." Grandpa William's fingers tapped against the side of his glass. "Didn't think she'd leave me over it. She had nothing when I met her, you know? I thought she'd forgive me, if for no other reason than to keep her fingers in the bank account. But she left me, like that." He snapped his fingers, then plucked a peanut out of the trail mix on the reclaimed-oak coffee table.

"Sounds like you didn't give her much choice." Caleb poured another finger of Scotch while he tried to imagine a younger Grandpa William being so callous about his wife's feelings. If he pictured him in a skinny blue suit with a fedora, it made the story more believable. Still, it was hard to believe. "That was pretty sloppy justification. What did you tell her about the other woman? That it was only business?"

"Something like that." Grandpa William downed the rest of his Scotch in one gulp. "She kept pushing me. What was the real reason? Why did I really do it? Honestly, hell if I knew back then. It was a mixed blessing when Rosie got pregnant. Easy to explain that I gotta take care of my kid, you know? Give him a family."

"Grandma Rosie was the other woman?" Caleb leaned back and shook his head. Grandma Rosie of the powder-soft hands and hair so white it was nearly translucent as the side piece? He couldn't imagine it, but there it was. He felt a tiny stab of betrayal. Not the paralyzing kind like when he'd realized the prosecutor was telling the truth about his father, but a gentler squeeze of the heart. He'd thought at least Grandpa William was who he said he was, that there were no ugly secrets waiting to escape. Sure, this was different. Personal. Not business. But it did make him look at his grandfather differently. *How can you know someone your entire life but not really know who they are?*

His thoughts must've shown on his face because a flush of color rose up his grandfather's neck. Embarrassment. After so many years? Very interesting. "And now? Would you give Gloria the same answer?"

Grandpa William rubbed at his flushed neck. "I don't know what I'd say if she ever gave me a chance to explain, but I figured it out after Rosie left me. Gloria, she's a big personality. Wherever we went, people flocked to her. Women and men, they all wanted to be in her circle, hear her stories, be her friend. I disappeared beside her. And I'm ashamed to say, I didn't like it. I should've been proud of her, proud to be with her. Instead, I broke her heart."

A long moment stretched between them, only the *tick-tock* of the mantel clock filling the space. Grandpa William looked lost in memories, his eyes half-closed, his shoulders drooping.

"She really is something." Caleb described how he met

Gloria, his Scotch sloshing dangerously in the glass when he used his hands to gesture. He ended with Gloria's grand exit, not mentioning the phone call with Lance. He didn't want to get his grandfather's hopes up.

Grandpa William chuckled, and his color returned to normal. "That sounds like her alright. Always thinks she knows what's best." He wolfed down a handful of trail mix from the bowl. "Good to know she's still in fighting shape."

"Her granddaughter seems like a fighter, too." Caleb filled him in on Riley's role at the Dorothy, and it finally came out, the whole debacle of the commissioner meeting.

Grandpa William snorted so hard, he had to grab a cock-tail napkin to cover his nose. "Wish I'd been there! Sounds like a hoot."

Caleb's nail dug into the arm of his chair. "It was a real setback."

"Are you kidding me? All that talk about community input isn't going anywhere. Stick to the plan, Caleb. Things never go smoothly at city hall. You should know that."

It was true. In all the projects he'd been involved in over the years, there had been many government obstacles. Permits, inspections, vendors. He knew to factor in time for the unforeseeable but unavoidable stalls and delays along the way. Why had he thought his work on the Dorothy would be any different?

"You're right, as always, Grandpa." Caleb helped himself to some of that trail mix. He hadn't eaten dinner, and the Scotch needed something to slosh around in his belly with. "I'll stay the course, but it would help if I knew more about the history of the building."

"Should've filled you in from the beginning. Guess I was

hoping we'd get through this without having to dredge up the worst part of my past." Grandpa William settled back and crossed his arms over the small bulge of his belly. "What do you want to know?"

"Why would Gloria tell her granddaughter she owns the building?"

Grandpa William chuckled. "Because she does."

Caleb blinked. Blinked again. "I saw the paperwork."

Grandpa William waved his hand. "Sorry, I should've said she did. Gave it to her in the divorce."

"But now you own it."

"That's right." Grandpa William nodded, seemingly pleased that Caleb was following along, but Caleb felt more confused than before.

"How did that happen?"

"What?" Grandpa William snapped a tiny pretzel in half with his teeth. A few crumbs feel onto his chest, and he wiped them away.

"Grandpa!" Caleb pushed the trail mix out of his grandfather's reach. "If you gave her the building, why is it in your name?"

"Nosy, aren't you?" Grandpa William eyed the trail-mix bowl but let it go with a sigh. "I let her have the Dorothy in the divorce settlement, so she'd always have a place to live and a steady income. But after me, she took up with some real characters. Her second husband was no better than me, always out with a new girl on his arm. And that third husband of hers lost the Dorothy in a poker game. Can you imagine?"

Caleb couldn't. "How do you lose an entire building in one game?"

"Not just any game, Texas Hold'em." Grandpa William rubbed his hands together, clearly delighted to be prompted into retelling the tale. "Some of the regular guys got together. I wasn't going until a buddy called me. He heard her husband talking about throwing deeds in the pot."

"Why? Isn't losing thousands of dollars at a time enough?" Caleb shook his head and watched a yacht power by, leaving long wakes in its path. The water churned then stilled.

"For some, they can't stop. It's in the blood, all that adrenaline." Grandpa William made a fist and raised it in the air. "Boy, was it pumping that night."

"What happened?" Now Caleb was even more curious. He'd always thought of his grandfather as a businessman, not this guy who cheated on his wife and gambled with fortunes.

"My buddies held him off until I got there, and then we started a new game. I was talking trash, like I always did, about the others not having enough money to go up against me. Hinted that I'd take other kinds of bets. Had that guy hook, line, and sinker." Grandpa William demonstrated by crooking his finger and hooking his lip like a fish.

Caleb smiled. "How'd you know you'd win?"

"I didn't." Grandpa William winked. "But I knew he was a gambler, couldn't help himself. So when I got pocket queens and a nine-nine-queen comes out on the flop, well, I figured that was my shot. I mean, there's still a queen out there; it's not a done deal, but my odds are good. Gloria's husband puts up a decent bet, so I call. Seven on the board, doesn't impact me. Him either, judging by his face. So I bet nothing. Lulling him into a false sense of security, right?"

Caleb nodded, following the story. He could almost see it. The dark room, the cigar smoke, the bell bottoms. Or maybe there weren't bell bottoms. He didn't want to interrupt Grandpa William's story to ask the year, so he added a few years in his mind, picturing them with side burns and bell bottoms, and let his grandfather go on.

"That loser ups the bet even more; I call again. Four on the river. Doesn't change a thing. Just to stir the pot a bit, I say, 'All in.' You should've seen the guy's face. So sure of himself. So eager to take my money." Grandpa William laughed and sipped his Scotch. "I do more of my trash talk. Too bad he can't raise. Too bad he doesn't have the cash. He thinks I'm bluffing. Throws the key to the building right in the pot."

Caleb waited for the end of the story, but Grandpa William merely smiled at him.

"You can't stop there. What happened?"

"You know what happened. I called. I won. The Dorothy was mine again, and when Gloria found out he'd bet her building? Oh, he was in big trouble. I heard he had to sleep on the couch for six months." Grandpa William looked delighted at the memory, smiling wide enough to show off his bridge and two crowns.

"Does Gloria know it was you?"

"God no. She never would've stayed in the building if she'd known. Woman's got her pride. And then some. You don't want to upset her." Grandpa William knocked back more Scotch. "She wasn't too upset at the meeting, was she?"

Caleb sloshed his own Scotch down on the coffee table in front of him. "Of course she's upset. She knows condo conversion means everyone's out. The building can't survive on what it's bringing in now, and from what I can tell, the current residents can't cough up any more cash. The place is teetering on the edge of bankruptcy as it is."

"You can't kick out Gloria. I promised her the Dorothy would always be her home."

"It's a little late to tell me that now, Grandpa. I already filed the paperwork with the city. Not five minutes ago, you told me to stay the course."

"And you should. Be charming. Be persuasive. Get the community on your side. Have you never had to get something through a city commission before? It's easy to flip them if you've got some voters on your side."

Caleb's jaw tightened. "Dad always handled that."

Grandpa William snorted. "Of course he did. Can't recommend following in his footsteps."

Both men took cautious sips of their Scotch. Grandpa William eyed Caleb over the rim of his tumbler, eyes still sharp enough he didn't need glasses except to drive at night.

"There's nothing for it then. I'll have to go to this next meeting. Show you how it's done."

Caleb thought about protesting, but truth was, things could hardly go worse than they had yesterday. Besides, he didn't think the heightened color in Grandpa William's cheeks was from the alcohol. No, Gloria was still on his mind. Caleb could tell by the way Grandpa William rubbed his empty ring finger and stared out over the intracoastal waters. He wasn't going to the meeting to push through the condo conversion. He was going to see Gloria, and Caleb couldn't help but think it would be even more disastrous than the first meeting.

Caleb knew he should stay away from the Dorothy until after his plans were approved. No good could come of engaging with Riley or her grandmother or any of the other residents, but he couldn't help it. He felt pulled. Besides, Riley'd still been limping on her bruised foot. What if she needed help? Okay, so that was *really* reaching. But there it was. Maybe it was the whirlwind of commotion he'd stirred up, or that devastating glimpse of betrayal he'd seen in her big, brown eyes. But bottom line: he wanted to see her.

It was a beautiful day, at least for late August. Slightly less muggy than usual, and this late in the day, the afternoon storm had already passed. More cars than usual lined the street, and Caleb had trouble finding a spot to park his Porsche. He finally found curb parking about a block away and, after arming the alarm, started his hike back to the building. If there was this little parking in the off-season, the Dorothy really did need its own parking structure. High-end residents wouldn't park their precious cars this far from sight.

His long legs ate up the distance quickly. Up ahead, a couple of women holding hands walked with a pug between them toward the empty lot. No doubt going to the so-called dog park. A twentysomething young woman in a sundress let herself be pulled along by two oversize mutts in polka-dot harnesses toward the lot. More dogs and owners slipped through the gaps in the fence. Some carried beach chairs, others coolers. All of them were greeted by Riley, who directed them toward where two folding tables were set up.

The lot was filled with more dogs than Caleb imagined

could possibly live in the neighborhood. One table was set up with plates of snacks—cookies, a veggie platter, a few homemade-looking pies—and bottles of soda. The other table was covered in paperwork, and a lovely woman roughly Riley's age sat behind it, urging people to sign with one of the many pens strewn across the table.

A gaggle of midsize dogs ran circles in the lot, banging into some of the people's legs and barking up a storm. Other dogs hung out closer to their owners, keeping a careful watch over everything. Riley stood off to the side, plastic glass of soda in one hand, smiling and laughing with Eliza while Lady leaned against her leg.

A family of three, parents in their midthirties with a kindergarten-aged daughter and a chocolate Lab, ducked into the lot. Riley greeted them warmly, gesturing toward the tables where people were now standing in line to sign the brunette's papers. Riley talked to the couple intently, gesturing toward the Dorothy. The mother tugged her husband toward the paper-signing line.

Caleb got a feeling in his gut. A bad feeling. A very bad feeling.

CHAPTER 11

THE IMPROMPTU DOG DAYS OF SUMMER dog park block party was going better than Riley could've imagined. Of course, now that people were gathered, she wished she'd arranged some sort of sound system and that the refreshments were a bit higher class. The manager in her couldn't help it; she loved a good event, loved making them happen, loved making sure people enjoyed them.

It would've been nice to have a face-painting station for the children and maybe set up some games with prizes. She could see it all in her head, how the lot would look decked out for a small street fair. Maybe local vendors and restaurants would want tables. It could be an annual event, a place where neighbors could bring their families and pets to enjoy the last days of summer before school started.

"What is this?" Caleb took her by surprise, striding up on his long legs, polo shirt neatly tucked into his jeans. Tucked. Into jeans. Who tucked anything into jeans? She needed to stop looking at his pants. He'd get the wrong idea.

Riley forced her gaze to his. "A little neighborhood get-together."

"On my property."

"I did a title search. It's not that hard, you know. I believe the property belongs to your grandfather?" Her lips twitched. She could tell by the flare in his eyes it was a sore spot.

"Grandpa William asked me to take care of things for him here."

"That's nice. Want a cookie?" She waved at the table. "They're going fast."

He opened his mouth, then closed it. "I do."

Caleb stuffed a chocolate chip cookie in his mouth and was about to take the last one when the kindergarten girl walked up to the table.

"Cookie?" Her hazel eyes widened with hope.

He handed the last one over to her. She chomped into it, half going into her mouth and half falling to the ground. Her Lab scarfed up the rest before she'd even realized it was missing.

"We were worried the dog would be jealous when we had Zoe, but the two of them are inseparable. Partially because Zoe is a never-ending supply of snacks." The mother smiled at her daughter. "It makes keeping the kitchen clean easier, too. Cocoa's always been part chowhound."

"They make a good team." Caleb watched Cocoa watch Zoe for any more scraps. "I'm Caleb. It's nice to meet you."

"Sasha. You new to the neighborhood?"

"You could say that."

"It's a great place to live. And this get-together is lovely, isn't it? Did you already sign the petition? It'd be such a shame to lose our dog park to a heartless developer."

"It'd be the worst. And I'd probably be out of a job." Riley joined the conversation, a half-eaten brownie in hand.

"You don't know that for sure." Caleb's stomach growled. The cookie'd only made him hungrier. "Maybe it'll lead to a better job."

"I like my job how it is." Riley stretched the truth a bit to make her point. The Dorothy wasn't her dream job by any leap of the imagination. What young girl dreams of pulling

chicken bones out of a garbage disposal on a weekly basis
and arguing with the cable company about internet speed?
Not her. During her hospitality studies, she'd imagined herself rising in the ranks of a swanky chain, helping to create
a luxury experience for weary business travelers and jaded
millionaires.

Maybe she'd even dreamed of being swept off her feet
by a billionaire—oh, why be greedy? a millionaire would
do—noticed for her effortless efficiency and determined
cheer. He'd find the swanky chain's requisite blazer and skirt
sexy, her tight chignon a mystery he wanted to unravel. At
first, he'd think it was a mere fling, but it wouldn't take long
until he realized he couldn't live without her. They'd be
married in the Grand Ballroom, honeymoon at the sister
resort in Tahiti.

Yeah, she'd thought about all of that, pulling midnight
shifts on the desk and comping guests' room service when
their morning omelets arrived cold. She'd thought about it
and dismissed it. Riley knew who she was, a hard worker
with a grandmother to keep an eye on and now a dog who
needed expensive prescription dog food to keep from devel-
oping more bladder stones. She watched LouLou enticing
Lady into galloping around the lot with a play bow and an
excited yip. Lady obliged, lumbering to her feet and chasing
the little poodle, tongue hanging out of her mouth.

A Dalmatian crashed into the back of Riley's legs, hitting
her knees at exactly the right angle to take her down.

"Careful." Caleb reached out and grabbed her elbow,
steadying her.

Riley caught her breath.

"Sorry? Did I hurt you?"

"No." She rubbed her elbow. It wasn't pain that brought the nerve endings in her skin to life. Why, of all the men in Miami-Dade County, did her hormones wake up for Caleb Donovan? She sidled sideways, attempting to put more distance between them without looking like she was running away. "The knockdown is an all-too-common occurrence at the dog park. I should've gotten out of the way."

The tiny pack of terrors was already halfway across the lot, yipping and yapping up a storm. Riley smiled. Dogs knew how to enjoy the moment.

"It'd be nice if there were some benches." Caleb scanned the lot, the assortment of humans as motley as the dogs they'd brought with them. Some stood, some sat in beach chairs they'd brought from home. Others squatted, petting dogs and speaking doggy nonsense to them. "Maybe a table or two?"

"And agility equipment." Sasha filled the space between Caleb and Riley. "In our old neighborhood, the dog park had an A-frame, and Cocoa loved to race up to the top and enjoy the view from there."

"An A-frame?" Caleb's forehead crinkled while he looked up the term on his phone. Riley admired his earnestness, that desire to get things right, even in a casual conversation.

"A ramp. Shaped like an A. And there could be tunnels and weaving sticks." Sasha clasped her hands together. "A real doggy paradise."

"It would be nice for them to have more stimulation." Riley shaded her eyes, forcing her gaze away from Caleb's quick fingers, and searched the patchy grass for her poodle. "And a water station, especially in the summer, would be incredibly useful."

"We could get a kiddie pool for the dogs who like to swim!" Sasha mimed the dog paddle, and Riley laughed.

"Poodles are supposed to love water, but so far, I haven't had a chance to see if LouLou's a swimmer or not. She doesn't mind a bath, but she's never seemed especially eager to jump into Eliza's pool the couple of times we've been over there."

"You never know." Sasha folded her arms over her stomach. "We had a Lab growing up we couldn't keep out of the pool. Every chance he got, he was neck deep. Loved to fetch things out of the water, too. He was quite a character."

"I'm sorry for your loss." Riley placed a hand on Sasha's forearm.

"When did he die?" Caleb looked up from his phone.

Riley cut her eyes at him. If he was going to hang out around dog owners, he needed to learn the etiquette. Every loss of a pet was a fresh wound for dog lovers.

"Years ago. After I left for college."

"I'm sure you still miss him." Riley patted Sasha.

Sasha inhaled deeply. "Yes, Cujo was the best dog."

"Cujo?" Caleb's thumbs tumbled over his phone screen. "Like the crazy Stephen King dog?"

Sasha giggled. "My brother named him, I'm afraid, and my parents had no idea until years later why everyone did a double take when they heard his name."

Riley laughed with her. "And now you have Cocoa."

"Yes, I can't imagine living without a dog." Sasha turned to Caleb. "Which of these gorgeous pooches is yours?"

"Oh, I, uh—" Caleb's thumbs fumbled, and he stuffed his phone in his back pocket.

"He's a guest." Riley didn't know why she wanted

to jump in and save him, but she wanted him to fit in. "LouLou's guest."

Sasha's eyes widened, bouncing between Riley and Caleb. "Oh. Riley, you never said anything."

Riley raised a shoulder. "Nothing to say. He wanted to check out the area. And LouLou, bless her man-loving heart, took a liking to him when he rescued her during a storm."

"How sweet!"

"What's sweet?" Sasha's husband joined them, and Caleb ended up retelling the story of finding LouLou in the rain.

"I'm Joe." He clapped Caleb on the back. "Welcome to the neighborhood."

Caleb ducked his chin, a move Riley found endearing, and said, "Anybody would've done the same."

"You'd be surprised who wouldn't." Joe launched into a story about finding a bag of kittens on the side of the 95, abandoned and starving. "Took 'em to a local rescue. Allergic as all get-out to felines but couldn't leave 'em out there to die."

Sasha snuggled into Joe's side and winked at Riley. "I got a good man in this one, didn't I?"

What could Riley do but agree? The truth was, she knew Sasha and Joe by sight, knew their daughter's and dog's names, even had a vague idea which direction their house was in. But she didn't really know them. This was the longest conversation they'd ever had, the only conversation where they'd talked about something besides the weather or their dogs.

"You don't have to own a dog to sign the petition, do you?" Sasha asked Riley. She gave Caleb an encouraging smile. "Every signature helps, right?"

"Right." Riley gave a clipped nod, interested to see how Caleb would handle it. Had he seen the petition? Did he know it was for the upcoming commission meeting?

But Caleb wasn't paying attention. He was frozen in place, watching as a black Dodge Ram slowly made its way past the park. It hopped a curb and parked illegally in front of Eliza's house, but with so many people coming out for the party, Riley didn't think Eliza would mind.

A tall, blond guy climbed out of the driver's side, planting two large cowboy-boot-clad feet in Eliza's front grass. He shaded his eyes and peered across the street.

"Lance?" Caleb whispered almost too softly to hear. Then he unfroze and took a few halting steps in the direction of the Ram. "Lance!" His voice grew stronger, and then he was half walking, half jogging to the fence. "What're you doing here?"

CHAPTER 12

"SAID I'D BE IN TOUCH." LANCE LOOKED ENOUGH LIKE their father that it was eerie. The same cool, blond locks, the same rangy build, same Grandpa William–blue eyes. He sauntered up to the chain-link fence, threading his fingers through the metal diamonds and leaning into the already sagging panel.

"So, hey." Lance kicked a booted foot into the dirt.

"Hey." Caleb stood about a foot back from the fence, noticing how Lance looked even more tired than when they'd video chatted. When Lance left the Donovan family business, he'd started his own construction company, Excalibur Construction, and he oversaw every aspect of the operation. Caleb remembered something about Lance's ex-wife encouraging him to "lean in" to his King Arthur–inspired first name. Across the street, Lance's truck had not only the company name but a logo depicting the famous sword in the stone and the slogan "We build your Camelot" in an old-fashioned scripty font.

Lance had taken his then-wife's advice to heart, that was for sure. And it made sense. Lance wanted to leave behind the Donovan name. No way would Robert Donovan have been associated with such a cheesy name, even if he had married—and quickly divorced—the woman responsible for naming her son after a man doomed to love from afar.

Lance's fingers tightened on the chain-link. "This is the empty lot?"

Caleb's lips twitched. "As you can see."

Lance surveyed the decidedly not-empty scene. "This is the property?"

"Yeah." Caleb pointed to the Dorothy. "The lot plus that building."

"Nice neighborhood."

"Yep. Why don't you come in? Meet some of the residents? I can give you a walk-through, tell you about what I've been thinking. Maybe you'll have some ideas?"

Lance's lips thinned into a line. "I don't think so. This really isn't my kind of thing."

"But I'm building my Camelot." Caleb knew as soon as the words were out of his mouth that he'd touched a nerve, gone too salesman, too like their father. He shook off the old training and tried again. "It would mean a lot to Grandpa William for the two of us to work together."

"I don't work for Donovans."

"Not for. With."

"I don't do that either."

"Then why'd you come by?"

"Can't a big brother check up on his little bro, see what kind of trouble he's getting himself into?"

Caleb rubbed the back of his neck and rocked forward on his toes, then back to his heels. "How'd you know there's trouble?"

"Why else would you call so many times?" Lance dropped his hands from the fence. "Looks like we're about to get some company. Some pink company?"

Sure enough, Riley was right behind him in yet another pink T-shirt. This one had a fluffy cloud across the chest with the word "Believe" written in silver glitter in the middle. Her hair was pulled back in one of her sloppy pony-tails with a glittery pink hair tie.

She smiled at Lance. "Hi there. You don't happen to be a Miami Beach resident, do you?"

He nodded.

"Wonderful! Will you help out by signing a petition to preserve our neighborhood? It'll only take a minute."

"Preserve it from what?"

Riley's eyes gleamed with mischief. "Why, one of those real-estate magnate types has his eye on tearing down my Grams' building and turning this neighborhood dog park into a parking lot. Can you imagine?"

Lance's eyes crinkled, proving his lines were as much from laughter as sun squinting. "I can indeed. And you mean to stop the march of progress?"

"For as long as I can."

"I'd be happy to help. Where do I sign?"

Caleb grimaced but ambled along behind Riley while she pointed out to Lance how to enter the so-called dog park. He followed them to the table where a perky twen-tysomething with a Chihuahua on her lap talked an elderly gentleman with a cockatoo on his shoulder through the petition steps.

"Sydney, please help this gentleman sign on the dotted line." Riley circled the table to stand beside Sydney, shoving a clipboard and pen in Lance's direction.

"Happy to." Sydney shot Lance a smile while her Chihuahua looked on with a weather eye.

When Lance reached for the pen, the tiny dog growled.

"Enough, Chewy. You can't scare away our supporters. Did Riley tell you what this is about?"

"She sure did." Lance took his time signing. "Not that she had to. I'd sign anything for you."

Chewy growled again, and Sydney laughed. "Let's hope it's that easy to get the signatures we need."

"I'm sure you won't have any trouble." Lance clicked the pen closed and rolled it back toward Sydney. Chewy gave it a suspicious sniff but allowed it to stay on the table.

"Thank you." Sydney examined the petition, then flipped the clipboard to a clean page before setting it out again.

"You need anything, you've got my number on that form of yours." Lance backed away with a slow smile.

"And on your truck. You can see that thing for a mile, can't you?" Sydney petted Chewy's head. "If I need construction, you're the first I'll call."

"You need a night on the town, you can call me for that, too."

"Stop flirting. Geez, can't take you anywhere." Caleb grabbed his brother's arm and pulled him away. Lance might look a bit ragged with his hair curling over his collar and two-day stubble, but he was apparently still catnip for females.

"Now that I've signed, I can go, right? No need for us to work together if you can't get the permits you need."

Caleb wasn't worried. A few signatures wouldn't change anything. Cities made decisions based on dollars, not emotions. Still, he eyed a few of the clipboards to get a sense of what he was up against. When he saw how many signatures Riley's party had garnered, he admitted to a twinge of alarm.

Lance smirked at him and turned the charm on Riley. "I wish you ladies luck with the City Commission. I hear those developer types have all kinds of nasty tricks they use to get their way, but I have a feeling they have no idea what they're up against."

Sydney giggled, and Riley thanked him for his time and signature.

"I'll walk you out," Caleb said, but Lance waved him off.

"I can squeeze through that gap all by my lonesome. Looks like you've got your hands full here. Do they know who you are?"

"She knows."

"The one in pink?"

"Yeah, Riley Carson."

Lance laughed and slapped Caleb on the back. "I'd wish you luck, too, but you know how I feel about Donovan real estate projects, so I'll just say, little brother, choose your battles carefully. Who are you really doing this for?"

"Grandpa William," Caleb replied automatically but knew it was the wrong answer. "Myself."

"Hope you figure it out." Lance strode away, and Caleb felt his whole project slipping through his fingers. Without Lance, Knox would never come on board. His brother hadn't stopped by to help, just to gloat, plant some seeds of doubt and dissent, and disappear. Like he always did. Caleb understood how his dad felt sometimes, watching people— wives, sons, business partners—walking away. But he wasn't his father. He wasn't doing anything shady or illegal. What would it take to keep someone by his side?

A sparkly "Believe" flashed through his mind. But what should he believe in anymore?

"I can't believe how many signatures we have!" Sydney scrubbed the underside of Chewy's chin with her knuckle, and he grunted in satisfaction.

"Eliza called in the troops, for sure." Riley ticked off the groups of people who'd never been to the dog park but had shown up today. "Her yoga class, bunco group, and a bunch of her lawyer friends!"

"And a few judges. That won't hurt when the City Commission looks at these signatures."

Riley remembered Lance's words. "Unless the Donovans have some trick up their sleeve we haven't thought of yet."

"Probably." Eliza plunked into the tiny plastic folding chair next to Sydney, and Lady immediately plopped her big head onto her lap. "But don't worry. I'll be at the meeting with you to counter any legal trickery they might try to pull."

Riley laid a hand over her heart. "You're the best."

"I am." Eliza snapped her fingers for Lady to sit, which she did, and leaned forward to shuffle through the signature pages. "Not too shabby. By the time the meeting rolls around, we should have a thousand. You'd need ten times that to get something on a ballot for voting, but for our purposes, a nice, round one-thousand will do nicely." Eliza neatened the edges of the stack and smoothed them with a finger.

"I hope it's enough." Riley spun in a circle, looking for her poodle. Of course, she was over by the fence, leaning against Caleb's leg. That male-identified traitor. She'd better go get her. "I'll be right back."

Riley flip-flopped her way over to the fence where Caleb still stood, watching his brother drive off. She'd never met a single Donovan when she worked for their chain, but now that they'd dumped her, she'd met two of the three brothers in as many weeks. Life was strange sometimes.

Even stranger was how she couldn't find it in herself to hate Caleb quite so passionately now that she knew him, knew his smell and how his lips tasted. She wouldn't think about those things now, or ever, but it did touch something deep inside her to see the blatant longing on his face as he stared into the distance where his brother's truck could no longer be seen.

"He seemed like a nice guy. Your brother."

"How'd you know?" Caleb scrubbed a hand down his face. "Never mind. We all look like chips off the old block, don't we? But yeah, I think he might be a good guy."

"You're not sure?"

"We didn't grow up together. Different moms. Different custody agreements and visitation schedules. I don't really know either of my brothers."

"That's sad."

"Are you close with your siblings?"

Riley crouched down to smooth a hand along LouLou's back. "No siblings. I'm a lonely only, as they say."

"Were you, I mean, are you lonely?" Caleb crouched, too, facing her across the poodle's back. LouLou's tail thumped happily against Riley's thigh.

Riley ducked her face, wishing her hair were loose so it'd cover the color she felt rising to her cheeks. "I've never felt it. Having Grams. It was always enough."

"I never felt lonely, either." He scratched under LouLou's collar, sending her tail thumping triple time. "Maybe I just didn't recognize the symptoms."

"Loneliness isn't a disease," Riley said, but then she

thought of the sisters, Doris and Merle, who lived in the unit right below Mr. Cardoza, who were always calling her up to fix things they could fix themselves, and how Grams made sure she had at least one errand or visit per day so she would, as she liked to say, "have a reason to get up in the morning."

"Luckily, I have LouLou." Riley scratched the poodle right above her tail, her favorite spot.

"You're lucky then." Caleb stood and brushed his palms on his thighs. "Maybe I need a dog."

Riley looked up the long length of him, head haloed by the sun setting behind him. "Maybe you do."

CHAPTER 13

RILEY WALKED INTO THE CITY COMMISSION MEETING room with much more confidence than she'd had the week before. For one, Sydney had dressed in her in a to-die-for pale-pink Chanel suit with adorable kitten heels. For another, she had her PowerPoint presentation memorized and ready to go on her laptop, along with a backup on a USB drive and a printed-out script in case of technology failure.

Eliza was already seated, her hand on the briefcase that contained the pages of signatures and whatever legal notes she'd prepared. Behind her, Mr. Cardoza escorted Grams, and although they were twenty minutes early for the meeting, Riley recognized a lot of the faces in the room from the Dorothy and the dog park. Eliza was right when she'd said, "If you ask people to show up, you'd be surprised how many will."

Riley was certainly surprised, and touched, that so many people she'd talked to at the party were already seated. She saw Sasha and Joe a few seats down from Eliza, holding hands. She waved at Patty where she sat with her walker parked next to Doris and Merle, the two elderly sisters dressed like they were going to church in their Sunday-best flowered dresses and big hats.

Sydney waved at Riley from the back row and gave her a thumbs-up, mouthing, "You look great!"

It was amazing what having the right suit could do for a woman. She was no longer the on-site manager of a run-down building. She was back to being Riley Carson, rising star. It felt right to glide into a seat near the front and pop open her laptop. The Wi-Fi connected easily and her PowerPoint loaded, no problem. Unlike with the presentations she'd dreaded giving in college, she was excited to get started. Once the city commissioners knew the neighborhood like she did, they'd shoot down the Donovans' plans in a heartbeat.

Riley took it as a good sign when Commissioner Jackson came over to greet Grams, exclaiming loudly, "Gloria, you never age!" which was something Grams liked to hear as much and as often as possible.

"Pish-posh, Claudia. Don't you look lovely today?"

They exchanged thoughts on various overnight creams until Commissioner Santos called the meeting to order. The other commissioners were in place at the front of the room, a screen pulled down behind them. A small projector with a blinking light sat between Santos and Jackson.

"Forgive us." A booming voice entered the room. "There was a bit of a kerfuffle with the parking situation." An older man, probably around Grams' age, entered the room. He looked slim in a dark pin-striped suit that camouflaged the small bulge of a belly. His bold blue tie matched the eyes under a pair of bushy white eyebrows.

"Billy!" Grams' hand flew to her chest. Her other hand gripped Riley's forearm hard enough to leave marks.

The older man's sharp gaze landed on Grams. He leaned a bit heavier on the cane in his right hand. "Glo?"

"Billy?" Caleb entered the room, equally well dressed in a light-gray suit and crisp white shirt open at the collar. "Grandpa Billy?"

"Don't even try it. I've never been a Billy." He walked toward Grams, one thump of the cane at a time. "Glo, it's been too long."

Grams dropped her hands to her lap and studied her nails. She didn't respond.

"And you must be that gorgeous granddaughter I've heard all about." He reached out a hand to Riley. "I'm William Donovan."

"Don't touch that greasy snake-oil salesman," Grams hissed under her breath.

Riley ignored her and stood to shake his hand. "A pleasure, sir."

"She has manners," William observed, whether to Grams or Caleb, it was unclear.

"And she can hear you." Riley removed her hand and made a show of getting hand sanitizer out of her bag.

"Good girl," Grams murmured.

"You're not going to talk to me? Still?"

Grams held out her hand for some sanitizer and hummed to herself.

Although Grams couldn't carry a tune to save her life, William clearly recognized the opening bars of Carly Simon's "You're So Vain." His eyes narrowed, and he thumped away to an empty seat a few rows away.

Caleb placed a hand on the back of Riley's chair. "Bad blood, I guess, but I hope you'll keep an open mind during my presentation."

"And I hope you'll keep an open mind during mine."

"Deal."

Riley felt the loss of his body heat behind her, could sense without looking his taking a seat near his grandfather. How she hated this awareness of him that she couldn't control, couldn't turn off. He was here to change everything about Grams' and her lives, and all she could think about was how close his hand on the chair had been to her shoulder. What if he'd closed the gap, slid a knuckle up her neck and into the neat chignon of her hair? She closed her eyes against the image. Focus, that was what she needed right now, focus.

Santos gave some general opening remarks about the importance of every neighborhood to the character of Miami Beach. "But we mustn't lose sight of the progressive nature of time and the importance of planning for the future. Miami Beach was founded on one man's dream of what could be, and it is our duty as representatives of the people to keep reimagining what our future can be."

"As long as it keeps him in office and his major contributors' pockets lined with cash, he means," Grams spoke loud enough that her words carried a few rows. William Donovan's shoulders noticeably stiffened.

Caleb was brought up to discuss his plans for the Dorothy and the adjacent empty lot. He smiled readily at Santos' introduction, shook hands with each commissioner, and hooked up his computer with ease.

"First, let me introduce you to the Dorothy." The first image on the screen showed the Dorothy from the street, the wide expanse of unmanicured lawn leading up to the front door. He flipped through slides of close-ups of sagging gutters, peeling paint, the stained terrazzo in the lobby. He showed the gaping gate at the empty lot, the patchwork grass, a shot of the dog park when no dogs were there, just some plastic bags blown against the fence and shards of broken glass buried in the dirt. "As you can see, the property has not been kept up, and although the current residents love their home, there's no doubt that a huge influx of cash is needed to bring it up to modern standards."

"And whose fault is it?" Grams muttered. "If he himself has been owning it all these years, why did he never swoop in with his checkbook and make things right? He was waiting for this, waiting to take it away from me in as public and humiliating a way as possible."

Riley patted Grams' hand. She couldn't argue. She didn't know why the Donovans had kept their ownership secret or why they wanted to repair things now. She only knew she couldn't let them.

"I've been working with a local architect on some designs that will respect the building's history while still bringing it into the current century." Caleb flipped to a slide showing a shiny new apartment building, three stories high, with nothing in common with the Dorothy except the original lettering of the building's name preserved and hung over the new doorway. It was sleek and modern-looking, but certainly not Deco or even Deco-inspired.

Grams gasped and held her hand to her heart again. "He wants to build that monstrosity?" Other neighbors grumbled their disapproval.

"Of course, as with many of the older buildings on the Beach, parking is wholly inadequate even for the current residents. With increased capacity, we'll need increased parking space, and that's where the pièce de résistance comes in." Caleb clicked, and a futuristic parking structure appeared, also three stories, the outside covered in greenery. "The building is enough to provide ample space for residents while still allowing for public parking on the first floor."

"The city is not investing in new parking structures at this time," Commissioner Jackson said in a quelling tone that could probably hush an auditorium full of rowdy students but didn't dampen Caleb's smile in the least.

"Of course not. We have to build the parking structure anyway. We're offering a partnership with the city, a potential long-term revenue stream."

"A bribe!" Grams hissed.

"And a good one." Riley drummed her fingers nervously on the briefcase holding her laptop. She didn't have shiny photos of what could be to show the commissioners, and Santos' surprised laugh made her uneasy.

"What's the anticipated revenue stream?" Santos tapped the tips of his fingers together.

Caleb pulled up a complicated graph of current parking garages on Miami Beach and their hourly and daily rates as well as occupancy history and projections. "It's hard to say for sure, given the variability by season, but we estimate that opening up the bottom floor for public parking will bring in a couple hundred thousand per year, if not more."

Santos rested his elbows on the table and templed his fingers. "And if we had two floors of the parking structure, that would double?"

For the first time, Caleb blinked. "Priority goes to resident parking, of course, and then the extra spaces will be used as public spaces."

"And if the city's approval depended on having two floors of the garage?" Santos pushed his point while pushing his fingers into the table.

"Not going to happen." Eliza stood and addressed the commission. "You should be advised, I've alerted the

Historic Preservation Board to these proceedings, and they have representatives in the room right now. We know they are unlikely to approve buildings higher than the ones currently in the neighborhood."

"But the Dorothy isn't an historic building," Caleb said.

"Not yet." Eliza sat down, her point made.

"Still." Santos regained control of the meeting. "This is a very promising proposal. I believe the commission will look favorably upon it. We can certainly give preliminary approvals, get the ball rolling as it were, until we hear from the Historic Preservation Board." Other commissioners nodded their agreement.

Rocks settled in Riley's stomach, the kind of rocks she'd run into when working on the Dorothy's landscaping. Immovable stones, hard as concrete. She didn't think she could stand, but when Commissioner Jackson called her forward, Riley rose.

She fumbled the setup, felt herself sweating through Sydney's smart suit.

"Uh, hi." She flipped to her first presentation slide, feeling the fear from every school presentation she'd ever given freeze her face into a mask. Smile, she had to smile. She tried to, really hard, but when Santos reeled back from her fierce expression, she understood it wasn't working. How she wished LouLou were here, sitting on her feet like she'd done while Riley was putting the presentation together. Her comforting warmth was exactly what she needed.

Grams gave her a thumbs-up from the audience, and Sydney's encouraging smile from the back row straightened her spine. She could absolutely do this. Then she did what she had promised herself she wouldn't do: make eye contact with Caleb, where he sat in the front row. She thought he'd be smug after Santos basically guaranteed him a pass with his plan, but he nodded his head encouragingly. The warmth she'd been seeking filled her, melting the heavy stones in her stomach and finally allowing her to speak. She didn't understand it, didn't like it, but she couldn't look away. She addressed the first part of her carefully rehearsed presentation to him.

"Yes, the Dorothy needs some work. Maybe a lot of work." Her first image was a picture from the day Grams moved into the building. Tropical landscape filled the front yard, windows sparkled in the sun, and women with 1960s bouffants and large sunglasses sat in deck chairs beneath the palm trees.

"But it was once a gem of Art Deco architecture here on the Beach." She flipped through interior shots showing the lobby in its midcentury heyday, pictures from various parties at Grams' apartment through the years, lots and lots of photos of residents hanging out in the lobby, in one another's apartments, laughing, arms around one another. "More importantly, the residents of the Dorothy have always felt like it was a true home, a place where neighbors become family.

"And that empty lot? Why, it's not empty at all." She showed pictures from the dog park party, the people eating snacks and chatting, the dogs running the field. "The lot has become an important extension of the Dorothy, a place where the neighborhood gathers. Neighbors not only have a place to exercise their dogs but also to meet each other and become a real community."

Riley reached into her briefcase and pulled out the

petition and the pages and pages of signatures, presenting them to the commissioners. "That's why we're asking that the Dorothy be left the way she is so she can continue to be the heart of our beloved neighborhood."

Eliza whistled her approval, and the neighbors in the crowd stomped their feet and clapped. Riley let out a whoosh of pent-up breath and plastered on a smile, eyes darting from one commissioner to the other, searching their reactions. Hoping what she'd said, what she'd done, was enough.

Commissioner Jackson took the paperwork from Riley. "You've certainly got a lot of signatures here."

Riley nodded. Now that her preplanned words were delivered, she felt a bit self-conscious at all eyes being on her. She glanced at Caleb out of the corner of her eye. He was frowning and checking something on his computer. Good, maybe she'd shaken him up. Or at least the community support shook him.

"No one likes change." Santos' words were as conde-scending as his tone. "But it's the responsibility of this body to encourage positive change in our neighborhoods. I don't see how we can say no to the Donovan proposal when it offers so much to the current neighborhood as well as the benefit to the city."

Grams raised her hand, and Santos called on her. "My sole income is Social Security, and many of the residents are in a similar situation. If the Dorothy is converted to condos, many of us will be forced to move. And what can we afford here on the Beach? We'll be forced to leave the city that we have called home for longer than some of you commission-ers have been alive. How are you serving your constituents if the choices you make today force the very people who voted for you to move away?"

More clapping erupted from the audience. Commissioner Jackson leaned into the microphone on the table. "Well said, Gloria. I couldn't agree more."

"Perhaps you're overstating the situation, Gloria." Commissioner Graves swiped the microphone toward him. "The parking revenue could do a lot of good in our community, and there is plenty of affordable housing in our fair city."

There were mumblings of "Oh yeah, where?" from the crowd, and Grams got that fighting look in her eye that usually spelled trouble, but she demurred with a "That's certainly an opinion."

"You said it. Too many opinions, not enough action." Santos banged his hand on the table. "I say we vote now."

"I say we wait for the Historic Preservation Board to weigh in." Commissioner Jackson leaned into her mic and enunciated each word clearly. "Nothing can be decided until the status of the building is settled."

Commissioner Santos tapped impatient fingers next to his mic. "Come, Claudia, everyone at the table knows how hard it is to get a building through that process, and the Dorothy is well outside the historic preservation district. It's a delaying tactic at best. We'll let it play out, of course, we have to, but we know which way this is going. In the meantime, there's no reason we can't take an informal poll to see how the commissioners are leaning. All in favor of the Donovan proposal?"

Each of the commissioners except Claudia Jackson raised their hands.

"There you have it." Santos rubbed his palms together. "There's obviously a more official process to come, but it's good to see we are in agreement." At Jackson's snort, he corrected himself, "Mostly in agreement."

"I'm sorry," Commissioner Jackson said to Riley. "I understand where you and the community are coming from, I do. But it's hard to stand in the way of progress. Or rather profit. Let's hope the Historic Preservation Board comes through for you."

"Right." Riley sighed. Why had she thought any of this would matter? She and Grams were the little guys, and the little guys never won.

CHAPTER 14

CALEB SHOULD BE ECSTATIC. IN FACT, GRANDPA William's "Good job. It couldn't have gone smoother. What shall we do to celebrate?" still hung like cartoon bubbles in the air.

But Riley. He couldn't get her out of his head. Her glum look as he'd presented, her nervous but hopeful energy as she talked about the building she grew up in and loved. Her utter devastation when the board took its informal vote. He should be over the moon happy that things were going his way. Why did he feel like he'd just kicked a puppy? And not even an annoying, ankle-biting puppy but one of those supercute yellow Lab pups with big red bows tied around their necks. Yes, that was who he was. Caleb Donovan, puppy kicker.

"You've got the Donovan instinct, that's for sure." Grandpa William clapped him on the shoulder, a surprisingly strong jolt that had Caleb fighting for his stability.

Caleb pulled out his phone. "One minute." He held his cell to his ear and walked around the corner for privacy. That was what he needed, privacy for the phone call he was pretending to take so he could get some for real space.

Behind the building, lush tropical plants sprouted out of planters, sheltering stone benches. Discreetly located ashtrays marked this area as a designated smoker's paradise, but no one was currently lighting up. Caleb inhaled a deep breath, held it for a few seconds, and then enjoyed the whoosh of air as it left his lungs. Finally, a moment of peace. He crossed over to the nearest bench and sat, forearms propped on his knees, and let his head droop.

Sniffle, sniffle. Someone else was having an alone moment on the other side of the planter. The sago palms rustled behind him. The sniffling grew louder. A strangled sob had him on his feet.

"Are you okay?"

Sniffle. "I'm fine."

He recognized that voice. He rounded the planter and there she was, Riley Carson, in her wilted pink suit, dabbing at her eyes with a tissue. A travel-size pack sat on her lap, and a small pile of damp tissues had collected on the bench near her hip. Unlike Grams' attempts to sway him with fake tears last week, Riley's real tears made mascara run down her cheeks. She looked like a sad raccoon.

"You don't sound fine." He perched next to her, on the tissue-free side, and stared straight ahead. "You gave a good presentation."

"Not good enough." Her words were muffled behind the tissue.

"It was good enough. You certainly gave me some things to think about."

"Like what?"

"The Dorothy was something else back in its day, wasn't it? Art Deco design is optimistic and futuristic, but that future is now the past. It made me think about preserving the past as a way of preserving hope for the future." He hadn't realized what he was thinking until he said it out loud, but it made sense. His father wouldn't see the value in an old building, would say it's better for the bottom line to simply start from scratch, but old buildings had memories. They had character. They had people who loved them. People like Riley. Perhaps there was another way forward.

"That's kind of you to say." She crinkled the empty tissue holder in her hand and sniffled again.

"I'm not kind. Not generally anyway." He reached into the inside pocket of his blazer and pulled out a handkerchief.

"Oh, I couldn't." She waved away his offering with a watery smile.

He pressed it into her hand. "It's what they're for."

"I'm not going to give it back to you full of snot."

"Don't give it back. Throw it away for all I care. My mother gives me a new supply every holiday." He pulled out another one from a different pocket for emphasis.

Riley's head tilted, and she quirked an eyebrow. "That's an odd gift."

Caleb stretched out his legs, balancing his feet on the back of his heel, ankles crossed. "I had a lot of allergies as a kid, and she thought sending me to school with a box of Kleenex was tacky."

"That's sweet." She folded the handkerchief into a smaller and smaller square.

"Yes, too sweet, I think." Caleb's hands rested on his belly, thumb tapping wildly against the muscle outlined by the tight fit of his button-down. "She's the only one of Dad's wives to stay with him. Even when she found out he was cheating on her, she didn't leave. Went with him on every business trip, to 'help him avoid temptation' she said."

"That's pretty extreme. Guess she's one of those rare stand-by-your-man kind of women, huh?" Riley used the handkerchief to dab at her eyes.

"Too much so. I've always hated how he treated her."
Caleb's jaw clenched, remembering the fights he wasn't supposed to overhear, the shattered glass when his dad threw things against the wall, always her things, her Lladró figurines and Swarovski Christmas angel ornaments, the crystal champagne flutes from their wedding.

"I never knew my dad." Riley fisted the handkerchief, tucking the mascara-stained section into her palm. "He walked on Mom when she told him she was pregnant."

"I wish my dad had walked out before I was born. My whole life, I wanted to make him proud. Like if I were good enough, he'd ease up on my mom." Caleb let out a long breath. "What a waste of all our time. He was never who he claimed to be."

"Is it really worse to know than to wonder?" Riley unfolded the handkerchief, smoothing out the wrinkles with her fingertips. "In a lot of ways, I'm like my mom and Grams, but in the ways I'm different, I always wonder if those parts are from him. Or are they my own? I wish I knew." Riley dabbed at her newly leaking eyes. "Even if he is an awful human being, I still want to know him."

"If? He left. There's no doubt he's awful." Caleb didn't like seeing the tears creep back. It'd been a long time since he'd wanted to comfort someone else. He searched for the right words. "It's something we have in common, then, their awfulness. Different paths, same result. We both have fathers out there, but neither of us really has a dad."

"But your dad, or excuse me," she corrected at his stern look, "father, would be proud of you today. You won." At least her tears had dried, but she continued to fold his handkerchief into twisted origami squares, doing and undoing them over and over again.

Caleb watched her fingers, long and dexterous, with short work-friendly nails painted a pale pink to match the suit. He'd never realized you could tell so much about a person from their hands, but Riley's said it all: feminine, competent, sexy as all hell. What were they talking about again? Oh right, her messed-up paternal relationship. And his.

"Grandpa William says I made the family proud, but it's too late. I don't care what Robert Donovan thinks of me anymore. He's going to rot in jail, and I hope I never see him again."

"That's pretty harsh." Riley leaned sideways, and their arms pressed together. Did she crave his nearness the way he craved hers? "Whenever I'd get mad at my mom for being away for her job so much, Grams always told me that the *f* in family stands for 'forgive.'"

"That's a nice saying. Harder to do in real life." Caleb leaned, too, and her shoulder dug into his bicep. The pressure made him hot enough to shrug out of his sport coat, but he didn't want to break contact with her. "Would you really forgive your father if he showed and wanted to be part of your life now?"

"I'm not sure, and it's not likely to happen anyway. But you, you'll have lots of chances. At least you know where you father is. It's not like he can run out on you if you decide to have it out with him." Riley let out a controlled breath, and her head fell against Caleb's shoulder. "Maybe someday you'll make peace with your father. You can't spend your whole life angry at him."

The muscles of Caleb's arm turned rigid under her cheek. "Why not? Sounds like a good plan to me."

"You're impossible." She sat up and nudged him with her shoulder. He nudged back, and she sniffed back the last of her tears. "So now you only have to make yourself proud. Are you?"

"Proud? Of what? You made clear in your presentation all that would be lost. If I get final approval, I destroy the Dorothy's history. But if Eliza gets the Historic Preservation Board to designate it as an historic building, I won't be able to use my designs. Grandpa William will say there's no money to be made in the status quo. He'll think I failed him."

"I'd say that's too bad, but well, that would be great. Not the failing your family, of course, but the Dorothy being preserved would be amazing." Riley tucked the handkerchief into the gold-handled clutch already bulging with girl stuff. If she had that many things to carry, why choose such a tiny bag? It did complement the suit with its subdued champagne shimmer, but it wasn't a practical choice. Just like trying to keep the Dorothy exactly the same wasn't practical, either.

"The Dorothy needs renovating, though." Caleb shifted, angling his body toward hers on the bench. "Even you must see that. It's not in the same condition you showed in those slides today."

Riley's head bobbed in agreement. "Renovation. Not replacement."

Caleb stared at Riley's feet encased in closed-toed slingback heels, wishing he could see her toenails. Same pale pink as on her fingers? Or something bolder? To cover up his odd fascination with her footwear, he changed the subject. To her feet. "How's your foot? How's LouLou's injury?"

"We're both recovered." Riley crossed her leg, tucking one foot behind her calf. "She's running around the dog park like the little boss she is."

"I'm glad for both of you." Caleb couldn't tear his eyes from where the pink skirt hitched up, revealing the skin above her knee. He wanted to trace that inch of skin with the tip of his finger, test the back of her knee for ticklishness, slide his hand up one more inch and then another until the skirt rode her thigh and those knees were around his waist. The image was so vivid in his mind, he had to shake his head to clear it. Remind himself where they were: in public, on a bench. Still, her skin called to him, and he tucked his hand under his thigh to keep from reaching for her.

As if feeling his gaze, Riley tugged her skirt down, and he almost groaned when her knee was once again covered. Great, now he had a thing for knees, or at least Riley's knees. He searched his scrambled brain for something to say. Something about business.

"You know, if I can't build the parking structure, there's no money for anything. Not even renovation. But maybe there's a compromise." He let his hands out of their thigh jail so he could gesture at the expanse of green space across the street, a little plot of land too small to be a park but big enough to host a small butterfly garden. "I could build a dog park. A really nice dog park. A world-class dog park."

Riley folded the handkerchief in her lap and crossed her legs, that skirt inching its way up her thigh again. "Why would you do that?"

"Because it's the right thing to do?"

"Since when do Donovans care about that?"

Their gazes locked. The image flashed in his mind again: his hand on her thigh, her knees clamped around his waist. He imagined her hair spread out in wild curls around her head while he leaned over her, in toward her, their mouths a breath apart.

"This Donovan cares." His voice was whisper-soft.

"Cares about what?"

Somehow, the space between them disappeared. His mouth was a mere inch from hers. He could feel her breath, the sigh when he brushed his lips against hers with the softest touch. "About you."

"You're going to bribe me with a dog park?" She pulled back but not away. Her hand drifted to his shoulder and smoothed its way down his arm.

"Half the lot for a dog park. The other half for a small parking garage." His lip twitched at the corner. He wanted to smile. He wanted to kiss her. He wanted to make her happy. "Would it work?"

"Probably."

He cupped her face in his palms and traced her cheek-bone with his thumb.

"Then let me build you a dog park."

She closed the distance, brushing her lips against his with increasing pressure. Her wide brown eyes watched him, wary, and he'd give anything to replace that wariness with trust.

"I'm going to hold you to it." Her lips whispered across his. Heat flooded him, his heart pounding hard enough to beat itself right out of his chest.

Then there was no more breath left in his lungs for

talking. His other hand slid to cup the back of her neck, and he pulled Riley toward him. This. This was what he'd been waiting for since their first interrupted kiss. She parted her lips on a sharp breath, and he swooped in, his tongue dancing with hers. His fingers fisted in her hair, and she wiggled closer to him on the bench, her hands reaching up to twine around his neck.

She kissed him back as ferociously as he kissed her, and he soon forgot where they were. When they were. Who they were. He wanted to get closer to her and closer still. She must've felt the same because she swung a leg over his, scooching onto his lap, sidesaddle-style since the skirt didn't have much give. He groaned his pleasure at the closer contact. She rewarded him by tilting her head back to give him access to the sensitive flesh of her neck.

"Caleb, the car's here. Are you—" Grandpa William's cane tapped its way around the corner.

Riley pulled back with a gasp. She struggled to remove herself from his lap, but he locked an arm around her waist and held her in place. She frowned at him. He smiled back.

"Give me a minute, will you, Grandpa?"

Grandpa William humphed. "You're a Donovan all right."

Riley pried Caleb's fingers off her waist and popped to her feet.

"This was a mistake. It should never have happened." She sprinted away as fast as her borrowed heels would let her, leaving behind her wadded-up tissues and a Riley-sized emptiness in his arms.

CHAPTER 15

STUPID, STUPID, STUPID. RILEY KICKED THE TOE OF HER borrowed high heel against the concrete curb and watched Caleb hurry to his grandfather's side, taking his elbow while they ambled back toward the front of the building. Why did Caleb's very nearness make her so stupid?

"That was quite a show."

For a second, Riley thought Grams meant Caleb's and her private moment, but Grams was just arriving, her sensible Dr. Scholl's ballet flats adorned with a smattering of rhinestones on the toes she'd added herself. Grams loved her glue gun.

Riley stood, straightened her jacket, and tucked Caleb's gently used handkerchief into the waist of her skirt. Grams didn't need to see any evidence of how stupid she'd been, letting Caleb near her again with his dreamy eyes and dreamier kisses. She'd felt good pressed against him, his heat seeping through her sleeveless silk blouse, her hands braced against the firm muscles of his chest. She couldn't help but wish they'd had a few more minutes and a lot more privacy. God, she was even stupid inside her own head when she thought of him.

A buzz from her purse had her rooting around for her phone. "Grams, we gotta go. Constantine's got a major leak."

"I wondered why he wasn't here today. He didn't try to fix it himself, did he?" Grams linked her arm through Riley's and steered them toward the garage where Riley's Mazda was parked. "You know last time he tried to do it himself, that mess leaked right through my wall, ruined my lovely cabbage rose wallpaper. You never have repapered that wall like you promised."

"I know, I know. It's on my list." Riley's stomach, such a hodgepodge of rocks and nerves today, growled with what was probably hunger, but she took as a harbinger of doom. Constantine was always so old-world polite to her with his thick Italian accent and ever-present smile. To send an abrupt *water everywhere come now please* was as unlike him as missing Mass at St. Patrick's on Sunday mornings.

Constantine's door was already open when Riley rushed off the elevator, leaving Grams to find her own way to her apartment. But of course she didn't. She ambled along behind Riley, always with a nose for news, especially the neighborly kind. The hallway carpet outside Constantine's unit was damp. Definitely not a good sign.

Riley squished her way inside. "Mr. Marino?"

When she didn't immediately get an answer, she pitched her voice louder. He didn't like to wear his hearing aids. "Constantine?"

"In the kitchen!"

She followed his voice and found him with shirtsleeves rolled to his elbows, holding a dish towel over his sink drain. The sink itself was half full of water. Constantine was barefoot, a sight she'd never seen before, and water gushed from the cabinet directly under the sink. He dabbed the perspiration off his shiny, bald head with a red-and-white-striped kitchen towel.

"This is not good."

"Not good." Constantine pumped his elbows for reasons

Riley couldn't figure out, but it clearly made him feel like he was doing something about the situation.

"Why didn't you call sooner?" Riley squatted in her heels and opened the cabinet doors. Water sloshed onto her borrowed skirt. She really should've changed before dashing to Constantine's rescue. Riley wasn't entirely sure what she was looking at, but the pipe's raggedy edge where it should meet the wall but didn't was probably a bad sign. A very bad sign.

"You said the building doesn't have a lot of money, that we have to tighten the belts." Constantine mimed cinching a belt over his own tub of a belly. "So I try to fix it on my own."

"Mmm-hmm." She surveyed the situation. What to do? Her phone buzzed. Can we talk?

Caleb. She ignored it and called the plumber she'd had to use when her shower kept backing up and no amount of Drano cleared the pipes. In a few minutes, the dispatcher assured her someone was on the way.

How about now?

She shoved the phone into her bag and squished her way back to the hallway. No one was going to be happy with her for turning off the water, but she couldn't see another choice.

"Let me flush first!" Grams hurried to her apartment when Riley told her the water would be off until the plumber arrived and fixed whatever was going on in Constantine's kitchen.

"You've got three minutes, Grams." Riley pushed the elevator button and leaned against the wall. First, she'd shut off the water line to the building. Then, she'd write Sydney a check for the shoes and suit she'd just ruined. Could this day get any better?

Her phone buzzed. She ignored it.

Riley had a credit card specifically for building emergencies. The bills went to Rainy Day, which had made sense when she thought they were the management company, but now she wondered who actually paid the bills. She didn't have access to the building's financial records, just the spreadsheets Rainy Day sent her every month of incoming and outgoing transactions.

"Geez." Riley smiled at the plumber, a nice enough man with a Marlins ball cap pulled low over his forehead and work boots that looked like they weighed more than her poodle. She white-knuckled it while he swiped the credit card, praying it wouldn't be turned down. There'd been the drainage issue in the laundry room last month that ran up quite a bill. "I hope you're getting a vacation home or something out of this arrangement."

"Not me, but my guess is the owner isn't doing too badly." The plumber grinned and handed back the card. "My advice if you don't want to keep racking up the emergencies is to redo the plumbing. These pipes look original to the building, which means they aren't up to code and certainly not up to the strain of modern life."

Riley signed her name on his pad with her finger, shaking her head. "I'm afraid new pipes aren't in the budget. At least not anytime soon." She knew exactly how tight the money was for the Dorothy. No reserves. Patty behind on her rent. All those empty units.

"In the meantime, then, don't let anyone install a dish-washer, garbage disposal, or washer and dryer. And if some-one's got one of those in their unit, tell them to stop using it. Stresses the whole system. Until—" He mouthed the word *kaboom*, using his hands to illustrate a bomb going off.

"I'll certainly keep that in mind." *Kaboom* certainly described how this whole day had gone so far. Kaboom at the commissioners' meeting, kaboom on her new outfit, kaboom to the Dorothy's budget. She smoothed a wrinkle out of her damp skirt. "And I'll send an email to the resi-dents right away about not using any appliances. They're not supposed to have them, but you know how it is. A few ignore the rules and do as they please."

"It's the same in every building." He handed her a busi-ness card. "You can call me directly next time."

"Next time?" Riley slipped the card into her purse. Why was she playing dumb? Of course there would be a next time. As he'd pointed out, the pipes weren't getting any younger, and Mr. Cardoza wouldn't give up his garbage dis-posal any more than Patty would give up using her washer-dryer combo. Who knew what else the other residents might've installed over the years?

She added a walk-through to her to-do list. She'd say it was a general maintenance check, and it would be. But it would also be a hunt to find the culprit who was clogging up their drains. Mr. Cardoza was high on her list, but she couldn't rule anyone out. Not even her own Grams, who'd had a dishwasher put in twenty years ago and still used it. She rubbed her temple with two fingers. Sometimes she felt like she was holding the Dorothy together with nothing but bubble gum and an optimistic attitude.

"Good luck to you." The plumber smiled, tipped his hat, and finally, finally she could go home and not be optimistic. Yes, she was due for some wallowing—a good, old-fashioned, pajamas-in-the-middle-of-the-day, binge-watching afternoon with a poodle on her lap was exactly what she needed.

LouLou was overjoyed to see her, yipping and spinning in delighted circles. Riley scooped her up, planted three quick kisses on her head, and dropped her bag on the kitchen counter. She heard the buzz and sighed. What if it wasn't Caleb? She was supposed to be on call for the residents. It was unprofessional to have her phone on silent during business hours. Her fantasy of a lazy afternoon evaporated as she braced herself for whatever the next emergency was.

Now?

The smile on her face was not because the message was from Caleb. She was only happy that it wasn't a resident with more plumbing problems, or a broken thermostat, or God forbid, Hilde Grant needing another ride to the ER because her heart arrhythmia was acting up but she couldn't afford the ambulance copay.

Caleb's *Now?* waited for a response. Did he want to gloat? Email her his presentation so she could obsess over every detail of his destroy-Grams'-home plan? Or worse, did he think the kiss meant that he'd won her over? It hadn't. She should text him back to prove she hadn't been affected. Or she should *not* text him to prove she hadn't been affected? Ugh, she hated how mixed-up she felt, as confused as LouLou when her squeaky toy stopped squeaking—even when she was the one who'd disemboweled the thing in the first place.

Riley ran cold water over the insides of her wrists at the kitchen sink, an old habit from when she was a kid and wanted to cool down on a humid, summer day. She pumped some verbena-scented hand soap into her palm and scrubbed away traces of whatever she'd touched in Constantine's apartment. Really, she should hop in the shower, but she was so drained she didn't think she could make it out of the kitchen without a caffeine IV straight to the vein.

She popped a cup into the Keurig, not even bothering to check the flavor, filled it with water, and started it up. She leaned heavily on the counter, not even wanting to go as far as the counter to sit on a stool. LouLou circled a few times, then settled herself squarely over the tops of Riley's now bare feet. She wasn't sure where she'd toed off Sydney's shoes. Probably out in the hallway, as was her habit. She should really go get them. And she would. Later. After caffeine. She propped her cheek against the edge of the overhead cabinet and made a list of the things she'd do later. Maybe even text Caleb back. Something cool and unaffected. An inscrutable emoji perhaps. Her phone buzzed again.

You ok?

Oh, Caleb. Her eyes drifted shut, and she remembered the feel of his arms around her, his muscled biceps under her palms, the way all her worries flew out of her mind when he kissed her, and the only thoughts swirling in her head were *more* and *now* and *yes, please.* She was strangely polite in the throes of passion. Aiden used to make fun of her, faking a British accent from one of the HGTV home design shows she liked to watch.

"Dearest Aiden, what a jolly good chap you are. Yes,

please, do pour me some more of your tea." He'd always waggled his eyebrows in a way that made her laugh, but it hadn't really been funny. It wasn't like she thought about the things coming out of her mouth in heated moments.

"Must've been a repressed Victorian in a previous life," Aiden had said on more than one occasion, usually after she'd said, *"Not tonight,"* after particularly long, hard days at the hotel when all she wanted to do was collapse into a bubble bath and not come out until she was as wrinkled as pre-Botox Grams.

Stupid Aiden. She should've realized earlier that he wasn't interested in actually getting married. He liked being engaged; she'd been his fourth betrothed. It wasn't like there weren't warning signs. But she'd believed his stories about how the other girlfriends had gone Bridezilla as soon as they had a ring. She'd been sure if she stayed the course, stayed herself, it would work out. She should've listened to her gut. Or at least her Grams. It wasn't like Grams hadn't warned her a hundred times. A hundred times a hundred times.

"Men like that," she'd say, clicking her tongue like she did when Riley was ten and Grams caught her scarfing down all the Weight Watchers diet cookies, "never settle down. You're wasting your time."

Riley did waste time. Years of it before she finally freed herself from whatever delusion had made her think that sticking it out with Aiden was virtuous. He'd shrugged off their years together and never even bothered to pick up his things she'd carefully boxed and labeled for him.

"Toss it," Grams had advised more than once, but Riley dutifully carted it from her apartment to Grams' and then downstairs to the manager's apartment. For what? So she could have the memory of how Caleb filled out Aiden's old sweats forever emblazoned on her memory? No, thank you.

The Keurig clicked off, and she chugged her extra-bold blend. She felt the caffeine course through her veins, stronger than blood, pumping her full of what she knew was false energy but would take advantage of anyway.

"Come on, LouLou." Riley led the way to her bedroom where she changed into her cleaning-day clothes—ripped jean shorts and a T-shirt from her undergrad days that used to say "Will Work for Cupcakes" but too many washings later and the *w*'s and *r*'s were gone, leaving behind "ill ok fo Cupcakes," which Riley felt summed up her current mood pretty well.

"Ill ok?" she asked LouLou after pulling down the hem in front of her mirror. She'd laid Sydney's suit carefully on the foot of the bed. The damage wasn't as bad as she'd thought back in Constantine's apartment. Maybe a good dry cleaner could salvage it.

For now, though, Aiden's box was a priority. She might not be able to control the plumbing in the Dorothy or convince herself that she wanted Caleb to stop texting her, but she could do this. She could get rid of the Aiden remnants. She marched to the hall closet, LouLou on her heels, and flung open the door.

Aiden was written in her neatest print in black marker across the box. It was a large box, but not so large she couldn't pick it up herself, though a little awkward, and haul it out to the dumpster.

She clicked her tongue for LouLou to follow, groping blindly for the front door and finding the handle by touch. She peered around the right side of the box to steer herself toward the back entrance and out to the dumpster. That was why she didn't see what was coming on her left.

"Riley? Need a hand with that?"

"I got it." She squeezed her eyes shut. She should've texted him back. Surely, there was some emoji that covered the trifecta of sure-you're-a-good-kisser, but I-can't-with-you-right-now, and yes-it's-complicated. The shrugging girl? The genie? The tango dancers? God, it really was complicated. "I'm fine."

"You're always fine."

Riley huffed and set the box down. "What do you want, Caleb?"

"You didn't answer. I was worried."

Her brain stuttered for a moment on his response. She fought the urge to lean forward until her forehead crashed into his collarbone. She imagined his hand stroking up and down her back, how good it would feel to let someone worry about her. She'd tell him how the building needed new plumbing. He'd be sympathetic, let her talk it out, maybe suggest a plumber she'd never heard of, one the Dorothy could afford. He'd offer to make the call for her since she was unbelievably tired. But that wasn't her life. She was paid to worry about everyone else, not the other way around.

"You don't need to worry about me."

"It's just—"

Riley sliced her hand through the air, cutting him off before he could say something that brought back those moments on the bench. "Just nothing. I told you it was a mistake. A big, stupid mistake." She kicked the box, forgetting her feet were bare, and jammed her toe. Tears sprang to her eyes, but she dashed them away with the back of her hand. "I told you to forget it."

"I'm not going to forget this afternoon." His hand cupped her face, like he'd done on the bench, thumb smoothing away an escaped tear.

Her toe didn't really hurt enough to justify the tears she felt building in her eyes. "I have to go."

"Trash emergency?"

She nodded and picked up the carton of Aiden's left-behinds.

"Let me." He supported one side of the box with his hand.

It was easier this way. She hated him for it. Hated how light the box felt and how relieved she was not to deal with it alone. Hated that things seemed easier when he was around. She remembered how she'd climbed onto his lap, pressed her breasts into his chest, pushed into his touch. How she'd moaned when he'd grabbed her ass and pulled her tighter to him. She was certainly easier around him. Too easy.

Did she really need to take the box to the dumpster now? Maybe she should load it into her car and donate everything to Goodwill. That way, Aiden's leftovers might do some good in the world. Then she remembered the way he'd looked at her as she'd stumbled through her carefully rehearsed breakup speech, clearly disinterested and dismissive, flipping through his social media feed. It hurt her so much to leave him, but he'd seemed unaffected. They'd been drifting apart for over a year, no doubt about that, but she'd hoped he'd show some emotion when she left him. She just hadn't wanted that emotion to be relief.

"Come get your stuff!" she'd texted a few days later and, when he didn't reply, sent him a photo of the box with a question mark.

Keep it, he'd texted back. You can sleep in my old clothes and adopt a few cats. Winky face.

That was when the box got banished to the closet, and it wasn't more than a few weeks before LouLou was snuggling up on her feet every night at bedtime.

The dumpster was definitely the best place for anything Aiden related. She bumped open the back door with her hip and crab-stepped her way to the side of the dumpster, Caleb mimicking her moves on the other side of the box.

"Mmpf." She dropped her side, signaling Caleb to do the same while she flipped open the dumpster lid.

"What's in here?" Caleb rubbed a bicep. A nice bicep that Riley found herself unable to look away from. Corded and strong, the defined muscle flexed when Caleb ran a hand over his short hair.

"Aiden's old things." Had she taken too long to answer? Did he know she was ogling his arms? The combination of exhaustion and the recent caffeine influx warred in her, made her hands a bit shaky. She clasped them behind her back.

"That's more than some old sweats." He bent to inspect the box, forcing Riley to notice the way his thigh muscles bunched and pushed against the material of his pants. Muscles. Muscles everywhere with this one.

The dumpster lid banged against the wall. "His hand weights, some electronics."

"What happened with this guy anyway? Were you that

serious?" He popped open the top to examine the contents like he could get an idea of who her ex was by looking at his things.

Riley slammed the box shut. "We were engaged. Two years. When it became clear he wasn't interested in ever setting a date, I broke it off."

"That must've been a tough decision to make." Caleb watched her face carefully.

She blinked a few times like something was in her eye and swiped the back of her hand over her eyes. "Let's just say I'm not a fan of long engagements. I thought he'd try to get me back or something. He never did."

"Well, good riddance to that idiot." Caleb crossed corded arms over his chest and rocked back on his heels. "You know, it gives us another thing in common. Besides our terrible fathers."

"Yeah, what's that?" Riley checked the dumpster to make sure there was room. It would take quite a heave-ho to get the box up and over the lip, but once that was done, it was an easy drop to the bottom of the container. One more surge of effort, and that part of her life would be gone forever.

"We were both loyal to people who didn't deserve it."

Riley sank to her knees beside the box, his words fluttering like moths in her stomach. Or maybe that was too much coffee and not enough food. "How do you know he didn't deserve it?"

"Because he let you go." Caleb crouched across from her.

Riley fussed with reclosing the lid. "That's kind of you to say."

"I'm not a kind person." Caleb reached for her hand. She let him take it.

"Sounds like you've had some experience." Riley turned her hand to run nails lightly across his palm, backtracking to trace each line individually. She liked his sharp intake of breath, how he held it and let it out slowly, watching her with those intent blue eyes. "Do you think you'll ever be loyal to someone again?"

"I don't think I can help myself." He tugged her hand, stopping her explorations, and pulled her forward. She balanced her weight on the box, bringing their faces close. Closer. Kissing distance. "I'm a loyal person. Like you."

"Like me?" She breathed in his words, soaked up the longing in his eyes, leaned into his touch. He was magnetic. Even knowing who he was, what he planned to do to her building, she couldn't stop her lips from meeting his. Her feelings were jumbled up inside her. Complicated, so complicated, but his touch, the way he cupped her jaw as he drew her in for a deeper kiss, wasn't complicated at all. It was easy. And so, so good.

LouLou bounded onto the box with an excited wag of her tail, nosing at their joined hands for some petting. Riley laughed and pulled away from Caleb, relieved for a reason to pull away. Disappointed that she had to.

"You're right. I am loyal. To Grams. To my job here at the Dorothy. To my pal, LouLou." Riley kissed the top of her dog's head, trying to play off the last few minutes. She had to keep it light. As addictive as she found Caleb's kisses, the timing couldn't be worse. So she deliberately broke the rules of dating someone new and brought up her ex again. Not that they were dating, but what better way to kill the mood that had grown fast and hot between them? "You're also right about Aiden. He didn't deserve my loyalty."

Caleb searched her face, and he apparently didn't need any kind of emoji—not an upside-down face or even a waterfall—to get the picture. He gave LouLou a firm rub under her collar, then picked up his side of the box again. "Alright, let's do this. Bye-bye, Aiden."

The box made a satisfying *thump* when it hit the bottom of the dumpster. Riley slammed the lid shut and wiped her palms on her thighs. LouLou jumped up on her back legs and placed her front paws on Riley's knees.

"Fine." She scooped up her pooch. She thought she'd feel triumphant when the last of Aiden was gone from her life. Instead, it felt as if she'd just trashed two years of her history.

"Hey." Caleb moved in closer and scratched LouLou behind the ears. "I've got an idea. It might cheer you up."

Riley pulled in her pouting lip and tried to force a smile. "I think I'll stay in the rest of the day. It's been a pretty eventful few hours."

Caleb's mouth quirked into a half smile. "Even if I said LouLou's invited and what you're wearing is perfect?"

Riley looked down at her shabby cupcake shirt and raised a skeptical eyebrow at him. Then again, he did kiss her next to a dumpster. His standards didn't seem particularly high in the aesthetic department.

"I swear." Caleb held up his hand like a Boy Scout. "Give me half an hour."

Riley pulled out her phone. "Siri, set the timer for thirty minutes."

Caleb threw back his head and laughed loudly. LouLou squirmed to be let down so she could jump on him. "Let's go then. Time's a-tickin'."

"Timer set," Siri said. Riley muted her phone and followed Caleb to his car.

CHAPTER 16

"COME ON, LOULOU!" RILEY SLID INTO THE FRONT SEAT of Caleb's Porsche and patted her lap for LouLou to jump in.

Caleb stood to the side, holding the door open, ready to swoop in if needed. He wasn't sure what he thought would be needed, but Riley seemed off her game this afternoon. Sure, the meeting this morning hadn't exactly gone her way, and what was happening between them was probably as surprising to her as it was to him, but there was something else. It could be his plans for the Dorothy. No, his instincts told him there was a deeper worry underlying her usual feistiness. That it had prompted her to dump the ex's stuff was an excellent side effect, but it didn't stop him from being concerned.

LouLou tilted her head and inched closer to the car, sniffing the low running board suspiciously.

"She doesn't get in a car with strangers?" Caleb clucked his tongue in an effort to lure LouLou closer. Much like Riley and his earlier texts, she ignored him.

"She's a smart cookie."

LouLou perked her ears at the word *cookie* and did that begging thing with her eyes universal to all dogs.

"Sorry, girl. No treats in the Porsche." Riley patted her lap again, and the poodle jumped in.

Caleb closed the door and circled to the driver's side. "Top up or down?"

"LouLou's never been in a convertible."

"Down it is."

They waited while the roof retracted and tucked itself away. Riley relaxed into the plush seat, her fingers dug into LouLou's fuzzy coat, scratching lightly along her spine. LouLou sat up, one paw on Riley's wrist.

In minutes, they were speeding south on Alton Road toward South Beach, and LouLou fully enjoyed the rush of wind past her nose. She turned her head left to right, sniffing, sniffing, sniffing, and pawing at Riley's hand in excitement.

Riley laughed. "Who knew LouLou wanted a convertible?"

"She's a dog of good taste," Caleb said with a smile. LouLou's enjoyment chased some of the sadness out of Riley's eyes. He wished he could go faster—really let it go, like driving the 75 across state—but Alton was a known speed trap, so he kept the Porsche to a sedate ten miles over the speed limit.

"Where are we going?" Riley held tight to LouLou. The poodle would not be picked up by a sudden gust of wind and swept out of the car in a flurry of furry tragedy, Caleb was happy to note. It might be a ridiculous fear, but he was glad Riley kept a firm grip on the dog. Better safe than sorry, or rather, better safe than irrationally worried. LouLou squirmed but overall seemed quite pleased with the whole convertible turn of events.

"You'll see." Caleb turned left onto a small street and wound through a neighborhood of older homes on tiny lots. They passed a one-story Mediterranean villa that took up most of a block, surrounded by a wrought-iron fence that zigged and zagged around mature strangler fig trees shooting their long roots from branch to ground with gothic beauty.

"What a gorgeous place." Riley craned her neck to get a better view, and Caleb obligingly slowed down. The house was set back from the road and covered in ivy. At some point in its history, the property must've been quite a sight, the estate of some local celebrity perhaps. Caleb imagined a Rat Pack–era singer hosting lavish parties on the lushly landscaped grounds. The villa reminded him of the Dorothy—good bones and in need of a huge influx of cash to restore it to its former glory. A pair of dachshunds rushed the fence, one barking so ferociously, its front legs lifted off the ground from the force.

LouLou planted a foot on the top of the door, and Caleb curbed the urge to roll up the windows to keep her inside. Riley pulled the poodle back into her lap and shushed LouLou's half-hearted growling.

"What a nightmare for those poor owners." Riley pointed out a blue tarp on the roof—leftover from the hurricane last year, no doubt. "Still working on roof repairs? That's never a good sign. I hate how long it takes to get anything done. You know, the Dorothy still has windows that need replacing. They're on order, but I've started worrying they'll never arrive. Which is just as well. There's no money to pay for installation anyway." Riley covered her mouth and spoke through her fingers. "I shouldn't have said that to you. It's too easy to forget you're the enemy."

Surprised, Caleb took a quick study of Riley's profile. "Because I'm not the enemy. We both want what's best for the Dorothy. We simply disagree on precisely what that is."

Riley's hand dropped to her lap and curled in LouLou's

hair. "That's not really true. You're more interested in what's best for the Donovan business."

"The Dorothy is a Donovan property. It's the same thing." He pulled to a stop at a crosswalk so two bikers and a woman with a baby in a stroller and a toddler by the hand could cross.

"I'm suggesting a new building for practical reasons." Caleb sped toward the next stop sign. "Remodeling is such a headache. It's easier to build from scratch. No surprises." He paused long enough to check for cars. "What am I saying? Of course there are surprises. Any construction job comes with its challenges, but older buildings are filled with the unpleasant kind of surprises. Expensive surprises."

"Since when is a Donovan worried about expenses?"

Caleb watched the house disappear in the side mirror, a twinge of sadness making him frown at the idea that his father wouldn't think that beautiful old home worth saving. In fact, before Riley's presentation this morning, he would've felt the same. Now he knew that sometimes a building wasn't about dollars and cents and bottom lines. Sometimes it was about the past and the people. It was memories and the potential for more. But more cost money, and he'd seen the Rainy Day accounts. More was something the Dorothy simply didn't have.

"Maybe not all Donovans are worried about money these days, but I've learned to count my pennies." Caleb pulled off his sunglasses and folded them into the cup holder.

"You lost a lot?"

He turned bleak eyes on her. "I lost everything."

"Not your car, apparently." It was meant to cheer him up, her little quip, but it had the reverse effect.

"No, not my car. They couldn't take that." His blue eyes darkened like a storm at sea, restless and bleak. "It was paid for. A gift, from my grandpa. But I lost my future. Everything I'd worked for, planned on."

"Wow, that's bleak." Riley turned and tucked a foot under her thigh, facing Caleb. "When my manager told me not to come back to work at the Donovan Resort and I couldn't renew the lease on my condo, I had to pack up my things and move to Grams'. For months, I sent out résumés for jobs that never panned out. I cried. A lot. I thought about all the other employees going through the same thing, but I never, ever thought about you having it rough, too."

Caleb shifted in his seat. He hadn't meant to trigger pity from her. This outing was supposed to be him finding out her deep, dark worry, not exposing his. Still, he couldn't deny that the way her face softened when she looked at him, the empathy she radiated, was balm on a wound he'd thought healed. He was wrong. His father's betrayal still burned. That his family's worst moments also hurt Riley made everything worse. He felt the anger he'd tamped down flare to life again. His father had destroyed so many lives. How could a prison sentence possibly atone for what he'd done?

"I saw you on the news, you know." Riley threaded her fingers in and out of LouLou's coat. "You, the golden boy. The heir apparent. You always looked blank, like how sharks seem completely neutral until they're chomping down on a tasty sea lion? I thought the whole thing rolled off you, that your money protected you from any consequences."

"It didn't." He blinked. Extra-long. His fingers flexed on the gearshift, his knuckles cracking from the pressure. His whole life had changed. So had hers. All because of Robert Donovan. Another thing they had in common.

Then, her fingers squeezed around his. LouLou turned in a circle and rested her chin on top of their hands. Caleb blinked again and let out a deep breath. The anger cooled, banked for now, her touch making him hot in a different way. He revved the engine and turned them onto a tree-lined street, eager to see her response to his surprise.

"Flamingo Park? Gosh, it's been forever since I've been here." Riley clapped her hands together in delight, and he smiled. He hoped her hand would land back on his, but it didn't. She kept a firm hold on LouLou instead. "Grams used to bring me here for swim lessons. And tennis. Basically anything they offered, she signed me up for."

"So you're an athlete?" Small talk would lighten the mood, wouldn't it? He didn't want to bum her out with any more Donovan family stories.

She laughed. "Hardly! I did love this park, though. Lots of good spots for cartwheels. It's been years since I've done one of those, too."

"No time like the present then. Shall we head over to the Bark Park, and you can show me your moves?"

"Can you believe I've never brought her here?" Riley patted the poodle's head, bringing her mouth closer to LouLou's ear. She whispered loud enough for Caleb to hear, "I promise to be better about getting out and finding new places for you to sniff." LouLou wagged her tail in agreement.

Caleb pulled into an angled parking spot near a baseball diamond where a group of young men played soccer. Because the convertible's top was still down, the sounds of the park rushed at him. The *thunk-thunk* of basketballs from the nearby courts, the soccer players' cheers when one side scored, the rustle of overhead leaves as an ocean breeze brushed by. LouLou soaked it all up with her nose and would've gone right over the top of the passenger side door if Riley hadn't kept a grip on her collar.

Riley checked that LouLou was properly hooked to her leash, but before she could open the door herself, Caleb was already there, hand on the door handle.

"You're fast." Not as fast as LouLou, who was already on the ground, straining at the end of the leash.

"Spent my high school summers working valet at Donovan Resort downtown." He winked. "Good tips."

"Yeah, it was a nice place to work." Riley stepped carefully out of the car, holding onto the leash with both hands. "I enjoyed the perks, too. Until I was sacked."

Caleb grimaced. This sore spot was getting a lot of poking lately. "I really am sorry that happened. Believe me, it was no picnic for me, either."

"You seem to be doing okay," Riley said in a voice too bitter after their moment in the car. Why did nothing ever go in a straight line, especially emotions? Especially his? That anger bubbled again. Just when he thought he was moving on, it seemed that the past wouldn't let go of him.

"Yeah, now. I could say the same for you." Caleb's carefully blank voice matched his carefully blank face. He recognized it as the defense mechanism it was. He regretted that he couldn't simply reach out his hand and lace their fingers together like in the car, follow this weird spark between them wherever it led. The push-pull between them intrigued him, and he didn't want to make a wrong move.

So he didn't reach out, and she kept her hands on the leash. He tucked his yearning away and reminded himself why they were at the park: to make Riley's day better. "About those cartwheels?"

She laughed and let LouLou lead the way into the park. "Not in a million years, buddy."

Caleb scanned the fenced-in area of the park where two golden retrievers chased birds off the grass. They never came even close to catching one, but they sure were excited every time one took flight. The birds didn't seem too worried about the doggy duo since they'd land in another part of the park a few seconds later, causing the goldens to scramble after them again. A young woman in running shorts sat on an aluminum bench, scrolling through her phone with earbuds in.

Caleb opened the gate and gestured Riley and LouLou through. Riley unclipped her dog, and LouLou beelined for the goldens, stopping a few feet short of them and executing an adorable play bow. They took her up on the invitation and were soon racing through the grass in giant figure-eights.

"She sure doesn't act like an older dog." Caleb led Riley toward a bench in the shade of a live oak tree, still so careful with her that he thought an ice pick could crack the air between them.

"Her bladder's really the only sign of aging." Riley smiled at LouLou's antics, running under the goldens' bellies and cutting sharp corners. "Sorry again about your shoes."

She slanted a glance his way, and he looked back. She really was ridiculously beautiful, those wild curls and the smattering of freckles across her nose visible now that the makeup she'd worn to the meeting this morning had mostly worn off. He could be friendly without crossing a line. Hadn't they had enough drama for one day? Still, his eyes kept roaming to her lips, their soft pinkness, and all he could think about was kissing her again.

"Sorry again about how you lost your job." Caleb strung his arm along the back of the bench, his fingers close enough to Riley's shoulders that he had to fight the temptation to shift a little to feel the brush of his skin against hers. Because the line. He was holding it. Oh, who was he kidding? Seriously. Without even thinking about it, he drew lines of his own, small swirls and circles, on her skin; it was hard to remember why he shouldn't. Business. They needed to settle the Dorothy thing between them. As long as she felt they were on opposite sides, she'd never trust him. And he wanted that, her trust. He wanted it a lot.

"I sincerely hope we can put the meeting this morning behind us. That's why I brought you here. Let's plan the Dorothy's dog park. If you're working with me, it'll get the support it needs." Caleb studied her, his face close enough that it wouldn't take much to brush his lips against her ears. When had he started being turned on by ears? But it was happening. She did things to him that no one else ever had. If he wanted to talk business, he really needed to move away from her.

"You mean, support for the changes to the building?" Riley flushed. Good or bad sign? He couldn't tell. "You know the neighborhood already supports a dog park. You're looking to use me to win them over for your building plans, aren't you? But what happens to your parking plan if the city doesn't think half the lot is big enough?"

Okay, her tone made it clear. Bad sign. She was committed to her vision of the Dorothy. He admired it, really. In his world, when a deal got too complicated, you walked away. He knew Riley would not walk away from the Dorothy. Could they find a path for the Dorothy that they could walk together? The dog park was his first step in her direction. Would she meet him halfway?

"That's a problem for the architect to figure out." Caleb waved his hand like a magician doing a trick, *Ta-da!* style. "I tell him what we want; he makes it happen. What do you think? Half the lot as a park like this?"

Riley squirmed away from his touch and inspected the aging agility equipment—a worn-out A-frame ramp, metal hoops of different sizes and heights, a raised wooden platform. The grass was in good condition, and the old-growth trees were beautiful and provided a lot of shade, which Caleb imagined would be especially nice in the summertime. The Dorothy's empty lot didn't have many trees, and he'd already seen owners in the lot with their own handheld fans and portable water dishes for their dogs.

"The trees are nice." Riley leaned back just enough that Caleb's fingers brushed the top of her shoulder. The fabric of her T-shirt didn't shield him from the impact of her touch. He wanted more. More of her attention, her skin against his, her help creating a grand dog park. But the line he was holding wouldn't let him admit it. He held perfectly still and pretended that he didn't notice the heat traveling up his fingers, spreading through his very nervous system. How could he be feeling warmer from an innocent touch on her shoulder?

"And benches." His fingertips moved in a slow circle, not

so innocently now. "Though these aren't particularly comfortable." He shifted, trying to find a better position, and their knees touched, her bare one against the smooth khaki material of his pants. It shouldn't make him jittery. He jittered anyway, leg bouncing on the ball of his foot, looking out over the park like he'd never seen dogs at play before. He should move away from her. He didn't. She didn't move away, either.

The woman on the far bench rose, calling her dogs, and soon LouLou was alone at the park. She trotted from tree to tree, sniffing and wagging her tail. How nice it was to see the poodle being her happy, doggy self. LouLou didn't let indecision weigh her down. She followed her instincts and made the best of whatever came her way. He really should be more doglike about life.

"The benches are definitely a good thing. Shall I make a list?" Riley pulled out her phone, clearly determined to make the best of this situation. "You want a world-class dog park? I'll help you. No matter what happens to the Dorothy, the neighborhood canines deserve a place to play and be free."

"Thank you." Caleb watched as she pulled up a fresh note and labeled it Dog Park. The park would need a distinctive name, something to draw people from near and far.

"No need for thanks. I know you've had it hard, too, but I'm not quite over my grudge yet. However, this is for the dogs. All for the dogs."

"Then by all means, we must have a list." Caleb's fingers stilled on her shoulder. If she moved a few more inches, she could tuck into his side, and he'd slide his arm around her. But no, focus on the dogs. He wrenched his gaze away from her and studied the layout of the park.

She opened up her notes and typed *benches*, then *trees*. "Anything else?"

"What else do you like here?"

Riley stood and turned in a circle, examining the enclosure. "The water fountains for the dogs." She added it to her list.

"What about the dog toys?"

"Toys? You mean the agility equipment?"

"Sure, if that's what it's called." He lifted a shoulder. Weird name, *agility*, but then, he wasn't a dog person.

Riley tapped her finger against the side of her phone. "Agility equipment is only good if you know how to use it."

"Do you?" He wouldn't be surprised if she trained dogs on the side. He suspected she had a lot of hustle in her.

"Not really." Riley tapped some more on her phone, brightening with each search result. "But we could have a trainer come by. Weekly lessons! Wouldn't that be fun?"

He hadn't thought much beyond giving the empty lot a facelift, but if Riley wanted classes, why not? "What kind of lessons?"

"Agility, obedience. We could offer lots of classes."

"That sounds—" he rubbed the back of his neck, "—like a lot of organization."

"On it." Riley added classes to her list and smiled at him.

He smiled back, and suddenly the moments on her couch, on the bench outside city hall, outside the dumpster, all rushed his mind at once. His heart picked up its pace, even while he chastised himself. Beside the trash bin? Really? What had he been thinking?

She turned a wide smile on, a dimple dancing in her cheek, and he remembered. He hadn't been thinking. Just feeling.

"Do you think?" He inched closer. She let him.

"Mmm?" Why did her eyes have to be so melt-in-them chocolate?

He reached toward her, but his hand diverted at the last moment to chuck LouLou under the chin. "Do you think you'd like to see more dog parks, LouLou?"

Riley took a long, loud inhale before responding. "Wait, are you asking my dog out on a date?"

The poodle licked his hand with her small, pink tongue. Caleb smiled. "She appears to be saying yes."

"A dog park date?"

He nodded, fingers still under LouLou's chin. "She'll be our consultant."

"Our?"

He nodded crisply. "Precisely. The dog park we're building together. What do you say?"

His mind flashed to her licking her agreement, like LouLou was, but it wasn't his hand he pictured her tongue on. He slammed the door on his X-rated mind and tried not to be disappointed when she nodded. Safer that way. Less germy.

"This weekend?" He frowned, thinking of his calendar. "Wait, I've got a thing. The weekend after?"

"Sure. In the meantime, I'll talk to Eliza about the half-and-half compromise we've reached." Riley kept nodding. She hadn't stopped, really, so her head kept bobbing as he suggested times and places, and before he knew it, they were back in the Porsche, on their way to the Dorothy, and he had basically just agreed to date a poodle.

CHAPTER 17

GRAMS PATTED HER RECENTLY SPRAYED-INTO-SUBMISSION coiffure and sniffed. "It doesn't surprise me. Those Donovans can be quite charming."

Riley made a noncommittal humming sound and prayed for an emergency text that would put an end to this torture. She'd gladly pull more chicken bones out of Mr. Cardoza's garbage disposal if this weekly round of bunco practice would come to an end.

"Oh, he's a charmer alright." Patty rolled the dice and sighed at her results. "He even flirted with me."

"Not even one bit shocking. The Donovans are quite shameless in their skirt chasing." Grams took a sip of chardonnay and snorted.

Patty's skirt was more of a housedress, quilted and worn at the cuffs, but Grams' words had her sitting straighter in her walker-turned-seat. She gripped the yellow handle bars that were now armrests. "Is that such a bad thing? Riley's all alone in that downstairs apartment. Wouldn't it be nice for her to have a gentleman friend?"

Grams rolled the dice. "Riley has terrible taste in men. And Patty, yours clearly isn't much better. A Donovan is not a suitable gentleman friend for Riley. She needs someone…" Grams trailed off and studied the popcorn ceiling.

"Handsome? Charming? Wealthy?" Patty rolled the dice and jotted down the points. With only one table going, it wasn't a true bunco party, but the ladies liked to keep their skills sharp for the monthly game at Patty's church. That bunco required little in the way of skill was no reason not to enjoy a nice afternoon snack-and-chat.

"Sounds like Caleb to me." Eliza filled the fourth seat. She didn't always come to bunco practice, but when she did, she brought double chocolate brownies and a bottle of red wine. Riley took a hefty sip of her store brand merlot and snatched another brownie for herself. It was her third, but she was behind Grams and Patty by at least two, so she took an extra-large one.

"What was it like, seeing Husband Number One again?" Riley used the name she'd grown up with before she knew that HNO was William Donovan. The quickest way to get Grams to stop talking about Riley's love life, or lack thereof, was to get Grams to indulge in a bit of her own drama.

"She ignored him," Eliza reported to Patty after her roll of the dice. "I was expecting fireworks, but all we got was a Cold War."

"He doesn't deserve my attention." Grams took a delicate bite of her fifth brownie. She cut them in fourths, acting as though she couldn't possibly eat a whole one, but there wouldn't be a crumb left in Eliza's pan when she left later that evening. "He knows why. He knows what he did."

"What did he do?" Riley asked around a mouthful of her own brownie. She'd heard the dramatized version, the kid-friendly version, the sly innuendo version, but she didn't think she'd ever heard the truth version.

"What didn't he do?" Grams sniffed and dabbed at her nose with a cocktail napkin left over from the Fourth of July. Bright-blue stars crumpled in her hand.

"If it's too painful to talk about it, I understand." Riley

knew Grams would rise to the bait. She never passed up the opportunity to tell a story, especially about herself.

"If you insist." Dab, dab with the star-spangled napkin. "We were newlyweds, not married even a year, before he took up with another woman. Dancing. So-called business trips. Boys' nights that kept him out until dawn. All while I stayed home and waited for him to come home." Dab, dab. "I thought we were happy. I didn't know. Not until—"

Riley gripped the dice in her hand. "Until what?"

Grams' face changed, became older, sadder. "She got pregnant. I didn't."

"Oh no." Patty reached over the brownies to pat Grams' clenched fist. "That's terrible."

"Said he had to choose his family." Grams spit out the words like the wound was still as fresh as the day it was inflicted. "Like I wasn't his family. Like I was nothing."

"But he didn't stay with her, did he?" Eliza's comment wasn't necessarily a silver lining, but it did cheer Grams up.

"Nope. That's how they are, those Donovans. They go through women like, like—" she grabbed another napkin. "—tissue. Like father, like son. Isn't that true?"

"Caleb's only been married once. And she left him." Riley didn't disagree with Grams, not exactly, but she did feel strangely compelled to defend Caleb. LouLou liked him, after all, and dogs were known to be good judges of character. Riley liked him, too, a fact she planned to keep to herself, along with how beautifully his lips fit against hers and how she was slowly being won over by his daily texts. No, Grams would not want to hear about how she scrolled through their very short history of conversations when she climbed in bed. Or how her fingers hovered over the keys, itching to send a late-night invitation. So far, all she'd done was slide her phone into its charger before falling asleep alone, but maybe one night she'd give in and give it up. A girl could hope anyway.

"He's young yet." Grams waved her star-spangled tissue. "Just you wait. He'll show his true colors soon enough."

Caleb hadn't seen Riley or her little flirt of a poodle, LouLou, in two weeks. Of course, he'd texted. GIFs of adorable dogs doing adorable things, like eating birthday cakes or falling asleep in their food dishes, and names and locations of the dog parks he'd found in Miami-Dade and Broward Counties. She'd texted back laughing emojis and GIFs of baby goats romping and a cockatoo that liked to dance to Taylor Swift songs.

Early last night, he'd sent her an itinerary for today, working their way up the west side of the two counties and then circling around and hitting a few parks on the east side on their way back down. It wasn't that he was so rigid that he couldn't enjoy a weekend drive exploring dog parks unknown to him before, but he'd seen how happy lists made her when they'd gone to South Beach. He'd made the list for her, and he felt like an overeager puppy for doing it.

LouLou bounced against the glass front door of the Dorothy before Caleb even attempted the steps. Riley pushed open the door, hair pulled up in a high ponytail and sporting one of what he was beginning to suspect was an endless supply of pink T-shirts. This one featured sleeves and a front pocket in a darker shade than the rest of the shirt. A hobo bag with an especially long strap crossed her chest, and she pulled on oversize shades as she shut the door behind her.

He squatted to greet LouLou. She placed her paws on his knees and stared at him intently. "Hello there." He chucked her chin, and her tail whipped frantically back and forth atop her back. "It's like she knows what's going on." He tilted his head up to where Riley now stood over him.

"Of course she does." Riley bent to clip the leash onto LouLou's collar. "Her English is excellent."

Caleb barked out a surprised laugh. "Well then, shall we, ladies?"

LouLou pulled Riley toward the Porsche. "I think that's a vote for top down."

"Not a problem." Caleb held the door open for them, and when both were settled safely, he rounded the car, noting that he hadn't felt this happy in weeks. Two weeks to be exact.

Even poodles didn't have an endless enthusiasm for dog parks. Now on their fifth stop of the day, Caleb and Riley sank onto a dog-bone-shaped bench in Hollywood, Florida's recently renovated Hollywoof park and surveyed the weaving poles, the separate sections for large and small dogs, and the mushroom-like platforms at different heights for what Caleb could only guess were doggy step classes.

LouLou didn't stray too far from them, exhausted from the frenzy of running at Snyder Park when she'd spotted turtles in the lake. She hadn't gone in after them, but she'd run the shore in anxious back-and-forths until Riley'd finally scooped her up and hosed her off. Caleb'd watched as Riley added *hoses* to her dog park wish list. He noticed that she didn't add *lake* or *turtles*. She'd been awfully worried that LouLou would catch a turtle, even though the poodle was never closer to one than ten feet.

"What would you even do with a turtle, LouLou?" she'd asked while hosing mud out of the poodle's curly coat. LouLou's response had been enthusiastic tail whumping and a roll in the soft grass as soon as Riley loosened her hold.

Now, LouLou inspected the base of a tree with some half-hearted sniffing and then, with a huff, flopped onto her side and watched them with one eye.

"I can't tell if that means she likes it here or if she wants to go to sleep so she can dream about catching turtles." Caleb didn't even try to cover up the giant yawn that over-took him.

"She's exhausted, poor thing." Riley hid her own yawn with a hand. "This is more action than she typically gets in a day."

Getting some action was not on the agenda today. Sadly. *Down, boy. Focus on business.* "What're your feelings about the big dog/small dog separation fences we've seen? Some parks seem to have them, some don't. Do you think it matters?"

"My guess is it depends on the dogs." Riley's head fell back, and she contemplated the clear sky. "If someone brings an obnoxious dog in, it's probably nice to have a separate area to take your dog to instead of being forced to go home."

"You don't seem to have that problem at your park." Caleb couldn't believe he'd called the empty lot her dog park. Well, that was what he was offering her—or rather the neighborhood—wasn't it? A compromise. And it was working. With each dog park, Riley relaxed a little more with him. If he'd longed to reach for her, to pull her into his arms a hundred times today, he tried to ignore it. She'd kept a careful distance between them, and he respected that. Last time he'd seen her, she'd been so vulnerable—after the meeting and then dumping her ex's stuff. She'd been raw, and it had made him raw, too. What Riley really needed was some fun. He draped his arm along the back of the bench and asked her if there'd ever been a fight at her dog park.

"Not recently, but there have been some incidents. I'm going to vote yes on having two separate areas." Riley got out her phone and added that to the list. Then she groaned.

"What?" Caleb didn't realize he was massaging the back of her neck until she leaned into his fingers with a sigh. So much for keeping his distance. But a massage was fine. Relaxing. He dug into a knot where her neck flowed into the shoulder, and she sighed again.

"Marco and Kent." She tilted her head forward to give him better access to her tense muscles. "Another plumbing problem. These pipes are going to be the death of me."

"What pipes?"

"The original pipes." Riley rolled her head, vertebrae cracking. "The plumber says we need to redo the whole building. We can't. I do what I can and call the plumber when it gets real bad."

"You've got plumbing skills? You're such a Renaissance woman." Caleb kept his hand on her neck, kneading, while she rolled her head again.

Riley smiled, but it didn't reach her eyes. "That's me,

only instead of a paint brush, give me a wrench. I'm holding that whole place together with a lick and a prayer."

"It shouldn't be that way. What about the reserves? Your maintenance fees?"

Riley flicked her wrist, fingers swishing like she was batting away a fly. "Gone with the wind, as Grams likes to say. Every penny seems already spoken for. Insurance, utilities. I paid for a hallway lightbulb out of my own pocket last month."

"It's that tight?"

"It's that tight."

It didn't make sense to Caleb, how the building could be running on such a shoestring of a budget. Management companies were supposed to make things easier on the owners and residents, not create the kind of stress he was feeling stored in Riley's body. He gentled his touch. "The Dorothy needs a change. You see that, right? You can't go on like you are."

"It'll get better. When we get some new renters. It has to." Riley's back stiffened. "I better head back. My wrench is calling me." Her attempt at humor made him smile, but he was still troubled by how much her job demanded of her.

"Five more minutes." Caleb trailed his fingers up to put pressure on the base of her skull. It was a dirty trick, meant to entice her into staying, and it worked. "You and LouLou could both use a bit more rest."

"No kidding." Riley closed her eyes and rolled her head from side to side, slouching on the bench. "That feels good. Amazingly good."

"I'm glad." He increased the pressure, enjoying how her muscles melted at his touch.

"But I'm worried you'll get the wrong idea."

He eased up on a knot, kneading it lightly with his knuckles. "What kind of wrong idea?"

"I'm not going to kiss you again." Her neck cracked, and she sighed. "It was a bad idea before."

"Which time?" He felt her muscles quiver at the memory. He soothed them with long strokes.

She leaned in to his touch. "All the times."

"So you remember them?" He certainly did. Every damn day for two weeks.

She hummed an agreement. "Bad idea. Ideas."

"That's not how I remember it."

"Then you have a bad memory." She sat up, and her ponytail whipped to the side when she turned her head his way. "It could never work. We're on opposite sides of the development issue. Plus we're practically cousins."

"What?" He dropped his hands from her neck. "We are definitely not cousins. Why would you say that?"

"Your grandpa? My Grams? Face it, there's some parallel universe in which we are cousins."

"I don't believe in parallel universes."

"Then you need to read more sci-fi."

"I don't read any."

"That's my point."

Caleb's head reeled. "You're saying this whole conversation has been about my reading habits?"

She slapped his upper arm. "No, you goofball. About our incompatibility, professionally and familially. You get it, right?"

"We are definitely not incompatible." He cupped the back of her neck and drew her toward him. "And I definitely know it because you definitely want me to kiss you right now."

She opened her mouth to protest but sighed again instead. "You're right. I do."

His blood surged in celebration. He knew it!

"But—" she put a finger to his mouth, "—we can't always have what we want. We have to do what's best."

"This is definitely best." He pressed his mouth to hers.

She placed her hand on his cheek, pulling away half an inch. "One last dog park kiss, and then we put it behind us. Deal?"

"Absolutely," he said, closing the distance. Right before their lips met again, he whispered, "Not."

CHAPTER 18

RILEY HATED HOW MUCH SHE LOVED KISSING CALEB. Really, it was ridiculous how good his lips felt, how their tangled tongues spread pleasure to every starved nerve in her body. She leaned in toward him, knowing she shouldn't, that she was sidetracking them from the road she'd decided was best: professional courtesy.

Well, he certainly was courteous, the way his hand shielded the back of her head from the sharp edge of the bench. And it was courteous when he moved his hand to her waist, caressing her side before wrapping his arm around her to pull her closer. He was a real gentleman, not groping her breast in a public location. The dog park was empty; he didn't need to be quite so courteous, but she appreciated the thought.

The kiss went on and on, and pretty soon she was sitting on his lap with no memory of having climbed up there. Her hands were on his face, and she couldn't get enough of his mouth on hers. She sucked in his bottom lip, and he growled playfully at her. She didn't stop kissing him, not for anything. If this was the last kiss, it was going to be the best kiss in the history of last kisses.

She felt LouLou's feet press against her thigh, heard the whimper that usually meant she needed to go outside. But they were outside, so Riley ignored her poodle even when said poodle scrambled onto the bench and tried to insert her body between Riley and Caleb. There wasn't an inch to spare. She settled for squeezing her nose in between Riley's hip and Caleb's stomach. She shook and pressed herself to Caleb's side.

At first, Riley thought she imagined the few drops of water she felt on her head, on her arms. Then a crack of lightning made LouLou jump and paw at Riley's shoulder, and the sky opened up like a faucet. In seconds, she, Caleb, and the poodle were soaked to the skin.

Riley broke the kiss. "LouLou tried to warn us. Thank goodness you put the top up when you parked."

"It was more theft deterrent than weather prediction." Caleb buried his face in Riley's neck. "Come on, I'll take you home. It won't be the first time I've rescued you two damsels in distress from a storm."

Riley smacked his chest.

Caleb laughed and stood, cradling Riley in his arms. "Shall we reenact it?"

"Put me down!"

"Aha, like our first time." But unlike the first time, he set her on her feet and they walked to his Porsche. He kept his hand on her lower back, and she felt the heat there long after he'd tucked her into the passenger seat and deposited LouLou on her lap.

On the drive home, Caleb laid his hand face-up on the console between them, and she placed her palm over his. He laced their fingers together, and she sighed. It was supposed to be the last kiss, but she couldn't pull away, couldn't stop touching him.

"How'd your Grams end up raising you?"

It wasn't a story she shared with a lot of people, how her mom hadn't exactly abandoned her but also hadn't exactly chosen a lifestyle that included a child. Working a cruise ship meant long stints out of the country with no cell service, and even when home, it still meant long days of prep and longer days of recuperating for the next run. But Riley shared the story with him, and his fingers squeezed hers in sympathy.

Caleb pulled into an empty spot in front of the Dorothy. "Here we are."

"We are here." She didn't take back her hand, was reluctant to let go of the physical manifestation of the tentative bond they'd built today. Caleb was right; they weren't ready for a last kiss. At least not yet. Her heart sped up at the thought, thumping hard in her chest. More kisses. More everything. With Caleb.

Riley needed to check on Marco and Kent and probably Grams, too. She had a whole host of responsibilities that gave her every reason to get out of the Porsche. Instead, she sat like a silly teenager in the front seat of the car, tongue-tied over saying goodbye.

So she didn't. She tried out one of the late-night lines she'd almost typed but never did. "Can I interest you in a cup of coffee?"

He brought her knuckles to his lips. "I'd love one."

Riley led the way, her fingers still laced with Caleb's and LouLou trotting at her heels. She was doing this, taking him to her apartment. It could stop at coffee. It totally could. But she wasn't planning on it.

She set up the Keurig. "Do you have a favorite flavor?"

"Strong."

"Okay then." She loaded a cup of Da Bomb while the poodle danced at her feet. She liberated a dog treat from its box and broke it in two. "Something for you, too, of course." LouLou grabbed the treat and dashed for the sofa.

Caleb stood beside her breakfast bar, hand braced on the black-and-pink-laced marble. "The Dorothy really does have its charms."

"Yeah, Eliza's pretty sure it'll be a shoo-in to get it declared an historic property." Riley chose two large coffee mugs from her cabinet. One read *Keep Calm and Get Your Hospitality On* and the other pictured the silhouette of a poodle and the words *Life Is Better with a Poodle*. She held them both out to Caleb.

He took the poodle cup and placed it in the machine. "That'll certainly put a kink in my plans."

"Indeed." Riley leaned against the counter, hands around her empty mug. "That's our plan."

"You don't have to seem happy about it."

"Why not? You want me to be pleased that you plan to kick out Grams? Her friends? All the people who've lived here?" The glow of the dog park make-out session was wearing off. She felt the press of wet clothes against her skin, that weird chilly feeling as the AC kicked on. Good Lord, even her panties were wet, and not in the good way. What was she thinking, making coffee?

Caleb rubbed the back of his neck. "I'm working on that."

Riley snorted. "I'm sure." But then her hospitality training kicked in. "Are you cold? I should've offered you a towel or something." She'd been stupidly distracted by her hormones, but now that they were calming down, she couldn't wait to get out of these clothes. And not in the way she'd been imagining on the way home, where they end up scattered in a trail to the bedroom. No, she was dreaming of shedding them in the bathroom and stepping into a hot shower.

Her phone vibrated in her pocket.

Are you back yet?

Damn it. Marco. How could she have forgotten? Stupid hormones must affect her short-term memory. Or maybe she was simply really, really tired of plumbing problems, and her mind was helpfully blocking her from remembering any new ones. The Keurig finished its cycle.

"Can you?" She gestured at the coffee maker. "Because I—" She pointed at her phone. "I'll be right back. Marco and Kent are just down the hall."

"Sure." He grabbed his poodle cup. "Can I set one up for you?"

"Yeah, hazelnut, please." She dashed out the door, leaving him alone in her home with her dog. Would he be there when she got back? She suspected he would be, and that made her smile.

———————————

It wasn't an illegal garbage disposal or dishwasher, thank God, but it was the toilet, one of Riley's least favorite types of maintenance jobs.

"It runs and runs and won't flush. Not at all." Marco guided her toward their bathroom, Kent trailing behind them. "We've been using the lobby restroom since this morning, but Kent insisted I text you. I said it's not a real emergency, let Riley have her date with that handsome young man. But he said, 'What if it's worse than we think?' So I texted, and here you are. And here it is."

"It wasn't a date." Riley swiped her still-wet hair out of her face and tightened her ponytail holder.

"Sure, honey. Whatever you say." Marco gave her an exaggerated wink. "We can keep a secret, can't we, Kent?"

"There's no secret." Riley knew it was useless to try to stop building gossip, but she had to try. "Because it wasn't a date. We were doing research."

Marco giggled. "That's what the kids are calling it these days. Have you heard that before, Kent?"

Kent shook his head, and Riley gave up. Time to fix this toilet and get home. Hot coffee, hot shower, and maybe, a hot Caleb would still be there. He shouldn't wait for her, but if he did, well, that would be something, wouldn't it? She turned her attention to the toilet.

Marco and Kent had decorated their bathroom sometime in the 1980s. The mauve-and-black tile work was meticulously maintained, as were the black porcelain sink, bathtub, and toilet. The towels and bath mat were black, too, and all the walls were mirrored. All of them. And also the ceiling. Riley found the effect startling, but Marco and Kent didn't seem to mind how crowded the bathroom felt with the three of them, plus their multiple reflections, in the small space.

Riley gave the handle an experimental jiggle.

"We did that." Marco sat on the edge of the tub while Kent hovered in the doorway. The two men couldn't look more different—Marco all rounded and plump, Kent tall and gangly—but they tended to dress alike. Today, they were in gray lounge pants. Marco's T-shirt strained across his belly, advertising a popular crab shack in Key West. Kent's Mickey Mouse T-shirt hung loosely on his frame.

Both were barefoot. "We jiggled and jiggled, but nothing happened."

Riley popped the lid off the tank. Marco nodded approvingly. "I told Kent you'd do that. Didn't I say so, Kent?"

Kent inclined his head. Riley'd heard him talk in the past; she just couldn't remember when. Maybe the holiday party? Typically, Marco did enough talking for them both, and she supposed, after thirty years together, the system worked for them.

Ah, the fill valve needed adjusting. It was an easy fix that helped calm Riley's nerves. Not a plumbing disaster by any stretch of the imagination. No need to call a plumber. Once again, her YouTube video training paid off. She washed her hands in the sink and followed Kent out of the bathroom, waving goodbye to her many reflections.

"You're a marvel. I always say so, don't I, Kent?" Marco ushered her to the kitchen and loaded her up with some of his homemade banana bread. "Things are much better now that you run the place."

Riley held the aluminum-wrapped, still-warm loaf of bread to her chest. "Thank you, guys. I'm glad I could help."

Marco hugged her, then hustled her out the door. "Now get back to that young man waiting for you."

"I don't know if he'll still be there."

Marco lifted the mauve curtain from his window. The window that overlooked the Dorothy's front yard. "One Porsche, still parked. Go get him, honey."

"It's not like that." Riley's protest was brushed away with another quick hug from Marco and a knowing smile from Kent. Okay, maybe it was like that.

Riley swallowed. Caleb in her apartment. And she still

hadn't given him a towel. Seriously, they should take her hospitality degree away. She imagined him dripping on her kitchen floor, sipping his high-octane coffee. Waiting for her. Even when they disagreed. Even when she had needled him about his plans for the building. He still waited for her. It shouldn't make her feel warm inside. She should be thinking about how a Donovan would do anything to get in her pants. That was what Grams would tell her, and on some level, she believed it. On another level, though, she kept replaying that kiss in the rain and started imaging her hot shower for two.

Then her phone buzzed. Mr. Cardoza. She headed for the elevator. That shower for two was getting awfully cold.

Riley folded up the three-step ladder and placed it back in Mr. Cardoza's hall closet. "You're all set." She flicked on the light she'd just replaced, and Mr. Cardoza beamed at her.

"You're such a resourceful young woman. Thank you. I do not like to stumble around in the dark."

"I know the feeling." All Riley'd been doing since meeting Caleb was stumble around in the dark. "Have a good evening."

"You want to see the pictures my daughter posted today? She made a paella that looks so delicious I can taste it through the computer screen." He kissed his fingers. "I'm thinking I should make one this weekend."

"Thank you, but I can't stay." Her clothes were still damp and yet somehow stiff at the same time. She doubted Caleb would still be waiting, not after this long, but she was still in a hurry to get home.

Mr. Cardoza jogged his thin eyebrows up and down. "The Porsche is still on the street. You're entertaining Caleb Donovan?"

It was? And seriously, these seniors and their watchful eyes. They didn't miss a thing. No wonder she'd never been able to sneak out as a teen. Grams had spies in every unit. "We've been talking about his plans for the Dorothy."

Mr. Cardoza sighed. "Change is always happening. Nobody likes it, but no one can stop it."

"We can try. Or at least get the changes on our own terms."

"You can try, if it makes you feel better. Me, I already told my daughter I'm looking for a new place."

"Mr. Cardoza, no! What would the Dorothy be without you?"

Mr. Cardoza shrugged his thin shoulders. "What can I do? I can't afford to buy into a condo conversion."

Riley placed her hands on her hips. "Don't give up so easily. Eliza is helping us with the legal stuff, and she has a few ideas for how to keep the Donovans from turning the Dorothy into one of their soulless properties."

She hadn't thought the Donovan Resort was soulless. She'd thought it was her ticket to upper management and the life she'd dreamed of since college—one that included long hours, sure, but that was rewarding both emotionally and financially. She liked trouble shooting, how no two days were ever the same, and most of all she loved putting a smile on a guest's face. Now, however, any change that meant Mr. Cardoza had to move was a soulless one indeed.

"Like what?"

Riley lifted a shoulder. "A few things." She felt guilty not telling Mr. Cardoza more, but Eliza had said the surprise element was an important part of their strategy. That was why they hadn't even given Grams many details. Gossip could make the whole thing fall apart if it gave the Donovans time to mount a counterstrategy. "We have to trust in the legal process, I guess, and that Eliza knows what she's doing. And hope for the best. Let's not give up hope, Mr. Cardoza."

He patted her shoulder. "Of course. We will all keep our hope. But we will also keep our options open. I don't want to be homeless."

Impulsively, Riley threw her arms around Mr. Cardoza's frail body. "You won't be. I promise."

It was a promise she hoped she could keep.

CHAPTER 19

CALEB HELPED HIMSELF TO A TOWEL FROM THE HALLWAY bathroom, patting at the water still clinging to his hair and skin. He smelled extra-girlie after using Riley's shampoo and body wash. The sheer number of bottles in her shower had at first confused him. What were they all for? He'd inspected a few and found multiples of the basics, plus body scrubs, bubble bath, shower gels, and something called a hair mask that looked nothing like a mask and was really just a jar of thick, green goo that smelled like something had gone bad in the fridge. He didn't touch the mask, choosing the plainest bottles for his own use, but he still smelled like a fresh spring day and possibly roses.

His khakis stuck to him in an uncomfortable way, but remembering how he'd helped her dump the ex's stuff, he knew his choices were be uncomfortable or be naked. It seemed a bit presumptuous to greet Riley in the nude when she returned from her managerial duties, although he was seriously hoping that was the direction they were heading. Coffee, more kissing, less clothing.

He kicked off his waterlogged shoes. Funny how being around Riley was hard on his wardrobe—and even funnier how much he didn't mind. New shoes were easy to come by, but moments like they'd shared at the park were price-less. She was something else, something outside his previous experiences with women. What was the word he was looking for? *Caring*? *Genuine*? *Real*? What the hell, all those words and more. Maybe the only word that described Riley was, well, *Riley*. He peeled off damp socks and stuffed them in the likely ruined shoes and padded back into the kitchen, towel around his shoulders, to finish his cup of coffee.

Riley's laptop was open on the small dining table, printouts and notebooks fanned around it. The top sheet caught his attention—financial records. A quick scan showed they were for the Dorothy, no surprise, and if he nudged the top sheet aside to look at the whole pile, it wasn't an invasion of privacy because they were in plain sight and the building belonged to his family so they were, in a sense, really his documents, right? Plus, her worries about the plumbing situation troubled him. Upgrades should've happened years ago. What was going on with the Dorothy's financials? Now was as good a time as any to investigate.

He automatically ran calculations in his head, troubled by how the numbers added up but unable to say precisely why just yet. Intrigued, he gave up on trying to be casual and spread the documents out on the table. The picture they painted was indeed grim.

But why? The residents paid on time, for the most part. Every building had a certain margin built in for late payments, and the Dorothy was well within that percentage. Sure, the building had expenses, but with lower occupancy rates, the electric and water bills should also be lower. But they weren't. Year to year, no matter the occupancy, the utilities steadily increased. And the insurance rates were the highest Caleb had ever seen for such a small property. There were variables to consider: proximity to the ocean, located in a flood zone, building in general disrepair. Still, the numbers seemed astronomically high. He snapped a picture with his phone. It might be worth a call to a few insurance agents to see if the building could get a better rate.

His phone dinged with an email alert. He cruised his emails with one hand, the other wrapped around his coffee mug. The usual junk mail, another note from his father's lawyer, and a message from Grandpa William with the subject line URGENT. He set the mug down on the counter and used both hands on his phone. Grandpa William didn't like email, never had, and he wasn't one to exaggerate. With anxious thumbs, Caleb brought up the message.

See below.

Typical Grandpa William terseness. Caleb scrolled to the forwarded message below and read it quickly. Then he read it slowly. Then he read it one more time to be sure.

LouLou ran to the front door and *scratch-scratched* at the seam where door met wall. She whined, a high-pitched sound that filled the entire apartment. The doorknob turned, and the poodle leapt backward, spinning with joy.

"Hey there, LouLou, did you miss me?" Riley scooped up her dog and buried her face in her fur. After a moment of doggy-human reconnection, she set the poodle down and put her hands on her hips. "Sorry about the delay. Marco and Kent's place didn't take long, but then Mr. Cardoza called. He always needs something." She smiled and walked toward him in the kitchen. "Is my coffee ready?"

Caleb didn't move, frozen as he was. She brushed past him with a lingering touch on his arm and grabbed her mug. She took a sip and smiled. "Perfection. You make a mean cup of coffee, Mr. Donovan."

"What is this?" Caleb shook his phone at her.

"Coffee?"

"This." He held the screen so she could see. Her eyes scanned the message, widened, scanned again.

"Oh, uh, yeah. About that."

"You knew?"

The mug trembled in her hands. "Not exactly."

"What exactly did you know?"

"Eliza has a plan. A few of them. I didn't realize she's already started."

"Started what?"

"To shut you down."

"You knew. You knew this whole time. All day today? You knew about the lawsuit, and you didn't tell me." His hand clenched his phone so tightly he was surprised it didn't crumple in his hand like a beer can.

"I didn't know when or the exact details." Riley peered at him over her mug with anxious eyes. "I didn't know it was today."

"But you knew something, and you didn't tell me." Betrayed, again. His dad, his ex-wife, now Riley. Grandpa William with his strings and conditions. No one was ever completely on his side. Fine. He shoved his phone in his pocket and slammed back the rest of the coffee.

"Why should I?" Riley put the breakfast bar between them, fussing with rearranging her K-Cups just so. "Don't try to make me feel bad when I haven't done anything wrong. You know I don't want you to convert the Dorothy into upscale condos. You know how much this place means to me. Did you really think bribing me with a dog park would make me forget the rest?"

He hadn't expected her to forget the rest. He hadn't expected anything. This whole day had been fun, and when she'd invited him to her apartment, he thought they were getting somewhere. That she trusted him. That he could trust her. It wasn't the first time he'd been completely wrong about someone, but he swore then and there that it would be the last.

"You'll be hearing from my lawyers," he said in his coldest, hardest business voice. His hostile-takeover voice.

"Guess you've already heard from mine." She offered him a shaky smile, and he wanted nothing more than for her to tell him it was all a mistake, that she'd asked Eliza not to do it, that she was on his side. The truth was, of course, that she wasn't on his side. Never had been. Once again, he was left on the outside, scrambling to understand how he could've been so wrong. Again.

Riley clasped her shaky hands around the warm mug and stared at her front door. She hadn't known that if you closed it hard enough, it would bounce against the frame. LouLou sat on the inside, nose pressed to the seam between door and trim, and whimpered.

"I know. He sure was mad." Not that Riley blamed him. Eliza had mentioned a lawsuit that the residents should file about Rainy Day not properly maintaining the building. She'd said it was an important counter to what the Donovans would no doubt claim—that the building was too old, not updated enough to preserve—as they sought permits to tear down and rebuild. What Riley hadn't known was that Eliza had gone through with it. Of all the strategies Eliza mentioned, why had she started with the lawsuit?

"Guess I'll go straight to the source." Riley set down her cup and changed quickly into some dry clothes, including some long-overdue dry underwear. That she chose a lacier pair than she normally wore was nothing to worry about. They were bound to come up in rotation at some point, and spending the day with Caleb had nothing to do with her choice. She clipped LouLou to her leash and set out to the dog park to get some answers.

Lady saw them coming before Eliza did and let out a low, welcoming woof. LouLou shot through the gap in the fence, straining at the leash until Riley finally set her free. Eliza waved but stayed engrossed in her conversation with Kiki, who was held in place by a slightly overweight Princess Pugsley sleeping across the top of both feet.

Eliza and Kiki were both bent over Kiki's phone, admiring sunset shots over a Venetian canal, when Riley approached. She watched as Kiki flipped through another dozen shots of her and Paula's Venice adventure before gently clearing her throat.

"Eliza? We need to talk."

Kiki pocketed her phone in her cream-and-navy-striped palazzo pants. "Is it about the lawsuit Eliza filed? She's been excited to hear the Donovans' reaction. Did you hear from them today?"

What happened to Eliza's demand for secrecy for her plans? Riley cocked an eyebrow at Eliza but answered Kiki. "You could say that. Caleb and I were working on the dog park plans when he got the notice from his lawyer."

"*Boo-ya!*" Eliza pumped her fist. "I knew that would get their attention. It'll keep the lawyers distracted while we wait for the historic property proposal to wind its way through the proper channels. That can take forever, and I was worried the Donovans would pressure the commissioners and push things through before the Historic Preservation Board got a chance to chime in."

Kiki high-fived the older woman. "You are a genius."

Eliza grinned. "I kind of am, aren't I? Tell your Grams not to worry. Everything is going to plan."

Riley folded her arms across her belly. "Great. That's great." It should be great. Wasn't she the most opposed of all the opposition? Weren't her grandmother's living situation and her own job riding on the outcome? Why, then, couldn't she get Caleb's betrayed face out of her mind? The way he'd looked at her, like she'd let him down—no worse, stabbed him in the back like a backstabbing backstabber— haunted her. Perhaps because she didn't disagree with him. They'd formed an alliance of sorts on their dog park outings, and kissing him... Well, perhaps that had confused the issue even more. For both of them. She couldn't tell Eliza to stop the legal shenanigans because she liked kissing Caleb Donovan.

Kiki and Eliza were deep in conversation again, this time about Eliza's next legal steps and her gleeful anticipation of the trouble she could cause. "It's even more fun than the women's march!" Eliza rubbed her hands together and invited Kiki to the next City Commission meeting to protest the Dorothy's demise.

"Of course." Kiki nudged her pug awake, and they were on their way.

"You're awful quiet." Eliza dabbed at her hairline with the tissue she kept stashed in her bra strap. "Aren't you happy things are going as planned? I know it takes a while.

The wheels of justice grind slowly, that's for sure, but at least they're grinding."

"Yeah, thank you for all you're doing." Riley smiled at the older woman. It wasn't her fault she couldn't stop thinking about the feel of Caleb's lips on hers or the way he held her against him like he'd never let go. "You know we never could've afforded a lawyer on our own."

Eliza preened and tucked a graying strand of hair behind her ear. "I may be retired, but I keep my licensure up to date especially for cases like this. Now that I don't have to practice for the money, I get to take on causes I really care about. And I care about this neighborhood and you, Riley, which is why I'm going to ask again. Are you okay?"

Riley huffed out a sigh. Lord knew she could never tell Grams about whatever it was that was going on between her and Caleb. And who else would she tell? It wasn't like she had that many friends. Sure, she video chatted with her college roommate, Marina, every month or so, but the truth was she spent more time with Mr. Cardoza and Grams than anyone. And Eliza spent several afternoons a week with Grams, so this urge Riley had to confess all needed to be reined in. As soon as she said anything, Grams would know. And she'd lecture. And be disappointed. Like she did so often, Riley sucked it up.

"Thanks for asking. I am a bit tired lately." She fiddled with a loose string on her shorts; she didn't want to look Eliza in the eye. Lawyers were trained to spot liars, weren't they?

"Poor thing. Those residents run you ragged, don't they? Why don't you take a hot bath tonight and turn in early? A good night's sleep cures many an ailment."

"Thanks, I will." Riley smiled and called LouLou over. She'd gotten the answers she needed, but she didn't feel any better. To help her Grams, she had to stay the course. Caleb Donovan would simply have to help himself. "Can you forward me what you've done so far? I don't want to be taken by surprise again."

"Sure thing." Eliza leashed Lady and let the way out of the lot. "I didn't send it before because I know you have a lot on your plate."

"Too true, but I'd still like the information."

"You'll have it by close of day." Eliza chuckled. "Listen to me, sounding like I'm back in practice. Old habits die hard, don't they?"

Riley thought about Caleb. "New habits don't go too easily, either."

CHAPTER 20

"PLEASE, COME IN!" SYDNEY OPENED HER CONDO DOOR with a wide smile on her face. A bracelet of tiny bells chimed at her wrist and matching though larger bells hung from each earlobe. She wore strategically ripped dark-wash jeans and a flowing white top. Riley felt decidedly underdressed in her usual dog park cutoffs and black tank top with hot-pink trim, but she stuffed down her uneasiness. She was here to make a friend, a friend close to her own age, a friend she could confide in. No insecurities allowed.

"Thanks for agreeing on such short notice." Riley set her poodle on the floor but left the leash on. LouLou and Chewy knew each other from the dog park, but here on Chewy's territory, it'd be best to wait and see how the dogs reacted to this encroachment.

Riley needn't have worried. Chewy was overjoyed to see his buddy, jumping on his hind legs in excitement and executing a few two-legged steps.

Sydney clapped her hands together. "Oh, he usually only does that for treats!"

For her part, LouLou seemed equally happy to see him. She twirled in a circle, successfully tangling the leash, and then held still while Chewy gave her a thorough sniff. Then he dashed off but was back in a flash with a small, stuffed lamb. He dropped it in front of LouLou.

"An offering! How sweet! What a little gentleman you are." Sydney pulled a treat from her pocket and rewarded

Chewy's hospitality. LouLou was immediately more interested in the contents of Sydney's pocket than the lamb in front of her. Sydney laughed and looked to Riley for permission.

"Of course. She's nothing if not a chowhound. Is it all right if I take off her leash?"

"Of course! They'll clearly be fine while you and I have a nice chat."

Sydney led the way through her tastefully appointed living room done in inviting shades of blue and green. The look was coordinated but not matchy-matchy, and Riley especially loved the two dignified greyhound statues flanking the sliding patio door.

"I wasn't sure what you'd like; I've got a bit of everything. Coffee? Tea? Wine? I opened a bottle of Malbec, and there's a bottle of pinot grigio chilling in the fridge. What's your poison?"

It was just before lunch but what the hell. "A glass of Malbec sounds amazing."

"Done and done." Sydney pulled out two large-bellied wineglasses and poured generously. "For you." She handed over one glass and then held hers up for a toast. "To dog park friendships!"

They both took a long sip, and Riley settled into a tall-backed dining chair. On the table, Sydney had already put out some snacks: tiny cubes of cheese, an assortment of crackers, and a pile of grapes.

"Looks like you knew I'd go for the wine."

"Well, I was hoping." Sydney clinked their glasses again and propped her elbows on the cherrywood table. "Now, what can I do for you?"

Riley took another sip of her Malbec. It'd seemed like a good idea when she'd called Sydney up. She needed someone to talk to who wasn't enmeshed in Grams' circle. Face it, she needed someone to talk to, period. And Sydney had been really nice, volunteering her styling skills and helping out with the party. Now that she was sitting here, though, it was unbearably awkward.

They weren't first graders on the playground who could just blurt out, *Wanna be my friend?* and have the other one agree and then skip off to take turns pushing each other on the swings. It'd be so much easier if they were six. They could share their lunches and whisper in class, grow up together, and still find themselves here, years later, sharing a glass of wine and a lifetime of memories. But Riley didn't have anyone in her life like that.

Sure, she'd had friends in school, but no one she'd stayed in touch with. No one she could call in the middle of the night and cry to when she and Aiden split. No one to binge-watch Hallmark Christmas movies while her broken heart healed. She'd done it all alone, and sitting in Sydney's home, sipping this gorgeous Malbec while LouLou and Chewy tore circles around the living room, Riley regretted it.

She'd put so much of her effort into her studies, staying focused and on track, that she'd never slowed down to appreciate the people around her. Never slowed down enough to make a friend. Well, it was fall, sort of. In the Florida way of the heat and daily rains gently easing up, but that didn't mean she couldn't use the season to turn over a new leaf.

"Wanna be friends?" It sounded ridiculous, Riley knew, even childish. She said it anyway. One, because she'd downed about half her glass of wine by now, and two, because she didn't know a better way.

"Yes!" Sydney clinked the rims of their glasses. "I was hoping that's why you wanted to talk. I've lived here a few years now and know lots of people from my work, but I've been wishing I had someone not in my field to chat with, you know? Don't get me wrong, I love to talk shop. But some days, I need a break from all that."

"Absolutely." Riley gulped down more wine, relieved that Sydney didn't think her awkward gesture too gauche. "But I also need to talk shop."

"Hit me." Sydney poured them both another round and leaned forward on her elbows. "I want to hear everything."

Surprisingly, Riley found herself dishing—about Grams, the building, the disastrous commissioner meeting, all of it. Even, it turned out, the kissing part. The multiple instances of kissing. The I-think-I'm-going-to-with-sleep-him-oh-crap-now-I'm-suing-him moment. Her complete and utter confusion about her own feelings.

"Oh, sweetie." Sydney reached across the glass table to cover Riley's hand with her own. "Have I ever been there." She looked up at the ceiling. "Not exactly there, of course. But in an adjacent neighborhood for sure. When I was first starting out, I had this client. Man, was he ever delish, and charming, and do I even need to mention rich? It was hot and heavy for a long time."

"And then what?" Riley sipped her wine more slowly since the buzz had already settled in and loosened her tongue. No need to get ugly drunk. Not like after Aiden. No, she'd never go down that road again.

"Then it was over. His wife came back from her six

months in an Indian ashram to find herself, and boom, they were back together and I was out." Sydney slugged back another gulp and pushed the wineglass away from her. "It sucked. Doesn't Caleb have a wife? I think I remember something about her from the news."

"Divorced."

"Well, thank the Lord for small favors. At least you don't have that to worry about."

"Did you know your guy was married?"

"Not really. The clues did pile up after a while. Like an idiot, I ignored them."

"So he lied to you."

Sydney shook her head, long blond tresses getting caught in the creases of her elbows. "Not directly. I was an idiot all on my own."

Riley clucked her tongue in sympathy, a gesture she recognized as one of Grams' signature moves. Most women worried about turning into their mothers. Riley worried about turning into Grams. Not that it would be all bad, but she really was hoping for a happily-ever-after that included a solid marriage and a kid or two to be proud of. Funny, she'd never thought of it so distinctly before, but thinking about Sydney's mishap helped put things in perspective. She wasn't looking for a boyfriend or a good time. A few weeks ago, she would've said she wasn't looking for anything or anyone. But she couldn't deny her attraction to Caleb, her addiction to the way he looked at her, the way he touched her. Yeah, she was in the market all right. She just hadn't realized for what until this moment.

"Shit, Sydney, what am I going to do?" She told Sydney about this long-dormant wish for a home and family, a loving husband. "I feel antiquated. Shouldn't I be more worried about my career?"

"Haven't you heard? We can have it all." Sydney stood, planting both hands on her table. "And I'll tell you what to do next. Highlights."

"What?" Riley'd expected some girlfriend wisdom about going for it or guarding her heart or some other cliché. She'd not been expecting beauty tips.

"Oh yeah, you need some honey streaks around your face. That'll do the trick."

"What trick?"

"The trick to get him on board the wifey train. Step one, make it so he can't stop thinking about you. And for you, my friend, honey highlights to brighten up your skin tone, well, that's the ticket. Trust me. I have a beautician's license."

Maybe it was the wine talking. Maybe she should've turned down the third pour, but it'd seemed a shame to leave that tiny bit left sitting in the bottle. "Okay." Riley stood, a bit wobblier on her feet than normal. "Let's do it."

"Perfect!" Sydney twirled her finger in a follow-me gesture. "I've got everything we need in my bathroom."

"I'm right behind you."

"Ready?" Sydney's excited voice was decidedly more sober than it had been an hour ago but hadn't lost any of its enthusiasm. "You're going to die."

Riley swallowed hard and turned to face the bathroom mirror. It was double the size of her mirror at home with makeup lights running up and down both sides. It was a no-hiding-anything kind of mirror, which was why she'd closed her eyes for most of the process. She sucked in a breath and opened her eyes.

"I love it." Riley marveled at the soft, honey-toned streaks running through her hair. She'd always thought of herself as a rather bland blond, but the subtle color Sydney'd added did lighten her face and made her skin luminous. Or maybe that was the happiness shining through.

Riley hugged Sydney. "You're the absolute best. I can't believe it."

"Oh, I've been dying to get my hands on your hair since the day you came to borrow the suit. Which, by the way, I do eventually need back. I'm styling a photo shoot next week, and the client loved that Chanel number."

Riley dug her toe into the plush bathroom mat, a subtle gray-to-black gradient that was both practical and luxurious. "It's at the cleaners. I'm not sure the shoes will make it back though. I'll add the cost to whatever you're charging me for this." She fluffed her hair.

Sydney arranged Riley's hair first one way and then another. "The highlights are a gift. As is the trim I'm about to give you. What happened to my shoes?"

Riley filled her in on the plumbing drama that day, and true to her word, Sydney pulled out shears, taking a half inch off Riley's hair and creating soft layers that framed her face.

"I love it even more now." Riley marveled at her own reflection. She looked like one of those young women who hit the clubs after midnight and brunched on Lincoln Road in the middle of the afternoon on a Sunday. "You're a wonder. Now I feel even worse about your shoes."

Sydney merely shook her head and laughed. "Look, come with me."

Riley followed her down the hall to a bedroom door.

"I had to have a two-bedroom. One for my bed and one for"—she opened the door—"my clothes. And shoes."

Riley spun in a circle, feeling like Belle in the library in *Beauty and the Beast*. Only it was shoes, floor-to-ceiling racks on two walls. "I had no idea!"

"I know it's a little overwhelming. That's why I brought things out to the living room last time you were here. But I want you to see that seriously, don't worry about replacing my shoes. What's a pair of kitten heels between friends?"

Riley covered her mouth with her hand, suddenly so overwhelmed with feeling she couldn't speak. Finally, she choked out, "It's too much."

"I know!" Sydney laughed and spun in a circle. "It's absolutely too much. I have a serious problem. It's why I became a stylist, to have a healthy outlet for my style-hoarding."

"No, I mean it's too much for me. First the suit loan, the wine, fixing my hair. I haven't given you anything. I don't know how to pay you back."

Sydney hurried to her side and wrapped an arm around her waist. "Sweetie, it's not a transaction. You said you wanted to be friends. This is what friends do. Don't worry. I'll have a crisis soon enough, and you'll get to step in for some drama control. That's how it works. There's no keeping score."

Riley wanted to blame the wine for the tears rolling down her cheeks, but the truth was, the buzz had evaporated before the timer went off for her highlights to be washed out. She hung her head. "Thanks, Sydney. I don't know what to say."

"Don't say anything. You've been taking care of so many people for so long, you forgot what it's like to be taken care of for a minute. It's okay. You'll be surprised how quickly you get used to it."

Riley blinked back the extra tears that wanted to fall. She hugged Sydney and backed away. "I should probably grab LouLou and get going. You've been too kind."

"Not at all. I'm sure Chewy would enjoy a walk down to the dog park. Why don't we walk you part of the way home?"

Riley linked her arm through Sydney's. "That sounds perfect."

CHAPTER 21

CALEB RIPPED THE PARKING TICKET OUT FROM UNDER the windshield wiper of his Porsche and cursed under his breath. Absolutely nothing had been going smoothly since that email from his lawyer. First, the tenants sue Rainy Day—and by extension Grandpa William—for improper upkeep of the property. Then a city inspector was sent to investigate the claim, and lo and behold, somehow it had been missed that the Dorothy hadn't had its forty-year inspection. It should've been done two years ago, but with Grandpa William's health at the time and what was going on in the courts, that tiny detail had slipped through the cracks. The head of Rainy Day at the time retired a year ago, so there wasn't anyone in the office to be mad at, either.

Perhaps even worse, the Historic Preservation Board had officially declared interest in the Dorothy, and therefore, his plans were on hold until they made their determination. Forty-year inspections he could get around. A failed one could even help his cause. He could claim that the building was in such disrepair that the logical thing to do was tear it down and build a new structure. But if the Historic Preservation Board decided the Dorothy was a priceless treasure of the Miami Beach tropical Deco era, well, then, bye-bye new building, bye-bye parking structure.

Caleb clutched his phone in his hand. He'd wanted to call Riley a ridiculous number of times, but each time, as he was about to hit her number, he'd remember getting that email, that flush of guilt on her skin that meant she'd known all along. She'd known on their dog park excursion. She'd known while kissing him on the bench, while holding hands in his car, while shyly asking him in for coffee. He'd seen nothing but invitation in her eyes, but behind all that, she'd known. Just like his father, she'd let him believe what he wanted while knowing his downfall was near.

He'd vowed never to forgive his father. He wouldn't visit his old man in jail again or answer his letters. No, the time for believing in carefully woven fairy tales was over. Why, then, did his fingers itch to dial Riley? Wasn't she just as bad as Robert Donovan? Just as undeserving of a second chance to explain herself?

What if there was an explanation? That was what preyed on his mind. What if he'd let the memory of his father over-shadow his reaction? What if he'd bolted too soon? What might've happened if he'd stayed and listened to her? Would she have convinced him she was innocent? Or that the email wasn't what it seemed? Would she have kissed his concerns away? Led him to her bedroom?

He wished he could get the taste of her out of his mind, the feel of her under his hands. He crumbled the parking ticket into a ball and tossed it into the passenger's seat. His meeting with Commissioner Santos had been precisely what he'd expected. Apologies and delays. Until the lawsuit was settled, until the Historic Preservation Board weighed in, they were at a deadlock. Well played, Riley and her merry band of geriatrics, well played.

Caleb sped away from city hall. If he told Grandpa William about the delays, he might feel guilty that he hadn't been on top of the forty-year inspection issue, and the last thing Caleb wanted was to put more stress on Grandpa William's already weak heart. No, he was all alone on this, and he needed to figure out what to do—and fast.

He didn't like the way his own heart beat hollowly in his chest. He found himself wanting to ask Riley's advice. What would she say? He shook his head as if he could fling the thought of calling her out of his mind. Grandpa William liked to go on and on about the importance of family working together. Why not try his brothers?

Knox's number rang and rang until he was informed that the voicemail box was full. At first, he'd found Knox's elusiveness annoying, but now he was worried. Why couldn't he get hold of him? Did he even have the right number? Perhaps he should ask Knox's mom, but no, that would mean getting her information from Robert, and he didn't want to be grateful to Robert for anything. Maybe the lawyers had her information. He made a mental note to check later and asked Siri to call Lance.

"Little bro." Lance picked up on the second ring. A miracle. "In over your head already?"

Caleb ground his back teeth together. "Merely looking for an expert opinion."

Lance chuckled into the phone. "Must be worse than I thought. Did the second floor collapse? The roof cave in? Tell me everything. I do love a good construction story."

"They missed a forty-year inspection."

Lance snorted. "Happens all the time. With so much turnover in management companies and such, these oversights occur. It's no big. Just call the city inspector and set it up."

"What if it doesn't pass?"

"From what I saw? It won't. They give you a list of things to fix, you fix 'em, and then you get a new inspection."

"Sounds straightforward enough." Caleb's shoulders stopped trying to climb up his ears. He always felt better when there was a plan.

Lance outright laughed in his ear. "Only someone who's never done a renovation project would say something like that. Those old buildings are never easy. Once you open up a wall, no telling what other things you'll find. You've got yourself a money pit there, no doubt about it."

Caleb's teeth gnashed a bit more, and he had to forcibly relax his jaw. He'd had to wear teeth night guards as a teen because he ground his teeth in his sleep, and the dentist claimed he was doing permanent damage to his bite. He'd broken himself of the habit, and now was not the time to lapse back into it. He took a few deep breaths and concentrated on Lance's words.

"I don't suppose you could be there for the inspection?" The words slipped out even though Caleb specifically told his brain it was not a good idea to ask. "To keep an eye on things? Make sure it's done right."

Lance laughed again. "You're not dragging me into this mess. I don't care what dear old Grandpa Will wants. I thought I made myself clear."

"I'm asking for me. We don't have to tell Grandpa William anything."

"You? Do something without family approval? I'm shocked."

"Shocked enough to help me out?"

A long pause. "Text me the information. If I can fit it in, I will."

Caleb flexed his jaw, feeling the tension release at Lance's tentative agreement to help. Damn it, he hated it when Grandpa William was right, but it turned out, Caleb did need his brother's help. Turned out leopards did change their spots and pigs could fly. Maybe the inspection consultation would be enough to satisfy Grandpa William's terms. Maybe Caleb wasn't seeing his options clearly yet. He'd already done some adapting of his original plan for the Dorothy. What if he tried some other angles? Found a way to update the building and make it profitable while still keeping the current residents on, pacifying the Historic Preservation Board, and getting Commissioner Santos that parking garage? He pulled out his phone and dialed the architect. Only one way to find out.

"Look, look." Mr. Cardoza called Riley to the window over his sink. With a sigh, Riley set down her café solo and joined him, her poodle pitter-pattering behind her. LouLou bounce-bounced against Mr. Cardoza's leg until he picked her up, and the three of them stared out the window. "See?"

Riley saw the usual assortment of neighbors, absent Eliza and Sydney, and their dogs. A few people stood in the corner closest to the fence gap, chatting with one another, while a Lab mix and golden played tug-of-war with a palm frond.

"See what?" Riley leaned on her hands and stood on tiptoe, pushing her belly into the counter's edge. That was when she saw two blond men walking the perimeter of the fence. They were tall and engaged in an intense conversation. "You mean the Donovans?"

"Yes, yes. You should go find out what they are scheming." Mr. Cardoza kissed the top of LouLou's fuzzy head. Her top mop was getting out of control. She'd need to go to the groomer soon for her bimonthly buzz.

Riley pushed away from the counter, her weight shifting back into the heels of her feet. "I don't know. He's pretty mad at me."

"He has the nerve! He's the one trying to change everything. You go find out what he's doing. Take your little spy with you." He transferred LouLou into Riley's arms. "No man can resist her charms."

Riley scratched LouLou under her chin, her favorite place, and then around her ears. "I don't think he'll tell me anything."

"You don't know until you try." Mr. Cardoza shooed her out the door. Riley cast one last longing look at the café solo left abandoned on his kitchen table. At the door, Mr. Cardoza winked at her. "He won't be mad forever. He likes you, I think, and you like him. Make it right between you two, and everything else will fall into place."

"H-how could you possibly—" Riley sputtered and set LouLou on the floor. The poodle quickly dashed down the hall to wait for the elevator.

Mr. Cardoza pointed at his face. "These eyes may be old, but they still see. At the city meeting, the way he looked at you. And you looked back. The Porsche is parked out front many times. It's not the building he comes to see, is it?"

Grams always said there were no secrets at the Dorothy, but Riley was still taken aback by Mr. Cardoza's conclusions. She tried to play it off with a low laugh. "Oh, Mr. Cardoza, are you watching telenovelas again? Are you seeing romance everywhere?"

Mr. Cardoza straightened to his full five-foot-six height and sniffed. "Romance is everywhere. Open your eyes, and you'll see."

Riley kissed his cheek. "Thank you for the coffee. See you tomorrow?"

"Yes, yes." He patted her back. "Come tell me what you find out."

Riley waved and caught up with LouLou at the elevator. It had been a while since LouLou went outside. No harm in going to the dog park, and if she happened to run into Caleb and his brother, she'd keep in mind that Mr. Cardoza was watching every move from his apartment window. Nosy neighbors indeed, but it was hard to be mad when she knew how much Mr. Cardoza cared. She and Caleb seemed to have a thing for kissing in parks. Maybe they'd really give Mr. Cardoza something to see.

"You're right about needing parking for the building." Lance stopped on the sidewalk outside the empty lot and turned to his brother, arms crossed over his bulky chest. Years working construction was more of a workout than any gym regimen. "Street parking is awful. I'm like two blocks away. Ridiculous."

"Yeah, yeah, I know." Caleb scanned the dog park crowd. No LouLou. No Riley. He told himself he wasn't disappointed, but he knew it for the lie it was. "I really wanted your opinion on the building. Renovations, upgrades, what your prediction is for the forty-year inspection."

"Sure." Lance reversed his steps back toward the Dorothy, work boots scuffing on the sidewalk. "Uh-oh, here comes trouble."

Riley walked toward them, her long legs eating up the distance in quick strides. Today's T-shirt read *Pink* in big, zebra-striped collegiate lettering. Her poodle trotted happily at her side, stopping every few feet to squat on the grass swale between the sidewalk and the street.

"Good morning!" She greeted them brightly, as if she hadn't betrayed him the last time they'd seen each other.

Caleb's jaw tensed, and though he told those muscles to relax, they did not. He'd wanted to hear her voice, wanted to see her so badly, wanted their last encounter to have ended very differently. How could she act like everything was fine? She was smiling. Smiling at Lance.

"Morning! Riley, isn't it?" Lance strode forward, hand outstretched. "Hear you're giving my brother a run for his money."

Riley shook his hand with a low laugh. "It's not only me. The whole neighborhood is in on it, really."

"But I hear you're the ringleader." He winked at her.

Caleb's jaw tensed more. Was his brother flirting with Riley, right in front of him?

Riley ducked her head. "Aw, you're too kind."

And she was flirting back? Caleb's back teeth worked back and forth, not unlike a dog with a bone. He shouldn't have asked for Lance's help. It was all a huge mistake.

"What're you boys up to today?" The leash slid through Riley's fingers, and the poodle took advantage of the extra slack to approach Lance and smell his work boots.

"Casing the joint." Lance used his chin to point toward

the Dorothy. "Little brother asked for some advice on demolition and such."

"Demolition!" Riley's eyes flashed and her grip tightened on the leash. She rounded on Caleb. "You can't do a thing until the Historic Preservation Board makes its decision."

"He likes to be prepared." Lance's voice indicated a level of amusement that made Caleb's back teeth grind harder. "Donovans are used to getting their way, you know."

Riley poked a finger in the middle of Lance's chest. "You tell your little brother that in this, he will not get his way. Demolition!" She tugged on the leash. "Come on, LouLou. I think we need to consult with Eliza again." She stomped off, LouLou at her heels.

"Why?" It was the only word that could squeeze out of Caleb's overly tight jaw. Nothing like family to bring out the worst in him, teeth grinding and all. Caleb jammed his hands into his pockets and took a few breaths. He was better than this. He couldn't let Lance bait him. "I never said anything about demo."

Lance threw back his hand and laughed. "Yeah, but did you see her face? Priceless."

"You are such an ass."

"Hey, you never said you liked her. How was I supposed to know?"

Caleb's previously locked-tight jaw sprang open in surprise. "I don't like her."

"Yeah, you do. What're you going to do about it?"

"I don't like her," Caleb repeated with more emphasis.

Lance eyed him up and down. "You may not like her right now, but you sure are in love with her. Man, those puppy dog eyes of yours. How does it feel to be such a sap?"

"I'm not—" Caleb wanted to tell Lance how wrong he was, but a sudden flash of the feel of Riley in his arms, the way she kissed him back like she never wanted to stop, the way his mood had lifted just seeing her heading toward him on the sidewalk. What was that? Maybe not love, not yet, but it was certainly more than like. And if he wanted her to like him back, he needed a new plan for the Dorothy.

"Lance? All kidding aside, I need some help figuring out what to do with this property." Caleb and Lance had never been close, separated by five years and a nasty divorce between Lance's mom and their dad that resulted in a custody agreement where Caleb and Lance only saw each other a few times per year. "Grandpa William said a condo conversion was the way to go, but now I don't think that's the best plan. At least not in the traditional sense. What would you say to a community-centered renovation?"

Lance's affable demeanor faded. "This was a one-time consult, kid. I told you I don't do business with the Donovans."

"But you are a Donovan." He'd thought Lance would like the idea of not doing what Grandpa William wanted, would at least give him a thumbs-up for thinking outside the Donovan box. No go.

Lance's face shuttered closed like a storefront boarded up before a hurricane. "Not anymore. Sorry, Caleb, you're on your own. I shouldn't have come today. I'll text you a list of guys you can trust to do the work, but I'm out. You hear me?"

Caleb remembered this feeling from when Lance and his mom would drive away after a weekend visit. "Yeah, I hear you."

Like always, Caleb was on his own. Had it ever really been any other way?

CHAPTER 22

DEMOLITION! RILEY BYPASSED THE DOG PARK AND headed straight for Sydney's place. Sydney wasn't home, which made sense since it was Wednesday and she'd been booked for a fashion shoot all week. Chewy greeted them with some fierce barking through the door, and LouLou yipped back at him. Riley pulled her away from scratching at the wood and retraced their steps toward the Dorothy.

Surely, LouLou was peed out by now, but she managed to find a few extra squirts along the way, getting especially excited at a telephone pole that had clearly been marked by many dogs passing by. Riley often wondered if marking was the canine version of tagging: *i wuz here*. She smiled at the idea of LouLou leaving messages for other dogs, that she was connected to a larger doggy community that Riley knew nothing about.

Walking up to the Dorothy, Riley tried to see it as an outsider would. The peeling paint. The boarded windows that she would absolutely have replaced as soon as the glass was delivered. The grounds weren't so much lush as barely surviving. They could use landscape lighting so the residents would be safer coming and going in the dark. The building needed too many things; it was exhausting really to think too much about it.

She'd survived as the building manager by taking one crisis at a time, one day at a time. If she stood back, like she was doing now, and tried to think long term, her mind clouded with the impossibility of it all. Without more residents, they'd never have enough money to make the improvements needed. If the Dorothy didn't pass the forty-year inspection, they were in big trouble.

She noticed the Porsche before she saw him. How did he always find parking close to the building? Her Mazda was on the other side of the block. Just inside the entry, he sat on the old rattan furniture Grams picked out decades before Riley was born.

"You're brave. I'll give you that." Riley stood in front of him while LouLou sniffed his shoes.

"For daring to come into your building?"

"For daring to sit on that." She nodded at the old rattan sofa. "It's more decorative than functional."

"Like much of the building."

Riley's shoulders slumped. "Like much of the building."

Caleb stood, bringing him close to Riley, only the poodle between them. "Can we talk?"

Riley took a backward step and bumped into the rattan coffee table with magazines from the 2000s neatly stacked on it. A young Tiger Woods stared up at them. "About what?"

"About everything."

Riley was tempted, so tempted. The Dorothy needed a huge influx of cash. Truth be told, she needed not a mere makeover but a significant remodel. Riley saw that now, knew that things couldn't go on as they were. But *demolition*. She shook her head. "I don't think that's a good idea. You can't promise a dog park on one hand and then tear down the whole building with the other."

"That's not what's happening."

"Then what is happening?"

He took a step toward her. Her knees bumped against the table. His hand reached for her, then dropped to his side. His blue-blue eyes caught hers, and he offered a lopsided smile.

"I can't stop thinking about you, Riley."

Her breath caught and then hiccupped out. She touched a hesitant finger to his chin. "Really?"

"Really."

He swallowed and she followed the bob of his Adam's apple with her finger. "Are you going to withdraw your plans from the city?"

He shook his head, eyes still glued to hers.

Riley sidestepped around the coffee table. "Then we have nothing to talk about."

She walked away.

And if it wasn't what she really wanted to do, well, Caleb didn't need to know that.

Caleb took Riley's words like a strike to the gut. Give up on Grandpa William or give up on Riley. Were those his only choices? Without Lance, Grandpa William wouldn't give him the property, and Lance had made it pretty clear that he would not be signing on anytime soon. Caleb was going to lose the Dorothy anyway. Did he have to lose his chance with Riley, too?

"What about the dog park?"

Riley stopped midretreat, one hand propped on a hip. "What about it?"

"Don't you still want to build it?" Caleb didn't know Riley as well as he wanted to, but he knew the way to her heart was through her poodle. And her community. Besides, if Grandpa William was going to shut it all down anyway, why not do as he pleased? The weight of a lifetime of expectation lifted from his shoulders, and he smiled. "Because I do."

"What about your parking garage?"

Caleb lifted one shoulder in a half shrug. "Who knows what's going to happen with the lawsuit, the Historic Preservation Society, permits? It could take months. It could take years. Improving the dog park is something we can start today."

"Today?" Riley squinted at him suspiciously.

He didn't blame her. It was a crazy idea.

"Yeah, let's do it. Let me grab my iPad, and we can get started." He tried his most charming smile on her.

Riley's squint grew more squinty, but she jerked her head up and down in what was clearly reluctant agreement. "You're on. Coffee?"

"Always."

Riley loved home improvement stores. It wasn't a feeling she'd been born with but rather one that evolved during her time working at the Dorothy. She loved the cavernous structures that seemed to stretch for miles in all directions, the extra-wide aisles, the sales associates who scuttled away at the slightest hint that a customer might ask a question. She loved the smell of freshly sawn wood, the sound of the paint mixers going at it, even the screams of young children desperate to be picked up and carried the rest of the way to checkout. What she hadn't realized was that she'd love roaming the aisles with Caleb.

"We need a mailbox. We totally do." He stopped at an especially patriotic one, stars, stripes, and the head of an eagle glaring accusingly from the housing. "For all the fan mail we'll get from around the world. 'Dear Dorothy Dog Park, what is your secret to keeping every dog in the neighborhood happy? From, Curious in Cairo.'"

Riley laughed. Really laughed. So far, they'd bought some wooden benches and a kiddie pool. Not exactly cause for international envy. "'Dear Dorothy Dog Park.'" She took a stab at her own advice-style letter. "'If one kiddie pool makes dogs happy, will two make them twice as happy? Sincerely, Waterlogged in Walla Walla.'"

"We can get another pool. Do you think we need one?" Instead of laughing like she'd intended, Caleb spun the oversize cart back toward pool supplies. "One for big dogs, one for small, do you think?"

Riley laid her hand on his arm just below the elbow. "It wasn't a criticism, Caleb. It was a joke."

"Right." He spun the cart back around. "We're joking around now. Got it." He stared up at the fluorescent lights shining down on them. "'Dear Dorothy Dog Park, how many doggy bags do you stock in the dispenser per week? Yours Sincerely, Pooped in Peoria.'"

"Pooped in Peoria!" Riley doubled over, laughing until she gasped for breath.

Caleb chuckled. "It wasn't that funny. We should think about what to call the park. For real."

"What's wrong with Dorothy Dog Park?" Riley leaned

against the end of the cart, metal digging into her belly. "Or were you thinking something more like Donovan Park? Your family does like to put their name on stuff."

"They do, don't they?" Caleb thought of Lance and how the word *Donovan* was definitely not in his company's name. "That doesn't seem right for the dog park, though. Neither do these mailboxes. What else is on your list?"

Riley dutifully checked her list. "Mature trees? That's not something we can do here. In fact, a lot of things on our list are more long-term goals."

Caleb snapped his fingers. "What about those doggy-bag dispensers. We'll need some, right? What do we need, a pole? Box? Does it matter what kind of bags we get? Are there different kinds?"

"Different sizes." Riley trailed her hand along the top edge of the cart. "Medium is probably best. I'm sure they have them around here somewhere." She angled her head up and checked out the overhead signs. Nothing clearly marked "Build Your Own Dog Park" in sight. "Do you even know how to install a pole?"

Caleb checked his iPad and added a note. "I'm sure there's a YouTube video about it, but I'm pretty sure we'll need concrete."

"There's a YouTube video for everything! That's my whole Dorothy management strategy." Riley fell into step beside Caleb as he steered them toward posts and concrete.

"You shouldn't have to do the majority of the work yourself." Caleb pushed the cart forward. "A manager manages."

"You'd think so, wouldn't you? The Dorothy doesn't have the budget for me to call people for every single problem. It's been challenging, that's for sure. A far cry from working for your Donovan Resort. Back then, I'd push a button on the phone, and someone would magically appear to take care of whatever problem a guest complained about. Noisy toilet? Neighbors too loud? Blinds askew? There's a button for that."

"You deserve buttons."

"Says the man who decided to single-handedly build a dog park. Why aren't you calling in people to help you? Like your brother? Doesn't he own a construction company?"

"Lance is…busy." Caleb parked the cart in front of an array of poles in a variety of materials and heights. "Besides, how hard can it be?"

"Many, many a project has blown up in my face when I asked that question!" Standing in front of dozens of choices of fencing, Riley turned on Grams' patented eyelash-fluttering technique. "I'll admit I don't know what I'm doing if you do."

"What?" He wiped at the corner of her eye with his thumb. "Do you have something in your eye?"

So much for using Grams' feminine wiles tips on him. She let her blinking return to normal speed. "No, I'm fine. Just thinking about things like, great, we have some benches. What will happen in a big wind? What will keep people from simply walking away with them? We're going to need to put in fencing. Do we need some kind of tool for digging holes? Is there already one in the bowels of the Dorothy's maintenance closet? Would I recognize it if I saw it? Is it easier to buy one here? How many holes are we planning on digging?"

Caleb started laughing halfway through her list of questions and didn't stop even after she wound to a finish. "Have a few worries, huh?"

Her grip tightened on the pole. "I could go on."

"We are reasonable, educated, experienced people who can figure this out." Caleb rubbed the back of his neck and rocked forward on his toes. "I've overseen major construction of luxury properties. I think I can handle a tiny dog park."

"You'll be digging the holes, then? Installing the fencing? Building and securing the benches? Planting our trees?" She ticked off the list items from memory.

"I—" He pushed the cart down the overly lit aisle at a determined clip. "You're right. This is ridiculous." He retraced their steps to the bench section. "How do we get plumbing to an empty lot for the dog water sticks?" He slapped the side of the plastic kiddy pool. "Where does the water come from to fill these things? I don't even know where to start."

Riley blocked the cart's progress with her body. "Wait. You're saying neither one of us knows what we're doing?" Her laughter got a little hysterical. "I thought the Donovans were such great builders."

"I know how to anticipate what humans want. But dogs?" Caleb pointed to the turtle in swim trunks on the side of the kiddy pool. "Do they even like anthropomorphic amphibians? Who knows? I usually have someone to call, a project manager or something. They do the market research." He waved his hand. "All the details. Then I crunch the numbers, make sure everyone has the budget they need to get their part of the project done."

"You're talking about having a staff, but I'm afraid our dog park is a bare-bones project. Pun intended. No budget for experts. It's you and me, buddy. How're we going to figure this out?" Somehow, knowing he was as lost as she was made her feel better. She felt her inner manager coming out, making lists, thinking about her contacts.

"I don't need a staff. Hell, I've been the staff." Caleb pulled the cart to the middle of the aisle and made a show of reading the aisle labels.

"Right, when were you ever staff, Mr. I'm-the-Number-Cruncher?" Riley rested her foot on the lower rungs of the cart, smiling as a dad passed them, his toddler son riding their lumber dolly like a surfboard.

Caleb watched the father and son until they disappeared around the corner. "I already told you about my summer as a valet? My father said I had to learn the business from the ground up, so my summers were always booked. I did a rotation in food and beverage, housekeeping, gift shop clerk, even night shifts on the desk."

"I had no idea." Riley's foot slipped off the cart and thunked to the floor. She'd worked her way up, too, along a similar path, minus the valet experience, but simply couldn't picture a young Caleb checking in guests or delivering room service. "You know, I supervised night shifts. Nothing like the joy of surprising someone during a riveting game of *Candy Crush*. I could've been your boss!"

"Yeah, some nights were pretty long and uneventful." Caleb grinned. "And you wouldn't have gone easy on me, would you? I bet you were a hard-ass."

Riley slapped her butt. "Nope, nothing hard here at all. Unfortunately." She regretted the joke as soon as she'd made it because his eyes followed her hand to her butt and stayed there, tracing the shape. Why bring attention to what her mother always called her bubble butt?

"My mistake." Caleb finally tore his eyes away. "Nothing hard to take about that ass at all."

Although she'd been joking around, he wasn't. She should crack some other lame joke, break the tension building between them, but somehow the image of him pulling her closer and cupping her butt took over her mind, and that was definitely not something to talk about in the middle of the fencing aisle. But it was the only thing on her mind, pushing away words and reason until the whole scene played like a movie in her head. His hands on her backside, his tongue in her mouth, her fingers curled around his biceps, pulling him closer.

"You know who was a hard-ass?" Caleb wrenched his gaze from hers, heat climbing into his cheeks almost like he could tell what she was thinking. God, she hoped not. "My favorite manager, the head of housekeeping. Stayed on me until I could tuck a tight bed and fold the toilet paper like nobody's business."

"The idea of you turning over rooms is nearly impossible to picture." She tugged on the edge of the cart, moving them forward a few feet and apart, creating some kind of distance between him and her overactive imagination.

"Mom hated it and pressured Dad into moving me into management during college. It was more interesting work, but I missed the atmosphere of being one of the crew, you know?"

Riley sucked in her bottom lip and reined in her imagination. "I miss it, too. The team hasn't stayed in touch since we were let go."

"I'm sorry." Caleb squeezed his eyes shut. "I know it doesn't help what you went through for me to keep apologizing. It's one thing for my father to screw up his own life, but it's a whole other level to have done the same to countless others."

"And to you." Riley laid a hand on his arm just below the elbow. "It's not your fault. You did the best you could." Her own words shocked her. Did she really believe them? Yes, sometime between *I'm here to fire you* and learning that he'd unclogged toilets and stocked bathrooms with tiny bathroom products, she'd stopped thinking he was responsible for her career derailment. The bitterness that used to burn her stomach when she thought of working at the Donovan Resort was gone. Sadness still lingered, of course, because it was hard to let a dream go, but her life was pretty good right now, all things considered.

"Thanks." He swallowed, and a long silence stretched between them before he cleared his throat and asked, "Where to now, Ms. Manager?"

"Let's go to the gardening section and check out some sod." She confidently led the way, pleased at taking the lead. She did like to manage things, even if she was having difficulty managing her own imagination, her own expectations when it came to Caleb Donovan. Navigate a home-improvement store, though? No problem. She might not know what to do when they got there, but she at least knew her appliance aisle from her dead-bolt aisle.

"'Dear Dorothy Dog Park,'" she narrated as they walked, attempting to lighten the mood again. "'However do you keep hooligans from stealing your adorable benches? From Your Furry Friends in Fairhaven.'"

Caleb stopped in the middle of the aisle and grabbed her arm. "Did you say Fur Haven?"

She looked at where his fingers gripped her below the sleeve of her T-shirt. The pressure wasn't uncomfortable, but it was unexpected. "No, Fairhaven."

"But Fur Haven." His hold on her loosened; his hand slid down her arm. "That's it, isn't it? The name for our park?"

Riley liked the sound of the words *our park*, and she liked even more how his fingers linked with hers, pulling her forward in his excitement. "Maybe. What about Bark Park? That's a popular one."

"Every town's got a Bark Park." Caleb brought their hands up; her knuckles grazed his chin. "We need a name of distinction. One that will have people coming from everywhere, bringing their dogs for an afternoon of play."

"It's a neighborhood dog park. Let's not get carried away." She chucked his chin with their hands. "You're such a Donovan. Always thinking big."

"I want the best for you." He kissed the back of her hand, a quick, almost thoughtless gesture that nonetheless brought goose bumps running up her arms. "Is that so bad?"

"No." She let their hands drop back to hang between them, a strange feeling in her stomach. She was such an emotional ping-pong ball around him. She liked him. If she were honest, she liked him a lot. But he was still a Donovan, and that part of him scared her more than a little. Right now, he wanted the best dog park in the world. Once it was built, though, how soon until he was on to his next project? And when he did inevitably move on, what would happen to all this *liking* that tingled her nerves and made her long to snuggle into him and tell him she didn't need the best of everything as long as she had him?

Walking into the humid, outdoor gardening section

cured her of any desire to cuddle or have any human contact whatsoever. Sweat pooled at the bottom of her spine. Even her feet felt hot in her polka-dot flip-flops.

Riley pointed to sod plugs across the far wall. "Shall we pick out some grass for your Fur Haven Park?"

"I knew you liked the name." Caleb smiled and pushed the cart down the long row of grass pallets. "Zoysia, Centipede, St. Augustine? This is crazy. There should be one type of grass. One. And we buy it, and it grows. End of story."

Though Riley shared his surprise at the variety of sod types, she couldn't help but laugh at his outrage. "Like there's one kind of car for everyone? One flavor of ice cream? One type of tree?"

"Right? Wouldn't life be simpler?" He planted a hand on a stack of St. Augustine squares. "Will we need to install a sprinkler system or trust the rain to take care of the new grass? I mean, really, who do we ask these kinds of things? We need some experts because we're clearly in over our soddin' heads."

She groaned at his terrible joke and pulled out her phone. "Maybe Sydney can help."

"The fashionista with the Chihuahua? How's she going to help?"

"Sydney styles for all kinds of fancy events." Riley scrolled until she found Sydney's contact information. Was it too early in their friendship to favorite her? Nope. Riley added Sydney to the short list. "She told me about a dog wedding where she dressed the entire bridal party, dogs and humans alike. She's got to know someone who knows this stuff."

"I hope so." Caleb leaned heavily on the cart. "Fur Haven Park needs any help it can get."

Riley put a finger over his lips. "She's picking up! Hi!"

He nipped the tip of her finger, and she pulled away, acting like he'd bitten her. "Ow! No, sorry, Sydney. Just ridding myself of a pest." She pointed at the snorkeling turtle on their doggy pool and then back inside at the pool aisle sign.

Caleb took the hint and rolled away while Riley got down to business with Sydney. Caleb might not realize it, but the more neighbors involved in the dog park project, the more support he'd get. She felt a twinge of guilt that her plans somewhat undermined Eliza's and Grams' careful scheming, but she shook it off. Anything for the dogs, whatever it took. Even if that meant collaborating with a Donovan.

CHAPTER 23

"GRAMS?" RILEY USED THE KEY SHE'D HAD SINCE SHE'D been ten years old and Grams had deemed her old enough for the responsibility of key stewardship. It was several more years before Grams felt similarly about Riley's ability to handle a cell phone. Riley was the last in her class to get one—all three Emmas in her class had one since the third grade, for goodness' sake—but like the key, when Riley finally earned that longed-for phone, she never lost it.

The door swung open with a loud creak that would be excellent if they were running a haunted house for the upcoming Halloween season—that crazy time when stores displayed pumpkins, witches, and skeletons, oh my! right next to turkeys, elves, and reindeer. Grams, however, was not a fan of spooky Halloween. She was more a fan of Glamourween, dressing up as a fairy or a princess for as long as Riley remembered. Riley added oiling Grams' front door to her never-ending mental list of things to do at the Dorothy.

Grams' favorite chair in the living room, perfectly angled for a no-glare view of the TV, was empty. Grams wasn't in the kitchen, stirring up a pot of her favorite stew or baking cookies for their upcoming bunco night. Riley checked the time on her phone. Odd. Grams knew she was stopping by. Where was she? It was pretty late in the day for a nap, but maybe Grams lay down earlier and hadn't gotten up yet.

The blood smear on the tile floor in the hallway was Riley's first clue that something was wrong. Very wrong.

It streaked from the bathroom and trailed into the bedroom. Riley's finger hovered above the 9 of 9-1-1 when she stepped across the threshold and found Grams.

She was lying face up, blood pooled around her head like a dark halo.

9–1-

"Riley?" Grams croaked in a raw voice. "Is that you?"

-1.

Riley knelt next to Grams' hip. "Don't move. I've called an ambulance."

The operator quizzed Riley on details and cautioned her not to move her grandmother.

"I'll be right back." Riley squeezed her Grams' hand and sprinted to the door to make sure it was unlocked for the EMTs. There was an emergency personnel code on the box, so they'd have no problem getting into the building. Thank God, the service people had finally showed up to fix the short in that thing. In moments, Riley returned to Grams' side.

"What happened?"

Grams' chin quivered. "I was getting out of the nicest bubble bath—you know how Wednesday is the perfect day for that—and I slipped. I don't know what happened."

Riley had a theory, and that theory involved the glass of chardonnay Grams liked to drink during her bubble baths. She'd told her grandmother a million times she needed to install handrails in the bathroom.

"Who has the money for that nonsense?" Grams always waved away her concerns. "And don't get started on me wearing one of those button things. Please. So cheap-looking and gaudy. They won't go with anything I wear."

"I love you, Grams," Riley said, rubbing her grand-mother's hand between her own. Now was not the time to bring up should-haves. "That ambulance will be here any moment."

Sure enough, not even two minutes passed before a team arrived. The first on the scene was a young woman, Riley's age or a year or two older, who took over and solicited more answers from Grams.

Yes, she'd been in the bath. Yes, she'd gotten completely out. No, she didn't remember the fall, just opening her eyes and realizing she was on the bathroom floor.

"Were you unconscious, ma'am?" the young woman asked. Her name tag said Cabrera. Riley assumed that was a last name.

"How would I know that?" Grams fluttered the fingers of her free hand in the air. "I've never been unconscious before."

"How'd you get into this room?"

Grams moved her head to the side and winced. "What room?"

"You're in the bedroom, Grams. How'd you get here?"

"Keep your head still." Cabrera flicked back her dark ponytail. "David, can you check the back of her head?"

"On it." A younger EMT stepped forward, handsome in his freshly pressed uniform. His name tag read Blanco.

Riley looked away. She didn't need to see every detail. Grams was talking and alive, and that was what she needed to focus on—not the ice that filled her belly at the sight of Grams on the floor. The blood. The quick thought that this was it. This was how it ended. She'd been a few minutes late, and it cost Grams her life.

Grams grunted at whatever David Blanco with his smoothed-back hair and long fingers was doing, but Riley kept her gaze on Grams' nails, recently painted a chipper orange for October. She'd change it to match her costume, of course, but there were several weeks until Halloween, so she'd play up the holiday color even though she'd never dream of hanging a skeleton on her door or organizing a Dorothy field trip to the haunted house at the race track.

"What?" Riley's head snapped up. Cabrera had said something, asked something, and she'd missed it.

"We're taking her to the hospital. You can follow in your car."

"Oh, of course." Riley's head started nodding and didn't stop.

Two more EMTs came in from the living room, taller than Cabrera, more handsome than Blanco. They loaded Grams onto a stretcher. Riley's head was still nodding.

Hey. Riley looked down when her phone buzzed. You busy?

Riley's thumbs answered Caleb before her head kicked in. *Grams fell. She's going to the hospital.*

Is she ok? Are you ok?

Yeah, but I gotta go

Which hospital?

Mount Sinai

I'll meet you there.

Riley stared at the words as if they were in a foreign language. She'd never had anyone to meet her there before. Even now, she knew she should text her mom and let her know what happened. But what would Mom do half a world away working on a twenty-six-night Mediterranean cruise?

It had always been Riley and Grams, with special guest star Mom whenever she was in town. No, Riley learned at an early age to deal with crises on her own. Even when Grams had her hip replaced three years ago, Mom hadn't thought Riley needed any help caring for her during the recovery.

"You've got a lot on your plate," Mom had said in an under-standing tone when Riley called her with updates. "Don't worry about me. I'll stay out of your hair until this is over."

I'll meet you there. Four short words that helped Riley take a deep breath, locate her keys, and lock Grams' door without breaking into great heaving sobs.

I'll meet you there. Why hadn't Aiden ever texted her something like that? To help with Grams' physical ther-apy sessions or sit with her during follow-up exams? She'd thought he'd been great, not making her feel guilty about the time she spent with Grams. In hindsight, always so per-fect, he couldn't be bothered. Not about Grams. Not about her. If it wasn't convenient for him, Aiden wasn't interested. Caleb was, and that kept her moving forward.

Finally, she texted back *Ok*, all the breath whooshing out of her lungs. She hesitated in the hallway. Elevator or stairs? Which would be faster? Because if she was going to follow the ambulance, she needed to sprint like LouLou chasing a squirrel up a tree.

Of course, it wasn't as simple as that. Before she could make up her mind, Mr. Cardoza waylaid her in the hallway.

"What's going on? Was that Gloria on the stretcher?" His kind gaze and gentle grasp of her hand brought the tears she'd kept tamped down thus far to the surface. "What's happened?"

"Grams fell. There was a lot of bleeding, but she's conscious. I'm sorry. I have to go." She tugged away from him.

"Of course. Of course." He didn't let go until he'd pulled her in for a hug. "You need anything, you let me know. These phone things? They work both ways, you know?"

Riley sniffed back the sob that wanted to escape her throat. "Thank you." Even LouLou wouldn't have made it to the elevator faster than she did, and thankfully the car was already on the second floor.

As soon as the door opened, Riley stepped into the lobby. But what about LouLou? She hadn't been out in hours.

Bang. Bang. Someone rapped on the glass front doors. Outside, Eliza stood there, Lady sitting at her heels. Riley hurried to let them in.

"Sorry, I can't talk right now. I—"

"Who is it?" Eliza guided Riley toward her apartment. "We saw the ambulance. I came to help."

"Grams." Riley sniffed back another of those runaway sobs. "She fell. I have to get to the hosp—"

"Mmm-hmm, I got you. Let's get you some shoes." Eliza perused the collection outside Riley's door. "Your sneakers? Hospitals can be really cold."

Riley kicked off her flip-flops and slid into the Skechers. She fished around in her bag until she found her keys. When her shaking hands finally managed to unlock the door, LouLou greeted her with a clockwise spin of excitement. When she spotted Lady, she looped an extra few spins in the opposite direction out of joy.

"She hasn't been out in hours. I'll put some pads down, and I'll—"

Eliza took the keys from Riley's hands, separating the apartment key from the tangle and pocketing it. "You just go. Lady and I will take care of your little poochy. Won't we, girl?"

Lady cocked her head, tongue lolling to the side in a clear sign of agreement. LouLou did another joyful spin.

"Okay, that's good. That's wonderful. You're wonderful!" Riley hugged Eliza, grabbed her purse, and was out the door.

Riley raced for the ER door, grateful for Eliza's insight into footwear so that she could fly without worrying about losing a shoe. It had taken an inordinate amount of time to find parking in the multistory parking garage. She should've valeted, but it hadn't occurred to her until she was circling the third floor, and by then, she figured she might as well keep going to the top.

"Hey." Caleb stood outside the doors, hands shoved into the front pockets of his dark denim jeans. He rocked back on his heels and greeted her with a hesitant smile. He was so handsome, like paramedic-hot but with more tailoring, and he looked at her like, well, she wasn't sure like what. But whatever it was in his eyes, it slowed her down and flushed her cheeks.

"Oh." She halted to a stop, skidding a bit and barely managing to miss stepping into a giant wad of pink chewing gum. She sidestepped it. "Hi."

"You okay?"

"I don't know." She pressed under her eyes with the pads of her fingers, as if pressure could keep the well of tears in place. "I've got to find her."

"Let's go." He popped out an elbow, and she threaded her arm through, surprised at how natural it felt to lean on him this little bit. She felt her head loll to the side, resting on his bicep. It was okay to lean a tad more. She was suddenly so tired it was an effort to lift one foot in front of the other.

After clearing security, Caleb steered her toward the desk where a white-coated nurse with an inordinate number of pins and stickers on her lapel greeted them with a smile.

"My grandmother was brought in by ambulance. How can I find her?" Riley found her teeth chattering even though she could feel more sweat pooling at the small of her back than when they'd been outside in the humid nursery picking out sod plugs. Grams had been sick in the past, sure, even undergone the hip replacement, but this seemed worse. So unexpected. So real. So much blood. She'd need to scrub the grout before Grams was released. Grams wouldn't want any reminders of today. Riley knew she sure wouldn't.

The receptionist-slash-nurse typed away at her keyboard. "I'm sorry. She hasn't been processed yet. If you take a seat, I'll let you know when you'll be able to see her."

"Processed? What does that mean, processed? Do you need her insurance or something?" Riley turned panicked eyes to Caleb. "I didn't think to bring her wallet. Why didn't I think of that? Of course, they'll need her insurance. She's on Medicare. Is there a way to look her up?" Riley turned the panic on the nurse-receptionist.

"We can take care of that later. Right now, they'll be

assessing her. Maybe running some tests. Hold tight. She's in good hands, and we'll get you back to see her as soon as it's feasible."

Feasible. That was her Grams back there, all alone, with only good-looking medics to take care of her. If Grams were awake, she would have appreciated the brawn on the young men who'd carried her out on the stretcher. What a bunco story she'd have next week! Grams was good at finding the bright side to dark moments. She'd turn this into an adventure.

Right now, though, Riley wasn't feeling adventurous. She was shaky with nerves and unshed tears and that weird teeth-chattering-while-sweating thing. Was she getting sick, too? It wasn't quite flu season yet, but she hadn't had her shot since she lost the excellent health-benefit package the Donovan Resort used to supply for her.

Today she had a different kind of Donovan support. Caleb urged her to a waiting chair, a mottled gray-and-pink-fabric cover on steel legs. She collapsed into it, leaning her head back against the wall. Caleb sat next to her and reached over to take her hand. He interlaced their fingers and held their hands on the armrests between them.

"She's going to be fine. They're the best here."

Riley nodded numbly, eyes closed against tears that would do no good to shed. Tears hadn't gotten her job back, hadn't convinced Aiden to love her enough to fight for her. She should at least text her mom about what was going on, and even though that seemed too much, she did send a quick update. Her head slumped to the side and landed on Caleb's shoulder. He scooted down a bit to give her a more comfortable angle.

"She can't die." The words came without thought, voicing the deepest fear she'd had since first seeing the blood. "I don't know what I'd do."

Riley felt the press of Caleb's lips against the top of her head. "She's a fighter, isn't she? Like you. You'll get to see her soon." He laid his cheek against the top of her head. "We'll wait here until they say we can go back. Do you want something to drink? I could try to find a vending machine or something."

"No." Riley snuggled deeper into his side, uncaring of the armrest pushing against her ribs. "No, I just want this."

Caleb smiled into her hair. "Good. I'm not going anywhere."

Long moments passed. Riley inhaled deeply, the hospital smell of antiseptic and worry overpowered by the freshly laundered smell of Caleb's polo sleeve, the warmth of his skin under her cheek, the comforting rhythm of his hand stroking her back—up and down in a lazy path that skimmed her spine and ruffled the hair hanging below her shoulder blades. Grams was in good hands. Riley briefly entertained the thought that so was she.

A few hours ago, he'd had her laughing at the idea of canine mail and dreaming of a deluxe dog park where her poodle could run and play with her friends. Riley imagined sitting on the benches with Sydney, watching Chewy and LouLou frolic in the cooling fall days. Wouldn't it be lovely to have a tree or two, long branches stretching out overhead to shade them? Riley closed her eyes and pictured it, the perfect afternoon. Free from her duties at the Dorothy, hands cradling a hot cup of coffee while Sydney regaled her with stories of her celebrity clients' foibles, LouLou collapsed at her feet after a good, long run. The hospital receded, and Riley felt the breeze ruffle her hair.

Wait, that was Caleb, hand stroking under her hair to massage the tight muscles of her neck. Oh, that was good. She sighed and let Caleb into her Fur Haven Park fantasy. Sydney was waving her hands around, telling a really good story about a really tall basketball player and his insistence that his socks never match, and Caleb sat beside her on the bench they'd picked out together, gently rubbing her neck like he was doing now. At the hospital.

Darn it. The slip-slap of feet on tile brought Riley out of the safe place in her mind. She straightened away from Caleb, his hand slipping from her neck, and stretched.

"Did I fall asleep?"

Caleb leaned forward, forearms draped over his knees. "Maybe for a moment. Nothing new yet. I would've woken you up if there were news."

"Thanks." Riley fought the urge to cuddle into him again. The crisis was over. Time to get herself together. She mustered her resolve and checked back in with the nurse at the desk. "Any idea when I can see her?"

The nurse's smile was stretched thin, as though it was an effort. "I said I'd tell you as soon as that was possible."

"Thank you." Riley tried not to be discouraged. Grams was getting the care she needed. She had to believe that. She shuffled back toward Caleb.

"Riley?"

As if conjured from Riley's imagination, Sydney appeared. Skinny jeans disappeared into ankle boots zipped at the sides, and the dramatic belled sleeves of her crop top billowed behind her as she rushed forward. She engulfed Riley in a belled-sleeve hug. Riley stiffened at first but then relaxed.

"Sydney? What're you doing here?"

Sydney released her, pulling back to take a long head-to-toe look at Riley. "Eliza brought Lady and LouLou to the dog park. When I asked where you were, she told me what happened. How is your grandmother? How're you holding up?"

Riley felt those unwanted tears rise again. "They've got her in the back, doing tests or something. I can't see her yet."

Sydney propped her hands on her hips. "In that case, no news is good news. If something bad happened, they'd come out to tell you. Probably waiting on results or something. Hospitals are the worst." She shuddered. "Can't stand them myself, so I brought you a little something to help pass the time."

Sydney reached into her oversize tote bag and pulled out a plastic container. She popped off the red top. "My famous—or infamous, depending on how you look at it—orange cranberry muffins."

Riley's stomach growled right on cue. When was the last time she'd eaten? Long before the visit to the home improvement store, that was for sure. "You are amazing. You made these?"

Sydney plucked out a muffin and handed it to Riley. "I'm a comfort baker. Couldn't cook a pot of spaghetti if my life depended on it, but bake enough pastries to fuel an entire elementary-school bake sale? I'm your girl."

Riley closed her eyes at the first bite. "Oh my."

"I know, right? The secret is cardamom. It makes everything better."

"Oh my, my, my." The muffin was gone in seconds. "You have no idea how much I needed that."

"Well, these are all yours. And I'm here to offer my services of distraction. Waiting in hospitals is awful, and Eliza told me to keep you busy. And to tell you that LouLou and Lady are having a grand time and not to worry about getting back. She can keep LouLou at her place as long as you need."

"I don't know what to say."

"Don't say anything. Have another muffin. And tell me about the stud muffin watching us from the waiting area. How long has he been here?" Sydney pressed another muffin into Riley's hand. Riley didn't fight her, just peeled off the paper wrapping and took another calorie-laden nibble.

"Sydney, isn't it?" Caleb rose to his feet. "From the Dorothy?"

"From the dog park." Sydney held out the container to him. "I live a few doors down. Muffin?"

Caleb took a long whiff. "They smell delicious."

"They are delicious." Riley took her second bite and enjoyed how it melted on her tongue.

Caleb plucked one from the container. "I'd say just like my mother used to make, but my mom has never baked anything." He chomped down.

"Not even chocolate chip cookies?" Sydney asked, choosing a muffin for herself.

"No. She was definitely not the homemaker type."

"That's awfully sad." Sydney pouted her berry-stained lips. "Every child should have chocolate chip cookies after a rough day of times-tables tests."

"Mmm," Caleb agreed around his last bite of muffin.

Sydney offered him another, and this one was gone in a few chomps. "Are you a professional baker or something? I've honestly never had better."

Sydney's muffins were good, and just because Riley's culinary expertise ran more toward things that could be microwaved was no reason for her to get defensive. She couldn't help but wish Caleb would look at her the way he was eyeing a third muffin. When he took it and ate this one more slowly, clearly savoring every bite, Riley gritted her teeth. She had other admirable qualities. Not everyone was a baker.

"Would you mind sharing the recipe?" she found herself saying.

"Of course not!" Sydney grinned and pushed another muffin on her, but Riley declined, patting her stomach. "It's a variation on a recipe I found online. It's really not hard at all."

"Thanks." The muffins she'd gobbled down felt like rocks in her stomach. She was never going to bake muffins; she should admit that she'd never understood the chemistry involved in baking before someone got hurt. But Sydney had already set down the muffins to text her a link, while Caleb licked the last crumbs off his fingers with slow deliberation. Whatever. She had time to let everyone down in the future.

Sydney told a story about Chewy's adventures in lizard chasing. "I don't know who was more surprised when he caught one, him or the lizard!"

"Poor lizard." Riley laughed at the image of the tiny Chihuahua with a lizard tail hanging from his mouth while the rest of the lizard scampered away. "I hope its tail grows back quickly."

"Me too!" Sydney flipped through her phone until she found the picture she was looking for, Chewy nosing a detached lizard tail on the sidewalk. "He dropped it as soon as I told him to, but he was pretty sad to leave it behind. I felt bad, not letting him keep it. He moped the entire afternoon." Another picture showed Chewy with his head propped on a couch pillow, staring morosely out the front window. "Luckily, a UPS delivery came, and barking insanely at the driver cheered him right up."

"LouLou is not a fan of delivery people, either." Riley pulled out her phone, ready to reciprocate pet show-and-tell with some cute poodle pictures of her own. She'd missed a few texts. She checked her settings and realized at some point she'd turned her ringer off. She scanned quickly. Sydney saying she was on her way with comfort muffins. Two from Mr. Cardoza asking after Gloria's condition. One from her mom. She thumbed it open.

Do you need me to come home? I can catch a flight tomorrow when the ship docks at the next island.

Riley's shoulders tensed, like they always did when dealing with her mom. Sure, she'd come home, and then complain bitterly the whole time about the hit to her paycheck. She'd blow in, a suitcase full of presents from exotic places and stories of the interesting people aboard her current cruise, and somehow in the midst of helping out, she'd make more work for Riley. But Grams was her mother. Maybe Mom really wanted to be here. That'd be a nice change of pace.

Of course, I could only stay a day or two. The next leg of the cruise crosses the Atlantic, and they can't do without me for such a stretch of time. I'm sure you have everything under control anyway.

Don't worry, Mom. Riley texted back. *I've got it handled.* Like always. *I'll keep you posted.*

Are you sure? I don't want you to be alone through this.

Riley looked up from her phone. Caleb scarfed down another muffin while Sydney showed him more pictures of Chewy on her phone. "That's a lot of personality for such a tiny dog," Caleb said around a mouthful of crumbs, and Sydney laughingly agreed.

Riley's shoulder relaxed, and she sank more deeply into the uncomfortable waiting-area chair. She watched Caleb and Sydney for another few seconds before texting back.

I'm not alone.

Great! I'll see you both when I'm back in Miami.

Be safe. It was what Riley always texted at the end of any exchange with her mom, and Mom always texted back: Be good.

When she was young, Riley'd known what that meant. Listen to Grams. Do her homework without complaining. Not bother Mom with too many texts. Now that she was grown, what was she supposed to do with that particular bit of maternal direction? She sighed and leaned her head against the cold wall.

"Look at this one." Caleb drew her into his conversation with Sydney, pointing to a picture of Chewy buried in a pile of white blankets, only his dark-brown nose sticking out.

"He's a cutie pie for sure." Riley took a deep breath, letting go of the stress any interaction with her mother caused. Nothing was a better distraction than cute dog photos. She pulled up some of LouLou when she'd had a rather unfortunate too-close body shave a few months ago and looked like a miniature shorn pink sheep. Both Caleb and Sydney laughed at the poodle's forlorn expression, and soon Sydney and Riley were in a cute-photo showdown, each trying to outdo the other. Caleb was breathless with laughter, his arm draped casually across the back of Riley's chair.

"Is there a Riley Carson here?" a nurse asked in a heavy Haitian accent.

Riley lunged to her feet, phone dropping to the chair, all laughter pushed aside to make room for the panic assailing her. "How is she?"

The woman held open one side of the swinging double doors. "Resting comfortably. Would you like to see her?"

"Yes." Riley followed the nurse, anxiety fueling every step.

"We'll stay here!" Sydney called.

"Unless you want us with you?" Caleb asked, voice rising on the last word.

"No need to wait for me." Riley didn't look back at them, afraid her resolve would crack. It'd been nice to lean on Caleb's arm, for Sydney to bring snacks, for them both to sit with her and laugh at ridiculous dog photos. But Grams wouldn't want anyone to see her at less than her best, especially not William Donovan's grandson, and she barely knew Sydney. Riley braced her shoulders, telling herself that "resting comfortably" was a good sign. Worse signs would've been "critical condition" or "ICU." She clenched her phone in one hand and her purse in the other. Whatever was at the end of this walk, she could handle. There was no reason to feel lonelier and lonelier with each echoing step.

The nurse's sneakered feet squeaked across the tiled hallway floor. She stopped and pulled aside a curtain separating

Grams' bed from the line of others in the busy ER. "Here you go. Someone will be by to talk to you soon."

"My Riley!" Grams held out her arms, and Riley came in close for an awkward hug. With one person lying down, IV in her arm, and the other standing and leaning over a railing, the cramped, curtained-off space wasn't exactly conducive to intimate moments. Riley kissed her grand-mother's cheek and planted her butt in the small chair pro-vided for visitors.

"How are you?"

"Right as rain, though I'm sure I look a fright." Grams patted her hair. Her usual pouf was decidedly less poufy, but she looked beautiful to Riley. "They're talking about keeping me overnight for observation, but I want you to tell them I'm fine to go home."

"I'm not a doctor, Grams. If they think you should stay, maybe you should." Riley's grip on her purse handle tight-ened until her fingernails dug into the cloth strap.

"*Pshh.*" Grams rolled her eyes. "What do the doctors know? I'm fine." Her shaky hand when she brushed back her bangs belied the point.

"Why don't we wait and see what they have to say?" Riley took Grams' unsteady hand in both her own, warm-ing her chilled skin. "What have you been doing back here all this time?"

"Waiting and more waiting." Grams looked small in the hospital bed, the white sheets making the gray roots of her carefully dyed dark hair more apparent. Her makeup was fading fast, bits of foundation caught in the smile wrinkles that bracketed her mouth.

Riley found a tissue in her bag and wiped away the last of

the foundation from around Grams' mouth. "They haven't done any tests?"

"Oh sure, they think I'm a bloody pin cushion." Grams licked her dry lips and grimaced. "Taking all kinds of samples. I had a CAT scan, and they keep asking me what my birthday is, like it's some kind of trick question. I give a different answer every time, to keep them on their toes."

"Grams! You can't do that. They must think you're confused."

Grams giggled her little-girl giggle, the one that meant she knew she was in trouble and didn't care. "The first time, they acted worried, but now they know I'm joking with them."

"The hospital is no place to joke around." Riley tried to keep her face stern, but Grams' delight was infectious. If she was cracking jokes, she really must be okay.

"If not here, where?" Grams raised a penciled-in eyebrow that had lost some of its definition this late at night. "Everyone is so serious. They could use a laugh."

"And you're a laugh a minute." Riley grinned. Something she'd learned long ago—when Grams had showed up at her high school to rail against some policy or another—was that Grams would be Grams. There was no stopping her.

Authoritative footsteps stopped outside the curtain, then marched in, carrying a young doctor with the word *Resident* embroidered on the lapel of his lab coat. "Looks like they have a bed for you upstairs, Mrs. Carson. I've started the admitting paperwork."

"I don't want to stay," Grams said at the same time as Riley asked, "Why are you keeping her?"

The doctor checked the chart. "The CAT scans came back fine, but she's unsteady on her feet. Physical therapy recommended a night of observation, and I concur. You can't be too careful with someone her age."

"My age." Grams' face flushed. "I didn't fall because of my age. I'll have you know I was perfectly drunk in my bathtub, a habit I've had my entire adult life. Age has nothing to do with it."

"And in your entire adult life, did you ever fall and injure yourself because of this habit?" The doctor might be young, but he'd perfected the I-know-better-than-you face.

"It was an accident." Grams huffed.

The doctor jotted something on the chart.

"What're you writing?" Grams narrowed her eyes at him, a sign that usually made Riley flinch and tell her everything, but the doctor merely hummed a noncommittal response.

"I'd feel better if you stayed." Riley squeezed her grandmother's hand. "It was really scary to find you. And all that blood. If you're here, it'll give me a chance to clean up your place, get everything back in order for you. You'd like that, wouldn't you?" Maybe Riley couldn't bake a mouthwatering muffin, but she could get bloodstains out of anything.

"I suppose," Grams conceded with a final glare at the doctor.

"Excellent. It'll take a while to get the parts in place, but as soon as everything's settled, we'll get you to your new room." He scribbled another note and ducked through the opening in the curtain.

"You go on home." Grams extracted her hand from Riley's to smooth her hair. "It's nothing but waiting from here on out."

"I'll stay until you're settled in your new room." Riley

leaned her head against the bed railing. She wasn't going anywhere until she knew Grams was safe.

Grams stroked Riley's hair like she'd done whenever Riley was sick and stayed home from school to watch cartoons in Grams' bed.

"I love you, Grams." Riley snaked her arm through the railing to hold her hand.

Grams gave her a squeeze. "Love you, too. You're a good girl, Riley Carson."

CHAPTER 24

IT WAS AFTER MIDNIGHT WHEN RILEY WANDERED OUT to the parking garage, not completely sure where she'd parked her car so many hours ago. Her head fogged with exhaustion, and every step she took felt like a major accomplishment. *Good job*, she told herself, waiting for the elevator. *You can totally do this.* The arrival *bing* jolted her out of a semitrance, one that meant she might or might not've been asleep on her feet, and she wished with fierce intensity for her poodle. She could use a good doggy cuddle, and LouLou's elevator enthusiasm would certainly cheer her up.

She remembered winding through the parking garage for forever on her way to find Grams, so she chose the biggest number, resting her head on the elevator wall after all the effort of pushing the button. The elevator groaned itself up, opening on the roofless top floor. It was a cloudless night, and the moon was almost full. A few scattered cars made her Mazda easy to spot, and she groaned louder than the elevator when she saw it. Home. LouLou. Coffee. All she had to do was stay awake a little while longer.

"How're you doing?"

Riley stumbled over her own feet, surprised someone else was on the roof this late. Adrenaline flooded her body, and she raised her fist of keys like she'd been taught in the self-defense class she took back in college. *Muscle memory. Good for me.*

"It's only me." Caleb raised both hands to shoulder height and took a step back. "Please don't key me to death."

"Oh. Hey." She relaxed quickly, and the keys dropped from her suddenly limp grip to the paved rooftop, jangling louder than her nerves.

Caleb was beside her instantly, picking up the keys and using them to open up her car. "Here, why don't you let me drive you home?"

She blinked heavy eyelids. "What about your car?"

He held the passenger door open, gesturing like she'd won a grand prize. "It's not going anywhere. I'll swing by tomorrow."

"I'm fine. I can drive." Sitting in the passenger seat negated her very excellent point. It took an awful lot of concentration to keep her head upright.

"Of course you can. I'm not saying you aren't perfectly capable of doing whatever you set your mind to." He pulled the seat belt across her chest, clicking it into place. "I'm suggesting simply you don't have to. I'm here. Let me help."

If her head weren't heavier than five gallons of paint, she might've protested. Instead, she put a hand on his chest and looked up at the way one of the parking garage lights created shadowed patterns on his skin. His eyes were dark pools in his face. "Thanks."

He smiled and touched his forehead to hers. "I've got you."

He does get me. Riley let herself be tucked into the passenger seat of her own car. She snuggled into the jacket he draped over her, pulling it up to her chin and inhaling the slightly woodsy scent of his cologne. "How did you find me?"

"I waited in the ER for a while, but then the nurse told me they moved your grandmother to the observation wing. Figured you'd eventually come out to your car." He clicked his own seat belt into place and started her car.

"You've been waiting this entire time?"

"Well, Sydney had to go. Some kind of client meeting, she said." He angled toward the down ramp, following the exit signs at a sedate speed. "She checked in with Eliza, who took LouLou home with her, by the way. So I decided to stay."

"It's been hours. How'd you know where I parked?"

"I had some emails to take care of on my phone, and a brisk walk through the parking lot helped me stay awake. It's fine, Riley."

"Why didn't you text?"

"I did."

Riley fished out her phone. Sure enough, there were several texts asking how she was, where she was, if she needed anything. "I didn't hear them."

"I figured."

"You're pretty confident I wasn't ghosting you." Half her mouth tilted in a grin. The other half was too tired to keep up.

"When Grandpa William was in the hospital, I worried so much I could barely remember my own name. If you wanted me gone, I figured you could tell me in person."

"So that didn't happen." Riley rubbed at her tired eyes. "Now here you are, driving my car."

"Yeah, I think you're starting to like me."

She blinked, midrub, and blinked again. "Oh my gosh, that might actually be true."

"Good, because I definitely like you." He kept his eyes on the road, but she saw the flash of his smile in the dark. It warmed her more than her blanket, more than a hot cup of coffee on a cool morning. More than a video of a wiggly puppy licking mashed bananas off a laughing baby's face. She was in trouble now, liking a Donovan, but she couldn't find it in herself to fight it.

She reached across the center console and placed her hand midthigh. He dropped one hand from the steering wheel to cover hers, and they drove the rest of the way to the Dorothy in silence, partly because he was concentrating on the drive but mostly because Riley was already asleep.

Caleb admitted to feeling a bit stalkerish waiting in the parking garage for Riley, but she'd been more relieved than anything to see him, and the weight of her head against his shoulder, uncomfortable console between them and all, made him smile. She was used to doing everything for everyone. It felt good that she let him take care of her just a little bit.

He was under no illusion that this was anything but an extreme circumstance. Her Grams was clearly the most important person in her life, and the thought that something might happen to her terrified Riley. He understood, having gone through a similar situation with Grandpa William, but he couldn't help but wonder what it must feel like to be the most important person in Riley's world.

Had he ever been the most important person to anyone? He knew his parents loved him, that Grandpa William was proud of him in his own way, that his ex-wife had claimed to love him until most of their assets were seized. But the devotion between Riley and Grams? No, he didn't think he'd ever experienced that. What would it take to win Riley's trust? To be even the second most important person in her life? Or third, if you counted LouLou, which of course he should.

After finding parking half a block from the Dorothy, Caleb waited a few moments to see if Riley would wake on her own. She would not. However, a night in the car with her head at its current angle would lead to sore muscles in the morning. It was a kindness to wake her, even if it did make him feel guilty as hell.

She mumbled something about puppies with bows in their hair while he guided her out of the car. Once on the sidewalk, she weaved like she'd had a whole bottle of wine to herself. He really had no choice but to wrap an arm around her waist and pull her in to his side. She let her head fall against him, a move he was growing to associate with her, and stumbled along still talking about her puppy dream.

"Do you often dream about puppies?" he asked when she paused in her rambling.

She slow-blinked sleepy eyes up at him. "Caleb?"

"Yes, still here. You have your key?"

She fumbled in her pocket, pulling out the bundle she'd threatened him with earlier. It only took a moment to locate the master building key, and soon they were tripping over the shoe pile outside her front door.

When the door swung open, she turned panicked eyes to him. "Where's LouLou?"

"Sleep over at Eliza's, remember? She and Lady are probably wreaking all kinds of havoc over there."

"I should call. Go get her."

"It's nearly one in the morning. Let Eliza sleep. We'll go get little LouLou in the morning. First thing. I promise."

"Okay. I feel funny."

"You are funny. Let's sit on the couch for a minute."

"No, take me to bed."

His whole body froze. How long had he been waiting to hear those words? It felt like his whole life. Blood flooded to parts of him that didn't do his best thinking, but he took two deep breaths and said, "Let's get you tucked in."

She leaned heavily on him during the short walk to the bedroom, and when she saw her bed, she exclaimed with delight and flopped on top of the patchwork duvet cover.

"Poor Grams can't be in her own bed tonight, but this is plain heavenly." She sprawled on the bed, then patted the space beside her. "Where's LouLou?"

She was so tired. It was quite frankly adorable. "At Eliza's, remember?"

"Right." Her head flopped heavily onto the pillow. "Doggy sleepover. Eliza's so nice."

"Yes, she is. Do you want to take your shoes off?"

"Usually take them off outside the door." She tried to toe off her maroon Skechers, but they didn't budge.

"I've noticed. Quite a collection you have out there."

"I like shoes." Finally, the left shoe popped off and hit him on the shin. "I like a lot of shoes."

"Let me help." He took her right foot in his hands and pried off the sneaker. He used a knuckle to rub the arch of her foot, and she groaned. "You like that, huh?"

"Oh my God." She threw an arm over her eyes. "I'll pay you a hundred thousand dollars to keep doing that."

"I don't think you have a hundred thousand dollars." But he kept up the massage anyway, standing beside the bed with her foot in his hands.

Her head rolled to the side so she could eye him. "Probably not. But I'm good for it. Eventually. Over a lifetime of earnings."

"That's a big commitment for one foot massage."

"You're going to do both, aren't you?" Her left foot bashed against his thigh.

"Of course, and for you, I'll give the friends-and-family discount."

"You think we're friends?" She propped herself up on her elbows.

"Aren't we?" He dug a knuckle into the tightest part of her arch, and she flopped onto her back again, head bouncing on her pillow.

"Yeah, I think we are." She closed her eyes, a smile tugging at the corners of her mouth.

He was tired, too, should probably get home soon. Just a few more minutes and he'd go. For sure. Her head lolled to the side, and she appeared to be dead asleep. He swung her legs around and placed her feet on the mattress. He took the crocheted quilt at the bottom of her bed and used it to tuck her in.

Riley opened one sleepy eye. "Where you going?"

"Home. It's been a long day, hasn't it?"

"But you don't have a car."

"I'll call a service. Don't worry. Get some rest."

She tugged on his hand. "Stay."

God give him strength. He stared up at the ceiling. "I'll catch you in the morning."

"You don't want to stay?" Her lips pouted, and all he wanted to do was lean in for a kiss.

"Too much."

"Then stay." She tugged again, and he let himself be pulled to her side. She lifted the edge of the blanket so he could scoot in. Then she rolled and pressed against his side, one arm flung over his chest. "That's nice, isn't it?"

She was asleep before he could answer. He kissed the top of her head and wrapped an arm around her back. It *was* nice, her heat and the way she fit against his side. He stretched his legs out and snuggled closer. A guy could get used to this.

CHAPTER 25

RILEY WOKE SLOWLY, COMFORTABLY WARM AND TOASTY with a body much bigger than LouLou's providing heat all along her back. Large hands rested on her stomach, and her head was pillowed on a muscled arm.

"Good morning." Caleb's voice rumbled in her ear.

"Mmm, good morning." She turned, and they were face-to-face. She traced the side of his face with her fingers, enjoying the tickle of early-morning stubble. "Thanks for staying. Didn't give you much choice, did I?"

"It wasn't a hard sell." He smiled and turned his head to kiss her palm, and her heart *thump-thumped* in response. "How're you doing this morning?"

"Better." She checked the clock on the nightstand, torn between duty—get up, get to the hospital, get busy—and the delicious possibilities right here in her bed. "A bit early to check on Grams. Hungry?" A compromise, then, to justify not rushing off and not being quite ready to let Caleb go yet.

"Not exactly." He grazed his lips along the line of her neck, biting lightly where it curved into her shoulder.

She shivered and pushed at his shoulders. "What're you doing? I'll feed you real food."

"I don't want food." He lifted his head, and their eyes met, blue to brown, sky to earth, him to her. A universe of possibilities swirled between them.

She stilled. "What do you want?"

"You."

Riley knew the world didn't freeze in that moment; it only felt that way, like the slow tick of minutes stretched until one second was the same as a thousand. She stared into Caleb's sky-heavy eyes, sure no one had ever looked at her like he looked at her now. Like she wasn't just special but everything. The earth and sky and universe all together, packed under her skin. She felt it, too, the possibilities waiting to explode out of her, what they could be together. If she agreed. How could she not?

She nodded, suddenly shy, and was relieved by the flash of his joyful smile.

She smiled back, and with a groan, he claimed her mouth. She loved the taste of him, and he held her so tight, drinking her in with long kisses that left her gasping. Already his hands skimmed her skin, searching out all the places that made her sigh, lingering when the sighs turned into low moans.

She placed her hands under the polo he'd slept in, tugging it up over his tight abs, feeling his strength, the flex of muscle as he sucked in a deep breath, dragging the air from her mouth into him like it was a nutrient he couldn't live without. She felt the same way, as if she'd been starving for him her whole life. He broke away from her mouth just long enough to strip the polo over his head, and then he did the same with her pink T-shirt and made quick work of her lacy blush bra.

"You're pink everywhere," he breathed out, taking in her rosy nipples, and she turned pinker with the compliment, resisting the urge to cover them with her palms like some shy maiden in an old-fashioned movie. *Take the compliment,*

Riley. But it made her nervous, all this open admiration. Suddenly, she was nervous. So nervous that she couldn't stop the babbling from escaping her lips.

"Grams raised me to have a signature color. It makes a woman stand out, she said." God, talking about her grandmother while they were naked. She was ruining everything. Caleb would make some polite excuse any moment now, and she'd be alone in her bed. Again.

"You don't need help standing out." Caleb cupped one breast in his hand and framed her face with the other, catching her gaze and holding her hostage with the heat she saw there. "God, Riley, you're beautiful." And then he was kissing her again, his words rolling around in her head until she felt beautiful, too, and that made her bolder. She pushed into his hands, showing him how much pressure she liked, and he got it. He got it really good. Her head dropped back, and she closed her eyes. No more direction needed, which was a good thing because her brain was out of ideas. Except one.

She tugged at the waist of his khakis, and he growled, "Yes," while she unbuttoned him. The rest of their clothes found their way to the floor, and she could feel him everywhere, the delicious heat of his skin on hers, the glide of his hands over her body. She kept her hands busy, too, tracing the ridge of muscle in his chest, fluttering down to dip a fingertip into his belly button, a move that made him smile. She smiled back while they explored each other with gentle strokes that gradually grew more urgent, more demanding. His fingers traced her entrance, testing, teasing. She arched into his touch, gasping as the tension grew tighter and her legs quivered.

When he entered her, she was more than ready and cried out from the sheer pleasure of how right it felt. She sought his gaze and found him already watching her. Stroke by building stroke, he took them both over the edge, and when he fell, she fell with him.

Clutching his back, her legs wrapped around his thighs, she kept her eyes open, not wanting to miss the expression on his face. He touched his forehead to hers, panting breaths that brushed her cheeks and matched her own labored breathing. "You," he said and stopped, arms half propping him up, half collapsing under his own weight.

"You." She smiled and pulled him all the way on top of her.

He buried his nose in her hair. "Too heavy?"

"Not yet." She wrapped herself around him and stroked his back until his breathing evened out and he fell asleep. She didn't join him, just listened to the thump of his heart against hers, counting each beat like a prayer.

The doorbell startled Riley out of her languid daydreaming, something about cool sheets and warm hands and the sound of her name on Caleb's lips. He snored softly beside her, but she still wasn't sleepy. Just very, very happy. Amazing what really good orgasms could do for a girl's mood. She slipped out from under the weight of Caleb's arm and walked barefoot to the front door.

"LouLou!" Riley scooped up her poodle and rubbed noses with her. LouLou licked her cheeks with slobbery enthusiasm.

"Good morning to you, too." Eliza strode in, Lady on her heels. "How's Gloria?"

"They kept her overnight for observation." Riley set her dog down. LouLou promptly went to her food bowl to check for kibble. "I'm going to check on her soon, right after I clean up her place. Hopefully, they'll send her home today. How was my LouLou? Was she a good guest?"

"An angel." Eliza sat on one of two stools by the breakfast bar. "An angel who chewed through one of my throw pillows, but an angel nonetheless."

"She didn't! It's been months since she's shredded a pillow. Of course, I'll buy you a new one." Riley offered Eliza a selection of Keurig flavors to choose from. Eliza pointed to the French vanilla, and Riley popped it in the coffee maker, lining up a hazelnut for herself.

"*Pfft*, who cares about a pillow? It's a small sacrifice considering Gloria's in the hospital. Do they know why she fell?"

So Riley filled her in, and soon they were both sipping their hot brews while the dogs lounged on the couch. She ended with "I can never thank you enough for taking care of LouLou last night. You're the absolute best."

Eliza preened at the praise, smoothing her short hair behind an ear. "I do try. Honestly, it was no trouble—unless you're a tasseled throw pillow—and I can watch her again today if you need to go to the hospital."

Riley's tears surprised her. Dry-eyed one minute, she was crying the next. She'd been on the go for so long, always on call, always with her to-do list and budget constraints. She hadn't realized how much of a one-way street she'd been living on, always giving and never letting anyone in. That a kind word or action could reduce her to tears? Well, she blamed that on the orgasms, too. She was raw this morning, an exposed emotional nerve, exposed and apparently weeping.

Eliza leapt from her seat and came around the corner to hug her. "Honey, it'll be okay. Your Grams is a fighter. And so are we! I hurried over this morning because I heard from my friend at the Historical Preservation Society. Things are looking good. Very good. She says the Dorothy should sail through the approval process and be on the national registry of protected buildings in no time."

Riley hugged Eliza back extra hard. "That's wonderful news! I can't wait to tell Grams."

"What'd I miss?" Caleb leaned against the arch between the main living area and the hallway that led to the bedrooms. He was dressed in his usual khakis and polo, so usual they were the same ones he'd worn yesterday. They were a bit rumpled from doubling as pajamas and then their time spent on the floor, as was his hair. All in all, Caleb Donovan looked pretty darn good to Riley, rumpled and with the stubble he'd tickled her with still dotting his face. She sighed at the memory, tingling in places she didn't want to tingle with Eliza standing close.

Eliza looked from Caleb to Riley. "It's like that now, is it? Well, Sydney will be happy. She's been rooting for you two all along, and her money was on you getting together before the end of October, which puts me out a fiver. Patty's still in the game, though. She bet on a wedding before Christmas."

"A wedding?" Riley covered her face with one hand. Could this conversation get more embarrassing? "You bet on us? I can't believe you."

"What'd you bet?" Caleb sauntered into the kitchen and raised his eyes at the K-Cup collection and maybe the whole idea of nosy neighbors and wedding bets. Who knew what was running through his mind? He had his amiable businessman face on. He wasn't a raw nerve, twanging with every shift of emotional wind in the room. Maybe he had mind-blowing sex all the time. Maybe this morning was business as usual for him. Riley found herself tearing up again. God, it was worse than puberty, this business of opening up her heart again.

Wait, was that what she was doing? Opening her heart to him? A Donovan? The man who fired her? He stood next to her, his hand to the small of her back, thumb tracing small circles on the skin between the soft fabric of her shirt and waist of her jean shorts. Goose bumps rose on her arms. Yeah, that was definitely what she was doing. Stupid or not—and she suspected stupid indeed—she had to admit Caleb Donovan was working his way into her heart, one body-melting touch at a time.

"Help yourself." Riley gestured at the array of coffees. She did pride herself on always having at least a dozen choices on hand. He chose a dark roast and rolled it in his hands before popping it in the Keurig. She flushed, watching those hands, remembering where they'd been a few short hours ago. *Focus, Riley.* "Yeah, Eliza, what did you bet on? Lust on Labor Day? Reckless during Rosh Hashanah? Homicide by Halloween?"

Eliza laughed so hard, coffee spilled out of her mug. "Nothing that dramatic. Humped and dumped, to be honest. No offense, Caleb. You don't make the greatest first impression."

"Something of a cynic, aren't you?" Caleb sipped his dark roast from a mug that said *World's Best Granddaughter*.

"Me?" Eliza chuckled. "Have you met yourself? Can't believe how long it takes young people these days to get around to admitting their feelings."

Since no feelings had been discussed this morning, Riley ducked her head, her hair shielding her flaming cheeks. Maybe they hadn't discussed any feelings, but she'd sure felt the feelings. All the feelings. She sneaked a side peek at Caleb. Had he felt them, too?

He knocked back his coffee in a few gulps. "Why don't we head back to the hospital? I'm sure you're worried about Grams."

"Sure, give me a few minutes to clean up her place first. Don't want the bloodstains retraumatizing her." How could she be worrying about what Caleb did or didn't feel when Grams was still in the hospital? Out-of-whack hormones were no joke, a lesson she'd learned during puberty but had apparently forgotten lately.

"Eliza, would you mind sticking around for LouLou? I'll text when I know what's going on."

Eliza saluted her. "Dog sitter on duty."

Riley kissed her cheek. "I appreciate you."

"I know you do." Eliza pulled her into a hug. "Remember you've got people, Riley. People who love you."

Stupid hormones and orgasms and raw emotional nerves. She sniffed back more tears. "I love you, too."

CHAPTER 26

HE WAS JEALOUS OF AN OLD WOMAN. AND A DOG. AFTER declaring her love to Eliza, Riley'd kissed her poodle's head, saying, "I love you. Be home soon," before gathering up cleaning supplies to take to Grams' place. What would it be like to hear those words from Riley? He pushed the longing away. There was no point in it.

As blessed as Donovans were at real estate deals, they were equally cursed when it came to love. Look at Grandpa William, a string of marriages and mistresses, and his own father on wife number four. Lance, who'd been so happy at his wedding that he'd said "I do" too early during the ceremony, causing the whole audience to laugh at his eagerness, was already divorced. Caleb's own disastrous marriage was the evidence that cinched his case.

He'd suspected that Lisa was as attracted to his family's wealth as she was to him, but her immediate filing for divorce as soon as his assets were frozen had proven him wrong. She'd loved the wealth *more* than she loved him. What more could he expect, though? Donovans were workaholics and womanizers. Hadn't he heard that line enough times from Grandpa William growing up? Like it or not, it was part of who he was, and when Riley realized it, she'd leave, too.

She hadn't realized it yet. She kept her eyes on the road, driving them back to the hospital, one hand on the wheel, one clutched in his, both pink from all the scrubbing she'd done at Grams' place. He'd offered to hire someone to come clean, but she'd refused, saying Grams liked things a certain way and it was easier for her to do it than to explain how to someone else. That was how she was, he'd learned. Generous and genuine, willing to do anything for those she loved, no matter the inconvenience. He'd like to be loved like that someday. The longing he'd forced away came back, nearly choking him with its strength. He didn't want some day. He wanted today. With Riley.

Was he holding her hand too tightly? She didn't seem to mind. He loosened his grip, just in case she needed some circulation in her fingers. He shouldn't be selfish, thinking of what he wanted from Riley at a time like this. She was worried about her Grams, certainly not thinking about this morning or what it might mean for them. He needed to give her space, yet he couldn't force himself to let go of her hand. A few minutes longer, he promised himself, and then he'd let her do her thing.

At the hospital, they were lucky to find a parking spot on the same level as his Porsche. The image of her walking solo into the hospital saddened him. Of course she could handle it on her own, but why should she have to? "Do you want me to come with you?"

She brought his knuckles to her lips and kissed them. "Thank you, but I'm not sure Grams is ready for this."

He nodded like he understood what she meant by *this*. Him? Them? Were they a thing now? God knows, he didn't want to let her hand go, let her walk away from him, even if it was to take care of her Grams. "Sure. I'll see you later?"

She leaned across the console, her lips touching his in a brief kiss that wasn't nearly enough. He caught the back of her head and brought her back for a longer, deeper kiss. One that made him wish she had a bigger back seat and that they weren't in a crowded parking garage and that they could take a break from life for the day. Or week. Or month.

Riley pulled away first. "I really need to check on her."

He nodded, nibbling at her lips one last time. "I'll call you later? I have an appointment with the architect early tomorrow at the Dorothy. Do you want to meet him?"

Riley's eyes shuttered. He'd said the wrong thing. He tried to make it right. "I'd love your opinions."

She squeezed her eyes closed, then opened them, blinking rapidly. "Sure, call me."

"I will."

Riley slipped out of the car, and he watched her walk away, wondering why the last few minutes had felt so wrong. Was it that he wanted to be with her? What if she got bad news about her grandmother? What if she needed to lean on his shoulder? He shook his head at the foolishness. Riley didn't need anyone, especially not him. He shouldn't make this morning more than it was. Still, he pulled up his calendar, double-checking the time for the meeting with the architect. He was eager to show her what they'd come up with. A business meeting, yeah, that was what he was looking forward to. Just business.

"It's good to be home. Never thought I'd be so happy to be in my own bed again, but I slept like a baby last night." Grams let out a drafty sigh and settled herself into her favorite corner of the couch. Riley helped her tuck a soft blanket over her lap. The Prince immediately jumped up and made himself at home, kneading her thighs with his front paws.

"Someone's glad you're up and about today." Riley gave the Prince an affectionate scratch behind the ear, thinking about how her own night had been long and restless. After only one night with Caleb, sleeping alone had felt wrong— her bed too wide, her pillows not as comfortable as his chest.

"Slept next to me all night." Grams stroked him from head to tail, and he purred his contentment. "Snug as a bug in a rug, weren't you, my Prince?"

"I'm glad you're feeling yourself again." Riley sat close to Grams, bumping their knees together. LouLou'd slept close to her last night, too, but it wasn't the same. Maybe she needed a cat. Or maybe she just needed Caleb. "You gave me quite a scare."

"You and me both, darlin'. I hardly remember what happened, but the pain when my head hit the tile? Ouch! That I'll never forget." Grams reached out and patted Riley's leg. "You took good care of me, and I'm grateful. But please don't think you have to hang around all day like I'm an invalid. I'm perfectly capable of taking care of myself."

"That's good to hear." Riley leaned over to kiss Grams' cheek, surprised that Grams was hustling her out the door. "I do have a few things to do for the Dorothy today, and LouLou could use a good run at the park. Please call me if you need something, okay?"

"You know, they nearly starved me at that hospital, waiting hours and hours for a cold bowl of oatmeal. Then last night, I simply didn't feel up to cooking, so I drank one of my Ensure shakes. Won't you make me a bite to eat, Riley, before you go?"

"Of course." Riley should've known the independence speech was all for show. She checked the time on her phone. Fifteen minutes ago, Caleb had texted, inviting her to one of the empty units to look at plans with the architect. Fifteen minutes ago, she'd thought she was minutes away from getting Grams settled in the living room, resting, and could step out for a little bit. *Sorry*, she texted now. *Don't think I can leave anytime soon.*

First, she'd make Grams a snack, then Grams would want something to drink. Then another blanket. Then help moving to the bedroom. Then the light would be too bright, then not bright enough. For the most part, Grams was an independent woman, but when the opportunity arose to play the invalid, she took shameless advantage. Riley still remembered Grams' bout with bronchitis a few years back. She'd started sleeping on Grams' couch. It was easier that way.

We'll come to you! Caleb's text was followed with a smiley emoji.

She looked at the text. She looked at Grams. Oil and water.

Ok, she texted back because the truth was, she missed him. Missed having him near, his hand on her lower back, his quick smile at her touch. She was falling fast; she recognized the signs. Would Grams? She'd keep it all business, a property manager consulting with an owner on proposed improvements. Grams would appreciate getting the inside scoop on the architectural plans anyway. Give her something to talk about at the next bunco night.

"Who could that be?" Grams asked when her doorbell rang, sitting straighter and pulling a crocheted blanket over her lap. The Prince immediately stood and headbutted her belly. "Tell whoever it is I'm too tired for company. I want to rest up after all that hospital put me through. A substance-abuse counselor, can you imagine? At my age! I'm sure I know when I've had enough to drink and don't need someone younger than my own granddaughter suggesting otherwise."

"You did insist your fall was wine-related." Riley took her time getting to the door. Grams would not be happy that she'd invited Caleb—much less some strange architect—when she was looking less than her best. On the other hand, it was a chance for her to see Caleb's plans, including the dog park they'd been working on, and there was some part of Riley that wanted Grams to like Caleb. This could be a start. "The hospital is probably obligated to counsel anyone with substance-related injuries. I'm sure it was simply a formality."

"Trying to take away my chardonnay? I should turn them in for elder abuse." Grams harrumphed and petted the Prince under his ear in that spot that made him drool a little. Riley crossed the living room to peek out the peephole. She couldn't stop the smile that spread across her face at the sight, distorted as it was, of Caleb in a blue polo that matched his eyes. Goodness, the man was so handsome, her heart actually stuttered. *Ba-ba-bum.*

"In fact," Grams was saying, "why don't we offer our guests a glass? And you can pour me one too while you're at it."

"It's not even lunchtime yet." Riley finally opened the door. "Caleb, thank you for coming." She shelved the idea that her Grams was an alcoholic for the moment. A glass of wine a few times per week did not equal substance abuse. Of course, she'd do some research before completely dismissing the hospital's concerns, but Husband Two, Riley's grandfather, had been a drinker, and Grams made no secret of her disdain for his overindulgence, especially when his drinking habits led to his early death. Riley'd never known him, but she'd certainly heard plenty from Grams over the years about fighting her (possibly) genetic tendencies.

"Caleb Donovan!" Grams sat straighter, straightening her hair, straightening the blanket, fussing so much that the Prince jumped off her lap in a snit and positioned himself on top of the TV to keep an eye on the new guests. "Why on Earth are you darkening my door?"

"Grams, I invited him. He's here for business."

Caleb totally sabotaged her attempt to keep things business casual by dropping a kiss to her cheek, a general greeting in Miami but one that sent her to blushing in a way Grams was sure to notice.

"Meet Adam St. John. He's the architect working with me on the project. We brought some plans to show you." His hand dropped to the small of her back, to that place she was beginning to feel was his, the way he was always touching her there. The way she missed his touch when he wasn't there. She let herself be guided to a seat beside Grams.

"An architect! How nice to meet you, Mr. St. John. Forgive me for not standing to greet you. I'm still recovering from a stay in the hospital." Grams fussed with her blanket, antsy as the Prince after rolling in catnip, before offering her hand, fingers drooping like she expected him to kiss the back of it.

Adam St. John was possibly one of the tallest people

Riley'd ever seen, and Grams had to crane her neck up and up to bat her eyelashes in the helpless-damsel way she sometimes adopted around men. Attractive men. It didn't matter that Adam was forty years her junior. In Grams' book, a little flirting was never wasted time.

"A pleasure." Adam stooped from his great height to shake Grams' proffered hand and sat in the chair across the coffee table from the women. Caleb pulled in a dining room chair, angling it between Riley and Adam.

"Mrs. Carson, I hope you'll forgive our intrusion." Caleb crossed an ankle over his knee and leaned forward. "I'm excited to show you both what the plans for the building are."

"Please, call me Gloria." She tucked the blue-and-green crocheted blanket more tightly around her lap. "I suppose a bit of show-and-tell will be diverting. I could use some distraction from the awful things that woman at the hospital said."

Caleb paled. "Is everything okay?"

Before Grams could launch into a tirade, Riley cut her off. "She's in good health, except for that cut on her head. She's going to take it easy for a few days, which is why I'm grateful you could come to us." She was using her placating-guests voice. "Grams and I are both eager to know the fate of the Dorothy."

Adam cleared his throat. "It's nothing dire. Such a beautiful example of Deco architecture! It's been my pleasure to come up with a design that will preserve the history while still moving residents into the current century."

"Nothing wrong with the last century," Grams sniffed.

Adam flipped open a laptop and spun it in their

direction. "Caleb told me the building is at about half capacity, and we looked into current buying trends. These old Deco buildings—"

"They aren't that old," Grams muttered, squinting at the screen. Riley knew it would be futile to suggest she put on her glasses. Wear them in public? Never!

Caleb pushed forward, eagerness in his tone. "The point is that many of the buildings were designed as vacation homes. Inadequate closet space."

Riley nodded emphatically. What she wouldn't give for a spacious hall closet or even a small linen nook, a place to store all her shoes in one place. Maybe not on the scale of Sydney's setup, but the importance of storage should not be underestimated.

"And typically, one bedroom. Now, the manager's apartment has two bedrooms while the rest of the building consists of one-bedrooms and studios. At some point, they must've renovated. How did they do it?"

Adam opened up a program, and blueprints appeared on the screen. "They combined a studio and a one bedroom, and that's what we want to do with the rest of the units. Two bedrooms, rare on the Beach, even more rare in Deco buildings. It will make the place irresistible to new buyers." He scrolled through plans that made little sense to Riley.

"I could use another bedroom," Grams mused. "It's not a bad idea. How about a second bathroom? Or half bath?"

"Adam thought of that." Caleb pointed out the different layouts possible with different combinations of units. His phone buzzed midspeech about making the building ADA-compliant while still preserving its charm.

"Excuse me." Caleb checked the caller ID. "I have to take

this." He ducked his head, a finger to one ear, saying, "Give me a minute. I'm just leaving a meeting."

Adam scrolled through pages of landscaping plans, talking them through his ideas in a deep voice that sounded a bit how Riley imagined God would sound if he were to call down from the heavens with some architectural opinions. Miniature people walked through lush tropical landscapes. There was a fountain, a lion spitting water into a basin where blue jays bathed. Egrets stalked through the liriope ground cover.

"It looks the same as it did in my day." Grams beamed approvingly at the outdoor plans. "How delightful! Show us more!"

The next screen stole the breath from Riley's lungs. It was the dog park. Except it wasn't. A mammoth eyesore of a parking structure filled the entire lot.

"And here's the moneymaker," Adam was saying. "Of course, residents will park for free, but I was able to get about four times more spaces than the building needs into the square footage, which means the city will make money hand over fist so are sure to approve the plans."

"Why, that's quite hideous." Grams squinted as though she couldn't believe what she was seeing. "Nothing Deco there at all."

"We'll do some plantings around it, help it blend into the neighborhood." Adam forged ahead like Grams wasn't raining on every step of his parade.

"That eyesore isn't going to blend." Grams' voice pitched high into her about-to-launch-a-tirade range.

Riley didn't care about the garage. She cared about the dog park. The dog park Caleb had promised. The one they'd been working on. But Fur Haven was most definitely not in the plans. No getting around the facts. She'd slept with a liar.

She sprung from her seat and flung herself out the front door. Caleb leaned against a wall, phone to his ear. She didn't care that he was busy.

"How could you?"

He held up the wait-a-minute finger.

Oh no, he didn't just shush her. Her eyes narrowed, and she contemplated swatting the phone out of his hand. But that would be childish. She did it anyway.

"Hey!" He scrambled after the phone, picking it up off the carpet and managing a quick "I'll call you later" before stuffing it in his pocket. "What is wrong with you?"

"What's wrong with me? What's wrong with *you*?" She was so mad tears sprang to her eyes. Yeah, that was why she wanted to cry. Not because he'd lied to her. Not because she'd fallen for it. At least Aiden had never pretended to be something he wasn't. "A parking garage? What happened to the dog park? Our Fur Haven?"

Caleb's eyes widened. "He showed you those plans?"

"Duh." So what if anger made her childish? It wasn't like she was trying to impress him. "Quite a way to drop the bomb, by the way. Nice touch, stepping out while Adam did your dirty work."

"Wait, wait, wait." Caleb ran a hand over his short hair, ruffling it in a way Riley did not find cute. She didn't. "Let me explain."

Riley crossed her arms over her chest. Aiden had explained a lot of things to her, and it always managed to paint her in the wrong somehow. Being explained to was not her favorite thing, but she gave a curt nod and twirled her hand like *go on*.

"Adam did the parking structure first, when I was trying to get the council on board, remember? I haven't had a chance to talk to him about the dog park yet. That's all. It's an oversight. A big oversight on my part. I'm sorry, Riley. I didn't know he'd show you that part. I was excited about the conversion plans. I wanted to share them with you as soon as possible."

Riley rolled her hand again because she was afraid to open her mouth, afraid she'd say something stupid about understanding and forgiving because he really was cute with his contrite face and worried eyes.

"We can talk to him right now. I also wanted him to see your Grams' photos. Do you think she'll show him? He'd love to see how the place used to be, I'm sure, and maybe that will help him with his planning."

"Hmm." Riley wasn't mad anymore, just cautious. Suspicious. "I almost believe you."

"Almost?" Caleb took a step closer to her, then another and another, until he was crowding into her space, crowding her against the wall. He slapped his palms above her head and lowered his face to hers. "Believe this," he said, and he kissed her.

He was angry and maybe she was still, too. Their teeth clashed, tongues tangled. It wasn't like the sweet kisses of that first night together; it was angry and rough, and Riley found herself pressing against him, eager for more.

Caleb broke the kiss, panting. "We can't do this in the hallway."

Part of Riley didn't understand why not. She'd never

known that part of her before. *Nice to meet you, naughty Riley.* The other part of her straightened the hem of her T-shirt and cleared her throat. "Right. We should go back."

"Back to bed," Caleb murmured low enough for her to hear, then louder, "We'll talk to Adam together. It'll be fine. I promise."

But it wasn't fine.

"A dog park? I don't design dog parks." Adam pulled his computer protectively into his lap.

"It's simply another kind of outdoor landscaping." Riley folded her hands, clasping her fingers tightly enough that they turned white.

"Those were mock-ups. We'd obviously get a landscape designer on board later in the project."

"Can't you mock up a dog park?" Caleb had squished himself onto the sofa next to Riley. Their thighs touched, and she kept thinking about that kiss in the hallway. And getting back to her place, her bed. Which reminded her that LouLou would need to go out, and the frustration of waiting even those few minutes longer made her twitchy. So she squeezed her palms together and tried to think happy thoughts about frolicking puppies in a brand-new dog park designed just for them.

"I wouldn't know where to begin." Adam slammed his laptop closed, his sharply defined eyebrows drawing together. "We never talked about this."

"I know. I'm sorry." Caleb leaned forward, arms on knees. "Riley and I did some field research. Show him the list."

Riley pulled out her phone and thumbed to the right note. She held it out to Adam, but he waved it away.

"I'm happy to work on buildings with you, Caleb, but you're on your own for the dog park."

Caleb fell back against sofa. "If that's the way you feel."

"I do."

Caleb held out his hand for Adam to shake. "Then we have a deal. You handle the building. I'll handle the dog park."

Adam shook on it and took his leave. The Prince walked him to the door, tail high and twitching at the tip.

"Touchy thing, isn't he? I guess architects are like artists, so sensitive." Grams patted her lap, and the Prince rejoined her.

"He's wrong about one thing." Riley laced her fingers through Caleb's, done caring if Grams noticed or not.

"What's that?" The smile he gave her made her wish Grams already had that spare bedroom. And was deaf or at least gone for the day. Who knew it would be so hard for a woman who lived alone to get some privacy?

She smiled back. "You're not on your own."

"That's right." Grams eyed their joined hands but didn't comment. A miracle in itself. "You've got us. We'll all work on the dog park with you."

"All?" Caleb echoed.

"Sure." Grams nodded like it was a done deal. "Me. Patty. Eliza. Riley, of course."

"Of course." Riley grinned. "Sydney's already helping, calling in a few favors. It'll be fun."

"Fun," Caleb repeated, apparently stunned into parrot mode.

"Sure." Riley stood and pulled him with her. "How hard could it be? Some sod, some equipment, a few flyers."

"Aren't you the one who said we couldn't do it on our own? That we didn't know enough? And what do we need flyers for?"

"For the grand opening."

Grams beamed at them. "Halloween is a few weeks away. What a perfect grand opening theme!"

"Yes!" Riley turned excited eyes to Caleb. "A pet parade. Costumes!"

Caleb took a shuddering, deep breath. "Whatever you want, Riley."

"A Donovan committed to keeping a promise? I like this boy," Grams declared, shocking Riley into speechlessness. "Now get going, you two. Dog parks don't build themselves."

"No, they don't!" Caleb laughed and tugged Riley to the door. She followed, lists already writing themselves in her head. Fall-themed décor, local vendors, booths, face painting for kids, snacks for dogs, ample seating for the humans. So many details to get right, but she was the woman for the job. She'd never met a to-do list she couldn't conquer.

CHAPTER 27

THE WAVES SLAPPED LAZILY AGAINST THE FIBERGLASS hull of Grandpa William's Super Sport. Caleb powered the boat out to sea, keeping within sight of land but far enough that Lance wouldn't be able to jump ship and swim for shore. Right now, both Grandpa William and Lance were being civil, each sipping his drink of choice and staring out at the horizon as if the other one wasn't sitting in the deck chair next to him.

At fifty-five feet, the Super Sport was the smallest of Grandpa William's boats but the one he took out the most often, usually with a few friends on the pretext of fishing. Today's agenda was different, but Caleb still went through the ritual of setting up lines off the back of the boat, even though he didn't bait them and didn't expect anything to chomp down on an empty hook.

"Beautiful day, isn't it?" Caleb stretched arms overhead and inhaled the sea air. He really did love being out on the water. The salt spray, the sun, the pelicans diving for a meal. His best memories of growing up were out on this boat, Grandpa William teaching him to steer, how to avoid manatees, how to throw a line, how to pop the top off a beer bottle without an opener.

"It is." Grandpa William sipped at his Scotch, stretching his legs out in front of him. "Lots of beautiful days lately. Why'd you get us out on the boat today? You know I hate to miss my regular tee time at the golf course."

"Can't we enjoy some family time?" Caleb stalled, rifling through the custom Yeti for a Belgian ale.

"False pretenses." Lance chugged back half of his Silver Bullet. "What's up, little brother? I know you have some kind of master plan. You always do."

Caleb held up his hands, a bottle of Orval pale ale dangling between his thumb and forefinger. "There were no false pretenses. Boat, ocean, beer. That's what I promised you, and you've got all three."

"You didn't mention Grandpa William would be here." Lance's fingers tapped against his beer can in an impatient rhythm. Not even twenty minutes together, and already Caleb could tell Lance was itching to go. He'd always been restless, never one to sit still for long, always on the lookout for a pickup game of basketball or an impromptu race with friends. He'd even convinced Caleb to pretend they were MMA fighters a time or two, a stunt that ended in black eyes and bruises for both of them.

"Please, you knew it was his boat. When has he ever let us take it out on our own?" Caleb set the boat to autopilot and popped open his Orval. How Lance could drink American lagers, he had no idea. But to each his own, he supposed.

"I'm sitting right here." Grandpa William poured himself another finger of Scotch and let out a long sigh. "Do tell us, Caleb, what's the plan?"

"Aren't you suspicious? Can't I just want to spend some time with you?" Caleb thought about how Riley didn't need a reason to see Grams. They were in and out of each other's lives on a daily basis. No need for formal invitations or official reasons. What was it like to have that kind of ease, not to feel as if every meeting needed an agenda and actionable items to justify their time together?

"Seriously?" Lance snorted and wandered to the deck railing, and he motioned Caleb over with urgent waves of his fingers. "Look, we've got dolphins!"

Two dolphins leapt out of the water in a perfectly synchronized movement that left Caleb feeling like a kid again—the best part of being a kid when the world was filled with these moments of awe.

"They're beautiful." Caleb and Lance stared out over the water, waiting for another glimpse of sleek, gray dolphins, but the pod had apparently already moved on. The wind ruffled the water, creating small white crests and tiny eddies. After a few long moments had passed and no more dolphins came into view, Caleb turned and leaned his back against the railing.

"Grandpa William, I've done some digging into the Dorothy's finances." Might as well get it over with so they could all go home.

"Finally, we get to the point." Lance propped his elbows on the railing and lifted his chin to catch the sun.

"I'd expect nothing less, Caleb." Grandpa William nodded curtly. "You've always been good with numbers."

A compliment? From his grandfather? Caleb and Lance exchanged equally shocked looks.

"Thanks." Caleb swished the beer in the bottle, ignoring the fact that his phone vibrated in his pocket. "The thing is, the Dorothy's numbers don't add up. I'm afraid it's not only that Rainy Day missed the forty-year inspection. They've been hosing you, Grandpa."

Grandpa William sat up straight, clunking his glass

heavily on the arm of the deck chair. "What do you mean?"

"Fraud. They've been skimming money. If I'm right, it's been years."

Grandpa William used his cane to push to a standing position. "One measly heart event, and the vultures close in to take everything they can." He thumped his way to the railing, pausing with the rock of the boat to catch his balance.

"It goes back longer than that. Possibly decades. I need to do a deep dive, but I wanted to get your permission first. If it's as bad as I suspect, we're going to have to press charges. And given we're involved, it'll be in the media."

"Great." Lance stormed to the cooler for another beer. "Just what my business needs. More corrupt Donovan publicity."

Caleb crossed his arms over his chest. "That's why I wanted us to talk this out together. Technically, we're the victims in this scenario, but that's not how the media is likely to play it. They loved watching our father get put away. They'll use any reason to bring all that up again."

Grandpa William stared out to where ocean met sky, that long stretch of flat horizon always inexplicably out of reach. "If what you suspect is true, what do you need from me?"

"Access to all the financials." Caleb stood close to his grandfather, worried about the slump to his shoulders, the gray cast to his skin. "I've already put in a call to the insurance company. Rainy Day is reporting yearly fees at almost double what we're being charged. I need all the records for as far back as I can get to see what else they're padding. Once I have my case, we'll go to the authorities."

Grandpa William clenched the railing in one hand, his other hand still firm on his cane. "I can't believe I let this happen. I should've known better than to trust a management company, but I didn't want to get too close to Gloria's building. She needed her space."

"It's not your fault." Caleb wanted to put his arm around his grandfather's shoulders but wasn't sure how that would go over with the old man. His phone vibrated again, but now was not the time to check messages. Instead he said, "The good news is that if they've stolen as much as I think they have, reparations will more than pay for the renovations the Dorothy needs."

Lance popped the top of his can and took a long swig. "I don't know. She's going to need a lot."

"Precisely." Caleb leaned against the railing and took a pull from his own drink. "I am talking a lot of money. Enough money that we wouldn't have to evict the current residents. We could offer them the option to buy in or keep renting like they are now, and we'd still have enough money to fix up the empty units for rent or sale. It's a win-win."

Grandpa William slashed his cane through the air, silver handle flashing in the sunlight. "I don't like it. The plan was for you three boys to work together to overhaul this property, make it truly profitable, enough that you could buy another property and then another. Rebuild the business together. Now your only plan is a facelift. That's not how you build a dynasty."

This time, Caleb did put an arm around his grandpa's shoulders. "That's another reason I brought you out here today. Lance, do you want to go into business with me?"

Lance snorted. "Hell no."

"See, Grandpa, Lance isn't interested. And Knox won't even return my calls. But I wanted you to see that I can do this on my own. I found the problem at Rainy Day, and I'll get it fixed. With that money, I can move forward on the renovations."

"No, it's you three boys together or no deal. I told you the terms up front, Caleb. They don't change just because they're difficult to fulfill." Grandpa William stomped toward the prow, shaking off Caleb's arm.

A pelican swooped close, nearly touching the deck, before diving into the ocean and emerging with a fat fish in its beak. It tossed the fish into the air, and in a single gulp, the fish slid headfirst down its gullet.

Lance crossed his arms over his chest, feet planted against the roll of the deck. "Why is it important to you? The three of us working together?"

It was quiet so long it seemed Grandpa William wouldn't answer, but finally, he let out a long sigh. "When I started Donovan Real Estate Group, it was with my brother, Eddy. You would've liked him. Everyone did. He was a real charmer."

Caleb was confused. He'd never heard of an Eddy Donovan. From the blank look on Lance's face, he was equally surprised.

"He died. Lung cancer, real young. We didn't know about smoking back in those days, you know? And he was a couple-packs-a-day kind of guy. Real life of the party. After he was gone, the business wasn't as fun anymore. I got tunnel vision, only cared about profits. That's how I raised your father and look where it got him."

Caleb's throat tightened. He'd never considered that his

grandfather might feel guilty for what happened to Robert. Never really thought about Grandpa William feeling anything but embarrassment for how it all went down. There was a sheen in Grandpa William's eyes that spoke to the truth.

"You boys have to work together, don't you see? Put family first and everything will be okay. You won't turn out like Robert. Or me. Because you'll have each other." Grandpa William wiped at the shine in his eye with a knuckle. His cane clattered to the deck.

Caleb picked it up and handed it back to his grandfather. "I didn't know about Eddy. I'm sorry."

Lance joined them, clamping a strong hand on Grandpa William's back. "Me too. That's a real sad story."

Grandpa William turned hopeful eyes to Lance. "You'll do it? Go into business with Caleb?"

Lance's nostrils flared. "Now, I didn't say anything about that. The past is the past, Grandpa William, and we have to move on. I've got my own business. Caleb has a sound plan for this property of yours, and Knox is off saving the world. You have to let us lead our own lives."

Grandpa William's knuckles turned white from the tight grip on his cane. "My terms are my terms. If you three don't work together, I'll sell the Dorothy to the highest bidder, and that is my final offer."

Caleb's phone vibrated again, and Grandpa William poked his cane angrily in Caleb's direction. "Answer the damn phone, Caleb. What is the emergency anyway?"

Caleb palmed his phone, scrolling through a thread of text messages. "It's Riley. I'm in some kind of group text about the dog park grand opening. They got a vegan dog treat baker to sign on, and everyone's very excited."

"Vegan dogs." Grandpa William chuckled. "This thing is going to be a disaster."

Caleb scanned the congratulatory texts and the many, many dog photos that were part of the thread. He smiled. "It's going to be amazing. Grandpa William, tell me you'll come. Let me show you why my plan will work in this community. Give me a chance."

"I'll be there." Lance swigged the last of his beer, wiping at his mouth with the back of his hand. "I miss my dog something terrible. Divorce sucks."

"Don't I know it." Grandpa William raised the last of his Scotch in a toast.

"You'll be there?" Caleb refilled Grandpa William's glass and tossed Lance another Silver Bullet.

Grandpa William eyed him over the rim. "I suppose."

Lance clicked his can to Caleb's bottle. "Cheers to that. Good luck, little brother. You're going to need it."

———————————

Caleb followed the sound of excited chatter to Grams' place. When he knocked, a frazzled Sydney opened the door and waved him in. "Come on, come on. We need more hands on deck."

Grams' furniture had been moved aside, leaving a wide swath of burgundy carpet as a work space. Grams sat on the sofa, her plump cat contentedly curled up on her lap, overseeing the proceedings. Although Eliza, Sydney, and some other women whose names Caleb didn't know but who he'd never seen without a pug between them were present, no dogs crowded the living room. He thought that it was a shame that the dogs couldn't be part of preparing for their own party. *Maybe it's better this way,* he mused, *more of a surprise for them.*

Riley sat cross-legged on the floor, finger-painting a large sign for, well, finger painting. When she spotted him across the room, her face lit with a welcoming smile. He checked the other occupants of the room. Nope, no one else was blinded by the sight. Just him. He held out a hand, and she hopped up to give him a quick peck on the cheek.

"It's about time. You don't want to miss the painting!" She pulled him down to sit next to her and pushed some finger paints his way while introducing him to Kiki and Paula. Kiki kept busy with paint markers and stencils, and Paula counted out raffle tickets in sets of ten.

Caleb had overseen the grand opening of the Tucson resort, the casino in the Virgin Islands, even a small reopening of a property in Orlando, and he'd never been asked to finger-paint a single thing. When was the last time he'd dipped a finger in a jar of paint? Kindergarten? First grade?

"Your signature pink is smearing." He traced the dot of pale pink on Riley's cheek as it streaked back toward her gleaming hair.

"I'll show you some signature." She scooped a blob of deep blue and dabbed it on his forehead. "Still not as blue as your eyes, but definitely your color." She leaned up and kissed the tip of his nose. "We've got work to do. Booth signs don't paint themselves."

"Show me what to do. I'm in."

They fell into a pattern. She outlined words in big bubble letters, and he methodically painted them in. He tried to stay focused on the work, but Riley's constant up and down to fetch glasses of lemonade for Eliza or a water bottle for Sydney made it impossible to stay on task. The women laughed and, if he wasn't mistaken, were also texting each other while talking. It was a whirlwind, so when the door opened and Mr. Cardoza walked in, he let out a relieved sigh.

"I come to help!" Mr. Cardoza brandished a large tray of tiny coffees and a box of empanadas. He circled the room like a waiter, talking to each person for a moment before moving on. When he got to Caleb he said, "Eh, Mr. Donovan, our Riley's brought you to the right side of this fight, I see."

"It doesn't have to be a fight." Caleb took a sip of coffee and almost groaned with pleasure.

"What else could it be?" Grams nibbled at an empanada, flakes of crust sticking to her bottom lip. "It's a fight for our home. For our way of life."

Nothing was definite. Caleb had a lot more work to do to prove his theory about Rainy Day, and even more work to compel them to pay the money back. Looking at the faces around him, though, he hated the thought they tolerated him only because of Riley. They still saw him as the enemy. Maybe that had been true at first, but looking at their paint-streaked faces, sipping Mr. Cardoza's amazing coffee, he just wanted it to be over. *Face it, Donovan. You want them to like you.*

So, against his better judgment, he told them about his meeting with his grandfather on the boat.

"I can't believe Lance won't help you out. That boy needs a talking-to." Grams sniffed and empanada crumbs trembled, then fell to her lap where the Prince quickly lapped them up.

"That's what you can't believe?" Riley capped a jar of paint too aggressively. "Rainy Day's been stealing from us!"

"Allegedly. Possibly." Caleb held up his hands. "We can't go around accusing them until we have more facts."

"But you're sure." Riley searched his face.

He nodded.

"Then you're our hero, aren't you? I can't believe I never thought to question the reports they sent me. I feel stupid."

"How could you have known?" Caleb soothed a hand down her back. "They're good at covering their tracks. I wouldn't be surprised if an investigation reveals ours is not the only building involved. I've seen the financials on lots of projects, and the Dorothy had the numbers of a much larger property. It didn't add up."

"I should've suspected." Riley leaned in to his side, and he liked the way she fit just so against his shoulder. "But if I didn't, I'm glad you did."

"Well." Eliza stood and wiped her hands down the sides of her ankle-length skirt. "I suppose I need to amend the lawsuit to name Rainy Day rather than the Donovans."

Caleb inclined his head toward her. "That would be much appreciated."

"I suppose there's nothing to it. You and I will have to work together to nail those bastards." Eliza held out her hand to shake.

Caleb had thought he'd be using his grandfather's legal team, and maybe at some point in the process he would. For now, though, working with Eliza was the best business proposition he'd heard in a long time. He shook her hand. "You've got yourself a deal."

Mr. Cardoza collected empty coffee cups from Kiki and

Paula. "Can the next meeting be at my apartment? All this excitement is good for the soul, I think. I can cook a nice dinner."

Sydney whipped out a massive planner, and before he knew it, Caleb was committed to dinner with Mr. Cardoza, a brunch at Eliza's, and drinks at Sydney's, all in service of the grand opening preparation, but watching as Riley dutifully updated her calendar and Grams looked over the group with undisguised pride, Caleb suspected that the project was secondary. These people really liked each other, and because of Riley, he was now one of them.

CHAPTER 28

RILEY MOANED AT THE SOUND OF HER ALARM, SO chipper and darn optimistic in the morning, and fumbled on the side table to hit Snooze. All she managed to do was knock her phone onto the floor, where the alarm continued to buzz its cheerful crickets-on-the-hillside greeting. She was about to swing her feet over, plant them on the floor, and do her grown-up adulting thing, when an arm snaked around her waist and pulled her into the heat of Caleb's body.

Oh yeah. That. Suddenly, the cricket alarm seemed further away. She wiggled into her favorite spooning position and let out a deep sigh. "That's nice. You're nice."

"I'm trying." His hand swept up her stomach and cupped her breast. Caleb hadn't spent every night of the past few weeks here, but enough that she suspected what was coming next and knew she had to hush the alarm or it would seriously spoil her chance to enjoy being the sole focus of Caleb's attention.

"Give me a sec." She tried jackknifing her body and hanging her shoulders over the bed. Caleb didn't seem to mind the extra pressure of her butt to his groin. In fact, he pushed back, helping her forward those crucial few inches so she could reach her phone. "Got it."

Thankfully, the crickets hushed. She flipped to face him, cupping his face in her hands, holding them nose to nose.

And nose. LouLou hopped onto the bed and pushed her snout under Riley's wrists, bumping for attention.

"'Morning, LouLou." Caleb patted the dog. "You need to go out?"

"I'll do it." Riley liked Caleb staying over, liked it a lot, but she wasn't ready to share dog-care duties yet. She wouldn't want LouLou to come to rely on him and then one day, *poof*, he disappears and LouLou never knows what happened or why. Yeah, it was LouLou Riley worried about feeling abandoned. She didn't have abandonment issues of her own, not at all. And they certainly weren't aimed at her ex, or dad or mom. No, they weren't. She dropped her feet to the floor, and the dog dashed out of the room.

LouLou seemed to know it was a special day. Before Riley even had the chance to hit Start on the Keurig, the poodle had her nose pressed to the front door, her tail thumping wildly against her back. At the sound of the coffee maker initiating its duties, LouLou whined and pawed at the weather stripping at the bottom of the door.

"LouLou, no!" Riley hated replacing the weather stripping, but unfortunately, life with this particular poodle meant it was a biannual chore. "Do you need to go out?"

Riley walked toward the back door to let LouLou out onto the patio, but the poodle wasn't having it. She amped up her whining, pawing more frantically at the door.

The doorbell rang.

Riley checked the clock over the stove. Who on Earth would come by this early in the morning? Maybe Sydney was swinging by with a dog park opening outfit, some kind of athleisure perhaps, with a matching outfit for LouLou. Riley chuckled at the mental image and opened the door without looking through the peephole.

"Sorry for barging in this early." It was Sydney, garment

bag in one hand, drink carrier in the other. "I'm really excited about today! I wanted to get an early start and figured you'd want to be the first to see the changes anyway. I can't wait for the temporary fences to come down so we can finally see everything. Did I mention I'm excited? Because I am!"

"Me, too, especially if one of those is for me." Riley swept the door open.

"Of course!" Sydney handed over a cup. "Mocha latte with coconut milk. That's how you know we're friends. I know your Starbucks order."

Riley would've laughed, but she was too busy sucking down caffeine. "Where's Chewy?"

"Right here!" Sydney spun around, showing Chewy dangling from a baby-type backpack, his itty-bitty legs sticking out in all directions. She knelt down to let him out, and soon he and LouLou were out on the patio having a good sniff. He even used her two-by-two box of grass to pee in, which meant she had to pee in it, too. Then he peed on top of that pee, and that kind of one-upmanship could go on all day, so Riley led Sydney to the couch.

"No one's coming for setup until eight," Riley reminded Sydney, although she couldn't be mad at someone who brought her lattes in the morning. "What exactly was your plan?"

"Pure nosiness. But then I figured you'd be curious, too. We can grab a sneak peek, then come back later with the supplies."

"Sounds great." Caleb entered the living room, tucking a dark polo shirt into the khakis he'd worn yesterday. "I'm excited to see it myself."

Sydney's eyes widened. She took a gulp of her coffee and

then another gulp. And another. Finally, she said, "Sorry I didn't bring you anything. I didn't know—"

Caleb waved away her concern. "Don't worry about it. I can fend for myself." He headed for the Keurig, which was almost done with the cup Riley'd started anyway. "Do you think we'll get many people today?"

"Are you kidding?" Sydney sat one foot under her, the other dangling to the floor. "It's going to be chaos."

"The good kind, I hope." Caleb smiled over his *Crazy Poodle Lady* mug. Riley's brain melted just a little, watching him sip out of the corny coffee cup Grams had brought back for her from one of her field trips to the outlet malls with some of the other women in the building. He really was a kind man. A good man. She hoped everyone would see that today.

"Dogs!" Riley called, and the poodle and Chihuahua came running in. "Let's do this, shall we?"

The morning was the very best type of South Florida fall day—not cool, but not sweltering and humid, either. The light breeze off the ocean made Riley wish she'd worn a T-shirt instead of her tank top. Florida problems, she reminded herself. She could always change later. The festivities weren't supposed to start for another few hours.

Yet even though the scheduled start time was hours away and the volunteers weren't scheduled to arrive for another hour, the dog park was plenty busy. Lady was on her back in the middle of the newly laid sod—St. Augustine grass—big paws wiggling in the air as she got in a good back scratch. Smaller dogs raced from tree to tree in a sniffing extravaganza. Princess Pugsley sat at the top of the A-frame ramp, regally surveying the goings-on.

Caleb unhitched the first gate. "After you."

Riley and Sydney unclipped the dogs and hung the leashes on the multihook leash rack in the holding area. After making sure the first door was secured, Riley opened the second gate. LouLou and Chewy dashed toward Lady, tails wagging a thousand miles per minute.

"So fancy with a gate!" Sydney wiped her palms on her yoga pants. "Imagine not squeezing through the crack in the fence anymore. And no more escapees now that there's the holding area. Antechamber? What should we call it?"

"I don't know, but it's sure going to give dog owners peace of mind. Everything looks fantastic!" Riley'd seen the sections, even paged through never-ending lists of equipment with Caleb, choosing the right accessories for their dog park, but nothing had prepared her for the reality of it.

The grass was a healthy green and stretched in an uninterrupted plain. A plastic-coated chain-link fence enclosed the perimeter, and another length of fence bisected the park into small- and large-dog sections. A gate at the north end allowed the two sections to be joined, and now the gates stood open, dogs racing from side to side with no regard for size. On the small-dog side, the agility equipment was sized for small to medium-size dogs. Jumps, weave poles, rings. Riley couldn't wait to see what LouLou thought of them. On the large-dog side, the ramps, tunnels, and a seesaw were big enough to challenge even Lady.

Right now, no one was using the agility equipment. The dogs sniffed and marked each piece, of course, but the owners gathered near the grouping of newly planted trees—placed to provide shade to both sides of the park once they grew to their full size—and enjoying the comfort of the dog-bone-shaped benches.

Riley checked her watch. "The volunteers and vendors should be here soon. Let's think about where everything should go."

Sydney pulled a tablet out of her see-through backpack. "On it, boss. I already have a few options sketched out."

After a few clicks, she tabbed through her designs until Riley said, "That one. You've been incredibly helpful, Sydney. What would I have done without you?"

"It was my pleasure." Sydney looped her arm through Riley's and steered her toward the other owners. "See, you'll get the hang of this friendship thing eventually. For now, let's make sure all these folks are coming back later to spend their money. Our Howling Halloween party must be a howling success!"

Fur Haven Dog Park. Caleb loved the intricate iron scrollwork that spelled out the park's name over the front gate. He'd overseen the construction of twenty-story high-rises, five-star resorts in foreign countries, even a luxury spa or two, but he couldn't be prouder of this dog park if he'd single-handedly built it himself. Oh wait, he had. Not actually, of course.

They'd eventually caved to necessity and hired a landscaper to deal with the sod and new plantings. A handyman Lance recommended assembled and installed the equipment and benches. Other than the actual work, though, this was Caleb's first project completed all on his own. Okay, not on his own, either, but his new partner was definitely not the usual Donovan conglomerate. He searched for her in the crowd.

Riley waved at him from across the length of the park, a hot-pink shirt with a rhinestone lipstick kiss helping her stand out from the other owners. No one brightened a day like Riley, and her organizational skills had kept everything running smoothly, no setbacks on her tightly managed schedule. With everything in place, today could truly be a celebration of what they'd accomplished.

"Your father would be proud of you. How I wish he could be here with us."

Caleb flinched at the sound of his mom's voice. He spun to find her directly behind him. "What're you doing here?"

"That's a fine way to greet your mother." She leaned in to let him kiss both her cheeks. "You didn't think Mr. Pom-Pom would enjoy your dog park?"

The Pomeranian in question rode in a custom Hermès bag, his fur freshly groomed, head peeking out of the gap between the handles. When he saw Caleb, he shivered with delight and pushed a paw out of the bag.

"Hey there, little guy." Caleb shook Mr. Pom-Pom's paw and got his knuckle licked in response. "How did you even find out about today?"

"Was it a secret?" His mom pushed her Louis Vuitton sunglasses on top of her head, her carefully kept ice-blond hair a perfectly straight curtain to her shoulders.

"No." Caleb rocked on his feet. Where was Riley? Didn't she need him for something? Anything? But no one came to his rescue. "I'm just surprised to see you."

"If you must know, you suspicious thing, your father told me." She lifted Mr. Pom-Pom out of the bag and held him under her arm. He squirmed a few seconds before settling with his head on her arm. "Though I can't imagine it would've been all that hard for you to pick up a phone and let me know yourself."

"Robert?" That made even less sense. "I didn't tell him anything. I wouldn't tell him anything."

"Your grandfather visited. When was it, maybe last week? Filled him in on the details." She ran French-manicured fingers through Mr. Pom-Pom's fur. "Of course I had to come and see it for myself."

"To see if I'd embarrassed the family, no doubt." He'd rocked so much on his heels that he'd dug an indentation into the new sod.

His mom narrowed her eyes at him. "How could you say that? When did I ever miss an awards ceremony? A graduation? I've always been here for you, Caleb. You know that."

"Except when you weren't." Now was not the time to get into it with her. He knew that. Too many people around, and she'd clearly come to be nice. Years of feeling like second choice bubbled to the surface, though. "If you were in town, you came to everything. You were gone a lot, though."

"You know why I had to travel with your father." Her mouth straightened into a tight line.

He'd upset her, but apparently he wasn't done yet because he found himself saying, "Yes, I'm well aware how all our lives have to revolve around him. Here's a change, though. Not anymore. This is my thing."

"You're still angry." His mom soothed fingers over Mr. Pom-Pom's head. "You have to forgive him someday."

Riley was walking toward him, LouLou trotting at her heels even though she wasn't on a leash. He let out a long breath. "Not today."

His mom looked him up and down. "No, apparently not. Eventually, though. I'll call you about setting up a visit."

Before he could tell her not to waste her time, Riley arrived, sliding in next to him and leaning in to his side. His arm came around her, and the jaw he hadn't realized was quite so tight relaxed.

"Mom, meet Riley. Riley, this is my mother, Christine."

"Nice to meet you. How wonderful of you to come today!" Riley kissed the air near his mother's cheek in greeting.

His mom took in the rhinestones, the stringy jean shorts, the pink-and-yellow polka-dot flip-flops. He feared what would come out of her mouth, but all she said was, "And who's this adorable fur baby?" and pointed to LouLou with her one free hand.

"This is my LouLou." Riley squatted to pet her dog. Mr. Pom-Pom wiggled so much that eventually his mom let him down. LouLou and the Pomeranian took a few moments to suss each other out, then LouLou took off at a run, and Mr. Pom-Pom followed, yipping in delight.

"Mr. Pom-Pom, come!" Caleb's mom called, but the dog ignored her, already halfway across the park with his new friend.

"He's perfectly safe," Riley assured her, eyes on the dogs. "Caleb's created a really great space here for the neighborhood, don't you think?"

Although he'd been thinking something similar earlier, he didn't like that she didn't mention her part in the process. "Riley and I planned it together. The whole community came together, actually. It was quite the collaboration."

"It's nice." His mom shrugged the Hermès bag up higher on her shoulder. "I mean it, Caleb. You've made something of your own here. We're proud of you."

He sought out Riley's hand and squeezed it, hard, because he loved his mom, he really did, even with her revisionist history and blind loyalty to his father. He'd always wondered why she didn't leave, like Robert's other wives had, but today, for the first time, he was glad she'd stayed. What would his life have been like without her?

For all the times he'd felt left out of his parents' tight twosome, there were also the memories of her beaming face at his graduations, her urging him to blow out candles on his birthday cakes, the soft touch of her hand checking his forehead for a fever. She'd done the best she could. He acknowledged that now. He didn't know what it would change, but something did feel lighter and brighter within him.

"Give her a tour." Riley tugged him closer to his mom. "I need to check on a few details with the vendors, but make sure she stops by the bakery booth. There are these cookies that are apparently good for both dogs and humans!" She dashed away with a jaunty wave, and he immediately felt the loss of her presence. Alone with his mother in the first time since forever, he decided the best thing to do was follow Riley's suggestions.

"Shall we?" He crooked an arm.

She placed her hand on his elbow. "We shall."

Caleb marveled at how the dog park really did bring people together. Or maybe, he reflected after showing his mother the dog bakery and splitting a pumpkin-spice cookie with her, just maybe, the magic was Riley.

CHAPTER 29

"What do you think?" Caleb tried not to let his nervousness show. His mom had acted impressed during his tour, even if she did scoop up Mr. Pom-Pom the second she saw a bit of mud on his paws and head for her car, promising to "tell your father everything." Before he even knew what was happening, he found himself agreeing to visit her.

"You'll see." She'd tweaked his nose like she used to when he was younger. "In no time at all, you'll be making up with your dad."

It'd been such a nice time with her, showing her around, that he hadn't even argued, which she took as agreement. She'd kissed his cheek, leaving a bright-red smear behind, pleased she'd pinned him down for a coffee date next Monday. Maybe Riley could come with him. Yeah, he liked that idea. A lot.

Grandpa William was a more difficult person to please. Besides, a fancy dog park was not at all what Grandpa William had had in mind when he'd challenged Caleb to turn the Dorothy into a profitable venture. The dog park, in fact, would not be profitable in terms of income. That it would profit the neighborhood, that it persuaded the Dorothy's residents and the surrounding neighbors to agree to the remodel and rebranding of the Dorothy should count, but Caleb was afraid it wouldn't. Grandpa William had sent him to accomplish a job, and that job was unfinished. However, his mom's reaction to the park gave him hope. If she saw the value in what he'd accomplished here, then Grandpa William could, too.

Grandpa William cleared his throat and then cleared it again. "It's a strange sort of condo conversion you've got going on here. Is it some sort of doggy hotel? Did you do the market research on that? It's never good to invest in a fad, you know."

"It's a dog park. For the neighborhood." Caleb felt his speech getting more clipped. He could gush about the park, the neighborhood, the way pulling all this together made him feel as though he belonged in a way he'd never felt before. But Grandpa William wouldn't want to hear that. He'd want to hear profit margins and bottom lines.

"And the neighborhood is very grateful." Riley appeared right at his most tongue-tied moment and twined her arm through Caleb's, smiling at Grandpa William. "You should've seen this place before Caleb came along—just a run-down, abandoned lot where people brought their dogs. Now, it's a real community space. Did you get a caramel apple yet? They are to die for." Riley steered the men toward one of the booths ringing the dog park. "This local husband-wife team makes specialty dog biscuits that my poodle can't get enough of! For today, they've branched out to human treats. Here, try one."

Riley thrust a caramel apple into Grandpa William's hand while shelling out more dollars for another round for her and Caleb.

"Implants." Grandpa William handed it back.

"Oh." Riley's face fell, and she held a caramel apple on a stick in each hand. "Maybe something else?"

"I don't care for sweets." Grandpa William strode forward, leaning on his cane for balance in the grass.

"Why don't we find you a seat? The costume parade's starting in about fifteen minutes. I can't wait to see what everyone's come up with!"

"Did you decide on a costume for LouLou?" Caleb kept an eye on his grandfather's balance while doing his best to keep this conversation alive.

"Oh yes. And if you'll excuse me, I need to go find her and get her ready." Riley dashed off with both apples, leaving Caleb to eat his in the frosty disapproval of his grandfather's gaze.

"She's Gloria's granddaughter, isn't she? You sleeping with her?"

Caleb choked on a mouthful of apple. "Yes."

"To which question?"

Caleb stuffed more caramel deliciousness into his mouth and merely hummed an agreeable sound.

Grandpa William snorted. "Figures. All this nonsense for a woman. You really don't have your father's killer instincts, do you?"

Caleb swallowed hard. Sure, he'd followed in his father's footsteps, shouldered those expectations, enough for three sons and then some. At first, Caleb hadn't thought the accusations against his father could possibly true. If anyone knew the company inside and out, it was him. If anyone knew how his father worked, it was him. But he'd been wrong, and he'd paid a hefty price for believing his father's lies. A few months ago, hell, a few weeks ago, he would've been insulted at the idea that he wasn't the businessman his father had been, but looking around at the happy neighbors and happier dogs, he felt a swell of pride instead. "No, sir. I sure don't."

Grandpa William humphed in displeasure. "What do your brothers have to say about all this? Never heard of investing in fixing up a dog park for a neighborhood. Where's the payoff? How will you boys get the business off the ground if you're giving away your money? Or rather, my money." Grandpa William's narrowed gaze focused on Caleb in the way that had made him squirm when he was younger.

Today, though, he rolled his shoulders and forced a pleasant smile to his face. "As you well know, my brothers decided not to be involved. Knox by way of not being reachable and Lance by choice. This is all my decision." And this portion of the build was all Caleb's money. Which he was sure his grandfather already knew, since the man counted every nickel.

"No help from your brothers." Grandpa William snorted. "Figures. You never did understand the meaning of family."

Caleb felt his pleasant smile slipping. He drew in a deep breath and looked out over the dog park he and Riley built. The ring of booths around the perimeter selling everything from vegan dog biscuits to handmade dog-centric jewelry. At the greyhound rescue table, two greyhounds leaned heavily on a young woman as she talked excitedly to a family of four. The youngest, a girl no more than three years old, reached out a hand to pet a greyhound. The dog dropped to the ground, rolling to its back, tongue lolling out of the side of its mouth. The little girl screeched with laughter and rubbed the dog's belly while the grown-ups kept talking, oblivious to the bond being formed. Caleb had no doubt who that dog was going home with today.

Children raced with their dogs, faces painted at the table Sydney'd set up with a makeup-artist friend. Even now, the woman worked on a young teen to turn her face into a butterfly mask. There were three more kids in line, ranging from ages five to twelve by the looks of it, and another line of kids twice as long at the snow-cone machine.

At the far side of the park, Sydney had set up a temporary gazebo arch with a black banner that read "It's a Howling Halloween Costume Contest!" in large orange letters. Chewy sat beside her, decked out in a tiny Han Solo costume. Other dogs joined the group, from a Dalmatian dressed as a fireman to Princess Pugsley in her princess finest.

"Let's gather for the costume parade!" Riley'd gotten hold of a bullhorn. The sound carried across the park, bringing all attention to her.

She was gorgeous, standing there in a fluffy, pink poodle costume. Big bows held her hair in ponytails to make her poodle ears, and a pink tutu completed the look. Next to her on a shiny silver leash, LouLou was dressed as a 1950s teen, complete with ponytail and poodle skirt. Grams stood a few feet away, filming everything on her phone.

Family? Caleb had learned a lot about family during this project, but he hadn't learned it from Grandpa William. No. He was looking at the only family he cared about right now. Riley, her poodle, her Grams, all her assorted responsibilities to the people around her. She'd brought him in, made him feel part of it, like he belonged. It was a strange feeling, this pressure pumping his heart faster and faster.

Her smile. Her determination. The squeaky sound she made when she first woke up and stretched her arms over her head. She was just so doggone cute. His heart thumped harder and harder.

He loved her.

It wasn't sudden, like a flash summer storm, but more of an unfolding. It'd been there all along, the bud of his feelings, and somehow Riley convinced it to bloom.

She and Sydney attempted to herd the motley participants into a semblance of a parade, and the group headed out to march around the newly christened dog park. Dogs and owners walked proudly, if not necessarily in an orderly fashion, while onlookers cheered. Riley and LouLou led the way in their poodle-human swap costumes, Grams trailing them with her camera the whole way.

At the agility platform, each contestant hopped up, and Sydney and her expert panel—Mr. Cardoza and Patty—oohed and ahhed over each dog. After dozens of dogs had been seen, Riley handed the bullhorn over to Sydney.

"We've got some wonderful prizes today, donated by our generous local vendors." Sydney went on to explain who'd donated what, but Caleb stopped listening to anything but the beat of his heart in his chest.

He loved Riley. And all the while, she kept up with the event, talking to neighbors, making sure everything ran smoothly. He stood here next to Grandpa William for what? Some kind of familial approval? Some sign that he was worthy of the Donovan name? Why wasn't he over there with Riley, having a good time?

"You know what?" Caleb turned to Grandpa William. "You're right. I'm not a real Donovan. Not anymore. And I think that's for the best, don't you? I started something new here. I'm building a community for people to live in, to be part of. Not a fantasy getaway vacation or some sort of status symbol for having made it, but a real place for real people. And that means a dog park for the neighborhood and renovating the Dorothy in such a way that the long-term residents don't need to be evicted for the improvements to happen."

"And I guess it means doing it without my money." Grandpa William leaned heavily on his cane. "The deal was you got your brothers involved in the condo conversion or you don't even get the building. All your so-called plans don't mean anything if I don't sign the building over to you. As far as I'm concerned, you haven't met the terms of our agreement. No deal."

"No deal?" Caleb staggered back a step. He'd been thinking of the project as his for so long, the words stunned him. He'd expected some resistance from Grandpa William, maybe a lecture, not a declaration of no deal. "What do you mean?"

"I mean"—Grandpa William coughed into his palm—"I'm going to sell the Dorothy to the first person who comes along. I'm disappointed, Caleb. Gravely disappointed."

"I'll buy it." The words flew out of Caleb's mouth.

"You can't afford it."

"What do you want for it?"

"Nothing you can give me."

"How about a dollar?" A new voice joined the bargaining session.

Both men swung their heads around in an eerily similar gesture.

"Gloria?" Grandpa William was the first to speak. "I didn't know you were here."

"Well, that's certainly a lie. You've been watching me since you arrived."

Grandpa William flushed, usually a sign he'd forgotten his blood-pressure medication, but Caleb didn't think that was the case this time.

"I've been watching you, too, Billy. And listening. Talking to your own grandson that way? Shame on you. Makes me glad we never had children." Grams lifted her chin and stared at Grandpa William.

To Caleb's surprise, Grandpa William was the first to look away. "Glo, you don't understand."

"I understand plenty." Grams tucked her phone into her bra strap to free up her hands and pointed at Grandpa William. "The Dorothy was supposed to be mine. You promised it to me, and at the first opportunity, you took it back. Holding onto it all these years, pretending like you were doing the right thing letting those idiots at Rainy Day run everything into the ground? What happened to you, Billy? We had our differences, sure, but I never thought you were the kind of man to renege on a business deal."

Grandpa William's mouth gaped open, much like one of the fish he was so fond of fishing for, and then snapped shut.

Grams pushed a finger into the center of Grandpa William's chest. "Do the right thing, Billy. Give the Dorothy back to me. Keep at least one promise you made to me in this lifetime."

Grandpa William's color reached an alarming shade of red. "Fine," he snapped, pushing Grams' finger away. "You can have it for a dollar."

Grams reached into her cleavage and pulled out a five. "Keep the change. I'm feeling generous today."

Grandpa William snatched the bill from her and shoved it in the front pocket of his button-down. "My lawyer will send over the paperwork."

Grams took a step backward, nodding with satisfaction. "Fine."

Caleb couldn't believe what had happened. All his planning, the work on the dog park, learning about the neighborhood, everything, was just a waste of time. Rather than listen to his plans, Grandpa William gave the building away for a dollar.

So much for keeping it in the family. So much for rebuilding the Donovan real estate empire. So much for Grandpa William's belief the family could be brought back together. He'd sold them out for a dollar.

"Hey." Riley slipped in beside him, tipping her head to rest against his arm. "What's going on?"

Grams snapped her fingers. "Our troubles are over, Riley. The Dorothy is saved!"

"That's wonderful!" Riley gazed up at Caleb with trust in her eyes. "I knew you'd come through, Caleb."

"No, no, dear, pay attention. I saved the Dorothy. Single-handedly, I might add." Grams fluffed her already fluffy hair. "And for a darn good price."

"What're you talking about?"

"The Dorothy is mine again! Can you believe it? Billy finally did the right thing. I mean, I had to bribe him, but he eventually did the right thing."

"Five dollars is not a bribe." Grandpa William's color was returning to normal.

"He gave you the Dorothy for five dollars?"

"Sold." Grandpa William corrected her. "You can't give away anything in business."

Riley looked from Caleb to his grandfather to her grandmother. "I still don't understand. What about Caleb's plans?"

"He didn't keep the terms of our deal." Grandpa William folded his hands against the small roundness of his belly. "He knew the consequences."

"Caleb?" Riley turned those big eyes on him, and he couldn't take it.

"I'm done." He pulled away from her. From them. "Done with this family. Done with this building. I can't believe I've been so stupid."

"Exactly." Grams gave a crisp nod. "All the Donovans can pack up and go home now. The Dorothy is saved. Isn't it wonderful, Riley?"

Riley's anxious gazed ping-ponged between Grams and Caleb. "Of course, Grams, I'm happy for you."

Caleb mumbled, "Of course," and strode away, out of the dog park. LouLou saw him from across the park and came running, bouncing on his leg to be picked up. Instead, he squatted and gave her a good scratch behind her years. "I'll miss you, LouLou, but it's clear I'm not needed around here anymore."

"Caleb!" Riley called, but he ignored her. It had all worked out how she wanted, hadn't it? Grams got the building. Everything could go back to how it was before, except now it had a premiere dog park to draw in more residents and finally fill those empty units. How would they pay for the renovations required for the forty-year inspection?

Who would they hire to do them? Not his problem. He'd been an idiot to think he could win his family's approval, an even bigger fool to think Riley would want him to be part of hers. Whichever way he looked at it, Caleb was a fool. Grandpa William set him up to fail, and in that regard, he'd fulfilled his expectations. Everything about this project was an epic failure, including Caleb himself.

CHAPTER 30

"I DO NOT UNDERSTAND WHAT JUST HAPPENED." RILEY'S rigged-up poodle-like ears drooped, and she scratched her waist where the tutu dug in.

Grams took her through it one more time, and of course Riley was happy for Grams. She knew she should be totally happy. Wasn't this everything she'd wanted since Caleb first set foot on the Dorothy's property? But things had changed since then. She'd changed. Frosty reception from his mother or not, she'd started thinking of Caleb's plans for the Dorothy as their plans. *Our plans.*

"Grams, what're you going to do with the Dorothy?"

"First"—she checked off her points one finger at a time—"I'm going to fire those lazy, no-good property managers at Rainy Day. Second, I'm going to hire you to run everything. Third, I'm throwing a party the likes of which the Dorothy hasn't seen in decades. Fourth"—she turned to fix a glare on Grandpa William—"I am not inviting him."

"Okay, that sounds like a really thought-out plan." Not as thought-out, of course, as Caleb's with his blueprints and architect consultations and brother the contractor. And of course, Caleb's plan lacked the glamour of a major party. That was how Grams was, though, very big picture. So big she hadn't maybe thought out issues of financing and renovations, but Grams was looking so smugly happy that Riley decided now was not the time to bring up real-world considerations. There'd be plenty of time to pop that bubble later.

For now, Sydney was calling everyone over to announce the costume contest winners, a job Riley was happy not to have. How to choose between the pair of whippets dressed as race horses with plush jockeys on their backs or Lady in her Viking helmet complete with horns and long orange braids? The Pomeranian dressed as a cheerleader or the midsize mutt with a dinosaur costume? Truly above her pay grade. While Sydney talked about how amazing every dog looked, Riley pulled out her phone and texted Caleb.

Hey. Come back. Don't you want to know who won?

No response.

"Of course," Sydney was saying, "none of this would be possible if not for the generosity and work of a few key people. Riley, come on up here. And where's Caleb? Caleb Donovan, everyone, let's thank him for our wonderful new Fur Haven Dog Park!"

Sydney's thanking you. Everyone's clapping. You should really come back.

Delivered, but not even a blinking three dots to indicate an attempted response. Just her own words staring back at her.

"Riley, want to say a few words?" Sydney thrust the bullhorn at her.

"No, I don't." She shoved it away, but Sydney was insistent. "Okay, then a few words. Thanks to everyone who helped make today possible. And Sydney is right; Caleb deserves the lion's share of praise. Or should I say doggy's share? Unfortunately, he was called away a few minutes ago, but I know he'd want you to enjoy the day. Have you had one of those caramel apples? My goodness." She shoved the bullhorn back at Sydney and checked her phone again. Still nothing.

She marched over to Grandpa William, poking him in the chest like Grams had. "I hope you're happy. This is all your fault."

"Isn't it always?" he mumbled, leaning on his cane. "Young lady, enjoy your grandmother's building. It has a lot of potential."

"So does your grandson, but I'm not surprised you'd give up on him. You handed the Dorothy over for five bucks. You're clearly not a man who values anything but your own convenience."

Grandpa William blanched, and Riley felt a twinge of guilt. He was an old man, after all, and she'd been pretty harsh, but as she walked away, she heard Grams saying, "That's my granddaughter. She has a good point, don't you think, Billy?"

He mumbled something in reply, but Riley didn't hear. She was already texting Sydney to ask her to keep an eye on LouLou while she went Caleb hunting.

"You were robbed." Grams' grip on her elbow surprised Riley and kept her from sprinting out of the park in search of Caleb. Grams' pumpkin-colored nails with black cobweb designs on the thumbs and ring fingers dug into Riley's skin. "No one was cuter than you and your little poodle. A visual pun! What were those judges thinking, giving it to some mutt in a ladybug costume?"

"French bulldog puppies are the cutest things ever." Riley tried to peel Grams' fingers off one by one, but Grams wasn't having it. She leaned on Riley's arm as if she needed support. Riley suspected it was an act, but what if it wasn't? Grams' fall wasn't that long ago, and it had been a tiring day. "Do you want to go home?"

"And miss all this? Not for the world. Walk me over to the booth with Dr. Morrow's daughter running things. What does she do again? Something with those old racing greyhounds?"

Riley slowed her pace to match Grams', her silent phone burning a hole in her pocket. "She's the rescue coordinator. After the tracks were closed, thousands of dogs needed homes. She's been rehabilitating and training them at the rescue center. You want to meet a few of them? They are the sweetest things."

"I suppose." Grams walked even slower, either a ploy to keep Riley at her side or a genuine sign of fatigue. Riley wasn't sure anymore what was drama and what was aging. Those hours in the ER waiting room had changed everything. She needed to keep a close eye on Grams to make sure she didn't overdo it. Caleb was a big boy. He would either text her back or not. Maybe he needed some space.

Riley's gut clenched at the thought. In her experience, needing space was a precursor to breaking up. Were they even really a couple? Sure, he'd been staying over more nights than not, but it'd barely been a month. Did what they were doing count as dating?

"Gloria! Riley!" Danielle stepped around the table to hug both of them. Danielle had been a few years ahead of Riley in school, but her petite stature, barely topping five foot three, and rounded cheeks always made her look younger. Danielle's father had been the veterinarian for Grams' many cats over the years, and Riley had grown up sitting in his waiting room to learn diagnoses for various feline illnesses. Danielle'd spent most of her high-school and college summers working for her dad. "How's the Prince? I haven't seen him in ages."

"He says hello," Grams said with the authority of someone who knows her cat is perfectly capable of speaking English but simply chooses not to. "He is not fond of the new diet your father put him on, though."

"I bet! Riley, how have you been?"

"Good, good." Riley's phone vibrated in her pocket. She snatched it out of her pocket, eager for Caleb's response. But it was only the CVS robotext reminding her to pick up Grams' medication. She thought about pretending it was something more serious back at the Dorothy, but before she could form a vague response that would give the impression she was needed elsewhere while not telling an outright lie, William Donovan walked up to the booth.

"What do we have here?" He pointed at the array of photos spread across the table, tapping one of an older greyhound with a graying muzzle and obviously crooked knees.

"These are our retired racers ready for adoption. That guy is a special one. A retired champion. Unfortunately, his advanced arthritis makes it difficult for him to get around, and they were going to put him down. My dad and I got there in time to save him."

William's eyes scanned the table but landed back on the old dog. "What's his name?"

"We've been calling him Pops. He's eight years old, which is getting up there for a greyhound."

"And people can just adopt them?"

Danielle smiled and picked up Pops's paper, putting it in

William's hand. "It's a bit more complicated than that. We do a home visit to make sure it's safe for the dog, interview the potential owner, that sort of thing. But if everything checks out, yes, people can just adopt them."

"I've never had a dog." William studied the paper, even taking out a pair of reading glasses to read the small print under the photo. "What kind of home does a dog like this need?"

"Usually, greyhounds need lots of space to stretch their legs, but his arthritis, especially in his knees, pains him, so he'd be happy in a low-activity household. To tell you the truth, I think he'd be the perfect companion for someone older, someone who might understand the challenges of his condition." Danielle gave a pointed look to William's cane.

Grams snorted. "Don't give this man a dog. He doesn't know how to take care of anything or anyone."

"His foster home isn't too far from here. Want me to give them a call and see if they can bring him to meet you?" Danielle was all smiles and sweetness, but she was clearly intent on closing this deal in spite of Grams' attempts at intervention.

Grams snorted again, loud enough that William offered her a handkerchief from his pocket, but she turned her nose up at it.

"Young lady," he said to Danielle, "I think I would like to meet this dog."

"Stars above, what a bad idea this is." But Grams didn't act like she was going anywhere.

"Wonderful!" Danielle was on her phone in seconds, brandishing the text reply proudly when it came in. "They're on their way!"

"I need to go!" Riley extracted herself from Grams' death grip. She did not have the time to oversee a whole adoption sequence. Hard as it was to picture Caleb's grandpa with any kind of pet, she hoped for Pops's sake that it worked out. "It was great to see you, Danielle! You do such good work for the greyhounds."

"You don't want to meet Pops?" Danielle was already pulling up more pictures of Pops to show William.

"I'll be back. I just have a—" Riley pulled out her phone and rushed away. No texts from Caleb. Should she send him another message? She didn't want to be a nag. If he wanted to talk to her, he would. There wasn't really anything she could do if he was avoiding her. But she also couldn't stay at the dog park like everything was fine. He'd run away from his big triumph. He should be here to enjoy it.

Your grandpa's going to adopt a dog.

There, that wasn't naggy, and it was true. *Speak now or forever hold your peace.*

See? She could be funny, too. But the screen stayed blank. She tried to think of the scene between William and Grams from Caleb's point of view. How disappointed he must be. It wasn't his fault his brothers weren't interested in William's plan. He'd done the best he could with the situation, and looking around her at the happy neighbors and happier dogs, he'd done a damn good job.

What had gone wrong? She needed to analyze the situation, and then she needed to fix it. Not only for Caleb but Grams, too.

In fact, she doubled back for Grams. "Come on. We need to discuss a few things."

"Oh, you've got your serious face on. You wouldn't be so

glum if you'd won the costume parade. I'm going to have a talk with that Sydney friend of yours."

"We're going to talk. All of us. You, me, Sydney, Eliza."

"Right! Now that I own the building, we should tell Eliza to drop the lawsuit."

"Among other things." Riley whipped out her phone and started texting. As soon as the Howling Halloween dog park party was over, they were having a major powwow. Or should she say bowwow? She smiled at her own joke before sending the calendar invite. Before that meeting, though, she and Grams were going to have a serious conversation.

CHAPTER 31

FIVE DAYS. THAT WAS HOW MANY DAYS HE'D SPENT BEING an idiot, not responding to Riley's texts. She'd given up after a few, but that hadn't stopped him from obsessively rereading them. Why couldn't he reach out to her? Hadn't he realized less than a week ago that he loved her? But what could he offer her if he didn't have the Dorothy to build the business on? His messed-up family? His messed-up life? She'd be better off without him, there at the Dorothy with her Grams and her residents and her dog park friends. Maybe she'd think fondly of him whenever she took her poodle to their dog park. Yeah, right. He knew men who ghosted were not thought fondly of. He should text her back. He would. After this stupid meeting with Commissioner Santos.

Caleb parked the Porsche a block away to give himself a chance to walk off the nervous energy he was feeling. If he stared at the bench where he and Riley'd made out after that memorable commission meeting, there was no one there to mock him. No one but his own brain, reminding him what an idiot he was being. He passed through security with little annoyance and took the stairs to Santos' office.

"Caleb." Commissioner Santos rose and shook his hand. The office was on the small side, tidy and modern with lots of grays and blacks giving it a masculine feeling. Caleb took a seat in a surprisingly comfortable guest chair but was forced to rise again when Commissioner Jackson entered the room.

"Commissioner." He shook her hand as well.

"Please, come with me. We'll never all fit in this tiny room."

"Always bragging about your corner office." Santos waggled an eyebrow at Jackson, and she laughed. "Did you book the conference room?"

"Where else?" She led the way down the hall in her sensible block heels. Santos sped up to catch the door and held it open as they passed through.

The conference room was a larger version of Santos' office, sleek and gray, with a large oblong table in a manufactured gray wood taking up the center. A telephone that resembled some sort of alien creature occupied the middle of the table. Santos held a chair out for Jackson, and they all took their seats.

"I'm always happy to see you, of course." Caleb rubbed the back of his neck. "I admit, though, that I'm curious why you asked me to come down."

"It's the holiday spirit!" Jackson announced, drumming red and green nails on the table.

It was only a few days after Halloween. When had she even had time to get Christmas nails done? Or maybe she celebrated Christmas year-round. He'd heard of people like that; he just didn't think there were any in the subtropics. Sweat and the Christmas spirit weren't usually paired, but the Christmas trees swinging from her ears implied a serious commitment to the holiday.

"I'm sorry. I'll have to check with my accountants"— who he didn't have on the payroll anymore—"before I can commit to any campaign donations."

"We're not here for campaign money." Santos rubbed his

palms together. "But if you're in the mood to give, I have a few ideas."

"I'm afraid I'm already maxed out on charitable giving, but if you give me the basics—"

Commissioner Jackson cut him off with a laugh. "That's not why we called you in. Look, William's here. Why don't you come on in?"

Speaking of people he was avoiding. Caleb turned his head to see his grandfather, leaning heavily on his cane, enter the room with a black-and-white greyhound on a thin lead. The dog's dark muzzle was peppered with gray, and it walked stiffly behind Grandpa William. At least Grandpa William didn't know how to text.

"Grandpa."

"Caleb."

"Is that a greyhound?" Caleb remembered the text Riley'd sent the day of the dog park grand opening, warning him, but he couldn't believe his grandfather had gone through with it.

"His name is Pops." Grandpa William settled heavily into the chair next to Commissioner Jackson, and the greyhound promptly dropped his five-pound head into his lap. Grandpa William stroked the dog's head while surveying the room. "He's good company."

"That's good. Great." Caleb shook off the surrealness of the whole thing and splayed his hands on the table. "But I still don't understand why we're all here. Why I'm here. Santos?"

"Hey, I'm not late, am I?" Lance strode into the room, workman's boots managing to clomp even on the carpeted surface. "And look who I brought with me."

"Knox?" Caleb stood and took a few lurching steps toward his oldest brother. Knox was lean and muscled, biceps bulging out from a Semper Fi T-shirt. "I can't believe it's you!"

"Hey there, Caleb. Aren't you a big boy now?" Knox's teasing grin was the same as it had been the day he came to say goodbye before heading out to the marines. What wasn't the same was his left leg encased in a pretty serious-looking brace, the kind with metals and straps so large they couldn't go under a pant leg.

Caleb went in for a hug at the same time as Knox stuck out his hand to shake. They met in the middle in an awkward backslapping compromise. "What're you doing here?"

"You've been calling, haven't you?" Knox settled himself awkwardly into a chair, leg held stiffly out in front of him. "And I had some time on my hands." He gestured at his leg. "Medical discharge. Where else am I gonna go but home?"

"I, for one, am glad to see you." Lance took the chair next to Knox. "Can we get started? I've got to get back to my job site. Bathrooms don't demo themselves, you know."

Caleb looked from one brother to the other. "What is this about?"

Jackson drummed her nails. "The Historic Preservation Board decision came in. The Dorothy will be added to the historic building register."

Caleb nodded. He'd figured as much. It was a beautiful building. He'd hoped to see it restored to its former glory and shining with a new light all its own. Whatever. Riley would take as good care of it as the budget would allow, although he did worry about what she and Grams would do about the forty-year-inspection improvements.

"And we've seen your plans for the renovations. Gorgeous. I'm going to want to buy into the building myself." Jackson patted the stack of papers in front of her. "That young architect you're working with has a promising future here on the Beach. He's captured the history beautifully, but it still feels fresh and modern." She spread the drawings out on the table for everyone to look at.

Lance whistled low through his teeth. "That's an ambitious plan, little brother."

"It was." Caleb couldn't look at the plans. Riley had loved them. That was all he'd cared about by the time Adam dropped them by the Dorothy. "They're perfect!" she'd said and kissed him. He'd felt such a sense of accomplishment, like this, this is what he was meant to do. He supposed he should send the drawings to Grams now, in case she was interested.

"And we approve!" Santos banged the table for emphasis. "All of us! The other commissioners couldn't meet today, but we were told it was an urgent matter to get this resolved. We wanted to let you know in person that you have the official city stamp of approval. That parking garage with the rooftop dog park? Phenomenal idea. Believe me, we'll be reaching out to your Mr. St. John for plans in the future."

"The what?" Caleb turned a drawing to face him. A three-story parking garage, the full size of the once-empty lot and not much taller than the Dorothy, was sketched out to show the outer walls growing bougainvillea and the top story filled with miniature people and dogs enjoying the view from the top. Grass, agility equipment, even palm trees. Caleb had never seen such a thing, but he loved it. Riley would love it.

Riley.

"Ingenious, isn't it?" Santos beamed at him like it was his idea. "A compromise that makes everyone happy. The city will, of course, expect the ground floor to be income-generating spots, right?"

"I wish I could." Caleb folded his hands in front of him. He was forced to say out loud the thing he could barely acknowledge in his head. "The Dorothy has changed ownership. You should be speaking with Gloria and Riley about their plans."

Commissioner Jackson squeaked, "What's this?"

At the same time, Santos belted out, "What kind of nonsense is going on here?"

Grandpa William tapped his cane against the hard plastic of his chair arm. "I'm afraid there's been a misunderstanding. Caleb, the Dorothy is yours. Lance and Knox let me know in no uncertain terms that you'd met the terms of our agreement. They claim to both be working with you on the renovation. Why didn't you tell me? Why did you let me think you'd let that Carson woman control everything?"

Caleb knew his mouth was hanging open, but he couldn't quite get it to close.

"You can be so pigheaded, Grandpa William." Lance leaned his chair back on two legs. "He was probably letting you stew, and then you went and sold the building for five bucks? That's what I heard anyway. Luckily, the new owner was happy to sell it to me, even if, as she noted multiple times during our negotiations, I'm not as handsome as Billy."

Caleb's mouth gaped a bit more, and he finally managed another "What?"

"She had to make a profit of course. Caleb, you owe me ten coconuts. I figure you're good for it, though. I paid her this morning; we're square. The Dorothy is officially Donovan-owned again."

"You own the Dorothy?"

Lance chortled. "Keep up, kid. Grandpa William's deal with Gloria hadn't gone through yet. No paperwork or anything. Essentially a handshake deal. For ten bucks, she shook on giving it back. You've met the terms of his crazy agreement, so he'll be signing the Dorothy over to you. To us. That's what you wanted, isn't it?"

Wasn't it? Two months ago, it was all he wanted. A chance to build the business back, to repair his broken family, to prove he was nothing like his father. But now, paperwork in front of him, gorgeous plans approved, his brothers aligned with him, all he wanted was Riley.

He shook his head. "Why would Gloria give back the Dorothy?"

"Sell back." Lance pushed a piece of paper with Gloria's signature on it his way. A quick scan revealed that she'd signed away any claim to the Dorothy. "Something about forty-year inspection repairs costing more than five dollars. Someone must've shown her the estimate I gave you."

That someone was Riley. His files were still at her place. "Riley did this?"

"Well, it wasn't Santa Claus," Lance drawled, evoking a surprised chuckle from Knox.

"Riley did this." Caleb searched his brothers' faces for confirmation.

"We'll lock it up all legal with the lawyers this week." Grandpa William tapped his cane authoritatively. "I'm proud of you, Caleb. You're going to bring pride back to the Donovan name."

Caleb didn't care about that. Not anymore. He shot out of his seat.

"Riley. I've got to find her."

CHAPTER 32

RILEY LIFTED HER FACE TO THE NOVEMBER SUN. AT A mellow eighty degrees, fall was her favorite time of year. Less humidity, more breeze, and the influx of tourists that kept the hospitality industry alive. Which would mean something if she were still in the hospitality industry, but she had a sinking feeling that she'd have to move on soon.

She couldn't work at a Donovan-owned property, not after all that happened with Caleb. She felt good that she'd righted the wrong done to him by his grandfather and was happy knowing that today he'd find out that his renovation was saved and his brothers were on his side. Not to mention, she'd saved her Grams from an unmanageable number of financial headaches. But she couldn't stay at the Dorothy, knowing she could run into Caleb at any moment. No, he'd made it clear at the Howling Halloween Party that what she'd thought was so special between them wasn't special at all.

LouLou darted around the new dog park, inspecting the base of each piece of agility equipment, wagging her tail frantically at whatever she smelled there. The chitter of a squirrel caught her attention, and she raced to chase it up the newly planted palm tree. The squirrels had wasted no time moving in on the new trees. Perched at the top of one of the struts still holding the palm tree in place, the squirrel turned its head from one side to the other, almost as if it were amused by LouLou's attempts to scale the tree.

"Hey."

It was the text she'd been waiting for, only delivered in person. She sucked in a deep breath and turned to face Caleb. He was rumpled, like he'd been sleeping in his clothes, and a few days' worth of stubble shadowed his chin. Bloodshot eyes traveled from her head to her flip-flop-clad feet.

"Hotter-than-You Pink?" He gestured at her toenails.

Riley looked down, surprised she hadn't changed the color since the night they'd sat on her sofa watching Netflix movies while she painted her toenails. He'd even helped with her tiny pinkie toe, always a challenge to do without smearing polish everywhere. He'd made fun of the name but had given her an amazing foot rub while the nails dried. It was a nice memory, one of many she was sure she'd revisit in the future as she beat herself up for being stupid enough to believe in a happily-ever-after. Again. When would she learn that men, at least men she fell for, never saw her in their futures?

"Yeah. How are you?"

"I don't know. It depends."

"I thought you'd be happy to get the Dorothy back. Your grandfather seemed especially pleased when I spoke with him."

"And my brothers? How on Earth did you get Knox to answer his phone?"

"Lance knew a way to get hold of him. They didn't realize Grandpa William's strings were so inflexible. They agreed to the project to help you break away from him. You know that, don't you?"

"By playing Grandpa William's game, we're in deeper

than they realize, I fear. In a few months, my brothers won't be thanking you for your part in this."

"In a few months, they won't be able to find me."

"What do you mean?"

"My mom is pulling some strings of her own to get me a job on her cruise line. Nothing's for sure yet. I'm sending out lots of résumés, too." She crossed her fingers. "Here's hoping something comes through. Soon."

"Any place would be lucky to have you."

"Yeah, thanks. That's nice of you to say." Riley looked anywhere except directly at Caleb. The crease in his khakis, the slope of his shoulder, that strong line of his jaw, the sky overhead.

"Riley."

His voice drew her gaze directly to him. He reached for her hand, taking it gently in both of his. He kissed her knuckles and dropped to one knee.

"What're you doing?" She pulled at her hand, but he held on.

"Where better to propose than our dog park? We built Fur Haven together. I want to keep building with you. For the rest of our lives."

Riley's eyes widened, her whole body as still as the moment when LouLou spotted a squirrel but seconds before she erupted into a barking and running frenzy. "You can't be serious."

"I'm on one knee. I am totally serious."

"No." She wrestled her hand free. "I mean you can't be serious, thinking you can waltz into my dog park and propose and everything will be fine."

"Our dog park."

She planted her hands on her hips. "I texted. I called. You ghosted me. Ghosted. And now you think I'm going to marry you?"

Caleb's head dropped. He dug around in his pockets until he pulled out his phone, thumbs dancing on the screen.

Her phone buzzed.

I'm sorry. I love you. Please say you'll marry me.

"You texted me!" she screeched at him, slapping at his shoulders. "You jerk!" She smacked him again for good measure. "How could you text me like that?"

"Wait, wait. Am I in trouble for texting you or not texting you?" He stumbled to his feet, phone dangling in his hand.

"Yes!"

Their excited voices drew LouLou toward them, and she jumped on Caleb with muddy paws, leaving an abstract pattern of paw prints on his thighs. Caleb scooped up the poodle, cradling her in front of him. "LouLou, I don't know what to do."

LouLou licked the underside of his chin sympathetically.

"Don't talk to my dog." Riley snatched her poodle out of his arms. "She doesn't know why you haven't been around. She doesn't understand what you've done."

"What did I do?"

Riley held her dog tight. "You broke my heart."

"No, no, I didn't. I'm right here."

"You ghosted me."

"I am really sorry. I was confused."

"If I hadn't talked Grams into giving back the building, would you even be here right now?" Riley's grip on LouLou loosened, but she wouldn't give in and reach for him.

"Of course. I hated not talking to you, not being around you."

She glared at his phone. "It was easy enough to fix."

"After enough time went by, I thought only an in-person apology would do."

She sniffed, rubbing her nose in LouLou's soft fur. "How could you text me that you love me when you've never said it? Dropping to one knee when I wasn't sure if we were even dating? You're confusing me, Caleb. I don't know where we are or what we are."

"I love you." His words were strong, sure. "I love your kindness and competence, that you can unclog a sink and balance books and that you change your toenail polish every week. I love how you love your grandmother and Mr. Cardoza and Patty. How you fought for your dog park. How you smell after you use the bazillion products in your shower and how you feel so soft and warm when you fall asleep in my arms. I love that you made me understand this neighborhood, that you made me part of it. I love little LouLou, even if I don't love how early she wants to wake up to go outside. Riley, I love everything about you."

Riley's sniff turned into a sob, and she buried her face in LouLou's curls. "You're such a jerk."

"Yeah, I know. But I'm trying to be better."

Riley bent her knees and released LouLou, then threw her arms around Caleb. "You really are a jerk. Disappearing for almost a week, then texting me that you love me while I'm standing right in front of you."

"I'm sorry. I should've told you sooner. I should've trusted you."

"Yeah, you should have."

"Do you forgive me? Are you ever going to answer my proposal?"

"Yes."

He smiled then frowned. "To which question?"

She laughed. "To both!"

He caught her mouth with his in a deep kiss, one Riley felt all the way to her soul.

"It's about time." Eliza's crackly voice broke them apart. "You'll make Patty a rich woman if you tie the knot before Christmas. She could use the cash. Think on it, you two. Why don't you?"

Riley looked up to find Eliza and Lady looking on. "Not that stupid bet again!"

"Got your Grams on FaceTime." Eliza held out her phone. "She wouldn't put any money in the pot. Bet you're regretting that now, aren't you, Glo?"

"I regret nothing. That's my life motto, you know." Grams waved at both of them. "You two better come see me right away. We've got some planning to do!"

"You're not mad? He is a Donovan."

"I don't suppose anyone is perfect." Grams flipped her hand. "Except me, of course."

Caleb squeezed his arms around Riley from behind and spoke over her shoulder. "Thank you. Your approval means a lot." He swung Riley around in a circle, LouLou chasing her legs.

Grams chuckled. "Get back to kissing. That's the best part."

Riley turned in his arms. "Don't I know it."

Caleb waited until Eliza and Grams hung up and Eliza settled on a bench a polite distance away. He cupped Riley's face in his hands. "I love you."

She smiled up at him. "I love you, too."

The kiss was the best of her life, so she protested when he pulled away. "What?"

Caleb looked down at his shoes. "She got me again."

Sure enough, LouLou had draped herself across his loafers, and when he wedged them out from under her, his left shoe was a bit damp.

"Oh my gosh, I'm really sorry." Riley covered her cheeks with her hands. "I can't believe she'd do that here at the dog park. She has all this space. I don't know what's gotten into her."

"I've been doing some reading about dog behavior."

"You have?"

"Yep, and I think—no, I hope—she's marking her territory. I want to belong to you two. I want to be a family, and I want to start right away."

"It's a good thing I'm willing to marry you then."

"Before Christmas." He smiled and kissed her again. "You know, for Patty's sake."

"Well, if it's for Patty, why not?" She laughed, pulling his face down for another kiss.

"Get a room!" Eliza called from her bench just as a rumble of thunder announced an afternoon storm.

"Good idea!" Caleb reached down to clip the leash onto LouLou's collar. "Come on, LouLou. Let's go before we get drenched."

Hand in hand, one tail-wagging poodle between them, they dashed home, one step ahead of the rain.

ACKNOWLEDGMENTS

I am so grateful to all the people in my life who have supported me on this rocky journey, with special thanks to:

My husband, Michael Crumpton, for always believing the luck wave was about to change, and my dad, Herman Geerling, for the pep talks and prayers.

Kaitlyn Ballenger for so generously sharing your expertise, and to Rebecca San Juan and Joyce Sweeney for beta reading some pretty rough pages. To Omar Figueras for your kind explanations about real estate law, with extra props for wading through an early draft with editing pen in hand. Katy Yocom and Jenny Luper, thank you for reading early drafts and sharing your helpful insights.

Laurie Calkhoven, a constant source of inspiration and motivation. Long live the Job Quitters' Club!

My Spalding University M.F.A. in Writing community, especially Sena Jeta Naslund, Karen Mann, Kathleen Driskell, Gayle Hanratty, Ellyn Lichvar, Jason Hill, Lynnell Edwards, Terry Price, and Nancy Chen Long for keeping the home fires burning. Your work means so much to so many.

My Spalding University M.F.A. in Writing mentors and workshop leaders: Luke Wallin, Joyce MacDonald, Rachel Harper, Robin Lippincott, Lesléa Newman, Beth Bauman, Kenny Cook, and Dianne April—your instruction and encouragement mean more than I can express.

My supportive Broward College colleagues and friends Erin Burns-Davies, Rowena Hernandez-Muzquiz, Jamie

Martin, Sandra Stollman, Amanda Thibodeau, and Judi Tidwell; thank you for listening to So. Much. Drama.

Deb Werksman for taking a chance, and to the wonderful team at Sourcebooks, with special thanks to Susie Benton, Rachel Gilmer, Catherine Baccaro, Jessica Smith, Jocelyn Travis, Diane Dannenfeldt, and Sabrina Baskey.

Julie and Shepherd Edelstein and Nicole and Ray Cabrera for sharing your hotelier experiences and expertise. Christopher Leser, thanks for the poker tips! Any mistakes are totally mine.

Kay Rico Coffee in Hollywood, FL, especially owners J.R. and Elizabeth Mendez and their barista sons, Daniel and Timothy Aleman. Could this book have been finished without your dirty chai lattes with oat milk? Debatable. Thank you for the space on your couch and the excellent music selections.

Read on for a sneak peek at book 2 in the
Fur Haven Park series by Mara Wells

Tail for Two

Available July 2020 from Sourcebooks Casablanca

CHAPTER 1

I'LL NEVER SWIPE RIGHT AGAIN. CARRIE BURNS EYED THE man waving her over to a small table-for-two wedged between a sickly potted spider plant and the large front window of the newest coffee shop in her neck of Miami Beach. The small neighborhood was, as her ex-husband used to describe it, "just north of the tourist trap" that was South Beach. The space was perhaps too intimate, as evidenced by the number of people Carrie bopped with her oversized shoulder bag when she squeezed by them on her way to lucky date number thirteen.

Not that this was her thirteenth date with him. Oh no. In her limited time in the online dating world, she'd never been on a single second date. But after a dozen first dates, she'd hoped that number thirteen would be the one. Not The One, with wedding bells and coordinated calendars, but at least a second date. So far, though, it wasn't looking good.

For one, the man, a banker named Daniel Merrifield, was significantly older than his profile picture and dating profile suggested. Late-thirties? Yeah, right. Not that there was anything wrong with aging. She hoped to live to a ripe old age herself, but she was really over older men who only wanted to date younger woman.

And it wasn't like she was so young herself. With a failed marriage behind her and a toddler waiting for her at home, Carrie often felt older than her actual thirty years. She hadn't yet found a gray hair amid her brown strands, but with the dual strain of maintaining her business and caring for her active son, she was expecting one any day. She glanced at her phone before sliding into the seat across from Daniel. No panicked messages from the babysitter, a teen girl who lived with her parents in the condo above Carrie's and who both Carrie and her son, Oliver, adored. No, the only one feeling panic was Carrie.

"Hello, Carrie." Daniel half-stood then quickly sat again, smoothing a palm down his paisley tie, and handed her a menu. "Order anything you like. My treat."

Carrie really shouldn't judge him on so few words. And yet. "I prefer separate checks."

Daniel frowned, salt and pepper eyebrows slamming together over his prominent nose. "The espresso is quite good."

"You've been here before?" Carrie kept her attention on the menu, scanning the double-sided laminate sheet for her favorite coffees—something with as much sugar as caffeine and preferably topped with about three inches of whipped cream. "Do you live nearby?"

"No, Brickell." Daniel picked at the corner of the

menu, shredding the laminate seal. Another strike, his making things worse for a start-up coffee shop in the ultra-competitive Miami market by defacing their new materials. Of course, the owners could've sprung for a more durable menu in anticipation of customers like Daniel, but folks new to owning and operating small businesses weren't always prepared for the idiosyncrasies of the public.

Carrie resisted the urge to take the menu from him with a gentle reprimand about respecting others' property, like she would've done with her son, and instead listened to Daniel as he gamely pushed forward with their date. "The espressos have good Yelp reviews. That's what I'll order, if a waiter ever deigns to give us some attention."

"The Beach is kind of famous for its poor service." Carrie forced a laugh. What's the point of dating if you don't have a good time? She would have a good time. *They* would have a good time. She folded her hands on top of her menu and smiled across the table at Daniel's serious face. "The upside is there's never a rush. We'll have plenty of time to get to know each other a bit."

Daniel checked his watch, a combo time keeper and fitbit-type contraption, clearly not charmed by her smile or her there's-always-a-silver-lining world view. "I have a meeting in less than an hour."

"Oh." Carrie schooled her features. It was four in the afternoon. Even if they only spent twenty minutes together, factoring in travel time, he should've counted on at least an hour, if not longer, for their date. What kind of banker had after-hours meetings? The kind who lined up multiple dates on the same night was her bet.

Daniel half stood again, scanning the crowded room

until he locked onto a server standing by the cashier. Daniel snapped his fingers and pointed at their table before sliding back into his seat with a disgruntled sigh.

Carrie didn't like Daniel's attitude about their server, wherever he or she may be. Carrie'd worked her way through college waiting tables at a diner near her campus. Serving was hard work, work she'd gladly left behind when she graduated, and she found herself bristling at his whole attitude.

In fact, everything about this date was one huge red flag. She should run while she had the chance. Pretend there was a babysitting emergency. Yeah, that's what she'd do.

"What can I get for you?" Their waiter couldn't be any older than Oli's babysitter, a hair shy of sixteen. He was gangly, the kind of tall a man grows into, but he'd need a few more years to look comfortable in his body. A giant Adam's apple bobbed as he recited some drink specials for the day.

Daniel ordered his espresso, but Carrie was swayed by the list of specials.

"May I hear them again?" She smiled at the waiter, and his cheeks flamed.

Daniel sighed like this whole thing tried his patience, which made Carrie want to ask more questions. But that would merely prolong the date, so she selected a salted caramel latte with extra whipped cream and let the waiter escape.

"What do you do again?" Daniel waved a hand, like the answer was a wisp of smoke he couldn't quite grasp.

"I own an interior design firm." She slipped him her brightly-colored business card out of habit. Single-mom, single-proprietor businesses required a lot of hustle.

"Right." Daniel fluffed a paper napkin on his lap,

leaving the card untouched on the table between them. "Decorating."

"Design." Carrie knew she shouldn't be annoyed. She took a calming breath and fingered the single pearl on the white-gold chain around her neck. "I create the feel of a space using color, shape, pattern."

"Like I said, decorating. I'm sure you're good at it." Daniel's gaze tracked over her face and down into her cleavage. She was always overdressed, but that was her thing. In her line of business, she couldn't afford to be seen with a hair out of place or an outfit not perfectly coordinated. Clients drew conclusions in a blink of an eye, and Carrie liked to think that the world was full of potential clients.

"Thank you." Carrie wasn't sure his comment was a compliment, but she decided to take it as one. It was clearer by the moment that they wouldn't suit romantically, but if she played nice and made a good impression, maybe he'd remember her name if his bank ever decided to redesign their lobby or upgrade their executive offices.

Their drinks arrived, his a tiny cup he downed like a shot, hers overflowing with whipped cream topped with a caramel drizzle. She took a long, hot sip. Her first true smile of the afternoon overtook her face.

"So what do you think of this place?" Daniel swirled his empty cup. "Design-wise, I mean."

Carrie took a moment to soak in the atmosphere, to review her initial impressions, to think about the Coffee Pot Spot as a client.

"First, no dying plants." She used her chin to indicate the failing spider plant behind him. "If you're going to have plants, they've got to be alive and healthy. Anything less is depressing and creates a negative atmosphere. Given they've been open less than a month, and that poor spider is already on its last legs, I'd say no live plants for them."

"Aren't fake plants tacky?" Daniel clinked his empty espresso cup on its miniature saucer.

"I don't love fake plants. There are other ways to bring color and life into a room. Some outdoor photography perhaps. I'd have to talk theme with the owner. And also room capacity. Of course, you want to get as many chairs in the room as possible, but not at the expense of safety. Anyone with a bag creates a fire hazard when they set it down." Carrie swept her arm to indicate the book bags, briefcases, and purses as large as hers blocking the aisles from where they hung on the back of their chairs.

"Why wouldn't their designer have thought of that?"

"My guess? The owners did the design themselves." Carrie took a long sip of her drink. Caffeine and sugar, such a heavenly combination. "It's always tempting for new business owners to try to save money that way."

"It makes sense." Daniel nodded like he was a design expert. "Tables, chairs, hang some stuff on the wall. How hard can it be?"

Carrie let out a long, controlled breath. This was part of her job, after all, educating people about why they needed her. "Let me put it to you this way. I've lived in homes my entire life. I'm very familiar with what makes a house: walls, roof, foundations, electrical, plumbing. How hard could it be, right?"

Daniel snorted. "It's not the same thing."

"Isn't it? I can watch videos about how to install a ceiling fan. Why should I hire someone else to do it?"

"I'm getting your point." Daniel drummed impatient fingers on the table. "There's more to it than meets the eye."

"Yes." Carrie nursed her coffee, perversely compelled to drink as slowly as possible in light of his haste. "If I do my job well, the effect should be effortless. I don't want clients to see the design; I want them to feel it."

In her eagerness, Carrie leaned across the tiny table. When she pulled back, the table wobbled. She grabbed the edge to correct it, managing to tip her coffee at exactly the right angle to pour salted caramel latte down the front of her silk lavender tank top and right onto the lap of her favorite pencil skirt.

Daniel stood like he was going to help her. But what could he do?

She shooed him back down with a wiggle of her fingers. "I believe that's my cue to head home to my son."

"Your son?" Daniel looked stunned.

She mentioned being a mother on her dating profile, but she'd found most men didn't do much more than look at pictures before deciding which way to swipe.

"He's two, almost three." She reached into her bag and pulled out Winnie-the-Pooh wipes and a stain remover pen. "Quite a handful." Using her son to scare off Daniel may have been overkill, but the look on the banker's face was worth it.

"Nice to meet you." He threw down a couple bucks for his espresso and fled the scene. The gangly server showed up with a damp rag and helped her put herself to rights. She left him a generous tip and squeezed her way out of the overcrowded coffee shop. Thirteen was definitely not her lucky number.

Lance Donovan pulled his work truck up onto the front lawn of the Dorothy, the decrepit Art Deco building his younger brother, Caleb, had convinced him to renovate. And it had taken some convincing. At eighteen, Lance left home and never looked back. He'd never wanted anything to do with the Donovan real estate legacy his grandfather built, and that his father so casually destroyed. One summer interning at the Donovan main office was enough to open his eyes to the truth: his father, real estate tycoon and pillar of the Miami community, Robert Donovan, was a crook. It'd taken another decade and a half before he'd been caught, but Robert was now serving time in federal prison. As far as Lance was concerned, Robert was exactly where he belonged, and he'd had no intention of ever getting tangled up in a Donovan scheme again.

Somehow, though, Caleb got through to him. Maybe it was earnestness, Caleb's real desire to make the building a better place for the people who lived there. Maybe it was genetics, as much a part of him as his Donovan blue eyes and blond hair; maybe it was destiny. Whatever it was, Lance now had one hell of a project on his hands. Step one: get the Dorothy up to code so she could pass her long overdue forty-year inspection.

While he waited for the diesel engine to cool, he flipped through the city inspector's notes. Roof, electrical, plumbing, elevator. All pretty standard stuff on an old building and easy enough to do in the next few weeks. Once they passed the forty-year inspection, if everything went according to plan, he'd be done with the whole remodel in ten, twelve months tops. What job ever went to plan, though? In fifteen years of construction, he'd learned to expect the unexpected—and padded time estimates accordingly.

Lance swung out of the truck in a practiced move, his steel-toed work boots planting firmly on the Dorothy's scraggly grass. His crew should arrive in the next twenty minutes or so, but he always liked to arrive early on the opening day of a new job. It was corny, he knew, but he liked to spend a few minutes with the building, letting it know they were here to help and to ask for its patience while they transformed it.

Inside the old-fashioned lobby with its stained terrazzo floors and fake palm tree in the corner, Lance took a seat on a sketchy rattan chair and closed his eyes.

"Sleeping on the job already?" A deep voice interrupted Lance's private moment with the building.

"That's how I make the big bucks." Lance stood to clap his brother on the shoulder. They were similar in height, though Lance had a few inches and a few pounds of muscle on his little brother. What marked them as brothers were the unmistakable blue eyes they inherited from their Grandpa William and the square jaws that hinted at their stubborn natures. They hadn't grown up together—different mothers, different homes—but in the few weeks he'd been working with Caleb, Lance had learned to respect his younger brother. He was a good guy, much too idealistic to be a true Donovan—a trait that made Lance feel protective of him. Ridiculous, of course. They were both grown men. Still, Lance hadn't been part of a real family since his divorce, and he had to admit that Caleb and his fiancée, Riley, felt like family.

LouLou, Caleb's step-poodle, jumped on Lance's knee and shoved her head into the flat of his palm. Lance scratched her head and grinned at Caleb.

"You ready for all the chaos?" Lance motioned toward the elevator with a dramatic sweep of his arm. It was the first major project, since it was the most urgent in the fifty-five-plus building. Between heart conditions, canes, and walkers, many of the residents would be unable to reach their second-floor apartments if the elevator went out.

"More chaos than wedding planning? Impossible." Caleb tugged on LouLou's leash. "We need to head outside. Little dogs, little bladders."

Lance shook his head, overgrown hair brushing his ears. "You love it all, don't you? The wedding stuff, the poodle."

"I love Riley." Caleb's face was so serene, Lance had no doubt of Caleb's sincerity. He bit his tongue to keep from telling Caleb what marriage was really like—how it starts out all sparkly and sex on every surface of your home but ends in bitter words, resentment, and divorce lawyers. Caleb pointed at the glass doors. "We'll be at the dog park if you need us."

"Wait!" Riley busted through the stairwell door and into the lobby, wild strawberry blond hair flying in all directions. "I want to go, too."

"Didn't Grams need you?" Caleb handed the leash to Riley. LouLou spun, managing to tangle her front legs in the nylon lead. Caleb knelt to untangle her.

"Classic Grams exaggeration." Riley rolled her eyes. "What she needed was batteries in her TV remote changed. We're good. Let's go before another crisis arises. I wanted to talk to you about maybe changing venues?"

"That's my cue." Lance strode to the glass front doors and held one side open for his brother and soon-to-be sister-in-law. "No wedding talk in front of the bachelor."

Riley turned wide eyes on Caleb. "You didn't ask him?"

Caleb stood, LouLou's leash free and clear. "When have I had the chance?"

"Now's a good time." Riley nudged him toward his brother. "LouLou and I will be outside. Catch up when you're done."

"Done? I don't like the sound of that." Lance crossed his arms over his chest, narrowing suspicious eyes at Riley.

Caleb ran a hand over his buzzed-short scalp. "Look, Lance, I know we haven't always been close."

"Like ever." Lance snorted.

"But we are brothers." Caleb ploughed on, clearly uncomfortable. He rocked back and forth on his heels. "And I do need a best man for this wedding."

"Me?" Lance rocked back on his heels, too. He'd almost forgotten to invite Caleb to his own wedding. It'd been his ex-wife, Carrie, who'd insisted on inviting his dad's side of the family. He was glad she'd forced the issue, but at the time he'd been angry at Caleb for doing nothing at his reception except drink by himself in the corner. No brotherly toast? What had he expected, though, from a brother he hadn't talked to in years? Families were complicated, no doubt. "Best man?"

Caleb smiled. "Yeah, you. My big brother. My business partner. Who else?"

"Knox?" Lance named their oldest brother, throwing him under the bus in his panic to get out of anything having to do with weddings.

Caleb's smile widened, the smug bastard. "Yep, Knox, too."

"Well, you can't have two best men."

"Yes, I can. It's my wedding. I make the rules."

"That's not how weddings work."

"It's how our wedding is going to work."

"You really don't want me." Lance didn't want to be the rain cloud on Caleb's sunny day. He decided honesty was his best policy. Or whatever. "I'll curse the whole day."

"It's important to me." Caleb kept that patient smile on his face, reminding Lance of all the times his mother had come to pick him up and Caleb stood outside the house waving and smiling until their car was out of sight. "It's important to Riley."

Lance sighed. He did like Riley. She'd done something to Caleb, made him less of a Donovan and more himself somehow. He sighed again because he knew how this conversation would end as soon as it started.

"Fine. I'll be your best man."

Caleb slapped him on the back. "Excellent. Wait 'til you see the cummerbunds."

Lance groaned. Weddings were so not his thing.

CHAPTER 2

"HOLD ON, YOU LITTLE PISTOL." LANCE TUGGED ON LouLou's leash, once again cursing himself for agreeing to poodle-sit for Caleb and Riley. They hadn't even left on their cruise yet, an extravagant affair they'd arranged for the Dorothy's second floor residents to get them out of the building while the elevator was being replaced. The two occupied apartments on the first floor hadn't wanted to be left out of the fun, so they got tickets, too. Leave it to his soft-hearted brother to foot the bill for a vacation. Then again, once the wheels of justice crushed the Dorothy's former management company for embezzling funds from the building, Caleb would be well compensated.

Why was he letting this bossy canine pull him to the dog park again? Oh right, Caleb claimed he needed practice. Riley was anxious about leaving LouLou. Apparently, since adopting the small dog, Riley and LouLou had never been apart for more than a day. Riley would feel better, Caleb had explained, if she knew that Lance and LouLou were already pals before the trip.

Lance could empathize. When he and his ex-wife separated, she'd kept their Jack Russell, Beckham, and he'd missed the dog more than he thought he would. He missed the warm lump of him under the covers, warming his feet in the night. He missed Beckham's excited yip when someone knocked on the door and the crazy jumping for joy when Lance came home. No matter how late it was, Beckham was always thrilled to see him. His ex? Not so much. She'd roll to the edge of the bed when he climbed in, her back to him, pretending she didn't know he was there.

It hadn't always been that way, of course. In the beginning, they'd burned up that king-sized bed in the bedroom she'd decorated in his favorite shades of blue. They'd doted on their puppy, taking long walks around the neighborhood and bringing him to weekend brunches on Lincoln Road. Waiters brought Beckham a bowl of water and a dog treat, and he'd settle under the table, happy to shred a paper napkin while he and Carrie shared a pitcher of mimosas. Not that he loved mimosas all that much, but they were Carrie's favorite so he sipped them and enjoyed how animated she'd get after the second one, waving her hands around and telling stories about work too loudly. Yeah, he'd loved that version of Carrie, and truth be told, missed her, too.

He shook off glum thoughts about his ex. Sure, there were things he'd do differently now, but ultimately, their breakup was for the best. One workaholic was tough on a relationship, but two ruined it. By the end, the only thing they'd had in common anymore was Beckham.

LouLou halted in front of the dog park gate, waiting for him to lift the latch. Inside, she wiggled while he unhooked her and opened the second gate. He hung the leash on one of the many hooks mounted on the fence, watching as LouLou sprinted for a large black Lab lounging near one of the newly planted palm trees. The big dog rose to its feet, greeting LouLou with a butt sniff and a nudge on her side. Lance missed how it happened—secret signal? habit?— but the two took off at a run, LouLou weaving figure-eights through the lush grass while her dog park buddy chased her.

"Good friends, aren't they?"

Lance had to look down to see who was talking. A small, steel-haired woman grinned up at him, a tissue crumpled in one hand that she used to dab at the perspiration gathering on her hairline. Her tropical print blouse was louder than the last rock concert he'd attended.

"Eliza." He greeted the woman warmly, kissing both cheeks in Miami fashion. They'd had a few encounters when he'd been doing the planning stages for the renovation. She and her dog didn't live in the Dorothy, but she enjoyed watching the goings-on from her house across the street.

"Is everything okay with Riley?" Eliza's crinkled eyes showed more smile wrinkles, but now they were furrowed with worry. "Why do you have LouLou?"

"Practice for the cruise."

"Ah." Eliza's face relaxed. "Me, I can't stand those things. Long lines. Too many people. Good food, though. I'll give 'em that."

"So I've heard." Lance couldn't remember the last time he'd taken a vacation. Was it? No, it couldn't be. Surely he'd gone somewhere with someone since his and Carrie's long weekend in the Keys right before the wedding. He simply couldn't think of it right now. Tampa maybe? No, that had been for a job. Man, he needed some time off and a plane ticket to somewhere far away. Greece popped to mind, but no, that had been Carrie's dream. The honeymoon they'd postponed and then never taken.

"Ah well." Eliza called Lady to her. "Got some family coming into town soon, so I'll have a full house. My brother, his kids, his grandkids. Amazing how time flies, isn't it?

Blink your eyes and the kids are grown. My oldest grand-nephew just made partner at a law firm, if you can believe that!"

Lance made sounds of agreement, understanding this was the type of conversation that didn't require a response, not unless he also had lawyer-type grandnephews, which he didn't. Though he might soon, the way Caleb and Riley carried on.

"Anything I should worry about here?" Lance pointed out LouLou snuffling in the grass, tail wagging while she gleefully shoveled dirt with her nose. Better to change the subject before he was made captive to an extended discussion about the life and career choices of all Eliza's extended family. "It's been awhile since I had a dog."

"That one can take of herself. Make sure you've got her leash on when you leave. She's a runner. Riley can tell you; once she gets going, she's hard to catch."

"Duly noted." Lance planted his hands on his hips and watched LouLou inspect the base of each weaving pole with her nose.

"Guess we'll be seeing you around." Eliza waved her tissue at him and strolled toward the gate, Lady trotting beside her.

Once both gates were closed, Lance relaxed onto a bone-shaped bench, tilting back his head with a long sigh. The past week had been a whirlwind of construction prep. And by whirlwind, he meant haunting City Hall, waiting on permits to clear, and spending hours on the phone tracking deliveries. His nightmare scenario was that the residents would return from their cruise, and the elevator wouldn't yet be operational. Elevators weren't his specialty so he'd brought in an elevator company, one he'd worked with before, to handle the installation but he was still the contractor and therefore, still in charge of the schedule.

A cold nose nudged his hand where it rested on the steel bench. Thinking it was LouLou, he casually petted the dog's head, but instead of the poodle-puff, he encountered the coarse coat of a terrier. Lance opened his eyes and found himself staring into the eyes of an adorable Jack Russell. It had the same brown mask as Beckham, with the same white stripe between his eyes, and the same white body with one large spot over his left hip.

"You could be Beckham's twin, couldn't you?" He scratched under the dog's chin, exactly the way Beckham liked, and the dog's tail beat wildly. "What do we have here?"

A mutilated tennis ball hung out of the side of the dog's mouth. Lance played a bit of tug of war to free it, a game that made the dog's tail beat even faster, and inspected the mangled toy. It was still roughly ball shaped, so he gave it a throw and the dog tore after it, springing across the dog park as fast as his little legs would take him.

"That's my dog." A muddy hand slapped down on Lance's jean-clad knee. A kid looked up at him with big, blue eyes set in a tiny but sharp face. His dark hair was cut short with a longer bang fighting back against the gel that was supposed to hold it out of the boy's eyes.

"He's a handsome fellow. Reminds me of my old dog." Lance gently pried the child's hand off his leg. He was in work clothes, so the dirt didn't bother him. The kid's parent was probably nearby, though, and he figured they didn't need to find their son cuddled up to a stranger in a park. Didn't they have programs in schools warning kids about stranger danger anymore? But this boy looked too young to be in school yet.

"My old dog," the boy repeated, leaning against his leg.

Lance scooted over on the bench. Really, this kid needed to learn some boundaries. "Yes, I had a Jack Russell just like this one. His name was Beckham. What's your dog's name?"

"Beckham!" The boy clapped his hands together. "Beckham is a good dog."

Lance didn't have a lot of experience with young children, or any children for that matter. "Your dog is also named Beckham?" It seemed incredibly unlikely, but hey, who better to name an athletic, driven dog like the Jack Russell after than the retired footballer who'd inspired a whole generation of American soccer players? He'd certainly thought it was the perfect name when he and Carrie found the dog bouncing off the walls, literally, of his pen at the local animal shelter.

The boy clapped again. "Beckham!" The terrier bounded back, jumping higher than the kid was tall. Lance laughed at the sight. This Beckham was so much like his old dog that Lance's laugh turned brittle. It *was* Beckham, his Beckham. His ex must've given his dog away to complete strangers.

Why? She knew he'd take Beckham back in a heartbeat, so the only reason that made any sense was malice. She'd fought to get ownership of Beckham and then given him away at the first chance, just to spite him. He'd never thought she was that cruel, but divorce showed you a lot of things about your mate that you didn't necessarily want to see.

"Oliver! Beckham!" A woman's voice caused both the boy and the terrier to spin toward the gate.

It couldn't be, but of course it was. Dark hair pulled back in a smooth, high bun, coordinated leggings and tank top with green and gold accents, dark running shoes with gold laces. Even dressed for a workout, Carrie still managed to be chic. She held a smoothie in one hand, cell phone in the other. A small knapsack rode low on her back. He had time to take it all in, the very realness of her. Straight back, long neck. Sleek sunglasses that hid the hazel depths of her eyes. Was pineapple-mango still her go-to smoothie choice or had her tastes changed in the years they'd been apart?

"Carrie." The one word felt awkward on his tongue. Too heavy. Too unused. Even in his head, he usually called her his ex. Carrie felt too intimate. Held too many memories, memories he'd done his best to obliterate. Still, here they were, popped into his mind as fresh as the days they were made, as painful as the conversation where she'd handed him divorce papers. Yeah, Carrie.

"Lance?" She whipped off her sunglasses and her gaze ping-ponged from where Oliver's hand rested on Lance's knee to Beckham's enthusiastic licking of Lance's work boots. "What're you doing here?"

Her voice was the same—that low timbre that strummed through him, soothing nerves he hadn't known were agitated until they calmed. Perhaps they'd been agitated for years, three years and nine months to be exact, but he pushed that thought away along with the other uncomfortable memories and forced a smile to his face. At least she hadn't given his dog away. There was that to be grateful for at least.

"Caleb owns that building now." He pointed toward the Dorothy with his chin. "Lives there, too. I'm watching his dog. Or rather, practice watching for when he and his fiancée Riley take all the old folks on the cruise."

"You're finally talking to Caleb?" Carrie shoved her sunglasses back on and took a visible breath, chest rising and falling, drawing his attention to how the workout wear outlined her breasts. Okay, he could admit he missed Carrie's breasts, their weight in his hands, the way her nipples puckered before he even touched her as if anticipating the pleasure to come. That part of their relationship had never been an issue, and as he felt an ill-timed erection pushing against the fly of his jeans, he was hard pressed to remember exactly what all their issues had been.

"Uh, yeah." His voice came out as awkward as his body felt. "We're partners, actually. With Knox."

"Well, that's something, isn't it?" She stood so still that he knew she was nervous. She'd trained herself to hide all signs of nervousness. Carrie was not a fidgeter. She clamped down on her muscles the same way she did her feelings— total control at all times.

"How've you been?" It should've been his first question. He knew how to schmooze clients, but his small talk skills scrambled at the glimpse of skin through the mesh cut out that ran diagonally across her leggings. Just as well. She ignored his attempts at polite chit chat.

"Oliver, come here." She held out her hand, and the grubby kid patted Lance's leg and hopped over to Carrie. She stepped so that she was between the child and Lance. "We'll leave you to it then."

"Wait." It'd been so long since he'd seen her, he wasn't quite ready to watch her walk away. "What're you doing here? Do you live nearby?"

Carrie shook her head, the movement unsettling her bun. It didn't fall, though. It wouldn't dare. "Not exactly. We like to take Beckham on adventures. You remember how he is."

"Our little Jack Russell terrorist." Lance quirked a real smile her way, quoting a Jack Russell blog they used to follow when they first adopted Beckham. He'd been such a handful that they'd needed lots of advice. Luckily, the internet was full of it, and Jack Russell owners loved to talk about their rambunctious pets. Saying terrorist instead of terrier referred to how the little dogs took over your life, and if not exercised and kept busy enough, could wreak utter destruction in the home. "Still doing the big walk every morning, huh?"

Perhaps sensing the adults weren't going anywhere soon, Oliver plopped onto the ground. Beckham trotted over and climbed into his lap, nudging the boy's hand with his nose for petting. Lance remember that move all too well. How many mornings had Beckham woken him up with demands for attention? Carrie was not a morning person by any stretch of the imagination, so Beckham learned early that Lance was his best bet for an early morning outing.

Carrie didn't answer his question. "We should be going."

Except Oliver and Beckham were now wrestling and oblivious to Carrie's attempts to get their attention.

"Cute kid." Lance didn't want to ask, but he had to. "Your son?"

Carrie's whole body stiffened. She nodded.

"How old is he?"

"Almost three."

Lance let out a low whistle. "Dang, Carrie, you didn't waste any time remarrying. And I guess husband number two talked you into kids, huh? Well, good for him."

"I did not remarry." Carrie's lips didn't move as she bit out the words.

"Oh." Lance's muscles tensed. He wasn't sure why. Maybe the shock. Carrie, a single mom? From the beginning of their marriage, they'd been in agreement: no kids. They had their careers to focus on, and neither one of them wanted to recreate the disasters to be found on both sides of their family. What happened to not only change her mind, but to also make her go for it on her own? He rubbed his temple, trying to imagine a scenario in which she ended up with a baby. He did not like the first option that popped to mind. "Wait a minute. How old is Oliver?"

"I told you. Three." Carrie leaned down to hook Beckham to his leash. He protested by sprinting away, one of his favorite games. Oliver took off after him.

"No, you said almost. Almost three." Lance wasn't the numbers guy his brother Caleb was, but he could handle the basics. Checking account, accounts payable and receivable. Counting forward and backward from nine months. "When's his birthday?"

Carrie mumbled something he couldn't hear.

"Did you say December?"

"Yes, he's a Christmas baby. Is that what you wanted to know? Are you happy now?"

Christmas Day minus nine months equaled a March conception, but he and Carrie split up in February. In fact, he'd sent back the divorce papers on Valentine's Day. Just because. So, Oliver wasn't his. He should be relieved, right? He'd never wanted kids, never would. That Carrie changed her mind didn't mean he had to change his. Good for her. Girl power and all that.

"Congratulations." Now he was the one biting out words. Deep down, he could admit he didn't like the idea of Carrie having a baby with someone else. *Tough cookies, Lance.* "He's a good-looking kid. Seems smart, too."

Carrie choked on a swallow of smoothie. "Oh please. Complimenting him is like complimenting yourself."

Lance's eyebrows crashed into each other. "What're you talking about?"

Carrie searched his face, her hazel eyes filled with messages he couldn't read. "You don't remember."

Oliver and Beckham bounded back, the dog sliding to a stop directly in front of Carrie and the boy clinging to her leg.

"Say goodbye to the stranger," Carrie coaxed her son with a stiff jerk of her chin that tipped the bun at an awkward angle. It dangled like it wanted to fall, but Carrie quickly rewound her long, dark hair and secured it with a green band.

Oliver looked up at him, those eyes as blue as Grandpa William's. As Caleb's and Knox's. As his own. But women weren't pregnant for ten months, and besides, Carrie wouldn't have his child without telling him. Sure, they'd been angry at the end, but not so much that she'd keep something like this from him. No, ten months put Oliver in the safety zone of someone else's problem. Lots of people had blue eyes, and in every other way, the kid was the spitting image of his mom complete with double dimples and her fine, sable hair.

"Bye-bye!" Oliver waved a dirt-streaked hand at him.

Carrie tugged on the leash, and Beckham followed her to the gate. Oliver followed, turning his head every few steps to look at Lance and wave again. Lance waved back.

You don't remember. Remember what?

And then he did. March. Grandpa William's birthday party. They hadn't told the family yet about the divorce, although Grandpa William knew they were separated. Even so, they'd been given the same bedroom they always shared when staying over and rather than make a fuss, Lance offered to sleep in the reading chair by the window. But he'd had a few too many at dinner, and after dinner. So had Carrie. He hadn't slept in the chair.

He'd reasoned that one more time wouldn't hurt anything. The ink was barely dry on their divorce papers, and they were both willing. Who knew? Maybe it was the start of a reconciliation. It was hazy, all the details, but one memory stood out crystal clear. Waking up in the morning with an armful of Carrie, her sweet body curled into his. He'd felt peaceful for the first time in months. God, he loved this woman. He tightened his grip, and she woke up, flipping to rest her head on his chest. She'd twisted her neck to look him in the eye.

"This doesn't change anything. You know that, right?"

Even with her warm body next to him, he'd felt chilled enough to pull a blanket over them. "Of course," he'd said, inching away from her. "Why would it?"

"Old habits." She'd swung her legs over the side, her back to him. "They're hard to break."

He'd wanted to say she was more to him than an old habit, but she'd already shrugged on her bra and was shimmying into her panties. She looked over her shoulder at him. "I'm sure your girlfriend wouldn't like to know about last night. I'll keep my mouth shut if you will."

He nodded, her words a blow to his gut. She knew about

Rachelle? How? They'd only been seeing each other for a couple of weeks, since he'd finally flirted back with his client's daughter. After he signed the divorce papers, what did he have to lose? He'd hurried to finish up the Florida room Rachelle's father wanted added to the back of his ranch-style home so there'd be no conflict of interest. As soon as the last screen was in place, he'd asked Rachelle out for drinks. They'd been having fun together, that's all. It wasn't like he'd posted about it on social media or anything. His relationship status was still married, a situation he needed to update but couldn't quite bring himself to do. Not yet.

"Well?" Carrie fussed with the bow on the waist band of her panties. The elastic stretched across her smooth stomach, and he couldn't take his eyes off the freckle that lived an inch south of her belly button. Lance shook his head, trying to get his mind right.

"Last night never happened." The words came out as a vow. He'd taken the whole episode and buried it deep in his mind.

"That's the spirit." Carrie had smiled at him and slipped into the emerald sheath dress she'd worn to the party. In their five years of marriage, he'd zipped her up a million times. That morning, she didn't even ask. Her fingers fiddled with the zipper until she'd pulled it all the way up, taking twice as long than if she'd asked for his help. And somehow, that was the moment he really knew it was over. The zipper said it all.

Watching Carrie now as she carefully closed the double gate and held Oliver's hand while they crossed the street to a small SUV across the street, it hit him harder than a ton of concrete pouring out of a mixer truck: Oliver was his son.

ABOUT THE AUTHOR

Mara Wells loves stories, especially stories with kissing. She lives in Hollywood, Florida, with her family and two rescue dogs: a poodle mix named Houdini Beauregarde and Sheba Reba Rita Peanut, a Chihuahua mix. To find out more, you can sign up for her newsletter at marawellsauthor.com.